SHE WAS BEAUTIFUL, RICH AND RESTLESS

. . . a brilliant prize in a city filled with beauty, wealth—and wanderers.

SHE WAS PART OF THE ESTABLISHMENT

. . . *a permanent luminary in a city of flashing and temporary stars . . . Washington, where men, women and careers are often made—and broken—in the course of a night.*

LENORA LATIMER HAD EVERYTHING

. . . until she set out to conquer the world and learned what she was missing.

The Best in Fiction From SIGNET

THE
RESTLESS
LADY

and other stories

by
Frances Parkinson Keyes

A SIGNET BOOK
NEW AMERICAN LIBRARY
TIMES MIRROR

SIGNET TRADEMARK REG. U.S. PAT. OFF. AND FOREIGN COUNTRIES
REGISTERED TRADEMARK—MARCA REGISTRADA
HECHO EN CHICAGO, U.S.A.

SIGNET, SIGNET CLASSICS, MENTOR, PLUME, MERIDIAN AND NAL
BOOKS *are published by The New American Library, Inc.,
1633 Broadway, New York, New York 10019*

FIRST SIGNET PRINTING, FEBRUARY, 1968

7   8   9   10   11   12   13   14   15

PRINTED IN THE UNITED STATES OF AMERICA

CONTENTS

FOREWORD

AS IN the case of almost everything I have written there is a story behind the story of "The Restless Lady."

Accompanied by my son John, who had just been graduated from Harvard, I visited every country in South America in my capacity as Contributing Editor to *Good Housekeeping*. I stayed at least a month in each and wrote at least one article in each. (These articles were later published in book form by Liveright, under the title *Silver Seas and Golden Cities*.) My route took me all the way down the East Coast and up the West Coast and when I say all the way, I mean this literally and not, as most persons do, no further south than Buenos Aires and Santiago. I went to the Falkland Islands, Magallanes, Tierra del Fuego and through the Chilean Canals and the Chilean Lakes. All in all, I spent six weeks in Patagonia. It is one of the most fascinating regions I have ever visited and the hospitality there is truly biblical in character, both at the great *estancias* of the wealthy and the small *fincas* of those in moderate circumstances.

Before leaving Buenos Aires, John and I were urged to delay our departure and join a cruise "around the Horn" on the *Don Quixote* that was starting shortly thereafter. It seemed best, for several reasons, to decline the invitation, but John and I covered all the same territory and all the same waters that the cruise did, after our departure. When we reached Chile, after we had been incommunicado for several weeks, we learned that the *Don Quixote* had been shipwrecked off Cape Horn, but fortunately with no loss of life, except for the captain who insisted on going down with his ship. A little later, the friend, whose invitation I had

7

declined, sent me a booklet, prepared by one of the survivors and his own detailed account of the wreck, with this tantalizing comment: "If you had only come along, you could have written a five thousand dollar story."

"The Restless Lady" was the result of this taunt. It was one of the few I have ever written that took a long time to find a welcome, but when it did, it was beautifully presented in *Family Circle* and well paid for— though not to the tune of five thousand dollars!—and also very well received by the public. Now, at last, it is really coming into its own. I have always felt it was one of the best things I have ever written and I am very happy about it. I shall continue to be happy, whatever its financial future proves to be, but I shall not be in the least surprised if my friend's estimate proves correct after all—not because of my own skill but because I had such unique and thrilling material on which to draw.

The other stories in this book also owe a great deal to background.

I have never been able to go into a house without thinking of what I would do with it if I lived there— what color I would paper the parlor, what pictures I would hang in the library, which bedroom would be mine. It has been a game I can play with myself, and one of which I have never tired. In the same way, I have always seemed to see every place in which I have stayed for any length of time—the Connecticut Valley, Boston, the Far West, the Deep South, certain parts of Europe, and finally Washington—not only as my own home, but as the home for countless fictitious persons, the background for a story. Such a story, though not "taken whole" from real life, almost invariably has some impression or experience of my own as a foundation upon which to build and enlarge the structure of an imagined plot. No one coming to Washington can fail to be impressed with the fact that certain sections of the city are extremely typical of the kind of people who live there, and the sort of life they lead. Sheridan Circle is distinctly "smart"; the fine houses of Lafayette Square are being cut up into offices and shops, but a few aristocratic families still linger there; the Speedway beside the Potomac River, where the famous cherry blossoms grow, is the favorite meeting place of thousands of young men and women who work for the Government and who have no less public place in which to see each other; Georgetown, the old "Court End of Town," deserted for years by the larger part of the "fashionable element" of the population, is being invaded and renovated. And so it came to me that a series of stories might be written about these and other similar localities, each story complete in itself, but linked to the others by the spell of Washington which hangs over them all, so that men and women everywhere, who cannot come to the Capital, might still understand some of its wonderful charm.

The plot of "The Cardinal's Nest" is based on the behavior of two birds in a friend's garden. The plot of "The Dixie Doll" is based on an actual incident which occurred in Virginia during the Civil War and is fictionized only in its minor details. "Mount Vernon—The Story of a Home"—the only other in this book with a Virginia setting—is, of course, fictionized fact. All names and all essential background are real; only conversations are, perforce, imaginary.

There are two subjects, above all others, which it seems natural to discuss in connection with Louisiana —Carnival and Bayous. " '. . . And She Wore Diamond Earrings' " deals with the first and "Bayou D'Amour," with the second. Both had their prototypes in reality.

The only story in the collection which deals with a psychic phenomenon, i.e., "In Need of Confession," was told in my presence as his own experience by one of the most prominent clergymen in the country. He had not previously been a believer in psychic experiences of any kind. This one was written by me with his permission and he approved the script.

Frances Parkinson Keyes

THE RESTLESS LADY

EVERYONE said that Leonora Latimer was the most restless woman in Washington.

She rose every morning at seven o'clock and rode horseback for two hours. Then she ran through half a dozen newspapers and an immense amount of mail while she drank her coffee. From ten to one she divided her time among her personal maid, her housekeeper and her secretary. At half-past one, she went out to lunch or entertained—never, so far as her servants or her friends could remember, had she taken a bite on a tray alone. After lunch she always played bridge, winning immense sums of money, which seemed rather a waste, because no one needed money less than Leonora. Late in the afternoon, she made innumerable calls, or received innumerable callers herself, until the vogue for cocktail parties put an end to this traditional custom of the Capital—a vogue which she was more or less instrumental in establishing; and after a round of cocktail parties, she either went to a dinner or gave one. Finally there was more bridge, or a dance; and when Amelia, her sour-faced English maid, was at last free to go to bed, she usually left her mistress propped up among lace-edged pillows, smoking cigarettes and reading travel articles.

For Leonora's restlessness was not confined to Washington. Often, while she was still playing bridge after luncheon, she would decide that she could not stand the Capital another minute and, ringing for Fernando, her butler, she would give a sudden order as an aside to her bidding.

"I double four spades," she would say pleasantly; and after a polite pause, too brief to permit her startled opponents to collect themselves, she would begin to gather in tricks with swift dexterity—"Oh, Fernando

10

—yes, I did ring. Please tell Amelia that I have decided to take the next boat for Spain. She may begin packing immediately. You and Luiz are down three, Ramón," she would go on, turning toward the table again and addressing the lithe, nonchalant, young *chargé d'affaires* of Argentina. "Those psychic bids of yours will land you in the poorhouse yet. My deal?"

Though she never admitted it, Amelia rather enjoyed these breathtaking departures, and the fiestas which followed in the wake of the cables which Miss Rhodes, the impeccable secretary, scattered to advise Leonora's Spanish relatives of her impending arrival in their midst. Amelia came to take them for granted, just as she did the castle in Spain, surmounting a tawny hill surrounded by purple mountains, which, in Leonora's case, was a reality and not a dream. For Leonora's father had married the daughter of a Spanish Ambassador; and later he had been sent as Ambassador to Spain himself. So, from childhood, Leonora had spent much of her time there. Indeed, she had herself been married in a beautiful dim Spanish cathedral, standing, veiled with priceless lace, before a carved altar of gilded wood. Her mother's uncle, who was a cardinal, had performed the ceremony and two royal princesses had been numbered among her bridesmaids.

So Amelia not only took Spain for granted, but gloated over it, with the arrogance of a faithful retainer whose employer is a great lady whom it is an honor to serve. But unfortunately, from Amelia's point of view, Leonora's travels were not confined to such pleasant countries as Spain: she cruised among islands in the Mediterranean. She caravaned across Iran. She went up the Amazon River. She throve on bad food, vile water, heat, cold, brigands, fleas and snakes; but Amelia returned from each of the expeditions looking more sour-faced than ever.

"It isn't within reason," she told Fernando, though she was careful to do her telling at a time when Leonora was out dancing the rumba at a fashionable "benefit" with Don Ramón, and therefore could not possibly hear her. "Bandits shooting at us, no further off than you are this minute, Mr. Fernando. And Madam laughing, as if it was funny, when any moment might have been her last—or mine, either, for that matter! It isn't reasonable for a lady to be so restless, say what you will."

Fernando did not say anything, because he agreed with Amelia. And Washington society was inclined to share her viewpoint regarding the unreasonableness of Leonora's restlessness. As long as Gay Latimer lived, it was natural that Leonora should do something—anything—she could think of to make her life endurable. For Gay Latimer had been a rotter if there ever was one, and why Leonora had married him was a mystery. The hard riding, the high stakes at bridge, the wild night clubs, the trips from Spain to Siam and back again—all these were comprehensible enough and excusable enough during his lifetime, since Leonora would not—or could not—divorce him, for, of course, she was a Catholic. But after he had died of delirium tremens, and she had emerged from the seclusion of her castle in Spain—where she had spent her mourning period—everyone had expected that she would settle down in Washington at last, and that in due course of time she would make a suitable second marriage. But she had gone on rushing about, and she had not married anybody. It was certainly very unreasonable.

It was not for lack of argument that she had pursued this course. There were, inevitably, the numerous fortune hunters whom a childless widow, who also happens to be a brilliant and beautiful millionairess, attracts. But there were dozens of men who would have been thankful to take Leonora without a penny, if they could only have her. And among the dozens was Ramón de la Barra, *chargé d'affaires* of Argentina, before mentioned, who could not, by the wildest stretch of the imagination, be accused of fortune hunting, since he himself was twice as rich as Leonora.

He was, incidentally, almost as handsome to look at, tall and supple and splendid, with a manner of moving about and of holding his head that no Anglo-Saxon could achieve. He had come to Washington very uncertain as to whether he would care for the post, having been transferred there from Paris, which to him was simply another word for Paradise; and then, two days after his arrival, he had been presented to Leonora at the White House Diplomatic Reception—Leonora wearing saffron-colored satin and topazes—and had decided that Washington was, after all, the only place worth considering in the entire diplomatic service.

"Does this seem something of a comedown?" she asked him whimsically. The Blue Room was full of "tumult and shouting" and her voice was as soft as it was mellow. But it had a vibrant quality, too, and he heard her perfectly. He bent his sleek black head and smiled with suave satisfaction.

"*Señora*, you cannot conceive how charmed I am that you should ask me that question! Every other woman I have met since my arrival here has said to me effusively, 'Don't you adore Washington?' Then she has gone straight on talking about something else before I could tell her that I did not!"

"Of course," said Leonora, still softly. "But you may like it better as time goes on. I hope you will. I feel you might be quite an addition to the diplomatic corps," she added, even more vibrantly, waving a casual hand in the direction of some of his most prominent colleagues.

Ramón laughed outright. "I like it better already," he assured her convincingly.

He would have enlarged upon this theme with true Latin subtlety and effectiveness, if the Vice President, who was jovial and rather blustering, and who doted on Leonora, had not come up just at that moment and preempted her attention. But ever since then, Ramón had contrived to see a good deal of her. Like Leonora he had a passion for early morning riding, for he had ridden from infancy all over San Mariano, the great *estancia* in Patagonia which his grandfather owned and operated. Like Leonora he had a passion for dancing, for he had danced the tango and the maxixe and the pericon ever since he was old enough to walk. Like Leonora he liked to play cards, for he had gone over to the casino in Montevideo from Buenos Aires every week end since he could remember when he had been at home. Indeed, their tastes were very congenial in many respects. So Leonora nearly always asked Ramón to "fill in" for dinner when a senator gave out because there was a night session; and lunched with him now and then at the Lido, where, according to the patriarchal custom of Argentina, fourteen near-relatives of his spent the season, and were likewise present at luncheon. But he could not induce her to see him alone; he could not make her listen to him; he could not make her love him.

Things were at this pass, and seemed likely to remain so, when Leonora's great-uncle, the cardinal, came to the United States to attend a Eucharistic Congress, and stopped off in Washington before returning to Spain. Ramón, swinging savagely up to Leonora's door late one dusky afternoon, found Fernando visibly affected. It appeared that His Eminence was in the drawing room with his niece; and the *Señora* had told Fernando that if Don Ramón should happen to call, he was to be admitted at once, in order that he might be presented to His Eminence.

Leonora had always declined to speak Spanish with Ramón, claiming, satirically, that all South Americans, and especially all Argentinians, spoke a "mongrel tongue" which no true Castilian would possibly understand. But this time, as she came forward, she said *"Qué tal?"* cordially as she gave him her hand; and, leading him toward the scarlet-robed figure seated in a carved chair by the great fireplace, went on, murmurously, *"Tengo un grand honor, amigo; mi tio—"*

It flashed suddenly through Ramón's mind as he knelt to kiss the cardinal's ring, that he had never seen Leonora in so gentle a mood; and when the cardinal had taken his departure to attend a banquet in his honor, Leonora, turning to Ramón, startled him almost out of his senses.

"Quieres quedarte?" she asked.

The instinct of the Latin is even surer and swifter than his intellect. Ramón gave no sign of the stupefaction that filled him because she had urged him to remain with her in the still, warm intimacy of the firelight, and—what was even more overwhelming—that she had used the familiar form of "thou" in speaking to him. He sat down beside her, and waited for her to go on.

"My uncle," she said, still speaking in Spanish, "was very anxious to meet you."

"I should not suppose that he would ever have heard of me."

"Someone must have mentioned you to him," Leonora went on, more nonchalantly. "Perhaps I did myself. At all events, he waited here expressly to see you. I told him that you were an idle and purposeless young man, and that probably you would drift in, for want of anything better to do. It appears that, when he was quite young, he spent a year in Argentina. I did not know it before. He never spoke of it until today."

"Was this before he had taken holy orders?"

"No, it was just afterward. He was connected with the staff of the Papal Nuncio. Well, it also appears that he knew your family, and that they were very kind to him."

"It is the custom of the country," said Ramón.

"It is the custom in every country for young men to fall in love inopportunely," said Leonora crossly, "that is what my uncle did. With a girl named Adela Carmen de la Barra."

"My grandmother!" exclaimed Ramón.

"Evidently. So he went back to Spain, and eventually became a Prince of the Church—of course, he was a prince anyway. But he became a cardinal besides. And he has spent the afternoon telling me, that it must be the will of God, and a real vocation, but that, unless he felt sure of it, life would seem extremely futile to him, compared to what it would have been could he have married Adela Carmen de la Barra."

Again Ramón, following his instinct, waited.

"So now," said Leonora, still more crossly, "he thinks it would be a good idea for me to marry you."

"I have always heard that the pronouncements of the Church are infallible," replied Ramón with commendable coolness, considering how he felt.

"Oh, yes! I was ecclesiastically assured that matrimony was a sacrament when I married Gay Latimer," exclaimed Leonora, so bitingly that Ramón was horror-stricken. He had never heard her mention her husband before; and now suddenly, she burst into terrible invectives against the dead man who had so bruised and broken her youth. And when at last, shivering, she pulled herself together, she covered her face with her slim hands and spoke in a whisper.

"So now you know. He's sorry, I think—my uncle, I mean. He's such a saint—so withdrawn inwardly, in spite of all his outward pomp—that he didn't realize what—what he and all the others who—who connived at my marriage were letting me in for. And he would like to make amends. So he—revealed this secret of his, hoping it would help me to find a solution. He seems to think it's fear that's keeping me from marrying, and he's tried to show me what—what love can —might be. I'm so touched—I'm all unstrung and shaken. Otherwise, you wouldn't have seen me like this. But he was much more moving than convincing. And now you know—why I couldn't ever risk it again."

"You are not afraid of me, are you, *querida?*"

"I am not afraid of anything," said Leonora coldly, speaking in English again, "and my name is Leonora."

"Is it that I do not stir you at all?" asked Ramón, and put his arm around her. The next instant, as if defying him to question her capacity for passion, she lifted her face, just as he pressed his own down hard against it. When he finally let her go, he could not have spoken to save his soul.

"So now that you know about that, too," said Leonora, still coldly, "I suggest that you go away."

"Your suggestion does not appeal to me," retorted Ramón, recovering speech. He was still taut all over, and there was something about his expression suggestive of a gaucho who decides to conclude an argument and reaches for the silver-scabbarded knife thrust in his broad belt.

"Leonora," he said impellingly, "do not punish me for what some other man did long ago—believe that the love of Ramón de la Barra is not like the lust of Gay Latimer! And do not punish yourself—confess that the kiss you offered defiantly brought you delight! Stop struggling and surrender! Not only your lips, but all your sweet secret self! My words sound cool and measured, I know, *querida;* but it is passion which makes me tongue-tied—a passion with which I long to transfigure your life!"

"Is passion all you have to offer me?" asked Leonora, standing very still.

"Is it all?" exclaimed Ramón. "It is not a hundredth part, of course, of what I am eager to offer you—of what I will offer you when you come with me to Argentina—that land of supreme splendor which you have never even seen!"

"I have never especially wished to see it," said Leonora with marked indifference.

"Because you have not realized its magnificence!" he retorted almost condescendingly. "Believe me, *querida,* that when the sun of this country has set, the sun of Argentina will still be rising! You jeer at our language; but some day no more Portuguese will be spoken in Brazil; it will be the tongue of Argentina instead! Some day the Andes will no longer mark the boundary of Chile—that will be our California! The destiny of Argentina is to dominate, and she will fulfill it gloriously!"

"I see," said Leonora, still speaking very quietly, "that arrogance has forsaken the province from which it takes its name and has become an integral part of Argentina—you will get into trouble, Ramón, with your own government, as well as with ours, if you permit yourself to speak to anyone else as you have spoken to me. I will regard what you have said as confidential, naturally. Nevertheless, I should advise you—"

She left her sentence unfinished and, walking away from him, pushed an invisible bell. Instantly, Fernando appeared on the threshold.

"Go and tell Amelia to pack," she said carelessly. "I shall need clothes for everything from camps to courts, and for every kind of climate and condition. And tell Miss Rhodes to look up the steamers going to British Guiana, and engage a *camerote de lujo* on the next one that leaves. I have heard," she continued, turning toward Ramón again, "that there are some waterfalls in British Guiana which far surpass Niagara—and Iguazu, too, for that matter—in beauty. I think I had better go and see them. Besides, I have been urged repeatedly to stay at Government House in Georgetown. This seems to me a most opportune moment for such a visit. *Hasta luego, amigo, y buena suerte!*"

In the year that followed Miss Rhodes and Amelia and Fernando all had reason to feel that their long suffering had been flagrantly abused.

In the first place, Leonora flew into a passion when the Governor of British Guiana promptly proposed to her, and sailed indignantly away to take a motoring trip through Venezuela, where the roads proved excellent. This expedition having seemed to her a success, she proceeded to take motoring trips through several other South American countries where there were practically no roads at all. And when at last she told Miss Rhodes to wire the Hotel Plaza in Buenos Aires for reservations, her exhausted staff felt much as the Israelites must have done when they finally sighted the Promised Land.

They little realized what was yet in store for them. The very day after her arrival in the splendid capital of Argentina, as Leonora walked out of the Hotel Plaza past the little shop where inferior vicuña rugs are sold at exorbitant prices, a poster, advertising a special cruise to the Straits of Magellan and the Fuegian Canals, caught her eye; and within a week she was on board the *Don Quixote* headed for the glacial currents that mark the approach to the Antarctic.

It was then that Miss Rhodes, acting as spokesman for her fellow victims as well as herself, finally summoned her courage to speak to her employer. She waited for a propitious moment, when Leonora, enfolded in furs, lay extended in her steamer chair, gazing out at gulls and albatrosses circling and dipping above the quicksilver water. She looked as if she were daydreaming, and as if her dreams were permeated with contentment. At first she did not notice the approach of her secretary; when she did, she spoke to her with unwonted gentleness.

"Won't you sit down," she asked softly, "and enjoy all this cool blue glitter with me? It seems to be all-encompassing. I never saw anything like it. It gives one a sense of release. I feel as if I were a million miles from everything that ever troubled—or—hurt me. I wish I never had to go back to civilization again!"

"Mrs. Latimer," said Miss Rhodes, hoping that her speech was unaffected by the shiver of nervousness which shook her spare body, "we *are* a million miles —to all intents and purposes—from civilization. The consequences might be very serious. I wonder if you are wholly aware of them."

"Just what do you mean?" inquired Leonora, speaking with slightly more reserve than she had before.

"It is very cold. Even with two hot water bottles in my bed, I cannot keep warm."

"You might try sleeping with someone," said Leonora flippantly. Then she laughed, not unkindly. "Do forgive me, Miss Rhodes, I didn't mean to shock you. It *is* cold. But you're not suggesting, are you, that the inadequacy of steam heat is a menace to life, liberty and the pursuit of happiness?"

"Indeed I do feel that these climatic conditions are dangerous," said Miss Rhodes, with pardonable resentment. Her voice *was* shaking now. "We might all easily contract pneumonia, and I have no confidence in the ship's doctor, none whatever. I suspect that he drinks—"

"Another way of keeping warm," murmured Leonora, "I might have suggested that instead of—do go on, Miss Rhodes, I am very much interested. The ship's doctor, under the influence of liquor, has forfeited your confidence, so—"

"Mrs. Latimer!" exclaimed the long-suffering secretary. "You know I did not mean. . . . My character is such—I cannot conceive how you can jest on such subjects—"

"Your conceptions are limited," said Leonora, still more wickedly. "Now, if you ever conceived a child. . . . Well, so you think we are likely to die of pneumonia, but that if we escape such a fate as that, the worst is still to come? Is that it?"

"Yes, Mrs. Latimer," replied Miss Rhodes, trying to collect herself somewhat. "There is grave danger of shipwreck. It is well known that more boats have gone to their doom in the Straits of Magellan, in proportion to the number passing through here, than in any other navigable waters. While as to the Beagle Channel—"

"I see," Leonora said. The gentleness had vanished from her manner. It was as frigid as the crystalline air about them. "And have you some practical suggestion to make for escaping a watery grave?"

"This—this boat," said Miss Rhodes, as if she could hardly bear to speak of such an object, "is to stop at Magallanes, I believe. The most dangerous part of the voyage comes after that. If you would only consider disembarking, Mrs. Latimer, and going directly north! I am told that there is a line of small, comfortable Chilean ships plying between Magallanes and Puerto Montt. I—as a matter of fact, I have looked up the connections. We could leave Magallanes the very day after our arrival there. Amelia and Fernando agree with me that this would be a very wise plan."

Without haste, Leonora rose, disentangling herself gracefully from the tawny vicuña robes in which she was wrapped. Mechanically, Miss Rhodes leaned over to rearrange them. As she straightened up again, she found herself eye to eye with her employer; and on

Leonora's lovely face was an expression which was, at one and the same time, mocking and relentless.

"Thank you so much, Miss Rhodes," she said, casually. "Now you may go and send a cable making reservations for yourself, and for Amelia and Fernando, on the nice, safe, little Chilean ship that leaves Magallanes the day after we arrive there. Then you may go to your cabin and pack, and you may tell the others to do the same. I will leave checks for all of you at the purser's desk. They will be adequate for your every immediate need. And references will be inclosed. I think that is all we need to say to each other."

But Miss Rhodes, horror-stricken, strove to say one thing more. "You can't mean it!" she protested brokenly. "Oh, Mrs. Latimer, don't send us away like that! After all these years! We've been presumptuous, perhaps, and—and cowardly, but we do love you. Indeed we do! And—and you *need* us! What will you do without us?"

"Do?" asked Leonora icily. "Why, I—I shall stay with the ship. I am only sorry that wrecks, in the Fuegian Canals and everywhere else, are as obsolete as hoopskirts. I think I should rather enjoy one."

She spoke sincerely, as well as satirically. She really felt, as she annihilated her secretary, that a shipwreck might furnish her with the supreme solution which she had sought for so long in vain.

But when the *Don Quixote* struck a sunken shelf in a small archipelago south of Cape Horn, and sank, bow downward, into the glittering Antarctic Sea, she really did not enjoy herself at all.

Ushuaya, the bleak convict colony at the tip of Tierra del Fuego, had been one of the *Don Quixote's* ports of call; and Leonora had spent the morning there so aimlessly, and with such a sense of utter desolation, that she was thankful when it was time to rejoin the ship. She had just finished her luncheon and had gone up to the social hall, where she was standing with her back against the starboard after bulkhead, smoking a

cigarette, when a sudden violent jolt threw her almost
off her feet; and, as she steadied herself, she was conscious of a muffled rumbling sound, followed by the
crash of falling glassware.

She turned toward a pretty Brazilian bride standing
near her, with an attempt at laughter which she realized, even at the moment, was not wholly successful.

"Has someone put brakes on the ship?" she asked
whimsically. "Or is this a young earthquake? I don't
know much about earthquakes! However, that rumbling—"

She received no answer. The Brazilian bride, giving
a long low moan as she dove out of sight, had already
scuttled away; and all the other passengers who, a moment before, had been standing companionably about,
had vanished as if by magic. Leonora was all alone.

Forcing herself to move quietly, she opened the
door of the social hall and walked out on the promenade deck. Ushuaya was almost out of sight. Long
strands of seaweed, rooted to the ship's bottom, were
streaming along the surface of the quicksilver water in
the direction of the wind. A jagged rock, rising gauntly
out of the ocean nearby, battered by the waves that
hurtled and hammered against it, accentuated the un-
canny sense of immobility. For the natural motion of a
ship afloat had ceased abruptly, and the peculiar feeling that she was no longer on a real ship was enhanced
for Leonora by the reflexes of her rebellious muscles,
which, up to that moment, had been responsive to the
ship's vibrations, and which now seemed paralyzed.
Though the deck was cluttered with confusion, she was
too bewildered to become a part of it.

The bow was sinking fast, the sluiced deck slanting
forward. A solitary shriek clove through the tense atmosphere. Leonora, setting her teeth, tried to dig the
rubber heels of her small shoes into the holystoned
surface under them, and keep her balance. But as the
ship filled, it listed heavily toward port, and she was
thrown, with a dozen others, into a huddle against the
outer wall of the bulkhead.

As she struggled to her feet again, intuitively aware

that if the ship did not come back there would be a disaster, she was curiously conscious of the fact that her paramount sensation, besides that of unreality, was not one of fear, but of loneliness. She was entirely composed, while all around her terrified women were weeping and crossing themselves. But her composure brought her no sense of superiority. For these frightened fellow passengers of hers had been quickly sought out by husbands and lovers, fathers and sons. They were being kissed and comforted, hastened across the slanting deck, guided to the after-end, where the crew, with furious haste, was beginning to unlash the lifeboats. In this hour of peril, all the men who had paid her persistent court from the moment that the *Don Quixote* had steamed out of the Rio de la Plata had deserted her for the drab creatures to whom she had felt they were fettered, and to whom she now saw they were bound by ties of tenderness stronger than any she had ever known. None of them was concerned for her safety. She, who had thrust Ramón de la Barra relentlessly out of her life and driven away the faithful servants who had followed her to the ends of the earth, was wretchedly alone. . . .

A cloud of thin brownish smoke was pouring out of the well deck, and a whistle was blowing short sharp blasts. Perhaps, after all, these might be heard in Ushuaya, though this already seemed so unreal and remote; and slowly, heavily, the ship was coming back, and passengers were surging out from every direction. But no one stopped to speak to Leonora. She wedged her way forward just in time to see a screaming sailor pitched into the sea from a lifeboat that had been precipitately released at one end.

The throng that had been pressing against the rail fell back, with a gasp of horror. There was a sharp outcry and a desperate demand for life belts rang out. Leonora touched a young officer, who was vainly trying to keep the crowd under control, on the arm.

"Tell them that I'll go below and find some belts," she said impellingly. "I'll get someone to help me. And

I'm not afraid. It doesn't matter when I get off. I'm all alone."

He nodded abruptly, and went on shouting with stern reassurance to the frightened, threatening mob herded about him, trying to make his voice carry above the clatter and din. When Leonora regained the deck, dragging a dozen life preservers after her, and followed by a cabin boy whom she had corralled and laden with others, two more boats had been lowered, with an ominous sound of creaking ropes and dashing water, but with no more mishaps; and helter-skelter, an officer, several stewards, and a score of passengers had scrambled into each of them and were shoving off.

"Those stewards are not seamen," Leonora heard a man standing near her say with tense conviction. "They'll never be able to handle the oars, and keep the boats headed into the wind."

She turned to look at him, and saw that he was a pleasant young merchant, who represented a large American firm in Buenos Aires, and who was taking his first vacation since his marriage. He was holding a wide-eyed, year-old baby tightly against his shoulder, and his wife, a frail girl whose hair blew in long damp wisps across her face, was clinging to his arm.

"Oh, Jim! What will happen if they can't?" she cried convulsively.

"The boats will get broadside and ship water," he said grimly. But he added quickly, "Don't worry, Elsie. There's plenty of time, really. We'll wait for a boat that isn't so full. You can hold the baby after we get in, and I'll row. We'll be all right. We'll be safe."

"I can row, too," broke in Leonora. "If your wife would hold the baby *now,* Mr. Mathewson, and you'd come and help me pick up life preservers, I think— pretty soon—"

"Oh, Jim, don't—don't go off and leave me! Not for a second! I couldn't bear it!"

"Well, now, I guess you couldn't." The young merchant looked steadily at Leonora. "Thanks a lot, Mrs. Latimer. Perhaps we'll make the same boat yet—I hope so. But I guess I'd better stay here with my wife. I guess she needs me."

He was still standing protectively beside her when Leonora came up on deck for the last time, carrying a small satchel in each hand. For nearly an hour she had kept on dragging up life preservers, the cabin boy whom she had galvanized into loyal service following close at her heels. Then she had been told by the curt young officer that no more could be used: as soon as the frantic crowds had recovered from the first shock of seeing the ill-fated sailor fall headlong into the sea, they had forgotten about the belts and had plunged toward the boats without them. Nearly everyone was off the ship now. She had better get ready to leave herself. She nodded and, going below decks again, waded her way along to her own stateroom, through a corridor where hats and bags, forgotten in the rush for safety, were floating on the mounting water. A deadly calm pervaded the passages which had been teeming with tumult only a little while before. In one of them she passed a grizzled engineer who was making soundings, and who did not even look up as she went by; and when she reached the saloon, she saw the Captain, accompanied by the First Officer, walking quietly about as if on routine inspection. He raised his cap and spoke to her.

"I must thank you for your courage and helpfulness, Señora," he said courteously. "They have been duly reported to me, and I am very grateful." Then he added, "And I must say good-bye to you."

"Hasta la vista, Señor Capitán," she answered, trying to speak lightly.

"It is not hasta la vista this time, it is adiós," he answered gravely.

"But the ship has righted herself!"

"Yes, for the moment. I think you will escape—you and all the other passengers—and find refuge. If our whistle was heard in Ushuaia, a coast guard and launches will come out. And even if the lifeboats are not all picked up, sooner or later they should reach shore. We are not far away. But the Don Quixote has made her last voyage. Tonight—or tomorrow morning —or tomorrow noon—as to that, *quien sabe?*—she will list again. And that time, she will sink. And the Captain stays with his ship, *Señora*. So it is *adiós*," he said again, raising her hand to his lips. "You must go to your lifeboat now."

Leonora's eyes blurred and her lips began to tremble. Involuntarily, she thought of the mocking way in which she herself had spoken of "staying with the ship" only a few weeks earlier, how she had satirically said that wrecks were as obsolete as hoopskirts. And now there had been a wreck, and she was leaving the ship that was going to sink. With a supreme effort she turned away, and walked resolutely toward the deck.

As the crowd had thinned, the uproar and confusion had subsided there, as it had below; but shouts and screams were still rising from the rocking lifeboats, where the frantic stewards were futilely struggling against the waves and wind. Jim Mathewson again looked steadily at Leonora.

"We waited for you," he said; and, for a moment, her heart leaped, because it seemed that, after all, she was not alone, that there was someone who really cared. "I thought my wife would be safer in the boat with you than with anyone else," he added with unconscious cruelty. "Shall we get along?"

"One—of—the—launches—may—pick—us—up!" he called gaspingly back over his shoulder to Leonora half an hour later. "They'll—take—all—the—boats—they —can—in—tow! Help—me—to—hold—her—in—the —wind, Mrs. Latimer! Till—the—cutter—comes!"

But all of Leonora's efforts, though she handled an oar as few women could or would, and was ably assisted by the curt young officer, the cabin boy, and the ship's chaplain, who at the last moment had sprung into the lifeboat after her, did not suffice to hold it in the wind. Hours later—long, cold, wet, hideous hours later—it was blown up against the rocks; and while the refugees were struggling toward the shore, waist-deep in icy water, the baby's food supply, to which Elsie had desperately clung throughout the wreck, was swept away as she was knocked down by the buffeting waves.

For her, this was the last straw. She had been desperately seasick in the pitching lifeboat; and nausea, which had devastated the chaplain and the cabin boy, also, had been actually annihilating for her. She sank down where she was, and began to shriek hysterically.

"Give me the baby," Leonora said to Jim Mathewson, through chattering teeth. "And pick Elsie up in your arms. We'll be all right in a minute—all of us."

It was a shivering, forlorn, little group of refugees that finally found a foothold among the cliffs. But they managed to build a fire from driftwood; for Leonora, somehow, had succeeded in clinging to her two little satchels, and when she undid them, and ripped open her rubber sponge bag, she tossed out, first of all, a box of matches and next, two packages of cigarettes! She had a flask, too, filled to the stopper with brandy, three thermos bottles full of fresh water, and a tightly corked bottle of malted milk.

"I thought we should probably need all these before we got through," she said encouragingly. "Can you mix a drink for the baby in this collapsible cup, Elsie? I imagine the rest of us won't want our drink mixed! But nothing except the cup is going to collapse! How far do you think we are from Ushuaya, *Señor Teniente?*"

"About fourteen kilometers, *Señora,*" the curt young officer replied, between gulps of brandy.

"What a nice invigorating walk! And when we get there, where do we stay?"

"There is the jail, *Señora*. And three bars and a pool room—"

Leonora laughed. Then, suddenly, she looked thoughtful.

"Is there a telegraph office there?" she asked, almost abruptly.

"But of course, *Señora!* How can you ask such a question? This is a civilized country."

"I am so glad you told me," she said a trifle drily. "And is there a 'track' too? You call it a 'track' in Patagonia, don't you? Is there any kind of a 'track' from Ushuaya to San Mariano?"

"The great *estancia* of the de la Barra family, *Señora*? There is sure to be!"

"Then we're going there," announced Leonora promptly. "All of us! Let's have another drink all around to fortify us for our journey!"

Forty-eight hours later, the ancient and monumental limousine, which had been put at Leonora's disposal by the governor of the penal colony, swerved off the "track" on which it had jolted and rocked across the pampas from Ushuaya, and lunged up a broad drive-way, past tennis courts, conservatories and gardens, toward a huge house overtopped by the tall white "windbreaks" that encircled it; and, as Leonora descended, with such dignity as she still retained, from the antique conveyance in which she had been shaken almost to pieces, her weary fellow travelers caught a glimpse of a curving, glass-enclosed portico, filled with bright flowers, beyond the broad steps which she mounted somewhat slowly and stiffly. Then they saw the front door open swiftly, and the tall dark form of a man looming up in it; and after that, they saw nothing at all except the black façade of the house. For the dark man gathered Leonora into his arms with a cry that was half joyous exultation and half angry amazement; and then the door closed with almost incredible swiftness, blotting out the two closely interlocked figures from the view of the Mathewsons, the young officer, the cabin boy and the ship's chaplain.

A year earlier, Ramón de la Barra had swung savagely out of Leonora's house after having embraced her passionately and bade her a furious farewell; and now that she had presented herself, with such apparent nonchalance at his, the first words that he spoke to her, after he released her, were furious, too.

"What do you mean by all this?" he demanded with rage. "What do you expect me to make of a message that reads, 'Escaping from jail arriving to visit you with my fellow convicts'? Is there no subject upon which you will not jest? What were you doing in Ushuaya?"

"I was taking a pleasure cruise," answered Leonora, still struggling for breath.

"A pleasure cruise! And how did you happen to land in jail on a pleasure cruise?"

"Because there was a shipwreck," she said, more calmly by this time. "A very futile sort of wreck, Ramón—not even exciting after the first few moments. And when we were rescued, the jail seemed the best place to stay. For the baby, I mean."

"The baby!" gasped Ramón, skipping over the shipwreck entirely. "Do you dare to stand there and tell me that you have a baby, Leonora Latimer, and that you have brought it to my home?"

"Why, yes. But I am sorry to say that it is only a borrowed baby, Ramón."

He glared at her with unabated rage and increasing scepticism. Then gradually his face cleared, and he laughed, putting his arm around her again.

"I have no idea how much of this fantastic story you are making up," he said, less angrily, "or how you ever found out that I was here, for that matter—"

"I would tell you, if you would only give me a chance, instead of first stifling me and then storming at me. I spent the day in Magallanes with your grandmother. She told me—a good many things about you. And I have not made up anything. Don't you ever get any news at all at San Mariano? Not that it matters —except that we are all pretty tired—and cold—and —hungry, Ramón—and that I have been so desperately lonely! Won't you let me bring the others in—and then explain all the details afterward?"

It was at this point that Leonora Latimer, who had never been known to shed tears, put her head down on Ramón de la Barra's shoulder and began to weep; and that was why the weary travelers, waiting dismally outside the *Casa Grande* of the *estancia* San Mariano in

the decrepit limousine, were so tardily and apologetically rescued. But at last they were brought in out of the
cold and the wind by a grave and courteous host. They
were ushered into a wide entrance hall where a great
coal fire was glowing. They were conducted to spacious bedrooms bright with flowered chintz. And, within an hour, they found themselves foregathered around
a groaning board chatting with the fellow guests: the
Spanish Consul, a Scotch manager of an adjacent *estancia,* an Italian journalist "covering" South America,
and a Chilean doctor, who, like themselves, had taken
refuge at San Mariano for the night, in true Patagonian
fashion.

Involuntarily, they found their eyes riveted on
Leonora. She was attired in a dress of wine-colored
brocade, which had been in the trousseau of Adela
Carmen de la Barra, and which had been extracted
from a huge chest of carved and painted leather. It had
a tight-fitting basque and wide, fringed flounces; it was
agreeably low, and it fitted Leonora as if she had been
molded into it. Around her neck, on a glittering chain,
was suspended a ruby cross. And, as she raised her
glass to propose that all the guests at San Mariano
should join her in drinking a health to their host, they
noticed that rubies glittered on her slim white fingers,
too.

At last she looked smilingly down the length of the
great white table, as if seeking Ramón's assent before
giving the signal to rise; and, as he bowed, gravely, his
eyes lingering on her lovely pale face, she rose and led
the way into the drawing room on the Consul's arm.
Then she turned courteously to the Italian journalist.

"I have heard that you are a famous musician as
well as a great writer," she said in that soft vibrant
voice to which Ramón had first listened at a White
House reception on the other side of the world.
"Would you be gracious enough to play for us a little
while? Then later, perhaps you will be my partner at
contract? It is the custom of the country to close the
evening with cards."

But though there was, as usual, a pile of silver and

bank notes at Leonora's place when the last rubber had been played, she did not, after all, close her evening with contract. She said good night to all the guests, standing at Ramón's side; and when, after a moment's hesitation, even the ship's chaplain had smiled a little quizzically but very kindly, and gone his way to bed, she slipped her hand into her host's.

"*Quiero quedarme,*" she said softly. "I want to stay."

Ramón's fingers twitched, convulsively, but they did not close grippingly around her own, and he did not answer her. His first sudden blaze of anger had died down long before; he had been all solicitude, all kindness and courtesy. But after the first violent embrace with which he had greeted her, he had not touched her again. He had played the host with whom a refugee had sought shelter, not the suitor whose long-lost love had walked straight into his arms. Even now, when the great house was hushed in sleep, and she was his for the taking, he did not speak or move.

Leonora, under lowered eyelids, gazed at him with curious tenderness. In the soft light of the warm fire, she noticed, for the first time, that he no longer looked arrogant. He looked, instead, as if all his gorgeous vanity and self-assurance had been wrung from him, as if some corroding process had eaten its way into his very soul.

"What is the matter, *querido?*" asked Leonora softly.

"You must be very tired," he said almost stiffly. "You have been through a terrible shock and strain. I hope that now you may have some rest. But before you leave me, I must beg your pardon for the way in which I greeted you this afternoon. I am very much ashamed."

"But why, Ramón? I thought it was a very nice way."

She spoke lightly, almost lovingly. But he disregarded her expression.

"And I must tell you that I cannot bear to have you

look—and act—as you have done tonight. As if you were really *dueña de casa* at San Mariano."

"But I am. Or I am going to be. So it is all the same. By the way, I must get off a cable to Miss Rhodes. She and Amelia and Fernando would be very helpful with all this company."

Ramón almost pushed her away from him. "You are not *dueña de casa* here," he said harshly. "And you are not going to be. I have lost my right to you through my own senseless folly. I have lost everything."

"Have you?" asked Leonora quietly.

This time Ramón raised his head and stared at her. There was something in her voice that he did not understand.

"You mean," she said evenly, "you were recalled from Washington because of your indiscreet boastfulness. You may remember that I warned you. So now your diplomatic career is ended, and your father feels this so keenly that he suggested you should leave Buenos Aires—indefinitely—and bury yourself in Tierra del Fuego. You thought you could occupy yourself with the direction of the *estancia,* at least. But the Scotch manager is so very capable that he really does not need much help. You are very lonely, with your nearest neighbor forty miles away; and you are so disheartened that you do not even try, any longer, to find out what is happening around you—even when a shipwreck happens!"

"How did you learn all this?" broke in Ramón. But Leonora did not answer him. She went on as if she had not heard him, locking her slim fingers into his lean ones and pressing them hard.

"I never shall forget this first ride of mine across the 'track,'" she said softly, "the whistling winds and the purple haze and the great solitary stones! The *guanacos* and the wild geese and thousands and thousands of little lambs! The endless miles of pampas gave me a sense of space that I'd never had anywhere else in the world! And I never had such a welcome as I did at the house where we stopped last night. It wasn't a *casa grande* like this one. It was just a simple, little white frame cottage. But the most wonderful person came out to greet us—a rugged old Scotswoman whose six sons have all been born here. You can't think how I want her for my friend! But I didn't stay with her long, this time, because if I had, I would have been late in getting to San Mariano. And I knew that there would be more than just kindness and hospitality. I knew that here radiance and fullness of life were waiting for me!"

"What are you trying to say to me?" Ramón asked hoarsely, finding his voice at last.

"Have you no imagination at all that you cannot guess?" Leonora retorted, her words coming with a swift stifled sob. "Do you think I would have ranged the world if my hearthstone hadn't been first desecrated and then desolate? Do you remember the story of the man who asked for bread and was given a stone? I have hoped for a long time that you would give me bread, Ramón. And instead, you offered me everything with which I was surfeited already—passion and wealth and power and adventure! Why didn't you offer me what I hungered and thirsted for in vain—tenderness and protection and loving-kindness; solitude and tranquillity; a home; children—" Suddenly, as if she were utterly spent, she bowed her head on his shoulder. "Won't you offer them to me now?" she whispered. "Won't you keep me with you in this lovely 'Land of Fire'—where I can have them all?"

For a moment, Ramón continued to gaze at her as if he could not believe his senses. Then he flung his arms around her. The blight of bitterness had faded from his face; it shone with reflected glory. He pressed it hard against her dark hair, holding her as if he would never let her go.

"Dulce amiga, vida mia, alma de mi alma," he whispered between his kisses. But Leonora was not even conscious of what he said or did. She only knew her wandering was over.

The restless lady had reached home at last.

THE OUTSIDER

MARGERY-ANNE Allen attended her first party at the Congressional Club in a white muslin dress, with hemstitched ruffles around the bottom of the skirt and a blue sash around her waist. She wore, moreover, low-heeled black patent leather slippers, somewhat the worse for wear, with white cotton stockings; a heart-shaped locket with one small turquoise embedded in the centre, and a turquoise ring.

There had seemed nothing wrong with the dress when, fresh from the loving, hard-working hands of Aunt Sally, it had been spread out, in all its spotless crispness, on Margery-Anne's big, four-poster bed, before she packed it in the little horsehair trunk which Father had carried down from the dim, dusty attic. On the contrary. It had seemed a very perfect dress indeed, exactly what the daughter of a newly-elected congressman might wear in Washington with credit to both herself and her position. But on the train doubts as to its fitness had already begun to assail her, dimming the glamor of her first long trip away from home. There were several girls of about her own age in the cold and dingy day coach, and Margery-Anne looked them over with an anxious eye as they went swaying up and down the dingy aisle to get water from the "cooler." She could not, somehow, picture any of them in ruffled white muslin, and this troubled her. Once she felt for her father's hand, and as his responsive fingers tightened over hers, she whispered,

"Father, are you sure that you won't be ashamed of me in Washington?"

Stephen Allen put his head back and laughed; and then he kissed her, right there in the train, and told her he reckoned she was his girl, all right, and they'd show the world together yet. This ought to have reassured her, absolutely. But someway, it didn't.

It was late in the evening when they reached Washington, and Margery-Anne was so cold and so tired that the blaze of lights in the office of the Ebbitt House made her feel very sick and giddy. Stephen Allen noticed just in time that she was "getting white around the gills" and hustled her into an elevator—the first elevator in which she had ever ridden—and down the long corridor to her room, and into bed before she could say "Jack Robinson." Then the next morning he appeared again before she was awake, laughing and shaking her gently, and asking her why she didn't answer the telephone.

"Where is it?" she asked, instantly obedient to his wishes though still stupid with sleep, "In the front hall? But Father, I'd have to get dressed first!"

"Why, Marge, it's there, right by your bed."

He put the instrument into her hands, and she was aware of the clear and pleasant voice of a woman who was addressing her. "Miss Allen? Ah, so you got in last night safely, didn't you? This is Mrs. Warwick speaking, Senator Warwick's wife. May I come in sometime during the course of the morning and see you, my dear? I knew your mother very well—we were at school together—and I'd like to have you think of me as your first friend in Washington."

It was when Mrs. Warwick, following closely in the wake of her telephone call, appeared in person, and Margery-Anne looked her over carefully, that the doubts about the white muslin dress began to increase.

Not that Mrs. Warwick failed to be kind. She was very kind. There was nothing in her manner to infer that she, the wife of the Senior Senator from the State, was doing a great favor to call upon the daughter of its most recently elected and most obscure congressman. Mrs. Warwick had been genuinely fond of Margery-Anne's mother, and the sympathy which she felt for the motherless girl, so abruptly wrested from her native surroundings, warmed to instant affection as she sat and talked with her. Both these factors combined to make her kind; and it was part and parcel of her kindness, of course, that she suggested the reception and dance at the Congressional Club that evening.

"We'll stop by for you about half-past eight then," she said gaily as she rose to leave; and was gone before Margery-Anne could voice those doubts that were assailing her.

Stephen Allen was delighted that Margery-Anne had been asked to go to the party. He saw that she looked almost as white as she had the evening before, but this, he decided, would wear off after things got going. He accompanied her to the door of the hotel when Senator Warwick's car was announced, and slapping her gently on the back, charged her to have a good time.

And now, instead of having a good time, she was miserable, more miserable than she had ever been before in her life.

For as she watched Mrs. Warwick shed a cloak of burgundy velvet lined with silver tissue and trimmed with ermine, she saw that, underneath, there was a dress to match the cloak, a dress of burgundy velvet embroidered in rhinestones. There was a glittering bandeau around Mrs. Warwick's silvery, waved hair, there were glittering buckles on her silver slippers. And every one of the women who were greeting her and chatting with each other, wore glittering ornaments too, and were dressed, either in velvet as gorgeous as hers, or in brocade, and satin, and laces that seemed more gorgeous still. The young girls, gathered together in one corner of the dressing room, and laughing, intimately, were, it was true, less elaborately gowned; but their pastel-shaded chiffons, so simply and so scantily cut, were insidiously lovely, just the same. And one of these girls, catching sight of Margery-Anne, stared, and then giggled, as she whispered to the pretty young creature standing beside her.

Mrs. Warwick, apparently, was oblivious to Margery-Anne's misery. At all events, she was presenting her to one of these beautiful ladies after another, calmly, cordially. "Miss Margery-Anne Allen, the newest acquisition to our circle—Mr. Stephen Allen's only daughter—*you* know what a landslide his recent election was—nothing like it in our state, at least within *my* memory. Weren't you at the Fort School when Margaret Tyler was there? Well, this is her child." And so on, and so on. They had rejoined Senator Warwick, who, plump and placid, was awaiting them at the foot of the curving staircase. They had passed the *Winged Victory,* banked with flowers, taken the right branch of the stairs, paused beside some fluted columns. A man in livery was bowing. "What name, Madam?" And then they were passing down a long receiving line—a receiving line made up entirely of smiling ladies carrying great bouquets of flowers, and one and all dressed in velvet, brocade, satin, and lace. Worse than this: in all the great white room, exquisitely decorated with ferns and flowers, and with the flags of every state in the Union floating in a frieze overhead, not one of the women and girls dancing so gaily to the music of the Marine Band, which, gorgeous in full-dress uniform was playing in the further corner, not one of these girls and women had on a white muslin dress, a blue sash, black patent leather slippers, cotton stockings or a gold locket!

Mrs. Warwick had been swallowed up in the receiving line; she was, it appeared, one of the numerous vice presidents of the club, and as such it was her duty to greet the guests, as long as they continued to arrive. Senator Warwick, mindful of the proprieties, invited Margery-Anne to dance; and puffing and panting, propelled her twice around the room, before coming to an abrupt stop near the dining alcove, where a candlelit table, in the centre of which a small flower-fringed fountain was playing over colored glass, was laden with tempting and delicious refreshments.

"You'd like some ice cream, wouldn't you?" he boomed joyously. "Of course! All young girls like ice cream. And then you must meet some of the boys here —not old century plants like me. Partners, real partners, that's what you must have. Eat your ice cream, my dear, and I'll keep a weather eye open for a likely partner."

Margery-Anne, swallowing hard, tried to protest that she did not care whether she danced or not. But just at that moment, the Senator, with an agility surprising in one so plump, pounced upon a very slim, very elegant young man, with sleek hair and a Grecian profile, who stood eating a lettuce sandwich with an air of complete detachment and great superiority.

"Archie! My dear Archie! I wish to present you—"

The gentleman so summoned finished his sandwich delicately before turning. Then he bowed, without speaking, in the general direction of Margery-Anne, and appeared to be about to proceed on his way.

The Senator, however, had no idea of being so easily thwarted; he kept a detaining hand upon his victim.

"—To Miss Allen. Stephen Allen's daughter—just elected from the second congressional district in the next state to yours—barely over the border—you've heard about the great landslide and so on. Miss Allen, I wish to present Mr. Foster to you, the best dancer in Washington, and incidentally the son of a shining light in the Senate."

Mr. Archie Foster, thus identified, waved a disclaiming hand. He could not, it appeared, escape. But before he asked the dowdy little thing in white muslin to dance with him—ye gods, where had she ever *found* such a dress—he had given her one swift glance of appraisal and decided exactly what he thought of her. Moreover he had been at no pains to veil the glance or conceal the decision. Margery-Anne rose in response to his reluctant invitation with her cheeks burning, and two great tears drenched the lashes of her eyelids, which she closed to hide them.

Such ability as the beautiful Mr. Foster had inherited from his illustrious father had gone entirely to his feet. He was, indeed, a matchless dancer. Even Margery-Anne, unversed as she was in the new steps, had not the slightest difficulty in following his skillful lead through the crowded room. Not once did they collide with another couple, not once were they out of time with the music or each other. Margery-Anne, whose eyes had dried by this time, glanced timidly up towards her partner's face, hoping to see a friendly smile on his lips, or hear a friendly word issuing from them. But

Mr. Archie Foster neither smiled nor spoke; and when the musicians paused, he did not clap for the encore. Other couples did, of course, vociferously; and correctly, coldly, he went through with the dance to the bitter end. Then, still without speaking, he led Margery-Anne to the corner of the room near which the musicians were stationed, bowed again, and turning on his heel, walked away from her.

In the first moment following her desertion, Margery-Anne's loneliness, her embarrassment, her shame, reached a pinnacle: Senator Warwick was nowhere to be seen, having escaped downstairs for a smoke; Mrs. Warwick, on the other side of the room, was still welcoming guests with official cordiality. Not one of the women to whom the girl had been presented in the dressing room had spoken to her since then or even seemed aware of her presence. It was unthinkable that in the brief intermission before the next dance she should rise and cross that endless, shining, slippery floor, in order to rejoin her hostess—such a course would have revealed, more pitilessly even than heretofore, the hopeless unsuitability of the white muslin dress and the blue sash. It was equally unthinkable that she should wait until after the next dance had begun, and then, unescorted, wind her way between happy, congenial couples. And certainly she could not remain, indefinitely, hidden behind the band. Twisting her hands miserably together, she looked about her for means of escape.

And, as she looked, she realized that she was not alone in her corner. Close beside her was sitting a young man who did not look much happier than she felt herself. He was a very big young man, who was not yet old enough for his size, and who appeared as loose-jointed and ungraceful as an overgrown puppy. His hair, instead of being fashionably sleek, broke into fair, undisciplined curls, and his cheeks were as rosy as a youngster's. These personal attributes, besides his unhappy expression, were the first things that Margery-Anne noticed about him. Then she became aware of something else.

He was not properly dressed; all the other boys of his age were in "Tux"; this one was clad in "swallow-tails." That, of course, was why he had hidden. He, like herself, was a social pariah.

Margery-Anne felt a wellspring of sympathy rising in her heart—a wellspring so strong that it drowned, instantly, her own self-consciousness and her own self-pity. No one, if she could help it, should be permitted to remain as unhappy as she had been herself. She turned to the awkward boy and smiled at him; and, as it happened, the awkward boy turned towards her at the same moment, met her glance, and acknowledged it by smiling himself.

"It's—it's very warm, isn't it?" said Margery-Anne, pleasantly, if without much originality.

"Oh, *rather,*" replied the awkward boy heartily, "I don't know how you stand it, really, this central heating."

"Well, I don't mind that, because we've had a furnace for several years now at home, though ours is just hot air; and of course anyone who hasn't had a furnace—"

She checked herself. This would never do. When she had meant to be kind, she must not brag about the comforts which she had enjoyed, and which, obviously, the awkward boy had not. She pictured the "air-tight" which probably heated the parlor of his home, the woodbox behind the kitchen stove, which, many times, he must have had to fill.

"You don't belong in Washington either, do you?" she went on quickly.

"Oh, rather not."

The boy spoke with emphasis. So he was homesick, too! Warily, as one who hesitates to give voice to the deeper emotions, she confided in him.

"We only got here last night, Father and I. I'd hardly ever been on a train before, and never to a hotel. Of course, the Ebbitt House is lovely, bit it *is* all strange at first, isn't it?"

"Oh, *quite,*" exclaimed the boy.

Margery-Anne began to like him very much. He

seemed an understanding sort of person. She became curious to know more about him, and decided to identify herself, thus encouraging him to do the same.

"Father is Mr. Stephen Allen. He's just been elected to Congress. His enemies said it was an accident, but it was really a landslide. He's wonderful. Is your father in Congress, too?"

"No, he's an outsider, don't you know?"

"Why, then you're even *worse* off than I am!"

The awkward boy looked at her intently. Not with that swift, cynical, appraising glance with which the beautiful Mr. Archie Foster had seared her, but with a kindly interest, even—surprising as that seemed—with admiration.

"Are you badly off?" he asked softly.

Afterwards, Margery-Anne wondered how she could have done it. But, at the moment, she did not stop to think. Above the blare of the band, she began to tell him everything: about the old house three miles outside the little country town where Father practiced law; about the long weeks alone with Aunt Sally, since Mother died, and the rare Sundays when Father was home all day; about Father's rise in local politics, which led to his rise in state politics, and finally to his election to Congress; about his decision to take her with him to Washington; about her preparations to go; about the white muslin dress. And when she had gone that far, the awkward boy listening all the time with attentive interest, it was easy to tell him the rest: about the day coach, which, as they afterwards discovered, should have been a parlor car; about the Ebbitt House, which, they afterwards discovered, should have been the Shoreham Hotel; about Mrs. Warwick's call, and the invitation to the party; about the white muslin dress again; about the handsome Mr. Archie Foster.

For the first time the awkward boy interrupted her. "That wax doll!" he exclaimed contemptuously, *"I* think your frock is *topping!"* Then he laughed, and before she knew it, Margery-Anne was laughing too. "My name is Eustace FitzMaurice," her new-found friend told her briefly, standing up, and looking, as he did so, much less awkward than he had before. "Would you do me the honor of dancing with me?" he continued, "Or would you prefer to have me presented to you properly first, and all that?"

"Oh, I'd love to dance with you, right away!" exclaimed Margery, almost breathless with joy.

"Jolly sporting of you," murmured the boy; and put his arm around her.

Lady Louise FitzMaurice, Countess of Carnor in her own right, cousin of the King of England, and wife of Lord Hugh FitzMaurice, Ambassador Extraordinary and Plenipotentiary from Great Britain to the United States, was, indisputably, the very perfect pattern of all that an ambassadress should be. Married when she was very young herself, to a young Secretary of Embassy with his spurs still to win, she, no less than he, had served her diplomatic apprenticeship in small, uninteresting and out-of-the-way posts; and, in the course of this apprenticeship, she had added to the store of tact, of charm, of brilliancy and of beauty with which she had been so liberally endowed from birth. After the apprenticeship, came better posts; Lord Hugh rose to become Second Secretary, First Secretary, *Chargé d'Affaires,* Minister, Ambassador. There was hardly a world capital which Lady Louise did not learn to know, and which did not learn to know, and to admire, her. And when, after a quarter-century of faithful service, her husband was given Washington—the greatest prize in the power of the Foreign Office to bestow—the universal verdict of approval with which the appointment was greeted was supplemented by the universal exclamation, "and how wonderful to think that Lady Louise will be the British ambassadress there!"

In Washington, as elsewhere, her success had been instantaneous; there was no obligation which she left unfulfilled, no occasion which she did not adorn; and to the casual observer it might easily have appeared that there was no nook and cranny of her time, no smallest particle of her interest, which was not claimed by her official functions. Only those who knew her very well—and Lady Louise, though a woman with a multitude of friends, had few intimates—guessed that she had a far more absorbing passion than that of her position.

This passion was her love for her only son. To her daughters she was, indeed, an affectionate and exemplary mother; but upon the boy she lavished all the devotion of which her ardent nature was capable. The one obstacle to her happiness was the enforced separation from him during his period of education; and her cup of joy ran full to overflowing, when he finally came down from Oxford, having won "firsts" in all his courses in spite of his absurd immaturity, and joined his father and herself in Washington for a holiday before beginning his own diplomatic career, in which he hoped to follow in his father's footsteps.

The Ambassador, wearied with the cares of office, went to bed and to sleep promptly at half-past eleven every night; but Lady Louise, in the chamber beside his, sat among the pillows of her *chaise-longue,* dressed in the most elegant of negligee attire, smoking cigarettes and reading French novels of doubtful discretion until such time as her son returned from whatever pastimes and pleasures had filled his evening. The hour of his return was the happiest in the day for them both, even if it chanced to be four in the morning; for Eustace FitzMaurice's love for his mother rivaled, if possible, her love for him, and there was no experience of his which he did not desire to share with her.

Lady Louise, hearing his step on the stair, looked up from a spicy paragraph, and waited for his knock. It came, almost instantly—three soft taps close together, their signal since his childhood. Then he opened the door quietly, and bounded across the room to her, grinning with affection.

"A good evening, darling?" she asked carelessly, putting the yellow-covered book down on a little inlaid table which had been given her by the Empress of

Japan, and running her fingers through his curls as he bent to kiss her.

"Topping. Looked like rather a frost at first, but in the end—got a tall drink here for me somewhere, Mother?"

"Right behind you. What seemed to be the trouble?"

"Well, I should have worn a dinner jacket in the first place. Not another male under thirty had on anything else. I felt an awful fool."

"My fault, darling. I should have warned you."

"All right, old thing. Then I missed the lady in question—she didn't meet me where she said she would."

"Mrs. Warwick?"

"Yes—deuced awkward. So I retired behind the band to recover from the sting of being at one and the same time, conspicuous and neglected—didn't know another soul in the place—then I was rewarded beyond my deserts. The prettiest girl I ever saw was dropped there by a damned cad, and I got the benefit."

Lady Louise's soft and lovely eyes dilated with interest.

"Bless her dear little heart! She was sorry for me. She thought I was in the same boat that she was. I was, of course, in a way, but not quite the way I gather she imagined." Vividly, tenderly, he described Margery-Anne and his meeting with her to his mother. "And after I had danced with her," he went on, "I found Mrs. Warwick in the receiving line—she'd come in late, which was why I didn't see her before—and discovered that this was the girl she'd invited me to meet in the first place!"

"How very jolly!" said Lady Louise.

"Rather! There was just one bad moment. Mrs. Warwick presented me, and all that, which was rather rot by that time. 'The Honorable Eustace FitzMaurice, the British Ambassador's son.' Rubbed it in, you know —how some Americans do love to put on side!—the blessed child went red as a rose. 'Honorable!' she exclaimed. 'I hope so,' I said; 'Since Mrs. Warwick stresses the point, perhaps she'd let me take you home—hours from now, of course!' "

Lady Louise helped herself to a fresh cigarette. "I expect," she said, "that you would be pleased if I invited Margery-Anne Allen to tea."

"Oh, quite," replied her son with alacrity.

Mr. Cyrus U. Foster, whose first claim to fame consisted in being the father of the best dancer in Washington, and whose second consisted in having served one term in the United States Senate, was retiring to private life because of the ingratitude of a constituency which had defeated him at the polls. This lack of appreciation told heavily upon the Senator; but more heavily still upon his son, Archie. How, in his native Rosamondville, was he to give scope to those talents which, for nearly six years, had caused him to be the honored guest at every dance in the capital (except a very few, given by some short-sighted "cave-dwellers" and diplomats who did not realize what they were missing by his absence). And how, moreover, was he to continue to press his suit upon the lady of his choice? There were, he was forced to admit, other claimants to her favor—interlopers whom he could keep at their proper distance as long as he himself remained upon the scene, but once removed to Rosamondville, he might not find this so easy. He had heard the ancient proverb that absence makes the heart grow fonder; but he had also observed that it did not always work out that way.

There were many reasons why he was anxious to win the lady in question. To begin with, she was very rich, her father having been most fortunate in his investments in oil and other commodities; and the Foster fortunes, never extensive, had been depleted in the effort to outshine other senatorial establishments. She lived in a pink palace on New Hampshire Avenue, a palace which was full of artistic treasures which she had collected in the course of several trips to Europe and the Orient and this pleasing establishment was quite large enough to shelter Archie, as well as her father and herself, provided she could be persuaded to accept him as a husband. In the second place, she was purported to have not a little political influence, and these rumors were strengthened by the fact that her father, who had come to Washington practically unknown, was now a member of the United States Senate —indeed, one of its outstanding senators; and since he lived very near to Rosamondville—just over the border in the next state, and had as much influence in one as in the other—it was highly possible that the father and daughter together might help Mr. Cyrus U. Foster to stage a comeback. In the third place, she was ravishingly pretty, with a Madonna-like loveliness which she set off with such garments as no other girl of his acquaintance would have had the money to buy, or the taste to choose, or the face and figure to set off. And last, but not least, he was frightfully in love with her, and would have taken her as she stood, without the oil-wells, or the pink palace, or the political influence, or the costly costumes, if he could only have got her. That, as he saw it, was the only hitch; so far he had not succeeded in getting her.

Meditating, in a luxury of woe upon his troubles, Archie Foster walked slowly up New Hampshire Avenue one afternoon, oblivious of the children playing happily around the Dupont fountain, and the balloon men crying their wares, and the magnolias blooming softly in narrow grass-plots, and all the other things that make Washington entrancing in the springtime. It was his lady-love's official day "at home" and he was on his way to see her—going, however, so late that he hoped he would have no difficulty in outstaying any other lingering guests who might still be there. For the matter of his suit was, he realized, becoming crucial, and he intended to bring affairs to a head.

He noticed, with annoyance, the congestion of cars about the pink palace. These were being skillfully directed by two police officers, evidently detailed for the purpose; but all their efforts were not sufficient to keep traffic moving, so great was the jam. There was a man in livery opening the doors of the automobiles as they drew up to the curb, and a man who was calling out the numbers of others whose owners were ready to depart. There was a man in livery at the front door, and another who was trying to keep the snowfall of visiting cards from overflowing a great silver bowl, and still another who was directing gentlemen to leave their wraps on the right, and ladies to leave theirs on the left. There was an orchestra of gypsy music, its members clad in tall boots, sky-blue trousers, and white blouses cross-stitched in red, green and yellow, which was playing in the curve of the hall; and beyond, the crowded dining room could be seen, with American Beauties rising in tall silver vases, and a cloth of Venetian point on the laden table; while up and down the stairway personages were moving, with a slow and stately tread: a Cabinet officer and his wife; the Vice President's pretty daughter; two Justices of the Supreme Court; one of the shining lights of the State Department and his sister; a dozen or more women of official importance.

Several of these dignitaries glanced at Archie, nodded, and then glanced away again. But one of them, a very beautiful woman dressed in dark purple, smiled cordially and extended her hand.

"Mr. Foster—I am so delighted to see you. Are you in very great haste to go upstairs? If not, I would so much like a word with you in the library."

Archie foamed at the mouth. He *was* in haste to go upstairs, though his haste, he realized, would avail him nothing as long as this awful crowd lingered. But he considered the British Ambassadress, who was addressing him, a greatly overestimated person, and had no desire to converse with her in the library or anywhere else. She had lately entertained, as a houseguest, a Royal Highness; and she had not invited him, Archie, to the dinner, or even to the reception which had been given for the Prince, although there had been dancing. However, he could not very well publicly affront Lady Louise; it would be better, he decided, to do this privately; and suffered himself to be led into the apartment which she had designated.

This was a cool and restful place, furnished in Cordova leather, and brightened by many flowers placed in clear glass bowls on small low tables near reading lamps; and it contained, moreover, a large number of books, for the girl he loved was surprisingly fond of reading. Lady Louise settled herself comfortably in one of the deep chairs, and lighted a cigarette. Personally, Archie disapproved of women who smoked.

"What a lovely house this is!" said the ambassadress, easily, "quite the loveliest, I think, in Washington. As our hostess is quite the loveliest woman."

"Young woman," corrected Archie, with an attempt at gallantry.

Lady Louise smiled and sighed. "Ah! women are always lovelier when they are young. Therefore no old woman, however lovely, can compete in loveliness with a young one. Especially a young one like the girl in question. The Prince was *tout épris* with her."

Archie's French was shaky, but he understood the drift of Lady Louise's remark. "It is a doubtful compliment, I think," he said stiffly, "to a young American girl, when royalty pays her marked attentions."

The ambassadress raised delicate eyebrows. "A doubtful compliment?" she echoed. "To be considered worthy of a throne? She might, perhaps, have been the first American queen—had it not been for a previous attachment."

"The Prince's marriage is, of course, already arranged."

Lady Louise's eyebrows went higher still. "Is it? I did not know. When I spoke of an attachment, I meant on the part of our friend. I believe that if she is not already actually engaged, her betrothal may be expected at any moment."

Archie's heart gave a bound of joy. The outlook was then, brighter than he had dared to hope. He beamed upon the ambassadress.

"An American woman," she went on thoughtfully, "would, without doubt, make a very queenly sort of queen, if one may use such an expression. She is the most adaptable creature on earth, and she would adapt herself to a throne quite as easily as to anything else. Because she is royal at heart, no matter how humble her first surroundings may have been. The outer trappings do not matter very much. It is what there is inside that counts. And the inside is very, very good indeed."

Lady Louise laughed lightly, and pressed the stub of her cigarette against a small jade tray to extinguish it. "This is a very suitable place in which to discuss the adaptability of the American woman," she said, "because our hostess is the personification of it. A little over five years, is it not, since she first came to Washington? And went to her first dance at the Congressional Club in white muslin and a blue sash, a forlorn little outsider. Not that she wasn't lovely then, though I have heard that there were persons so blind that they couldn't see it at first. How they must have regretted their shortsightedness since she became a *succès fou!*"

She rose, "I mustn't keep you," she said, "if you really wish to go upstairs. Though I should advise against it. I think the reception is virtually over, and Margery-Anne ought to have an opportunity to rest before dinner, for which I know she has an engagement."

The ambassadress slipped gracefully out of sight, her faint, slightly mocking laugh following her as she went. Ye gods, how he hated the woman! After all, for what had she detained him? To murmur glittering generalities on subjects that were either unwelcome or incomprehensible to him—except for that one glowing remark about a previous attachment. Archie hurried towards the now-deserted stairs, and took them two at a time.

A strange, pregnant silence greeted his ascent. There was not a sound of any kind, except the soft singing of burning wood in an open fireplace, which made itself heard and felt even though it was unseen. But somehow he knew, in spite of the stillness, that the drawing room was not empty. He lifted the brocade portière, embroidered, as only the Chinese know how to embroider, in white and flying birds.

Except for the fire, and one soft, shaded lamp which glowed like a huge dusky ruby, the great, gorgeous room was unlighted. But in the centre of it he could see standing, motionless and unbelievably close together, a man and a girl in each other's arms. The man's head was bent and the girl's head was lifted; and they were kissing each other with all the ecstasy that love and youth can bring to passion.

Slowly, lingeringly, as if reluctant to unclasp each other even for a moment, and yet instinctively aware of an alien presence, they dropped their arms and turned. The girl took a step forward, and as she did so, the sheen of the white brocade which fashioned the medieval dress which she wore, the sapphires set in silver which formed her hanging girdle, shimmered and glittered in the dim light; she raised her hand, and let it rest for an instant on a heart-shaped pendant which hung at her breast—a pendant carved from one great yellow diamond, revealing a ring flashing with sparkling stones—a ring which had first been given, centuries before, by a king to the lady whom he loved, and which their descendant had given to this girl. For a long moment she stood silently, glancing first towards one man, and then towards the other. At last she spoke, looking at Archie.

"I think you know my fiancé, don't you, Archie?" she asked quietly, "The Honorable Eustace Fitz-Maurice, Secretary of Embassy! He has just returned to Washington on leave of absence from his post at Madrid, and when he goes back there, I am going with him. Perhaps, since he is here so seldom, you may not remember him, though he and I have been fond of each other for a long time; but you met him, I recall, at least once—at the Congressional Club, several years ago." She paused, smiling, and slipped her arm through the tall Englishman's again. "You may excuse us if we did not notice you when you first came in. We did not realize that there was an outsider present."

THE SENATOR AND THE SEÑORITA

NO ONE would have dreamed of disputing the preeminent position in official Washington of Mrs. J. Montgomery Ellington. She had first come to the capital, a girl still in her teens, to act as hostess for her husband, who was more than twenty years her senior, when he was elected to the United States Senate. She was a second wife, rich, lovely and intelligent. She was also inexperienced, but she acquired experience painlessly, rapidly and gracefully. She proved to be an immediate and entire success. Even her step-daughters loved her; and when she married them off—one to an English duke, the other to an Italian prince—they publicly gave her the credit for it. No greater tribute could be paid to any woman.

It is hardly strange, then, that she was adored by her only child, a son, who in due course, fell heir to his father's place in the Senate Chamber and elsewhere, after the first Senator Ellington died of apoplexy at the conclusion of a five-hour speech he was making in a famous filibuster. J. Montgomery Ellington, Jr., who was the very glass of fashion and mold of form, did not marry. He continued to live with his mother in the mammoth red-brick mansion, which his father, at the time of his second marriage, had erected on Massachusetts Avenue. And, in this imposing residence, his mother continued to entertain the great of the earth for him, as she had entertained them for his father over a period of thirty years. He seldom needed so much as to say, "Oh, by the way, Mother, I should rather like to give a dinner in honor of so-and-so." Before the thought had fully formulated in his mind, his mother was apt to remark, very casually, "By the way, Monte, if the fifth of next month would be agreeable to you, I think that would be a good night to give a dinner in honor of so-and-so." And that was all there was to it. The household machinery ran with

51

smooth and noiseless perfection. Every morning, he found beside his plate a small pink slip torn from one of the plump memorandum blocks headed "United States Senate," on which had been written in his mother's flowing hand, "Dinner tonight with the Secretary of War at eight-thirty. Musicale at the French Embassy afterwards."—"Dinner with the Vice-President at eight. Children's Hospital ball at the Willard afterwards."—"Dinner at home with bridge."—And so on. When he returned from the Capitol, his evening clothes were already laid out on his bed. If he were dining out, the limousine was waiting at the door, prompt to the minute, to take him to his destination. Mrs. J. Montgomery Ellington issued all the necessary orders, and, what was more, saw to it that these orders were executed without any effort on the part of J. Montgomery Ellington, Jr.

This had gone on, without variation, for so long that it was with a distinct sense of shock that Monte, who was taking his ease in the cloakroom, received a summons from a page, who stated that the senator's mother would like to speak with him on the telephone. It had never been her habit to interrupt his unremitting labors in his country's service; and he foresaw nothing less than a death in the family—a death occurring most inopportunely, on the very day when the new Ambassador from South America, *Señor* Don Ricardo Honorio Miguel Accosta—was dining with them for the first time.

His mother's voice, carefully controlled and cultivated, did little to reassure him. There was not a death in the family. There was a situation rather worse. Blair, the undependable young British attaché whom she had never liked, had "given out" because of an acute attack of appendicitis and they were a "man short" for the dinner. Prolonged efforts on her part—efforts which had cost her an entire afternoon of official calling, which it would be difficult for her to make up later —had met with no result, in the way of "filling in."

She did not know where else to turn—she had asked everyone of whom she could think. She was actually asking him to help her out.

"I am distressed to annoy you, Monte, to put such a burden upon you,"—it was plain that she was suffering, as much as he, from her first inadequacy—"but is there some bachelor, among the senators, whom you could—?"

"They'll all have dinner engagements already. Why, it's after six, and we're on the point of adjournment, after a terribly hard day—"

"I know, Monte, I know, but perhaps there is *some-one*—"

Monte turned from the telephone, and re-entered the Senate Chamber, trying to remember that a gentleman is always calm, even in the face of calamity. As he did so, he collided with an inferior person who was plainly very angry at something, and who was making no effort whatever to be calm, and could not, by any stretch of the imagination—Monte's imagination—be called a gentleman.

This inferior person was Ralph Olson, the youngest man in the Senate, a "progressive" from one of the western states, who, through some hideous political mistake had recently been elected by an overwhelming majority—it might almost be called a landslide. He was uncouth in appearance, a great raw-boned clumsy oaf, his thick blond hair sticking up like a scrubbing brush all over his big head, his face burnt to a permanent brick-red by the unrefined elements. He was even more uncouth in dress; for he wore, day after day, a sack suit of a strange coarse tawny material, which certainly had never been either cleaned or pressed. And most of all he was uncouth in manner. He had a loud resonant voice, and he spoke with an accent which betrayed his Swedish ancestry. He was forever charging into situations and challenging individuals, instead of remaining silently in the background, as a new senator ought to do. The Vice-President, who was an undependable sort of a person, and a few of the other "progressives," who did not know any better, rather liked him, though many of his colleagues disliked him heartily—none of them, perhaps, as heartily as J. Montgomery Ellington, Jr. Nevertheless, even at the moment when the unwelcome contact with this inferior person took place, Monte remembered that Olson was unmarried, and it was, of course, inconceivable that he should have a dinner engagement.

"I was just looking for you," he said pleasantly, before the "progressive" could apologize for having nearly knocked him down—perhaps Olson did not mean to apologize, but under the circumstances it was just as well to give him the benefit of the doubt. "I was wondering if you'd dine with me. Er—tonight. At—er—eight o'clock."

Olson fell back a pace and glared at him. "What's up?" he asked shortly, "Getting friendly awful sudden, aren't you?—I'm not dependent on you and your kind for favors."

"Of course not, of course not," murmured Monte soothingly, "it will be quite the other way around. I mean, it would be a favor to *me.*"

"Well, I don't know as I'm under any obligation to grant you favors," Olson muttered, looking at Monte with a shrewd expression in his eyes which made that gentleman vaguely uncomfortable. He tried again.

"My mother is terribly upset," he said gently, "she is an elderly woman, you know, and not very strong, and well, she just telephoned me asking me to help her out. To bring a—a friend home to dinner with me."

"Can't she face the prospect of eating alone with you?" asked Olson brutally.

Monte swallowed his natural resentment. "She's giving a party," he explained gently, "in honor of a new South American Ambassador and his wife and daughter. One of her guests has just given out, on account of illness, and she hasn't been able, at such short notice, to fill his place. She'll have an uneven number at the table unless—she's really very unhappy—"

He paused. Olson, for some reason, seemed to be galvanized into sudden interest. No doubt that eloquent plea for the feeble mother had touched the fellow's heart. For Olson, with another of those shrewd, disquieting glances of his, had nodded his head.

"All right," he said briefly, "I'll be there"—and disappeared into the cloakroom just as the Vice-President's gavel fell, announcing adjournment.

"But Mother, you can't—you simply can't—send *Señorita* Accosta into dinner with that roughneck."

"I *must*—what else can I do? Without breaking all the rules of precedence? He's a Senator, isn't he, even if he *is* a roughneck? I haven't been seating official dinners for thirty years without learning—"

There was actually a little edge—very little, of course, but still there, in Mrs. J. Montgomery Ellington's controlled, cultivated voice. Monte noticed, too, that the tiara which adorned the smooth permanented waves of her hair was the tiniest bit on one side, that a flesh-colored shoulder-strap showed above the silver brocade of her gown. Certainly, his mother must be suffering, suffering to a very unusual degree, or such things would have never come to pass.

"Of course, if she were her father's hostess, I could put her on your right which no doubt you would enjoy—"

"I should, very much," interrupted Monte, laying down the offending table plan with dignity.

"But since she is *not*," his mother continued, "since her father, the Ambassador, has a living wife—"

"Who is fat and frumpy," interrupted Monte again.

"The place for *Señorita* Accosta is as I have indicated—beside Senator Olson," ended Mrs. Ellington triumphantly, as the first dinner guest came into the room, and effectually put an end to further fruitless discussion.

Monte had known, of course, that it was fruitless, from the beginning. And yet, as the distinguished ambassadorial family appeared in the doorway of the drawing room, the feeling that he would like to take *Señorita* Accosta into dinner himself increased with a sudden tumultuous bound. The Ambassador, ema-

ciated, grizzly and bristling, his shirt-front banded with
ribbon from which a medal hung, his chest covered
with decorations and orders, was bending over Mrs.
Ellington's hand. The Ambassadress, a little heavy, a
little untidy, as the uncharitable Monte had indicated,
but nevertheless a handsome and urbane woman, was
bowing pleasantly in every direction, her smiling eyes
sizing up the importance of the gathering as she did so
—this was quite the most "select" dinner to which they
had been asked since their arrival in Washington.
Señorita Accosta stood behind her parents, saying
nothing, looking at nobody, her hands clasped loosely
in front of her, the very picture and pattern of a *jeune
fille comme il faut,* modest, sweet, and self-effacing.

Dark waves of smooth hair, parted in the middle,
framed the pure oval of her face; dark eyes, large and
liquid, gazed gently into space. Her brow and cheeks
were as softly white as the blossoms of a camellia, her
lips scarlet as hibiscus. There was a little string of
tight-fitting pearls clasped closely around her slim
throat; the tight-fitting bodice of her white satin dress
was cut low over her creamy shoulders, and its shimmering skirt hung full around her satin-shod feet.
There was something about her so virginal, so lovely,
so remote that Monte, looking at her, caught his
breath. For the first time in his life he saw a girl who
might, perhaps, be worthy of becoming his bride. He
made a straight line in her direction.

She greeted him with just the right amount of blushing confusion—how he hated bold, screeching debu-
tantes with painted faces and knee-length skirts and
loud voices! Her voice was very sweet and gentle, and
she spoke English with the most adorable accent imag-
inable. He had to draw her out, of course, but she
answered him very intelligently—she was not stupid or
insipid. Yes, she had enjoyed the ocean voyage im-
mensely; and the landing in New York had been most
interesting—all those tall buildings! And the Embassy
was very comfortable. She was sure she was going to
like Washington. Already she had visited the Lincoln
Memorial, the Amphitheater at Arlington, the Con-

gressional Library, the Capitol. She had sat in the Diplomatic gallery of the Senate Chamber. She had already met several delightful persons, several senators, in truth. One whom the Vice-President had presented to her parents and herself, they had especially liked. A Senator Olson—

At that moment, as Monte in a flash, realized the extent of the roughneck's duplicity and culpability in coming to the Ellington mansion under false pretenses —implying that he was sorry for Mrs. Ellington, when, all the time, he had been grasping at a chance to see *Señorita* Accosta again—the sonorous voice of the second man was heard, like an echo to the *Señorita's* gentle voice, announcing,

"Senator Olson."

The roughneck charged into the drawing room with as little ceremony as if he had been entering a cowpen. He had on a rumpled dinner coat and a black tie, carelessly knotted, which had swung around under one ear. His hair, which he had evidently not taken time to comb, looked more like a scrubbing brush than ever; his hands were grimy, and one of them was adorned with a large carbuncle ring. Singling out his hostess, he proclaimed his presence.

"I guess I'm kind of late, but little Ellie didn't give me much notice. We call him little Ellie, down in the Senate, you knew that, didn't you, Ma'am? Seems to suit him, sort of. I guess I had ought to have worn a soup and fish—oughtn't I? Well, to tell the truth, I haven't got one, and you see there was not time—if only little Ellie had of given me more notice. Out where I come from, I can take in everything I want to go in a tuck, same as I can take a tuck in everything—no offense. Pleased to meet you again, Mr. Accosta, I'm sure, and wife and daughter."

He had actually grasped the *Señorita's* lily-like hand in one of his great paws, turning his back on his host as he did so. But Monte, his creeping horror increasing with every second, could hear him saying,

"I'm going to take you into dinner—of all the luck; I started right into the parlor, as soon as I got my overcoat off, but I was ahead of the game, it seems. One of those statues in fancy-dress out in the hall suddenly came to life, and stuck out a silver tray with little envelopes on it, right in my face. 'What's the big idea?' I says. 'Your escort card, sir' he says as smooth as cream. I took one of the trifling things just to humor him, and blamed if it didn't have my name on the outside and yours on the inside! A new-fangled kind of 'post-office,' I'll say!—Well, when little Ellie came shining up to me tonight, with his hard-luck story about an aged mother—just look at the lively dame, will you?—and a place to fill and all that rot, I didn't tumble—not far enough to notice. But when he let on who else was coming to dinner, why believe me—"

"I am very pleased to see you again, also," said *Señorita* Accosta.

Cocktails and relishes had been passed. There was no chance to go to the beautiful maiden in distress and rescue her. Monte, foaming at the mouth, gave his arm to the Ambassadress; and her daughter, by a slight restraining pressure on her escort's arm, succeeded in keeping him in his proper place in the line which filed out to dinner. Once at the table, their position was such that Monte could not keep his eye on his last-minute guest, or hear what this roughneck was saying. For the moment, he allowed his attention to be absorbed by caviar, served in great blocks of ice from which a shallow square had been hollowed out, and accompanied by curling wafers of "fairy toast."

Olson, who had never eaten caviar before, took one mouthful and decided that it was disgusting. This, however, did not trouble him. If he were not eating he would be freer to carry on a conversation with the young lady beside him. Scattering the silverware, in order to give himself more elbow room, he leaned towards her.

"What's your name?" he asked abruptly, "your first name, I mean, *Miss Accosta* is an awful mouthful."

The girl crumbled a bit of fairy toast. The expression on her scarlet mouth did not change. "My name is Mercedes," she said gently, "in my country, however, it is not usual for a young man to call a young girl by her baptismal name unless—in short, it is hardly usual."

"But you're in *my* country now!" boomed Olson happily, "and here it is usual. Among friends. By the way, my name is Ralph."

"It has a musical sound," volunteered *Señorita* Accosta in her sweet gentle voice.

"Well, it would have, the way you'd say it," the proud possessor of the musical name continued. "Say, what do you do for exercise in the smug, stifling city? Ever get a chance for a ride?"

"But assuredly. Almost every morning. I ride in the park of Rock Creek with a groom who has been with us many years. In fact, he was in my grandfather's service."

"Getting along in age?" asked Olson hopefully. "Can't keep up with you always, can he?"

"He is indeed somewhat aged," said *Señorita* Accosta smoothly, tasting her consommé, "and, as it happens, he is poor. He longs in some way to gain a little extra money to send home to his daughter, who is lame, and who is married to a poor shepherd in the Basque country. They are really in great want."

"They must be," said Olson, gulping, "now if someone made it worth his while for this groom, d'you see, to lag behind a little, now and then, and not to mention to Pa and Ma if you happened to meet someone when you went to ride—that would be just what he'd need, wouldn't it, to rest his old bones, besides supplying him with something substantial for that basking daughter of his?"

"It is evident," said *Señorita* Accosta, helping herself to terrapin, "that the good God has blessed you with a kind heart."

"I'm glad you get me," said Olson, helping himself in turn.

There is no need to follow the dinner, course by course—though these were perfect and delicious—

through to the end. No need to follow the ladies into the drawing room where Mrs. J. Montgomery Ellington contrived to seat the Ambassador's daughter beside her on a low stool, and to take in, with approval, every detail of her appearance, from the crown of her smooth, dark head, to the soles of her smooth white slippers. But we might, for a moment, pause in the library, where Monte, offering the roughneck a Corona Corona, offered him, at the same time and in a low voice, a little good advice.

"I feel I ought to give you a word of warning," he said, coughing apologetically, "having sent you into dinner with *Señorita* Accosta, I feel, in a way, responsible. Though of course you wouldn't make the mistake of approaching her as if she were an American girl, from your own state. Girls in Latin countries lead a very secluded life. This one is just out of the convent, utterly unsophisticated, of course, utterly innocent. And even if she had the inclination—which a pure, lovely girl like that would not—to indulge in light flirtations, she would have no opportunity. Her marriage will be carefully arranged by her parents with a man who, in their opinion, is eminently suitable. She herself will have no voice in the matter. They handle things very differently, these Latin Americans, from the way we do in the United States, especially—er—in the West."

"You don't say!" exclaimed Olson with that queer look which Monte did not like, tugging at his tie.

We do not need to linger, either, at *Señora* Accosta's days "at home" through the winter, for these were, after all, much like other official days at home in Washington; though they had the peculiar distinction of being attended, almost invariably, by J. Montgomery Ellington and his mother; nor at the other social functions, which, one after the other, followed each other in quick succession, and at which the beautiful daughter of the new ambassador, always sweet, always demure, always gentle, was to be observed with the most desirable of Washington's officials respectfully attendant upon her. But we might, perhaps, linger for a time in Rock Creek Park; for that entrancing spot might well repay our lingering.

As January melted into February, and February widened into March, and March blossomed into April, Mercedes Accosta found the Park increasingly beautiful. She loved the snow—the first snow she had ever seen—lying so softly on the wooded slopes; she loved the weeping willows, bending, featherlike, over the gray stream; she loved the dogwood shining, as stars shine, in the quiet groves; she loved the old stone mill by the ford of the river, and the rustic benches where children came to eat lunch; she loved the bridle paths, so still, so secluded and so winding—so winding that old Jaime the groom, was forever losing his way in them, and finding her again only when she emerged into Connecticut Avenue through the Zoo. There was a policeman whose beat took him past this gateway, and with him the old Basque made friends and whiled away many an early-morning hour which would otherwise have been empty.

But most of all Mercedes Accosta loved Ralph Olson.

She learned to listen for the steady clop, clop of his horse's hooves, galloping towards her from the distance. She would turn in her saddle, and watch him approach, straight and strong on his steed, the sun shining on his golden hair, his blue eyes gleaming in the early morning light. He seemed to her as beautiful as some splendid warlike saint, emblazoned on a cathedral window. But when he came close to her, she forgot about saints and stained glass, and remembered only that he was a man. For he brought his horse abreast of hers, and he always looked at her, full in the face for a moment, before he touched her; and that look sent thrills of joy pursuing each other all over her body. After that, without a word, he leaned over, and put his arm around her waist, pressing her closer and closer and closer, until she could feel his heart beating against hers. And then he kissed her. Kissed her eyelids and her brow, kissed her cheek. Kissed her mouth. . . .

It had been like that, from the first, from the very morning after the Ellington's dinner. They had understood each other so perfectly, from the beginning, that there had been no need of marring that perfect understanding by the clumsy intrusion of speech.

Afterwards—after he had kissed her, and she had returned his kisses, with the glow of fire that burns beneath snow—they went forward side by side where the bridle path was wide enough, or with him in the lead where it was not. And then they did talk to each other, pouring out their hearts. No impression, no experience was too unimportant to share. They discovered, not only a mutual passion, but mutual interests. Mercedes had an instinct for politics; Ralph could tell her what was going on in the Senate, and she could grasp the littlest detail of what he sought to explain. Ralph had a gift for tongues; he picked up, in no time at all, enough Spanish to make eloquent love in that language. Not that his lovemaking in English would have been called tepid—

It was a long time before any cloud dimmed the brightness of their horizon. And when that cloud appeared, Mercedes pointed it out to Ralph, frankly.

"I think that capable lady, Mrs. J. Montgomery Ellington, is considering me with favor—as a daughter-in-law," she told Ralph one morning after they had observed their ritual of meeting.

Ralph stared a moment, swore a moment, and then chuckled. "I presume that would be agreeable to you?" he suggested.

"Oh, Ralph, desire of my heart! And how can you say a thing so cruel?"

"Look here, Mercy—" he had shortened her name to suit himself, and she loved the form it had taken, "you mean to tell me that you wouldn't hanker to have little Ellie for a husband?"

"Soul of my soul!" she exclaimed. And this time he saw that there were tears in her eyes.

"How quickly, by special election, could I take that office, if I were a candidate?" he inquired gently.

They had, as has been stated, already observed their morning ritual. But Mercedes lifted her face. And Ralph seemed to find nothing tedious in the repetition.

It was, as it happened, this very day, that J. Montgomery Ellington and his mother jointly decided that the time had come when he might with propriety—and advantage—go to the Ambassador and offer—by proxy—his heart and hand to the Ambassador's daughter. He wrote, asking for an appointment, "on a matter of the gravest consequence," and was surprised that there was a slight delay in receiving an answer. At length a secretary telephoned and said without the apology which Monte felt to be his due, that the Ambassador had been very much occupied, but that he would be glad to see Senator Ellington the following morning at eleven.

J. Montgomery Ellington, upon his arrival at the Embassy, was ushered into a drawing room which seemed, to his refined and conservative taste, somewhat over-decorated with roses, lilies, and other costly and sweet-smelling flowers. These were, moreover, not wholly fresh, but rather savored of some past celebration. It was difficult for him, in such an atmosphere, to be as impressive as he would have liked. In fact, he became aware, almost immediately after the Ambassador's greeting, that he was not progressing as he would have liked. And, in a very few minutes, this dignitary interrupted him.

"My dear Mr. Senator," *Señor Don* Ricardo Honorio Miguel Accosta was saying, "if I understand you correctly, you are doing me the honor to ask for my daughter's hand in marriage. Or rather, you are explaining to me that such an alliance would be an honor to my house. I feel therefore that I must tell you, without allowing you to proceed, what you would know already if you had glanced at the morning papers. My daughter is married."

Monte, bereft of words to show his stupefaction, stared at the Ambassador as if hypnotized.

"Your distinguished colleague," *Don* Ricardo went on blandly, "Senator Ralph Olson, who was first presented to me by the Vice-President, and with whom, shortly afterwards, you gave me the great opportunity of becoming better acquainted at your hospitable home, impressed me, from the very first, as a young man whom I should be glad to welcome as my son-in-law. I made the discreet, thorough searching inquiries natural to a parent. I found that his character was without a blemish, and that his fortune was considerable. As far as his career is concerned, I am informed, from most reliable sources, that he will eventually very probably be a candidate for the presidency. Evidently, all this was not displeasing to me. After the somewhat eccentric manner of many of your countrymen, Senator Olson has seen fit to carry on his courtship in a way which seems to my compatriots singular, to say the least. But both the Ambassadress and myself, fully informed of the progress of events by an old and trusted servant who has been carefully watching over my daughter, were, on the whole, satisfied that these were taking a natural and—ah—wholly proper course. When Senator Olson came to me a few days ago, and told me that matters of immediate concern to him demanded his presence in the West, and that he would like to be married at once, I saw no insurmountable obstacle to the fulfillment of his wishes, especially since they seemed to exactly coincide with the wishes of my daughter. The ceremony was performed, in the presence of the immediate family and the Embassy staff, but the Archbishop of Washington yesterday afternoon."

Mr. J. Montgomery Ellington rose. "I wish," he said somewhat stiffly, "that I had been informed, a little earlier of this—this engagement. That much, I think, was due me." And as the Ambassador, without replying, turned a somewhat supercilious gaze upon him, he faded, with such grace as he could muster, from the room.

At home, in the imposing red-brick mansion on Massachusetts Avenue, his mother, he knew, would be waiting for him—the mother who was so preeminently satisfactory. It had been a mistake—an interlude—to imagine that anyone else could take her place as the perfect hostess, that anyone else could fully understand his needs and his importance. He was well rid of the roughneck—and the little Latin hussy who looked like a plaster saint dressed by Worth and that wily old intriguer, the Ambassador. Stifling a sob and straightening his shoulders, he started home to tell his mother all about it.

LAFAYETTE SQUARE

ON A Sunday morning in early July, as hot and humid as such mornings can be only in Washington, a young girl shut the black walnut front door with its etched glass windows slowly behind her, and went down the steps of the house where she lived. It was a tall, flat, narrow brownstone house, wedged in between a gift shop and a tea room representing the genteel form of trade which first dares to insinuate itself into aristocratic sections of a city, and seemed as subtly aloof from its neighbors as an austere elderly woman suddenly jostled by a pair of painted soubrettes might have looked. Across the street, where two or three cheap cars were standing, looking as disconsolately dingy as if they, too, had been affected by the heat, and where one shabby and antiquated victoria was wheeling mournfully past, lay a little park, its trees drooping under boughs laden with heavy, dusty, dark green leaves. The girl glanced quickly about, as if trying to discover an empty bench where she might sit down. There was none. Men and women, in every possible stage of disorder and discomfort, were sprawling everywhere; babies, sticky and sleepless, wailed from baby carriages drawn up against the seats from which their parents jerked them listlessly back and forth; older children hurled themselves against their mothers' laps, and then sank fretfully down on the gravel, munching ice-cream cones. The prospect seemed as hopeless as it was revoltingly disgusting. At last, probably because it was half hidden by shrubbery, the girl discovered a settee where only a solitary man, wearing a tropical suit and looking almost uncannily cool and crisp in the midst of the torrid disorder about him, sat reading a newspaper. She hesitated, glanced back at the brownstone house as if to be sure that no one was watching her, and then walked over toward the sheltered bench. The man looked up from his paper, nodded pleasantly, moved a little nearer one end of the bench, and went on reading. The girl sat down beside him.

She was very young—not more than eighteen or nineteen—but her pretty little white face, under the heavy braids of dark hair wound about her head, was drawn and lined with a fatigue that seemed very closely akin to suffering. Her thin little hands, clasped in her lap, twisted and untwisted a small, cheap cotton handkerchief back and forth between her fingers. She was hatless, and her white blouse and skirt were of the flimsiest ready-made variety. Even her stockings were of coarse weave, and her white shoes ill-shaped and shabby. For some time she sat silently staring ahead of her, twisting the handkerchief. Then, without a particle of warning, she suddenly and vehemently burst into tears.

The man beside her threw his crackling newspaper to the ground, and turned towards her in alarm.

"For heavens' sake," he exclaimed, "what's the matter? Are you—are you hurt or something?"

"I'm not hurt," she gasped, "I'm—I'm hot."

"You're *hot!*" he said, more puzzled than ever, "why, of course you're hot! You don't cry, do you, whenever you feel hot in Washington? If you do, you must spend about six months out of every twelve in tears."

The girl dabbled at her eyes, blew her nose softly, and looked up, with almost a suggestion of a smile on her white lips. "No," she said, "I don't usually cry about anything. But these last few days seem to have been unusually hard somehow. I haven't been out of the house in a week, and the house has kept getting hotter and hotter all the time, and there's been nothing to do in it except sit and think of how hot I was. Do you ever do that?"

"No, I'm too busy."

"Well, there doesn't seem to be anything for me to be busy *about*. And at last I couldn't stand it any longer, so I came out here and this is hotter still!"

It looked very much as if she were going to begin to cry again. The man gazed at her attentively for a minute, and then suddenly asked, "How would you like to go out for a ride in the country? That ought to cool you off."

"With—with whom?"

"Why, with me. I was just going to start myself. I only sat down here to read the paper first. You'll excuse my saying so, but you look very ill and tired. I'm sure it would do you good to come. Please do."

The color that suddenly flooded her face seemed all the more vivid because she had been so pale before.

"I suppose it was natural, that you should say such a thing to me," she said, looking him full in the face, "because I came out here alone and sat down beside you and, and answered when you spoke to me. And because I'm dressed the way I am. But I'm not what you're thinking, I'm a lady."

"I am sure you are," said the man smiling, "or I shouldn't have asked you to go out to ride with me."

"You don't understand yet," she said rather desperately. "I'm not a—a shop girl, or a telephone operator, or anything like that, who's had to 'lay off' because she was sick. I'm Camilla Montgomery."

"Camilla Montgomery," repeated the man, still smiling, "that's a pretty name. But. . . ." Then suddenly it dawned upon him that he had heard, that more than once it had been remarked. . . . He glanced from the shabby little figure beside him to the gaunt old brownstone house across the way. "You mean," he said, "one of the Montgomerys of Virginia? Your grandfather was Secretary of State, wasn't he? Or something of the sort? And he and your parents are dead, and you live with your grandmother in the old family house in Lafayette Square?"

The girl nodded. "And so—"

"And so I shouldn't have asked you to go for a ride with me?"

There was no doubt about it, the man had a remarkably nice smile, and nice eyes, crinkly and brown, that smiled too, and fresh, ruddy color. "I wonder why I've never met you before."

"Well," she said a little haughtily, "you wouldn't be likely to, would you? Of course we are dreadfully poor —you probably know that, since you seem to know all the rest—but still we're—"

"You're 'cave-dwellers,' and I'm an outsider. Is that it?"

Camilla flushed again. "Yes. I'm sure you're awfully nice. I can see that. But Grandmother. . . . What *do* you do?"

The man became rather vague. "Oh, I work for the government."

"I thought you probably did. There's no one left in Washington at this time of year except the poor government clerks."

"And 'cave-dwellers.' "

"Only the poor ones. The others—the ones who have stopped dwelling in Lafayette Square and gone up to New Hampshire Avenue and Sixteenth Street to *really live* are all in the country. I can't afford to go to the country, not even for a week-end visit. It takes too many clothes."

"I suppose," said the poor government clerk thoughtfully, "that you had just received a perfectly wonderful invitation to go for this very Sunday when it suddenly began to seem to you so hot you couldn't stand it. And that you've sat indoors wishing and wishing that you could manage it, and not even telling your grandmother that the invitation had come because that would make her feel badly, too, knowing you couldn't go, and so—well, finally you came out here and sat down on a bench and cried."

Camilla nodded. "Yes—how did you guess? The invitation was from Lisa Harrison—Justice Harrison's daughter, you know—for Bar Harbor. *Bar Harbor!* Just think how cool it is there! She's my best friend, always asking me to do nice things, and I never can—I can't even go to balls with her in the winter. Tulle is so expensive in the first place, and then it just *melts* when you dance. And she has lots of beaus—and—and all that sort of thing—and I never have any! I don't see what any man would want to call on *me* for! The parlor would depress any man that wasn't over ninety! It has a hideous carpet, and marble-topped tables, and portraits of the Montgomerys back to the time of Charles the Second—most of them very plain—on the walls. And the back parlor has no windows at all in it, and there are stuffed birds and glass flowers in the dining room."

The man threw back his head and laughed. Camilla gave a little snort.

"You wouldn't think it was funny if you lived there," she said. "Upstairs it's even worse. There's only one bathroom, and that has a horrid tin tub in it. And there are mottoes—'God bless our home' and things like that—and ugly black walnut beds with bunches of carved fruit on the head boards, and one old servant with her head done up in a red handkerchief."

If she expected the man to laugh again she was disappointed. He seemed to have suddenly become thoughtful.

"I think," he said slowly, "that I should like to call."

"Oh, I would love to have you! But who would introduce you?"

"Well—I might find someone. I have quite a few friends. And then we could have our ride after all."

Camilla began to twist her handkerchief again. "I'm sure you have," she said, as if she were trying to speak kindly and considerately, "but, don't you see? I don't want to hurt your feelings, but they probably wouldn't be *our* friends. Still—"

"Still," said the government clerk, "I think I'll risk it. Right now. Your grandmother couldn't do worse than turn me out, could she? Let's walk across and see."

Lying quivering in her ugly black walnut bed that night, over and over again Camilla rehearsed the scene that had ensued. How, in spite of all her protests, the stranger had gained his point and gone home with her. How he had given his card to the slatternly old servant, and told her without qualm to take it to Mrs. Montgomery. How her grandmother, after a long wait, during which Camilla knew she was getting out of her muslin dressing sack and into her one respectable black silk, came into the ugly parlor smiling graciously, and saying, "Mr. Senator, I'm sorry to have kept you waiting. I hope my little girl has offered you something cool to drink." How glad she had been to slink away—he "worked for the government," did he! Well, of course that was true, but what an *awful* blunder she had made—all the time she had kept thinking his face was vaguely familiar—of course, she had seen his picture in the newspapers over and over again! And she had said she wouldn't be likely to know him! Well, that was true enough, too; she couldn't afford to go to the smart "official" parties that he did! And she had snubbed him, and patronized him! She squeezed lemons and squirted the juice in her eyes, and was glad that gave her an excuse to cry again with mortification and rage. How Mr. Lloyd Carroll drank the punch which she finally took in to the parlor, praising it, and talking to Mrs. Montgomery about all the Virginians he knew—the very best Virginians there *were*—and then suggested, as if it were a brand new thought, that he would like to take her and Miss Camilla for a little ride. How he went off, and returned in a beautiful sportscar that shone and glittered, and drove them out into Maryland, through miles and miles of cool restful country, stopping for lunch at one lovely little inn and for tea at another, and finally left them at their door, promising himself the pleasure of seeing them both very soon again. Promising *himself!* What, thought

Camilla, hugging herself rapturously in the dark, about promising *her?* Think of being able to write to Lisa, who never had anyone more important than some young foreign attaché or some feeble light in the State Department to brag about, that the famous orator, Senator Carroll, had been to see her! It was all too perfect!

Before another day was over, there was more still to write to Lisa about. A big box of candy, an armful of roses, a sheaf of magazines and music, another ride after dinner when the session at the Capitol was over, an offer of seats in the Senators' gallery if she "ever cared to go and listen to the speeches." Her little thin white face bloomed into sudden radiance with pleasure, and Lloyd Carroll, watching the change come over it, felt something strange and powerful clutching at his heartstrings. The child had starved, had she? Well, everything which had been denied her should be showered upon her now. He made her understand that. If it was hot that Monday, Camilla forgot to notice it.

There came, after that, a long succession of miracles as July dragged itself torridly through to the time when the weary Congress adjourned early in August. And the greatest miracle of all happened, of course, on the night before Lloyd Carroll started for home to make the most of the few weeks that lay ahead of him in which to build up his political fences before the primaries took place.

"But you'll win, of course!" Camilla told him, standing beside him in the long, open parlor window looking out at Lafayette Square.

"Oh, of course," he answered lightly, "the Solid South, you know! Though the Republicans have been very active there this year! Still, I hate to leave Washington. Can't you guess why?"

Of course she could guess why. But she waited, breathlessly, for him to tell her.

"I'm so much older than you, nearly twenty years. You ought to have some nice boy. But I love you. And I can give you things, honey. All the things you've had to do without—good times, and pretty dresses, and jewelry. I want to see a string of pearls around your little white throat, and diamonds on your pretty little white hands. Will you let me put them there?"

It was he, and not she, who trembled as he drew her towards him.

Lloyd won at the primaries without a struggle; there was not even a contest for the nomination. And that being over, the election, in his state, was a foregone conclusion. As soon as it was over, they were to be married—and that was only three months away, two months, one month. There was no money for a trousseau, no money even for a pretty wedding, in the drained coffers of the aristocratic Montgomerys. But what did that matter, Lloyd laughingly asked Camilla in the brief, blissful visits that he managed to snatch with her during the campaign? They were to stay on with her grandmother in the old house—any other plan would have been too brutally selfish—but an old house transformed from garret to cellar with electric lights and porcelain tubs and hardwood floors and a new furnace! With new furniture—ivory bedroom sets and carved Florentine oak for the drawing room and oriental rugs everywhere! And a new staff of well-trained servants for next winter. Camilla would have her "Thursdays" like every Senator's wife, her formal lunches and dinners and gay little dances! And meanwhile the pearls and diamonds came from Lloyd, and wedding gifts from all her relatives, and envious letters from Lisa at Bar Harbor.

Camilla was wakened to consciousness on the morning after election day by the raucous shouts of newsboys tearing up and down the street, and darting across Lafayette Square. At first the words that they were screaming were unintelligible. She was too sleepy, too happy to pay attention. At last the names "Harding and Coolidge" began to force themselves on her consciousness. Well, Lloyd had told her that might happen, and Harding had already achieved recognition all over the country, she turned over, burying her head on her pillow. Then these names were followed by a phrase repeated over and over again:

"Solid South broken at last!"

She sprang out of bed, threw her robe around her, and rushed to the window. Just then the doorbell jangled through the silent house. There was no telephone in it, but Lloyd had promised to telegraph her the happy results of his election as soon as he knew, himself, the exact size of his majority. That must be his message now! She ran from the window to the staircase, and waited until the slatternly servant, puffing and panting, lumbered up to her and handed her the yellow envelope. Camilla tore it open.

> "Defeated by Jackson Fifty Thousand.
> Lloyd."

Not another word! Not a word about being sorry, not a word about coming to her! She crept down the stairs, and picked up the morning paper from where it lay on the hall floor, the likeness of the successful candidates smiling at her from the front page. And underneath those presidential pictures were Lloyd's and his opponent's! The man who had broken the "Solid South" and the man he had defeated! Lloyd's downfall was important enough for that! The headlines were almost as large as those about Mr. Harding! They told something else, moreover, besides the news of the political upheaval.

"DEFEATED CANDIDATE SAID TO HAVE LOST LARGE SUMS OF MONEY IN UNSUCCESSFUL CAMPAIGN."

"The private fortune of Lloyd Carroll, less large than was popularly supposed, is understood to have suffered gravely during the campaign in which he has been engaged, and which he has carried on in the lavish manner customary with this well-known orator. Although it is still too early to form an estimate of his losses, a conservative guess would probably—"

Camilla read no further. She crumpled the newspaper into a big untidy ball, and flung it from her with all her strength. Lloyd was *defeated!* Lloyd was *financially ruined!* Her beautiful fairy prince was changed by a wicked magician, her fairy palace was crumbling like a house of cards around her! There would be no more packages of shining jewels, no "improvements" in the dingy old house, no corps of servants, no "Thursdays," no more envious letters from Lisa! Her lips trembled. She gathered her robe around her again, and started for her grandmother's room to wail out her sorrows on that kind old shoulder.

Halfway up the stairs again, she stopped, her face burning with shame, far more painfully than on the morning, four months earlier, when she had discovered that the man who "worked for the government" was a famous senator. What *had* he been to her, this kind, honorable, sensitive gentleman, with the wonderful smile and still more wonderful voice? Only a means of escape from conditions she hated, only a source of supply for luxuries that she craved? Lloyd loved her, loved her dearly, she knew that. Her flush deepened at the thought of the tenderness and ardor of his love. He must, at that very instant, be suffering intolerably, because he knew that, for all his love, he could no longer pour his riches into her lap, could no longer make her existence all rose-colored for her. That was what the brevity of the telegram meant. He felt so much that he could say nothing. But did she love *him?* Up to that moment she had never questioned herself. Of course, girls were fond of the men to whom they engaged themselves, or else they would not become engaged. But what did "being fond" mean? Lloyd wanted to do everything for her. But what had she ever wanted, what did she want now, to do for him? She came of a race that had seen everything that it held precious and sacred wrested away, and yet had never faltered. Was she alone to prove false to the traditions of Lafayette Square?

Her grandmother, coming down an hour later, stumbled over her where she still sat, huddled against the railing. She rose, and looked the older woman in the face.

"Grandma," she said, "is there any money *at all?*"

Mrs. Montgomery was not the type of woman who counters with a "Why?" when asked a direct question. She answered it.

"There is very little."

"Would it be enough to take you and me to Lloyd's home?"

"No, my dear."

"Enough to take one of us?"

"Yes."

The girl threw her arms around her. "Grandma," she said brokenly, "Lloyd's been defeated. He isn't going to be senator any more. And he's lost money. He's poor, perhaps almost as poor as we are. I don't know yet. He won't come to me. He thinks I only cared for the money and position. And I'm afraid that's what I did care about at first. But now I care for *him.* I've thought it all over—and I'm going to him."

The old lady straightened herself. Then she brushed back the soft hair that had fallen over Camilla's cheek, and kissed her.

"You are perfectly right, my dear," she said.

The trees in Lafayette Square had turned to gold and crimson, and then to a dull and rusty brown, quivering on dried branches, or scurrying in the wind over the gravel walks, so that they no longer screened and sheltered the settees, where, indeed, few persons lingered to be screened and sheltered. But, on an unseasonably warm evening in mid-November, a man and a girl came down the steps of the flat, brownstone dwelling wedged between the gift shop and the tea house and, crossing the street, went and sat down, unnecessarily close together, on a bench near which there was no street light. And the man bent his head, and gathered the girl into his arms.

"Are you sorry?" he asked at last.

She laughed, a little catch in her voice. "Sorry for what?"

"For *anything?*"

"There isn't," she answered, "anything to be sorry *for,* that I can think of! Sometimes, though, when I imagine, just supposing *I hadn't* gone to you, and *forced* you to marry me, and to bring me back here for our honeymoon, I get so frightened that it nearly stifles me, thinking what I might have lost!"

She was very near to being stifled from other causes than fright. But when at last she managed to look at the man with the wonderful smile, he was smiling more wonderfully than ever.

"Honey," he said slowly, "there doesn't seem to have been any chance to tell you before, but things aren't half so dreadful as you thought they were. I can practice law, and make twice as much money as I ever lost! And I'm not absolutely strapped now, not by any means. Of course we'll have to be careful for a while. We can't do all the things we planned. I guess we'd better put up with the tin bath tub and the stuffed birds and the glass flowers a little longer."

Camilla laughed.

"Yes. And the hideous carpet, and the marble-topped tables, and the big black walnut bed with the carved fruit on it—"

There, suddenly, she stopped. Lloyd's fingers tightened around hers. Before he could prevent it, she leaned over and kissed his hand.

"It's all become so beautiful, since you came there to live," she whispered. "If you hadn't been defeated, I wouldn't have found that out."

"I don't think it matters much," Lloyd whispered back, "whether I was defeated in the Senate or not— as long as I won on Lafayette Square."

CHERRY BLOSSOMS ALONG THE POTOMAC

JOHN MERRILL grew up in Hamstead, Vermont. His mother was the sort of woman who sang in the choir of the Congregational Church on Sunday morn-

ings, and led the Christian Endeavor meetings in the
vestry Thursday evenings; who always had geraniums
and begonias growing in her spotless kitchen windows,
even when the Merrill finances ran so low that flowers
had to be planted in tin cans instead of earthen pots;
who beat every rug and cushion in the house each Friday, and aired and sunned the bedding the first of
every month; who scrubbed the cellar stairs once a
week, and scalded her dish cloths after every meal;
and who made great batches of doughnuts and apple
pies and fragrant bread before the rest of the family
was up in the morning and, as all Hamstead rises by
six, that was very early indeed. John, therefore, was
raised not only in the odor of sanctity, but also in that
of growing plants, and spotless cleanliness, and excellent cooking. The only trouble with such a background
for the career of a rising young American is that he
becomes not only sensitive, but actually unhappy
under less immaculate surroundings. After he had
worked his way through Middlebury College, and
taken a course—also self-earned—at a business college
in Boston, where he boarded with his mother's twin
sister—whose standards were also twin to hers—all
Hamstead said that John was wonderfully lucky:
through the Congressman of his district, he secured a
position as a stenographer to a choleric senator from
the Midwest who had recently arrived in Washington,
and who had been strangely unsuccessful in his attempts to retain in his office any young man who was
willing to work hard and long for twelve hundred dollars a year and the privilege of hearing just what the
Senator thought of his lack of ability all the time he
was trying to do it.

John Merrill, when the news of his appointment first
reached him, was inclined to agree with the rest of
Hamstead—twelve hundred dollars seemed, in the
Connecticut Valley, quite a princely sum; Washington,
the wonder city of all his dreams, which he had
longed, and supposed he longed vainly, to reach. But,
at the end of his first week there, he laid his head on
the dirty "art-square" that covered the table in his

room at the second-rate lodging house into which he had stumbled after finding that even two or three nights at a first-class hotel would devour all his savings, feeling numb all over, and choked. Partly perhaps with the dust, which covered not only the "art-square," but the dingy bureau with its cracked glass, and the rattling window pane, and the lumpy bed, and lay in rolls on the grimy floor, and even in a dusky rim around the inadequate wash basin; partly because the food he had tried to eat at one sloppy restaurant after another had choked him too, at the time, so that now he choked at the mere memory of it, and at the thought which mingled with that memory of the fish balls, and brown bread, and baked beans which, at that very moment, his mother must be putting, smoking hot, on the spotless kitchen table for the family's Sunday breakfast; partly because it *was* Sunday, and there was no familiar church to which he could go, no girl whom he had known from primary school to walk home with afterwards, no library book to read after this agreeable, though hardly thrilling promenade was over. But most of all because he doubted, even if he could suit the choleric Senator, which seemed unlikely—his stupidity and awkwardness and slowness had been cursed out a hundred times already—whether he could possibly stand the Senator, although the Senator represented twelve hundred dollars a year—a sum he had already discovered to be not princely in Washington, as it had seemed in Hamstead, but almost beggarly—and because the wonder-city did not seem wonderful to him at all, from what little he had seen of it, but unfriendly, and extortionate, and tawdry.

There was a tap at the door. It was, he supposed, the slatternly, overworked little man who came—every few days—to "spread up the bed." How the vigorous way in which his mother flung over the mattress, and drew the sheets taut, came to him when he watched him! He choked harder than ever, lifted his head, and began to read a fingered, year-old magazine with elaborate unconcern.

"Come in," he said, with a carelessness that was slightly overdone.

The door opened slowly, but nobody entered. After a minute, he turned and looked towards it.

On the threshold stood a girl, whose high color, which seemed to be growing higher every moment, was of a very different quality, John saw instantly, from that which he had noticed, with disgust, on the cheeks of most of the young persons whom he had passed in the streets. She wore a simple sailor hat with only a suggestion of soft fair hair showing beneath it, and she had on a plain suit of navy blue jersey, with a white blouse whose immaculate collar and cuffs were folded over her coat, and fastened with trim gold pins. She looked a little frightened, but aside from that her appearance was not only friendly, but distinctly attractive.

"How—how do you do?" she said in a rather frightened voice, "you're—you're John Merrill, aren't you?"

"Yes," replied that mystified but somewhat pleased young gentleman with equal shyness, rising and advancing towards the door, "what's your name?"

The girl smiled, a glimmer of bright teeth. "Sally Hunt," she said. "Our landlady told me about you. She said you came from Hamstead, Vermont, in the Connecticut Valley. I'm from New Hampshire, myself, just across the river, five miles south—Wallacetown."

"You *are!*" exclaimed the boy, a rising note of joy in his voice, "why, you must be Ephraim Hunt's niece! I heard he had one who left home six months ago to come and work in the War Risk Bureau. How awfully good of you to come and look me up! It's wonderful to see someone from home! Won't you come in?"

The bright color grew deeper still. "I guess I won't do that," the girl said, though with no diminution of friendliness, "but I thought that it was such a lovely morning and if you hadn't anything else to do, we might walk down to the Speedway, and see the Japanese cherry blossoms along the Potomac. They're just at the height of their bloom—a wonderful pink color —and I've heard that they're beautiful."

John Merrill caught up his hat. "Don't get your gloves soiled on this dirty banister," he said, "better let me go first, it's so dark."

They chatted like old friends as they walked down Seventeenth Street and across the Ellipse, of the people and the places that they both knew so well, though they had never met before; it was only after John had gone away to college that Sally, suddenly left an orphan, had come from the eastern part of the state to live with her uncle in Wallacetown. And this uncle had been having such hard sledding himself that she had not "gone out much," even after her own heavy little heart had become lighter, and finally she had decided that she must go away, and try to support herself.

"I was so happy when I got the letter saying I had passed the civil service examinations that I didn't know what to do," she said. "It seemed too wonderful to be true to think that I was coming to Washington. But since I got here—"

John's heart contracted, but he decided that it was still too early in their acquaintance to reveal his understanding and sympathy.

"What is your work?" he asked casually.

"I write all day long. It's pretty mechanical and monotonous. I put down on little slips of paper information that we get from the discharge papers of the men who've been in service—their age, and where they enlisted, when they were discharged and why, their rank and their company; this is used to compile statistics. When I do a good day's work, I can write about six hundred slips. But oh, how my head aches by five o'clock! All this work has to be gone over by two people to be sure no mistakes are made."

"I say, that's more tiresome than what I have to do down at the Senate Office Building."

"Oh, it's awfully tiresome! One thing that has to be designated is the cause of a man's disability, if he's disabled, and there are about sixty different diseases, and as many different kinds of accidents, and about fifty different locations where the trouble can be! I'm beginning to feel as if there wasn't a sound spot on a single member of the A.E.F.!"

John Merrill put back his head and laughed. It was the first time, he realized afterwards, that he had laughed since he had reached Washington.

"And the salary," said Sally, faltering a little, "sounded so big before I left home."

"I know—*didn't* it! And here! Why, I don't see how a girl can manage!"

"They manage different ways," said Sally slowly. "Some of them are cold, and hungry, and dirty. Some of them have families that can help them. Some of them—" the flush that had colored her face as she stood in his doorway flooded it again. "And the worst of it is, there's so little ahead of a government worker in the way of promotion! Why, I've met women, middle-aged, gray-haired women who've been doing such work for years, and they're only getting two or three hundred dollars a year more than I am. And they're not stupid, either, or uneducated. They're nice women, bright women. It makes me feel dreadfully hopeless. I felt especially hopeless this morning someway. I—I guess that's why I went to find you."

"I'm so glad you did. I was feeling sort of hopeless too. Oh look! Gosh, isn't that pretty!"

It was beautiful. No one, not even a homesick government worker, could have felt hopeless looking at it. Along the wide, smooth, curved drive of the Speedway, thick with cars—rackety Fords crowding shining limousines, elderly dowagers taking the air jostled by merry parties of boys and girls out joyriding—stood the blooming cherry trees, fragrant as roses, fleecy and fluffy as pink clouds. In the distance, on their right, rose the noble pillars of the Lincoln Memorial; on their left, the spearlike shaft of the Washington monument pierced the sky; across the sparkling river, rose the wooded slopes and lofty mansion of Arlington.

"Oh, John!" the girl cried suddenly, and it seemed to them both entirely natural that she should call him that, "it *is* a wonder-city, after all! I'm so glad we came, aren't you?"

Of course that was only the beginning. The following Sunday the cherry blossoms, thanks to favorable weather, were still fresh and rosy; and though, by the next, they had fallen to the ground, Sally and John found fresh beauties on the Speedway to make up for the loss of that first one they had discovered together, at their lunch at the Girl Scout Tea House at the bend of the Drive; sat, as did dozens of other young couples, on a welcoming bench to watch the sun go down. There was good news to tell each other that day.

"The Senator's secretary is thinking of leaving," John informed Sally. "He *says* it's a sick wife, but I *think* it's the Senator's temper. Anyway, that may mean a promotion for me. I don't mind the man's nerves, if it means a bigger salary and more responsibility."

"Of course you don't!" agreed Sally, "I don't wonder senators get cross—the hours they keep! Why, no 'laboring man' would work the way they have to! And it's thrilling, isn't it, to feel that you're a part—even if it's only a secretarial part—of the splendid work they're doing! And I've had a promotion myself! I've been made a 'group head.' That means that I have to keep track of what the other women in my group—from three to ten of them—do each day, help check the work and show the new girls who come in from time to time from other departments how to do *our* work. And I'm having a change from those everlasting slips! I'm going through correspondence—doctors' certificates, discharge papers, things like that—and filling out *cards*. The coding for the slips is done from the cards. I can do fifty cards a day."

"Have you had a raise?"

"Yes—I've beat you to it!"

"Good for you!"

But when John got his raise—for, whether it was because of a sick wife or a senatorial temper, the secretary resigned and John secured his position—it was a larger one than Sally's. So they agreed that evened things up, and celebrated the event—since they felt they couldn't wait till Sunday to go to the Speedway

—by having dinner at the Café Madrillion together, and going to the movies afterwards. They couldn't, of course, afford it, even though Sally insisted that it must be a "Dutch treat party," but, for all that, they both agreed that it was worth it. And, as they parted in the gloomy hall of the lodging house, where one feeble gas jet sputtered in a red glass globe held aloft by an imitation bronze virgin, Sally revealed a further piece of good news.

"I've got one real friend in Washington."

"You bet you have!" said John with almost unnecessary emphasis.

"I mean *besides* you, of course, silly! This friend and I went to school together in Portsmouth when we were girls. Now she's married to a member of the Supreme Court—just think of that! She's ever so much younger than he is—a second wife—and she has a lovely house, on one of the loveliest streets in the city, and whenever she can—of course her time is awfully full, official parties which she can't avoid and to which she couldn't ask me—"

"Why not?" asked John bluntly.

"Why she just couldn't! I wouldn't fit in. Not that Elsa herself is any different—she seems just the same as ever to me—but her guests wouldn't feel especially complimented to be asked to meet a girl that works in the War Risk—Ambassadors, and Cabinet Officers, and people of that sort. You must see that."

"Well, I don't."

"You ought to. Anyway, as I was saying when you interrupted me, she has invited me to dinner next Tuesday night, and she asked me to bring you along."

"How did she happen to know about me?"

"I—I guess I must have mentioned you."

John burst out laughing. "I guess you must," he said, "bless your heart! But what about clothes?"

"Can't you *hire* something?"

"Go to a Justice's house in a hired dress suit? No, Sally! I've got one, thanks, that I had in college—I'll be all right. I was thinking about you—"

"I've just got my bonus money. I'm going to have a

pretty dress if I starve! I haven't had a new one since
—Oh, John, you don't know how I want it! If you did,
you wouldn't think I was silly to spend so much that
way."

"I don't think you're silly," said John hastily. "I
think you're"—but just then there was the sound of
the latch key of another lodger turning in the front
door, and Sally fled.

The new dress was certainly pretty. It was pink and
fluffy, with touches of pale green. The sight of it, with
Sally's erect little head raised above it, and Sally's firm,
slim, white neck and arms emerging from it, had an
extraordinary effect upon John. He stared at her
shamelessly all through dinner, and when they started
home, he suggested that they should walk down to the
Speedway before they went back to the lodging house.
Sally demurred.

"I don't like to go down there in the evening."

"Why not?"

He could see her blushing under the street lamp they
were passing.

"Well, lots of fellows and girls go down there and
neck. They park their cars and devote their entire attention to it! It's disgusting!"

John laughed. "We haven't any car to park," he said
gaily, "and I suppose lots of them haven't any other
place to go. I've got some sympathy for them! We
haven't, either!"

"But we are not—we don't intend—"

"You look like one of those cherry blossoms we saw
down there yourself," he whispered. "Were—were
you thinking of them when you bought that dress?"

"How did you guess?"

"I sort of knew you were thinking about them, and
that first Sunday—did it mean as much as that to
you?"

Sally tried to laugh. "Before you ask me that," she
said, "I think you ought to tell me how much it meant
to *you!*"

It was very dark, and warm, and silent everywhere.

John drew her down beside him on the curved stone bench of the Circle through which they were passing.

"All right," he said softly, "I will."

But, after cherry blossom time in Washington comes summer—torrid, brassy, unrelenting. The extra session of Congress that year displayed none of the brevity that extras are supposed to have as a distinguishing characteristic. The nerves of the sharp-tempered Senator, who had always been used to a cool and breezy climate, jangled more and more. The boy from Hamstead, Vermont, grew white and thin under the strain of the heat and the jangling; and the girl from Wallacetown, New Hampshire, fingering her cards and slips with tired, sticky hands, from nine until half-past four every day, lost the buoyant freshness that had blown her straight into John Merrill's heart. They made the most, of course, of their infrequent leisure; but their two weeks' vacation did not come at the same time; and fall found them not only unrefreshed but unexalted. They had, indeed, had their *jour d'extase* but it seemed to their discouraged minds to have lasted no more than that. The present was bitterly hard and the future looked harder still. The hours which, could youth have had its birthright, should have been spent in blissful dreams of still more blissful realities yet to come, were passed, very often, in practical and anxious figuring with pencil and paper. The very least expensive flats, in the most unattractive parts of the city, rented for sums which seemed to them to be within the comfortable reach of only millionaires. The prices of food, as computed at second-rate cash markets, would eat *them* up, as John said, trying hard to joke about it. And besides, there were gas, and carfare, and clothes, and possible doctors' bills to think of.

"I can go on with my job, you know," Sally said over and over again. "Lots of married women do, nowadays."

"Oh, yes, I know," John answered bitterly, "and what kind of a home would we have, when you need to be at the office at nine, and wouldn't get back much before six? There would always be unswept rooms, and unwashed dishes, and laundry hanging around." The vision of his mother's spotless fragrant kitchen rose before him. "And you'd be so dog tired all the time, trying to fill two places at once, that you'd develop a temper like the Senator's. I can live with one like that, if I have to, but I'm hanged if I think I can live with two of them!"

Sally's eyes filled with tears. Men—even John— were apt to put things so crudely. She knew that what he said was true, and yet—

"And supposing—well, supposing you had a baby?"

"Oh, *of course* we couldn't have any children!"

"Well, starting out with that for a plan doesn't sound like marriage to me. It sounds like something we call a very different name."

Sally sprang away from him, cut to the quick. He succeeded, eventually, in comforting her, and thoroughly contrite at having hurt and grieved her, resolved that he would not allow his weariness and discouragement to get the better of him in the future. But the next time that they tried to talk their problem over, he made an even greater mistake.

"We might go home," she suggested at last. "It wouldn't cost us much of anything to live there."

"Well, it would cost us *something*, wouldn't it? And we haven't got that something! Besides, it would be acknowledging to everyone that we'd made a failure here. You don't want to do that, do you?"

Sally was silent.

"Do you?" he persisted.

"I want to get married," she said at last in a low voice. "I want to belong to you. You don't seem to see how I feel."

"Don't I?" he asked roughly. "Well, I know how *I* feel! I've tried to keep you from seeing, but if you're going to talk to me that way—" he took her in his arms, crushed her to him, kissed her until her neck, her mouth, were seared and smarting. "That's the way I feel—partly," he said when he finally let her go, "and if you ever tempt me again, I'll show you more."

She was crying bitterly, her fine, brave spirit all gone.

"I wasn't trying to tempt you," she said brokenly. "I was only trying to tell you that even if everyone did think we were failures, I wouldn't care; that no matter how hard things would be, I could stand them."

"Sally, darling, I'm a perfect devil. Please, please forgive me."

"I—I can't."

John suddenly felt as if he were freezing to death. A horrible numb, coldness spead all over his body, over his brain.

"Do—do you mean that?"

"Yes."

"You won't be engaged to me any more?"

"I can't."

"I can't even see you any more?"

"No."

It was winter again, and John shunned the Speedway as if the bubonic plague were lurking there. His only walks were the ones that he took—to save carfare—to the Senate Office Building down Pennsylvania Avenue, bleak and unlovely now that the last clinging leaves were gone from the sheltering trees. He did not meet Sally, even casually in the hall of the lodging house, for weeks at a time; when he did, she passed him so quickly, with just the merest nod of recognition, and the quick rush of color in her cheeks that he had learned to love so well, that he did not see her expression of suffering; if he had, nothing would have kept him from her. But, as it was, Christmas came and went with no sign of relenting on her part, and the notes that he thrust under her door, he found, unopened, thrust back under his. At last she disappeared altogether. Then, one dreadful night, his landlady told him why she had gone.

"Did you know that girl who came from up your

way—the one that had the fifth floor front room—was
awful sick?'

John leaned against the imitation bronze virgin carrying the red globe, feeling suddenly very weak.

"No," he managed to say, "I didn't. Is—is she in
a hospital?"

"She was. Flu she had and then pneumonia; she almost died, I guess," said the landlady, with evident rel-
ish. "Now that swell friend of hers—the one that's
married to the supreme judge, or whatever you call
him, has fetched her over to her house. She's given up
her room here, but she's paid her rent, which was
more'n I ever expected, when I found how low she was.
Her friend's housekeeper's a cousin of mine—that's
how I heard all about it."

Fifteen minutes later, John was ringing the doorbell
of the house where he and Sally had dined so happily
together on the night that she had worn that fluffy,
cherry blossom dress, the night that she had let him
tell her that he loved her, and kiss her for the first
time. The correct manservant who opened the door—
John had hated him at sight on the previous occasion
—informed him that his mistress had gone south that
afternoon, and had taken Miss Hunt with her. They
were to remain on the Justice's houseboat until Miss
Hunt was fully recovered.

"The young lady 'as been hawful hill," the butler
concluded, "if they wait until she 'as fully recovered, I
should s'y they'd be gone till the autumn."

The next day—it seemed to John as if the universe
were losing its health, just to spite him!—the bad-tempered Senator also came down with the flu; and during
his convalescence, he suddenly insisted that his secretary should move to his own house, "to help him catch
up with his confounded work." John left the lodging
house without many regrets, and so hastily that he
took with him only enough clothing for his immediate
needs, jammed into a suitcase. When, after a week's
sojourn among surroundings more luxurious than he
had even imagined before, he ventured to suggest to
his employer that, if he were to remain much longer,

he must return to his former abode at least long enough to pack his trunk, the Senator glared at him, and pointed a menacing finger in his direction.

"Sit down," he bellowed.

Without argument, John sat down, quaking slightly.

"You think I'm a damned disagreeable man to work for, don't you?" demanded the ornament of the upper house of Congress.

"Yes, sir, I do," replied John flatly. To his amazement, the Senator burst out laughing.

"Go get your trunk," that dignitary thundered. "You'll live here indefinitely, as far as I'm concerned. You've made good. I know what I am to work for. You've done damned well. From now on, your salary's doubled. When you need the money, it'll be trebled. All you'll have to do will be to tell me you need it. A young fellow like you ought to be thinking of getting married one of these days," and, at the telltale look that went over his secretary's face, "ho! so you *have* thought of it! Well, I'll give you a bungalow in Cleveland Park for your wedding present, then, *and* the trebled salary. Who's the girl?"

"There isn't any girl," said John, very miserably for a young gentleman who had just come into unexpected wealth, and the first thing he knew, he was telling his employer all about it. When he finished, the Senator was blowing his nose.

"Why in hell didn't you tell me all this before?" he shouted accusingly. "I lost my own girl—that's what made me what I am—I don't mean a United States Senator, I mean, so damned disagreeable. I'd have helped you in the first place. What do you think a thousand a year, one way or the other, matters to me? Go back and get your damned trunk. Then we'll set out to track the young lady down."

Whistling, John folded rolls of unmended cotton socks, and piles of ragged underwear and bundles of shirts with frayed cuffs into his little tin trunk. As he was strapping it, there was a knock at the door.

"Come in," he called cheerfully.

The door opened slowly, but nobody entered. After a minute, he turned toward it.

Sally was standing on the threshold. Her cheeks were blazing, and she was very thin, and looked rather frightened. But her arms were outstretched.

"I've—I've come back," she faltered. "And if you'll forgive me for being intolerant, and stupid, and everything, and if you still want me, I'll *stay* back this time, no matter what you do or say. Oh, John, I've nearly died without you. We'll manage somehow."

"Manage somehow!" he cried. "You bet we will!" He pulled her into the room, slammed the door, and sitting down on the tin trunk, gathered her into his arms, "Sally—Sally—Sally—"

"It's spring again," she whispered at last, though, even then, he had not had a chance to tell her about the true character of the bad-tempered Senator, and the bungalow in Cleveland Park because there were so many more important things to do and say. "The dreadful summer and hard winter are both over—and I hear the cherry blossoms are in bloom again along the Potomac."

"We'll go down and see them together," he said.

DOGWOOD IN ROCK CREEK PARK

DURING the two years of invalidism that preceded the death of Senator Anderson's wife, everyone in Washington said that Mrs. Anderson must have given more painstaking thought and valuable time to the training of her only daughter than had been generally realized. The young girl, during this trying period, showed remarkable self-control and poise; her anxiety for her mother never deteriorated into a visible depression, which would have made the situation doubly hard for her father; and while she neither shirked nor evaded the burden of responsibility which she was called upon to bear, it did not appear to crush her, or even tire her. And, at last, when the long dreaded time had come—

and gone—and the first great emptiness in the silent, stately house had passed and the quiet months that followed seemed gradually less poignantly pierced with grief, she began to take her place in the great world as her father's official hostess as quietly and efficiently as she had comforted him in his sorrow and solaced him in his loneliness. The housekeeping was accomplished, as it had been ever since her mother had first made the huge establishment one of the most justly famous in the capital, without friction and without apparent effort; the service was perfect, the entertaining as lavishly dignified as ever; and Patricia, sitting at the head of her father's table, was a far lovelier sight than even her mother had ever been, her soft arms curving over the dark, polished wood of the massive, carved chair, her hair dressed soft and high, and looking higher and softer still because of the tall Spanish comb that held it, her filmy black draperies floating away from her white shoulders, her grave, beautiful face, very white, too, except for the deep red line of her lips. The new Scottish attaché to the British Embassy, the Honorable Andrew Gordon, looking towards her from his place half way down the table—the position in which an unimportant young diplomat invariably finds himself when his hostess is dividing her attention between the Vice President and an ambassador—suddenly felt himself wishing that she held a rose as red as her lips in one of her slim, unringed hands, and that after dinner she would give the rose to him.

"And I do think Washington's just too awfully thrilling, don't you?" the debutante at his side was cooing, "it must be perfectly wonderful for you coming here this way—didn't it nearly *kill* you when you got your appointment? It's perfectly fascinating, I think, this wonderful interesting official society—the most marvelous people from everywhere make the whole thing so absolutely stunning, and—"

The Honorable Andrew Gordon, who was a serious-minded young man, gave a sigh, which, as he was also a very courteous one, he immediately hoped had not been audible. Patricia was rising. The liveried manservant behind her carved chair had drawn it silently back over the heavy carpet; her lacy dress was fluttering a little. As she passed Gordon, on the Vice President's arm, she paused for the fraction of a second.

"You were thinking of something lovely just then."

"I certainly was!"

"By-and-by, I want to hear about it—"

There was little hope of that, he felt. It was late before the men left the dining room; then his host, a violent partisan in politics who by no means underestimated his own importance, singled him out as the one man in the party who would be willing to listen to an account of the misdeeds of the senators "on the other side of the Chamber" and of his own valiant—and successful—efforts to triumph for the cause of righteousness.

"A very dangerous person that man Glover," he kept repeating with emphasis. "His election is considered—ahem!—to have been merely an unfortunate accident by all thinking persons. In my last rebuttal of his—er—outrageous and unpatriotic charges I held the floor for five hours. Of course you have heard of my speech on that memorable occasion, my dear—ah—Gordon. But I shall be glad to send you a copy of the Congressional Record for that date—the sixteenth, as I recall it—no, I believe it was the seventeenth, that you may preserve it. As a newcomer to this country it is important that you should realize at once the horrible conditions that exist here, and the attempts of the—er—most prominent statesmen to combat them."

Gordon was beginning to feel that the Senator was again quite likely to hold the floor for five hours, when, at half-past ten, the Vice President gave the signal for departure. The young Scotsman had been no nearer his hostess than the width of the great drawing room. It was unreasonable of him, he argued with himself, as he waited his turn to say good night to her, to feel so disappointed at not receiving a favor which he had not expected; it was natural that being so newly arrived at his post, he should underestimate Patricia's well-known efficiency—until he realized that, apparently by pure accident, he was the last to make his farewells, and that he had already taken leave of his host before reaching her.

"What was it?" she asked softly, as he took her hand.

Being very inexperienced, as a man no less than as a diplomat, he told her shyly, but without hesitation or circumlocution. Then he stood appalled at what he had done. But Miss Anderson appeared more reflective than offended.

"You must come here to dine again some time," she said quietly, "it's been so pleasant having you. Good night."

He did not see the connection between his own confession and her remark, until having been asked, a few weeks later, to "fill in," at another dinner, the place of a young Congressman who had been suddenly smitten with the grippe, he saw her carelessly take a crimson rose from one of the silver-gilt vases that decorated the table, hold it for a few minutes, and as she left the dining room, drop it near the place where he was standing.

Patricia's mourning, though it had been lightened enough to permit the giving of official dinners, still precluded her from dancing; but Andrew Gordon completed his day's work—as befitted a rising young diplomat—by attending two balls before, at three o'clock in the morning, he sank into bed with the not unreasonable hope of obtaining a little well-merited repose. He was distinctly irritated to find, when it was time to get up again, how little he had slept. The crimson rose, rescued from the pocket into which it had been hastily and ruthlessly thrust, and placed in a tumbler of water on his dressing table, pervaded the room with its bruised fragrance. It pervaded his thoughts still more persistently. Why, in the name of all that was strange and wonderful, should Patricia Anderson, at that vaguely formed desire and presumably expressed request of his, strew flowers in his path, going so far, even, as to create the opportunity to do so? And, now

that she had done so, what was his next move? He
hardly knew her—had not seen her more than a half a
dozen times—though, from the very first of these times
he had felt irresistibly attracted by her; and how, under
the light of heaven, was he to get to know her any better? He would make his dinner-call, of course, on her
next Thursday at home, but there would be at least a
hundred other visitors present on that occasion. A note
asking her to receive him alone would fall into the
hands of a private secretary and be answered with a
courteously chilly refusal; a telephone message, trans-
mitted through a butler, would hardly meet with a better fate, and would savor too much of informality, or
actual impertinence. And yet—could he let the favor
go unacknowledged, and thereby reveal himself as un-
grateful and unchivalrous? That, of course, was unthinkable.

He thumped his pillow, muttered a mild oath, and
drew the bedclothes more firmly under his chin. But
these vigorous measures produced no sensations of
drowsiness; at last he arose, almost determined to
throw the rose out of the window, and at least rid himself of its visible presence and its insinuating fragrance.
Instead, involuntarily, he lifted it, and drew it softly
across his cheek. As he did so, one of the sharp thorns
on the long stem pricked his fingers. He dropped it
hastily into the tumbler again, sucked his injured member resentfully, and glanced at the clock—after seven
—no use trying to get any sleep now. He took a cold
shower, dressed in tweeds, and struck out on foot in
the direction of Rock Creek Park, determined to walk
off his perplexities, since he could not think them out.
He strode up Connecticut Avenue, across the million-
dollar bridge, through the Zoological Gardens, where
even the animals seemed to regard this intruder upon
their early morning calm with mild surprise, past the
old stone mill by the ford where the shallow water of
the Creek rippled quietly over smooth brown stones,
and finally plunged straight up a hillside starred with
flowering dogwood, its long branches, with their delicate, exquisite blossoms closing about him as he

climbed, enveloping him with their snow-white petals. He did not stop until he reached the top of the hill; then he turned to drink in the full beauty of the fragrant freshness all around him—and found himself looking straight into the eyes of Patricia Anderson.

She had on a soft hat of dark gray felt pulled down over her ears, a suit of rough gray homespun, a plain and somewhat tumbled white silk blouse, no gloves, and heavy walking shoes; she looked a little shabby, and rather untidy. Her pale face was flushed to a rosy pink, and strands of soft dark hair had escaped from under the close little hat, and strayed across her soft cheeks and slim neck. Instinctively, she began to tuck these back into place. Then she held out her hand.

"Good morning," she said composedly, "did you ever see anything so lovely in all your life?"

"Never," replied Gordon promptly.

"I meant the dogwood."

"I didn't," he flung back without hesitation.

Patricia laughed. Gordon could not remember that he had ever heard her laugh before.

"Do you know," he said gravely, "that this—this meeting—is an answer to prayer?"

"Of course I do." She laughed again. "But how did you know that I had been praying?"

"Why, I didn't! I never dreamt of that! But I had!"

"What for?"

"I wanted to thank you for the rose—to have a chance to tell you that—"

"Well, you seem to have your chance," said Patricia with surprising calm. "Suppose we sit down?"

For a moment they sat silently, looking straight ahead of them at the flowering dogwood. Then Gordon began.

"You see—that divinity which doth hedge in a king which Shakespeare or some other old codger talks about isn't in it with the divinity that seems to hedge you in."

Patricia did not answer. She broke off a bit of dogwood, and appeared to be deeply absorbed in it.

"It—it makes it hard for a man that wants to see

something of a girl! I feel most awfully fresh, saying this to you. I don't mean to be, honestly. But if I could make you understand—"

"I don't think you're fresh. I do understand. You see—"

She hesitated a minute. "It makes it hard for a girl, too," she went on softly, "who wants to see something —of a man."

"I—I hadn't thought of that," he stammered, "there isn't any reason why a girl—any girl—particularly a girl like—I mean the kind of girl that—of course, if I were my elder brother it would be different."

"Who is your elder brother?"

"Didn't you know? He's the Duke of Dunkirk."

"Oh," said Patricia indifferently. "Well, he may be very nice—probably is—but I'm sure he wouldn't attract me. I wouldn't be able to help thinking all the time that he represented conditions even worse than those I'm trying to—forget once in a while."

"What conditions?"

Patricia tossed the branch of dogwood away from her. It fell to the ground, lightly and silently, a few yards from them. Then she faced him squarely.

"Don't you suppose I feel those barriers you call divinity too?" she asked with a vehemence that startled him. "Don't you think I have—always—day and night —ever since my mother was first taken ill, when I was only sixteen years old? *Barriers!* If you called them *chains* it would be nearer the truth—not hedging me in, but actually fastening me to—my prison."

"Your prison?"

"Yes—first a prison-house of grief! Then one of care; now one of responsibility. Do you think those are pleasure-houses for a young girl? I've tried to be a good sport, to play the game—everyone seems to think I've succeeded pretty well, and Father's rather more than satisfied—I believe he's actually quite proud of me. That's worth a great deal, of course. But it isn't worth to me what freedom—and happiness—and—"

"And love would be." Those were the words, he knew, that were surging to her lips. She did not say them. But both felt the power of them as much as if they had actually been uttered.

"So you see why a coronet wouldn't attract me," she went on more lightly. "Being a duke's wife would be just one step worse than being a senator's daughter. You see, too, perhaps, why I run away sometimes. I come out here so early in the morning that I can still get back in time to begin my day as I am supposed to, and never be missed—to have breakfast with Father and see the housekeeper, and look through the mail with my secretary, and then go out—or receive people at home—or accomplish whatever it is necessary that I should do. No one but the butler and my own maid—very old servants whom we've had a long time—know that I come, that I need to come. They seem to partially understand that—if I didn't do something like this, I'd—I'd go mad."

She got to her feet, and held out her hand. Gordon took it in both of his.

"These last weeks," she whispered, "I've been wishing I could see more of you. And when you told me about the rose—I knew you liked me a little."

"A *little!*"

"So I managed to give it to you. But I didn't know how much more I could manage—how much more you'd want me to manage—"

Again that strange strangle hold upon his throat!

"And last night I—I worried about it. It didn't occur to me that you weren't doing more managing yourself because—you weren't a duke! So I came out here, even earlier than usual—and then, in this beautiful, quiet place, with the dogwood blooming all around us —so safely hidden that no one could bother us, or interrupt us, or prevent us—you came and found me— as if you had heard me calling to you. Nothing—lovely —has happened to me for so long that it—it seems too good to be true."

"It is too good to be true!"

"What?"

"That I have found you."

If she hesitated, it was only for an instant. Then she

walked straight into his outstretched arms, and flung hers around his neck.

"We'll make it true!" she whispered, and pressed her face against his.

Their secret was to be all their own, they agreed, as long as the dogwood was in bloom; then they would share it. Gordon demurred a little. It wasn't quite square of him, he argued, not to go to her father at once. But Patricia was insistent. Tell her father, whose mind ran to nothing loftier than committee meetings and investigations, and rules of cloture and precedence, about these wonderful meetings in the spring dawn, with the silent woods for a trysting place, and the snowy blossoms for a bower? He wouldn't be interested; he wouldn't understand; he wouldn't approve.

"That's exactly why we ought to tell him—because he wouldn't approve, I mean."

"Would you rather see me in the drawing room than here?"

A vision of the drawing room, with its heavy gilt chairs upholstered in crimson brocade, its formal walls and crystal chandeliers rose before Gordon.

"Of course not."

"That's the only place he'd think we ought to meet. In fact, he might not think we ought to meet at all—under the circumstances."

"Exactly."

"Would that suit you?"

Gordon endeavored to explain to her how little it would suit him. He was reasonably successful.

"Well, then—"

"All right, darling, just as you say. While the dogwood lasts—"

It lasted, thanks to crisp, clear weather, much longer than usual. Every day they met a little earlier than the day before, parted a little later.

"These white trees all around us—they seem like the guardian angels of our love, angels with beautiful folded wings, don't they, Andrew? If we hurt each other, they might fly away—"

"We won't ever hurt each other."

"Are you sure?"

"Absolutely. Aren't you?"

"I'm afraid to feel too sure."

"Would anything make you feel sure?"

"One thing."

"What is it?"

A week earlier, she would have told him outright. What reticence there had been between them had been all on his side. Now, feeling more and more deeply, she was able to say less and less. But suddenly he knew.

"You—you don't mean?"

"Yes."

"When?"

"Right away. Before anyone can delay us or stop us. Don't you want me—now?"

If he tried to tell her how much he wanted her, he would have failed. Instead, he bowed his head on his hands. Then she understood.

"You think it wouldn't be honorable to do it—and tell afterwards?"

"I know it wouldn't, darling. I—I wish it would. As soon as we let people know we're engaged, part of—of all this is going to be spoiled for us. Even if there's no opposition—and there will be—we'll have to wait— and the waiting will be a ghastly sort of masquerade—"

"What do you mean?"

"The entertaining—putting us through a lot of strain, and sham—and artificial excitement. My emotions seem to be powerful enough without anything to stimulate them."

"I've been rather looking forward to the gay part of it," Patricia confessed almost shyly, "you see I never came out—and an announced engagement will put an end to mourning, of course, Andrew, think how wonderful it will be to dance together!"

"Yes, but—"

"All right then, do what I want—*first.*"

But he shook his head. "No. We'll stick to our bargain. As long as the dogwood lasts, we'll come here, alone, this way. Then—"

So, when the last petals had fallen from the trees, and lay, as soft and white as virgin snow on the ground, they stayed so late in the Park that all the world saw them walk back together, breakfasted in the sunny alcove of the great oak-paneled, tapestried dining room, and drove, in Patricia's roadster, down to the Senate Office Building to tell her father.

The immediate result was very much what she had foretold and expected. Their arrival, in the first place, was ill-timed. The Senator was on the point of starting to a very important committee meeting. That he should be delayed in this laudable purpose with the announcement that he was expected to hand over his invaluable daughter to an unknown young attaché who could not possibly need her, either in a private or an official sense, as much as he did, could hardly be expected to please him. Besides, the whole idea was so disagreeably and violently sudden. He had expected of course that sometime—fifteen or twenty years hence was his indignant inference—Patricia might think of something of the kind. But she was entirely too young.

"I'm twenty-one. Mother wasn't any older than that when I was born. It was lovely for me, having her so young. I don't want to be old when my children are little."

The Senator, who belonged to a more discreet and less normal generation had the grace to blush at her inference, which was more than either Patricia or Gordon did.

"Ahem! Well, well, my dear girl, I must say—er—and I had thought that one of my own colleagues—of the proper political party of course—as your choice—when you made a choice—"

"Oh, *Father!* You wouldn't expect me to *marry* a senator! Why, I've had to live with one all my life already!"

"You know, Patricia, my opinion of international alliances."

"You might change it," she murmured, "you did, about the League of Nations."

"I am talking about matrimony, not treaties—"

"Yes, Father, I know. But if you could come to see the lesser thing clearly, you might the greater, too."

The clock struck eleven. The Senator rose.

"Really, Patricia, really my dear—er—Gordon—as I have already told you, I am late for a committee meeting, and I am afraid there will not be a quorum if I do not hasten away. Of course, sir, you realize that I shall need—er—to investigate your qualifications—"

"Of course, Father dear, Andrew realizes that. I have told him that making investigations is your specialty. But you don't usually hold up things indefinitely by making them, do you?"

The Senator snorted slightly, and glared at Gordon. But before he went out of the room, slamming the door behind him, he kissed his daughter.

After the slamming had been accomplished, Gordon kissed her, too.

The investigations revealed so little that was damaging to Gordon, and so much that was, after all, reasonably satisfactory, even to the Senator, that, in the course of a few weeks, the engagement was announced. Patricia stood on her feet for five hours at a stretch, against a constantly growing bank of magnificent hothouse flowers, while dozens of hearty wellwishers—and possibly a few who wished her slightly less well—filed through the crimson and gilt drawing room and shook her hand or kissed her, according to the degree of intimacy with her which they possessed or wished to imply that they possessed, and then passed on into the stately dining room and ate up the excellent food which she had provided for them. For the first time in public, she had laid aside her black clothes, and was dressed entirely in soft white; and Gordon, when the last guest had departed and she had crumpled into the nearest chair, saw that her face was as white as her dress.

"Darling, you're terribly tired."

"Yes, rather. I must pull myself together. You know we're going to Aunt Sybil's to dinner."

From the dinner, they went to a ball at Rauscher's and danced together, of course, over and over again, under the smiling indulgent gaze of Aunt Sybil and the other patronesses. As he held her in his arms, his pulse beating high, he thought suddenly of the way she had clung to him and nestled against him in the sweet, silent woods of Rock Creek Park. They were even closer together now, and the diaphanous ball-dress, with its sleeveless, low-cut bodice, revealed her very differently from the way the rough little homespun suit had done; and there had been a good deal of champagne at the dinner. Involuntarily, he thought, too, of his own phrase, "my emotions seem to be powerful enough without anything to stimulate them," and felt, or thought he felt, her shrink a little from him.

"Did I hurt you, darling?"

"No."

"What is the matter then?"

"Nothing—I haven't danced for so long, it seems strange, that's all."

"It seems wonderful to me, just as you said it would."

It was three o'clock in the morning when he took her home, fiercely reluctant to part with her.

"Can't I come in for a minute?"

"No."

"Just a *minute.*"

"Why?"

"I want to kiss you."

"You *have* kissed me."

"I know, but not enough. Please, darling—"

He had his way, of course; and during the next few weeks, as they accepted the steady stream of invitations that flowed in upon them, lunching gayly at the Shoreham or the Willard, finishing the afternoon with a *thé dansant,* dining at one great house after another, and going on afterwards to a big charity ball or a small smart dance, they found it was often only at such stolen moments as those which Patricia had at first hesitated to grant that they were really alone together. The details for her trousseau and the plans for the big wedding at St. John's occupied her mornings; and she rose to face them with increasing weariness of both body and spirit. She did not care whether her bridal cake was built in three frosted tiers or in five, whether her wedding guests ate lobster Newburg or chicken patties; lace-edged sheets, embroidered tablecloths, lingerie as fine as gossamer, soft satin that shimmered under the touch—she looked at them through a veil of fatigue that seemed to grow thicker every day, blinding her vision altogether. The arrangements went on smoothly, under her competent guidance; but she faced them with decreasing joy, then with indifference; finally with a kind of terror. She forced herself to go ahead; and when she had driven her strength as far she felt she possibly could, she still had before her the dinners and balls, the teas and luncheons. She still had before her, too, Gordon's encircling arms and insistent kisses. There was excitement in her response to them, a thrill of triumph; but the well-spring of tenderness and joy and thanksgiving which had, at first, risen within her at his slightest touch, seemed to have run dry. At last, white to the lips, she told him so.

"You—you mean you don't love me any more?"

"I do love you."

"You say you're—*afraid?*"

"Yes. Things loom up ahead of me. I can't see where I'm going."

"I'll show you."

"You can't—any more. I'm afraid of you, too. I thought you were going to deliver me from bondage. Instead of that, you keep—tightening the fetters. It's hideous."

"Our love is hideous?"

"No—but the necessary accessories to it are."

She put her head suddenly against the back of the sofa and began, very quietly, to cry. Gordon bent over her, laying his hand across her shoulder. She shivered.

"Don't you want me to touch you?"

"No—I did want to have you. I *needed* to have you. But you've spoiled it all—by the *way* you've done it. Don't—don't come near me."

"Perhaps you'd rather I went away altogether?"

Her quiet crying had become hysterical.

"Would you?"

"Yes. If you had only married me when I wanted you to, this wouldn't have happened."

Gordon, without another word, walked out of the door. Then suddenly he turned, and came and stood over her.

"Look here," he said, "I'm afraid what I'm going to say will hurt you dreadfully but I've got to say it just the same; I didn't want all these accessories. I told you at the beginning how I dreaded the masquerade we had before us, and you told me you rather looked forward to the gaiety of it all! I told you, too, that I felt my emotions didn't need stimulating, and the fact that they have been—stimulated a good deal—hasn't been the best thing in the world for either of us. But someway I ought to have managed to save you from working yourself to death in order to carry through our engagement and our wedding in a conventional way. I feel pretty well cut up to think that I haven't; and it's a thousand times worse to feel that my love—or at least my expression of it—has become a torment to you instead of a refuge. I—I don't believe I'll ever get over that as long as I live—"

He stopped, his voice breaking. Patricia did not raise her head, or speak.

"I ask your forgiveness from the bottom of my heart."

He waited, and waited in vain for an answer. Then he went on more steadily.

"Just the same, I was right not to marry you that time. It wouldn't have been square in itself; but what's more, it wouldn't have been square to help you run away from the job that's been given you to do. It isn't right for you to talk about it, or even think about it, as bondage. I've been wickedly stupid not to see how much you needed help, not to try to make things easier for you; but I never had any right to help you escape from them. You used to have a current saying in the States that 'politics weren't fit for gentlemen'; and because 'gentlemen' were too lazy, or too indifferent, or too dull, to cope with them, the saying became partly true—*but it was the 'gentlemen's' fault that it was!* Now politics are in better repute than they used to be, because after a while 'gentlemen' woke up to their own blindness and stupidity and got into the fight and made it a clean one—you can't honestly say that the majority of men you know in public life today aren't honest and intelligent and hard-working!"

"I haven't said so!" cried Patricia suddenly, springing up, "that hasn't anything to do with us."

"Hasn't it? Haven't women as well as men a part in politics today? Haven't you—as the head of your father's house—any responsibility in carrying out your share of the work? Haven't you any obligation to the political side that's so mixed up with the purely social side that they're like—like the Siamese twins? You can be a 'lady' of the same type as those defunct gentlemen —and say how oppressive and wearing and empty and wicked it is—and it will go on being oppressive and wearing and empty and wicked—because you, and women like you, are willing to be *such damned slackers!* It takes money and intelligence and charm and beauty and position to do your job; lots of women would be glad to do it if they could, and they haven't got the tools; and you've got 'em—and want to lay 'em down!"

"You—you have no right to talk to me like that!"

"I haven't any right because I've failed you; but I'm not going to stand back and see you fail me—and your father—and your country for all that. You're big and strong enough—even if I wasn't—to keep our love for each other as—as—beautiful as it was at first. Even I don't need to see—those white blossoms we loved so much—to remember that they were there, and what they meant to us. Can't you fold their fragrance around your heart—and keep it there always? If you can't it's—it's you who have made our guardian angels fly away!"

It was raining an unseasonably cold, harsh rain, that made the June night black and ugly; but Gordon did not go home; instead, he turned north, and alone in the wet darkness, sought out the trysting place where he and Patricia had been so happy together, and sat for hours, doggedly miserable, thinking, fighting, at last inarticulately praying. It was daylight when he went back to his rooms; as he entered them, the telephone rang sharply. Gordon unhooked the receiver and took the message. For a moment he leaned, unsteadily, against the wall; then without changing his drenched clothes he sat down and began to write.

"Dearest" the letter began.

"I don't think, after last night, that you want me to call you that. But I can't help it, this once.

I've just had most dreadful news. My brother has been killed in a horrible accident. I cared for him more than anyone in the world except you. Now I've lost you both. I haven't forgotten what you said about not being willing to assume more care than you had already. So even if you hadn't already decided against me, this would have done it.

I'll leave as soon as I can get passage, so you won't have to see me again at all.

Yours forever,

Andrew Gordon."

He folded the letter into an envelope. Then before he sealed it, he slipped between the sheets a soft, white flower that had lain for a long time pressed in a little leather case against his heart. Then, under his simple signature, he added his new title—the title of the Duke of Dunkirk.

Three hours later, his hasty preparations for departure were interrupted by the appearance of his Japanese servant, bearing upon a silver tray a senatorial visiting card, engraved, without initials, simply with the last name of the dignitary to whom it belonged, and that of the state which he represented.

"Tell Mr. Anderson that I'll be out in a minute."

He found the Senator in a visible state of excitement.

"My dear Gordon—I mean, my dear Dunkirk—"

"Don't," said the boy wincing.

"Well, well! my dear—er—Andrew. This is very sudden and sad of course, very upsetting—"

"I was a good deal upset before I got my cable. Patricia probably told you—she's thrown me over."

"As I was saying, she—"

"I'm afraid I didn't hear what you were saying, sir—"

"She didn't give me the impression that she was—er—thinking of throwing you over. Indeed, she came into my—er—apartment very late last night—ahem—in tears and—er—urged me to go to you at once, in spite of the unseemly hour and the fact that, as she is aware, senators do not call upon attachés to—er—tell you that she was sorry. She did not enlighten me for what, and naturally I did not—ahem—accede to her wishes. Then this morning she received your note by special messenger and—really forced me to hasten to your side—at the risk of being late to a very important committee meeting. I feel I could hardly do justice to her remarks but I may say that they were sympathetic and affectionate not to say—er—intense. The gist of them was, however, that she was waiting for you."

"Where?" asked Gordon. But he knew.

"She—ah—did not say. In the drawing room, I presume."

Gordon presumed nothing of the sort. He escorted his distinguished guest to the door with scant ceremony, and turned his footsteps in the direction of Rock Creek Park.

He saw her a long way off, watching for him; but she did not wait for him to join her. He was not half way up the hill before, hearing his footsteps, she had rushed to meet him, drawn his tired head against her breast, clasped her strong young arms around him as if she would never let him go again. And when at last she had comforted him for his brother's death as only one lover can comfort another, she spoke again of themselves.

"Darling, I have been an awful coward—a 'damned slacker,' just as you called me—but I won't be again."

"You'll be what you've always been, wonderful and lovely—"

"And efficient."

"Yes," he said, slightly surprised, "efficient, of course."

"Just to prove it to you, I've got our plans all made."

"Our plans?" he echoed. "What plans?"

"Well," she said calmly, "at two o'clock the Bishop of Washington is going to marry us. At four o'clock we're going to take the Congressional Express for New York. We'll spend the night—"

She hesitated for a second. Gordon caught her to him.

"At the Plaza. Tomorrow morning we'll sail on the 'Olympic.' I've engaged a cabin-deluxe. I think we'll manage to be comfortable."

"Patricia—you're going with me!"

"It sounds that way, doesn't it?" she said softly, "and by and by—some day—you'll come back with me. But whether we're in Scotland—or Washington—or Rock Creek Park—whether we're sad or joyful, or alone or in a multitude—those white trees that are the guardian angels of our love are going to keep on blossoming in our hearts forever!"

THE COURT END OF TOWN

ALAN AMES was a philanderer. Everyone said so, and, for once, everyone was quite right. He would pay conspicuous attentions to a girl—attentions which included not only huge boxes of chocolates, and enormous orchid corsages and orchestra seats at the best plays in town, and long rides in his distinctly "snappy" roadster, with luncheon and tea in sheltered corners of expensive hotels thrown in, but, it was rumored, other even more marked tokens of apparent affection as well, whenever he had, or could create, the chance—and Alan was adept at creating chances if he wanted them; then, suddenly, he would stop calling on her, he would even walk past her at a dance with some new vision in tulle by his side, apparently unaware that she existed at all, and never remember that existence again, at least to any degree that counted. He should, of course, have been ostracized for such shocking conduct. But unfortunately for his own good he was not the type which the female of the species is prone to ostracize. In the first place, he was outrageously good looking, vibrant with perfect health and high spirits, possessed of a smile that flashed wide over snowy teeth, of a fresh color, and of a remarkably fine figure; then he had a voice which could be as gay as the song of the lark at sunrise, and tender as the notes of a cooing dove; he was, as all the girls expressed it, "a heavenly dancer"; and, in addition to all this, he rejoiced in a bank account which was apparently as inexhaustible as the widow's cruse. Under these circumstances, it must be confessed that Alan was in a position to give any maiden upon whom he had a "crush," however fleeting, an extremely good time. This was so hard to ignore, that, so far as anyone knew, it never *was* ignored.

It was while Alan was in his senior year at Yale that he accepted an invitation from Tom Fairfax, a classmate from Washington, to spend the Christmas holidays, at the capital; and, for the better part of a week, the happy philanderer pursued his usual course with the usual results. Then, in the cold gray dawn after a Charity Ball at the Willard, when the weary Thomas was sinking into a placid slumber, his guest, from the twin bed beside his own, roused him.

"Who was that girl," demanded Alan suddenly, "who came in late with some old codger who looked as if he must be an intimate friend of the family, or a distant cousin, or something like that? I tried two or three times to get introduced to her, and I always seemed to get balked."

"Lots of girls came in late," murmured Tom drowsily, "how the deuce should I know which one you mean?"

"Oh, hell! You'd know this one all right! Couldn't miss her! Little—awfully straight and slim—carried her chin up in the air, had on a queer slinky yellow dress, a corker, cut something like the ones in medieval portraits and stained glass windows, square low neck, girdle round the hips, you know. All she needed was a lily in her hand or a roll of vellum, and the idea would have been complete."

"Oh, you must mean Rose-Aimée."

"Rose-Aimée what?"

"Fairfax. She's a distant cousin of *mine*. That chap you saw with her is a senator who's got an awful case on her."

"Well, I like his taste. Why didn't you introduce me?"

"Dunno. Didn't think of it. A fellow doesn't, you know, with cousins. She's only seventeen—this is her first season—girls come out younger here than they do in New England. I hear she's cutting quite a wide swathe. She's been down in Virginia for a Christmas house party, that's why you haven't seen her before. Do let me go to sleep."

"I have a hunch I'd like to meet her."

Thomas emitted a sound that might have been a chuckle, only, as there was no reason why he should chuckle, Alan decided that it must have been a curious kind of yawn.

"All right. You're likely to find the scene rather crowded already, but I'll take you out there tomorrow afternoon. She lives in Georgetown—the old court end of town, you know. That branch of the family located there more than a century ago, and hasn't ever moved with the modern trend of fashion here. The house is what's called a gem of colonial architecture, I believe —yellow brick, fine specimen of a doorway, beautiful garden in the rear."

"I wasn't so specially interested in the *house*."

"But the garden—things have been known to happen in gardens!"

"Not in December, you blithering idiot!"

"December will have flown before anything happens in that quarter," prophesied Alan's host. "You interrupted me. There are also cobblestones in the street, hard on tires, devil of a way out there. She may not be in anyway, probably won't."

"You'll telephone first," observed Alan drily.

A slight snore was the only answer. But, the next afternoon, turning a deaf ear to various other invitations that had been showered upon him, Alan persisted in his determination to call on Miss Fairfax. In fact, the subject seemed to intrigue him.

"Curious name," he observed as they bumped along the further end of M Street.

"Fairfax?"

"Of course not, you darned fool. Rose-Aimée."

"Got it from a Creole grandmother. Were you thinking of calling her that, the first thing?"

Alan endeavored to express what he thought of his host.

"Well, I wouldn't, if I were you, that's all," said Rose-Aimée's cousin, emitting again that sound which was so curiously like a chuckle. "The kid's queer. You may come a cropper. If you do, don't blame me. I wash my hands of you, the minute you get into hers."

"What do you mean, cropper?"

"You wait and see."

The cropper that Alan Ames encountered was the fact that, less than an hour later, and for the first time in his life, he was head over heels in love.

There were only a few days left at his disposal before he was obliged to return to the institution of learning which he graced with his presence, and, as Thomas had predicted, the scene was crowded already.

In addition to several callow youths like himself, and the somewhat seedy-looking and middle-aged senator who had been Rose-Aimée's escort at the ball, and who was considerably more of a personage than Alan guessed, there was an Under Secretary, a foreign attaché, and three or four officers, who all seemed to find something strangely attractive about the old yellow brick house at the court end of town. Alan had not only been used to less competition, but the little which he had encountered had been of a very different calibre. In spite of the excellent opinion he had of himself, he had sense enough to see that Rose-Aimée, with the flower of Washington chivalry, so to speak, at her feet already, was not likely to be unduly impressed with what he had to offer. Still he was a little piqued when, demure, passive, sedate, she carelessly accepted his overtures without either surprise or elation. However, he was not daunted. He redoubled his efforts, but to no avail. He took her in to dinner, and she talked to the man on her left. He bespoke her for dances, and she forgot, and floated off with someone else. He sent her a huge boxful of yellow roses, with a graceful note intimating that he considered the flowers expressive of her own exquisite personality, and when she failed to wear them, or even mention having received them, he questioned her almost desperately about the matter.

"Roses?" inquired Rose-Aimée vaguely, "yellow roses? I didn't know you could get them at this time of year."

"It's very hard, but I did it," said Alan with satisfaction. "I thought they'd please you."

"Perhaps they were sent to the wrong address?" she ventured.

"I took them to your house myself."

"Oh, then perhaps my maid forgot! There are so many coming all the time, she gets careless. I'll speak to her."

Alan ground his teeth.

He "fished," shamelessly, for an invitation to visit Tom again at Easter, and landed it. And, as they swung up Massachusetts Avenue after leaving the

Union Station, he suggested that they should go straight out to Georgetown.

"I wrote your cousin I was coming down," he said importantly, "and told her I'd be out around five."

"Ah!" said Thomas pleasantly.

"I may as well tell you, I think she's a perfect peach. I've been writing to her ever since I went back at New Year's."

"Oh!" remarked Thomas agreeably.

"She hasn't answered often, of course, and then only little notes. But she's expecting me today."

"Yes?" queried Thomas. "Funny then—she went to New Orleans day before yesterday."

That night saw Alan ensconced in an upper berth of the Southern Express, with a crying baby in the lower, and a man who snored across the aisle. When he reached New Orleans, and sought out the address which Thomas had obligingly given him, he was informed that Miss Fairfax had been suddenly called back to Washington.

It was not until late June that she gave him an hour, an hour all to himself in the garden back of the old yellow brick house. She had refused his invitations to come on to the Senior Prom, to his graduation, to the Harvard-Yale boat races. But she received him now with a little soft, elusive smile, that sent his blood racing, and slipped a little soft, elusive hand into his for the fraction of a minute.

"I'm—I'm awfully glad to see you," he stammered stupidly, devouring her with his eyes, realizing her tantalizing aloofness and sweetness more keenly than ever. "I'm—I'm so glad you've got on a yellow dress. I always like to think of you that way, because you had on a yellow dress that night I first saw you, when you knocked me over straight away."

"Not really? It's cooler out in the garden. Shall we go there? We're going to have a mint julep, and some frosted cakes."

"That'll be fine."

It would have taken more than one mint julep, surely, to go to his strong young head. But they had not been in the garden ten minutes before he lost it, for all that. He caught her up, without the warning of word or gesture, pressed his face against hers, and kissed her over and over again.

"Rose-Aimée," he murmured, "you lovely, sweet, precious little flower."

Suddenly he knew, with sickening certainty, that he had made a fatal mistake. There was no answering flame, and worse than that, there was a spiritual withdrawal far more isolating than any mere physical shrinking could have been.

"You don't understand," he stammered, releasing her. "I wasn't doing that just to be fresh. I'm—I'm in love with you."

"Do you think I don't know that?" asked Rose-Aimée evenly.

"I want you to marry me."

"You have forgotten yourself very far indeed. But, even so, I did not so far insult you in my mind as to suppose anything else."

She was looking him straight in the face, entirely unembarrassed. Crimson, he floundered hopelessly.

"You mean—it doesn't make any difference to you —that I'm not fooling, that I'm awfully in earnest?"

"Not the slightest. You may be in earnest—"

"I *am* in earnest."

"But that does not alter the fact that you are very presumptuous."

"Presumptuous!"

"Very. A man with a record like yours has no right to assume that no matter how—successful—he considers himself in the matter of love affairs that every girl he looks at is going to fall into his mouth like a ripe cherry."

"Darling, you've been listening to silly gossip—"

"You know my name," said Miss Fairfax crisply, "and I happen to know more than one girl who—did get to care for you. I don't know what you said to them—though I can imagine. I don't know whether you ever touched them, or even tried to—though I can imagine that, too. But you made them conspicuous by the attentions you paid them, and you made them *think* you cared too."

"This time I do care," said Alan hoarsely.

"And then you threw them over!"

"Good God, you don't think I'll throw you over!"

"I certainly do not."

Her meaning was unmistakable. Alan winced under it. But, somehow, he managed to ask her a question.

"Are you turning me down because I'm a poor sort, or because you don't like me anyway?"

"I don't like you anyway."

"You lie," said Alan Ames distinctly.

In spite of her self-possession, Rose-Aimée took a step backward and gave a slight gasp.

"You wouldn't have bothered," went on Alan, finding his voice, "to run away from me the way you have if you'd been perfectly indifferent to me. You avoided me at first—made it hard for me to see you—just to spur me on. You knew things had been too darned easy for me with girls before, and thought that would attract me. Well, it did. Then you found that you couldn't avoid me, and what's more, that you didn't want to, and you got scared, so you decided to run. You little coward."

Rose-Aimée gasped again.

"I love you," said the boy, "and you know it. I'm not good enough, I've been a general ass all around, and worst of all where you were concerned. But for all that, in spite of it, in spite of yourself, you love me, and I know it. I'm going to do better. I'm not going to make a lot of fancy promises, because probably I wouldn't be able to keep them, right off, anyway. But I'm going to try. And I won't bother you, or hurry you, or—disgrace you. If I give you my word of honor on that will you just say that sometime—a long way off—if I do make good—you'll marry me?"

"No," said Rose-Aimée, but the little yellow rose had grown very white indeed.

Alan turned on his heel.

"Good-bye," he said, "some day you'll send for me."

"Never, never, never!"

"You will! *And I won't come!*"

"I'll never send! But if I did, you'd come so quickly that—"

"Never, never, never!" he mocked savagely, "and I hope you feel the way then that I'm feeling now!"

The garden gate clicked behind him, and he walked, blindly, down the drowsy, deserted cobblestoned street.

This story, being a true one, has no moral. Alan did not stop philandering, enter the ministry, and become a missionary to China. And Rose-Aimée did not cast aside her personal pride and the traditions of the court end of town, beg his forgiveness and ask him to name the day, and, upon being disdained, give up the unusually agreeable life of a belle in Washington to engage in settlement work. Instead, for a time, Alan philandered rather more than less, and his progress down the primrose path not infrequently took him to Washington, which he made no effort to avoid. Rose-Aimée, when she met him at a ball, walked straight past him with her head in the air, as if she had never seen him before which, as her cousin Thomas pointed out, made things, "damned awkward."

"I think you are too hard on Al. He may have needed a lesson, but you gave it to him all right. You cut straight to the bone."

"The wound seems to have healed."

"It's skillfully bandaged, that's all."

"If he had—cared at all—he wouldn't have gone on the way he has."

"He's gone on the way he has because he cared so darned much. He doesn't know any other way—being Al—to cover up that skillfully bandaged wound. And he's doing awfully well at law school."

"He'll need all the knowledge he gets there to extricate himself from breach of promise suits."

Later, Thomas wrung a reluctant promise from her that she would at least bow to his friend when she happened to see him.

"Did he ask you to make me do that?"

"You bet he didn't! He's never mentioned your name. I guess he's got over his crush. He seems to be through chasing girls, anyway—at least, he plays around a little, but he does it differently. He's absolutely on the level."

"Then he wasn't always?"

"Well, perhaps not. But a fellow as attractive as he is—and as rich—has the devil of a time keeping straight. I think it's the girls' fault often."

"Men always stand up for each other's awful conduct!"

"His conduct isn't so very awful, I tell you!"

After a while, Thomas gave up arguing with her. Her time continued to be fully occupied with her train of official admirers, and her cousin decided it was hardly worth while to mention his friend. But, when he did do so, on rare occasions, it must be confessed that there was little enough in the reports he gave her to warrant the impression that Alan was eating bitter bread. He was taken into an excellent firm upon his graduation from the law school, and was to all appearances, prosperous, respected, and happy. In 1914 he increased the general esteem in which he seemed to be held by resigning his easy, lucrative, and agreeable position, and enlisting in the Lafayette Escadrille.

From that time on, it seemed to Rose-Aimée, as she admitted to herself with exasperation, that she could not pick up a magazine of current events without seeing an extremely attractive full page picture of Alan in uniform, or read a daily newspaper in which his name did not appear in headlines an inch high. He was decorated for valor after a thrilling escapade, he was slightly wounded; he was said to be betrothed to a French countess; he had become a Captain,—a Major —a Lieutenant Colonel—then he was missing.

He was missing a long time; and, when he was finally found, he was found in a condition that necessitated his immediate return to the United States, and the sending of a communication from the War Department to his family that there was very little hope for him. The country watched the daily bulletins about him, expecting every day an obituary notice. There was a serious operation, followed by another still more grave, months of care in the hands of skilled surgeons and nerve specialists. He came out of it with the fresh gaiety all gone, a look in the blue eyes that seemed constantly to be seeing horrors which went straight past all the kindness of his friends, a slight limp, and the loss of his right arm; also, in possession of numerous medals, and before very long, of a seat in the lower House of Congress, fairly thrust upon him by a home district that insisted on calling him "one of the greatest heroes of the war" and rewarding him with what, according to its lights, was the greatest honor it could give him.

There was, inevitably, more or less a flourish of trumpets when he appeared in Washington. He yielded to Tom Fairfax's plea that he would "bunk with him" until he could find a suitable establishment of his own; and, at the first opportunity that they had for a chat on the subject of desirable locations, Thomas broached the subject of Georgetown.

"Funny, everyone seems to be moving back there again. There's a regular rush to get hold of those old places, and stick bathrooms and sleeping porches and garages onto 'em. Quite a boom in real estate. How'd you like one of those?"

"I don't know. It might be a good idea. Have you heard of any especially attractive?"

"Well, there's my cousin's. Her father and mother have both died, and it's a big place for her to live in all alone. I believe she'd like to sell. She hasn't a red cent, of course—never had much, as money goes nowadays, and Aunt Valerie was a helpless invalid for years before she died. That eats into family funds awfully. I know Rose-Aimée has sold a lot of the china—pink lustre and things like that—and most of her jewelry, even the pearls that she got from her godmother." Then, as Alan did not answer, "You remember my cousin, don't you? You had a kind of affair with her once."

"Oh, yes, I remember her. You say she isn't very comfortably fixed?"

"Gosh, no. She's taken up some kind of work—interior decorating, I think. Goes out very little. Can't afford to I suppose, for Lord knows she's still run after enough, though she's no chicken."

"Twenty-seven," said Alan laconically.

"How did you remember? Well, she came out so young, and was such a huge success, that I thought she'd kind of peter out, as long as she didn't marry—but she hasn't. It's her own fault that she stays at home more and more. She took the war awfully hard—I can't imagine why, for she had no very near relative in it—and slaved for the Red Cross and the Liberty Loan Drives until we all thought she'd lose her looks entirely; but she didn't. She was a pretty girl. Now she's beautiful."

"Yellow roses," remarked Alan enigmatically, "are lovely buds—but they're magnificent flowers. So she didn't marry?"

"No. I can't imagine why. She certainly has chances enough, ambassadors, and generals, and all that sort of thing. Well, how do you take to the Georgetown idea?"

Alan knocked the ashes off his cigarette. "I think I do, rather," he said, "but I'll stay here with you for a while before I look around, unless I'm a frightful nuisance."

"Oh, go to hell," said Thomas affectionately.

Alan had done well in the law—and well in the war; he did better still in Congress. Before he had been there six months he had made a mark which few of the "youngsters" could equal. His maiden speech was printed not only—as was inevitable—in the Congressional Record, but in every newspaper in the country, in many cases with favorable editorial comment. He was still too young and inexperienced for the Senate, of course, but that he was built of senatorial timber, there did not seem to be the shadow of a doubt—and after that—everyone began to say, if he kept on, he would soon be standing in the shadow of the White House, just as everyone, ten years before, had said he was an outrageous philanderer, and, again, everyone was right. But if the former flattery had gone to his head, the latter did not—it did not even drive the haunted look from his eyes. He was singularly free from either conceit or elation, which added tremendously to his popularity; but he was also singularly free from any touch of joy. He accepted the wining and dining tendered him as a more or less inevitable part of the life of a public official, and returned it gracefully and lavishly. In the course of this, it was inevitable that he should meet Miss Fairfax again. Little as she "played around," much as she might devote herself to interior decoration, empty as her purse might be, she "belonged," and this being the case, she could not withdraw from society altogether. The night came when Alan found her name on the card in the tiny envelope which the manservant tendered him on a silver tray upon his arrival at the Embassy where he was dining; he realized that he was to take her in to dinner, and wondered just how she would meet the situation. Afterwards, he told himself, he ought to have known. She met it with no trace of self-consciousness, with a courteous display of interest in his career—and with absolute impersonality. After that, he encountered her more and more often. She made as little effort to avoid him as she did to see him. And she was quite the most beautiful woman he had ever beheld.

He sent her, at last, from his office, a dictated and typewritten offer for her house, written on official stationery. A week later, he received a reply from a real estate company, which informed him, that, as Miss Fairfax's agent, it was empowered to inform him that, after all, she had decided not to sell. Within a few days, a bit of gossip overheard in the cloak room informed him that a little property had been left her by one of her relatives in New Orleans, that the worst of her straitened circumstances were over. He strode back into the House, delivered a speech which, by its power and eloquence threw everything he had said before into the shade, and, in a roar of applause, made for the door. A page stopped him.

"I've got a note for you, sir," he said politely.

"Thanks," remarked Ames mechanically; then, as he tore it open, and glanced at the single sheet which it contained, "Wait a minute," he said shortly, and pressed into the palm of the surprised youth a ten-dollar bill. The page shifted his gum skillfully from one side of his mouth to the other, and sought out his boon companion.

"Look what that guy, Ames, give me," he whispered hoarsely, "gee, but I like that feller! I bet he gets to be President some day. And say, I wish I knew what was in that skinny little letter. When he read it, he stopped looking like he was seeing ghosts for the first time since he's been here."

The "skinny little letter" had run:

"Dear Alan,
I shall be at home, all the evening, in the garden. Will you come to me there?
Rose-Aimée."

The gate clicked behind Alan, and, as he limped down the mossy path, a stray branch from a thorny, fragrant yellow rose bush caught him suddenly about the legs. As he stooped to disentangle himself, hampered by his one arm, he heard a soft rush of footsteps coming towards him, felt two capable little hands setting him free.

"You told me," a rather tremulous voice was saying, "that you'd never, never, never, never come."

He straightened himself and faced her. "Well, if it's any satisfaction to you," he said grimly, "you may as well know that there's never been a minute, all these ten years, when I wouldn't have come if you'd given me the chance. But you said you'd never, never, never send, and Good Lord, I was beginning to think you meant it! I never quite gave up hope until I heard you'd lost your money, and then I knew you'd starve before you'd send for me, because you'd persuade yourself you were asking for charity, and that I'd fling that in your face some day. When all the time it was I that was starving, I that needed charity, an ugly-looking cripple with his nerves all shot to pieces—"

"Don't," she said with quivering lips, "you know what you are—what I think of you—why I couldn't send—"

"That everlasting pride of yours! You *do* belong to the court end of town!"

"You do, too," she whispered, "I've—I've suffered dreadfully, but thank God I'm not going to be punished any longer because I couldn't see that ten years ago."

"You couldn't see it," he said slowly, "because I— didn't then. You were right about me, absolutely right. I wasn't fit for your royal presence, my dear. I'm glad you made me learn that I'd got to be, before I could even kneel before your throne."

He knelt then, burying his face in her dress. She leaned over him.

"I—I don't want you to kneel," she said softly, "I want you to—come and sit beside me on my throne."

Alan looked up, with a little happy laugh, and put his arm around her.

"In that case," he said whimsically, "perhaps you won't have me put out of the coronation chamber if I tell you that I want most awfully to kiss you!"

SHERIDAN CIRCLE

MRS. Edward Appleton was "having her day at home." Ever since four o'clock, a stream of cars had been coming over the Q Street Bridge, or up Massachusetts Avenue—depending upon whether their owners lived in Georgetown, the old "court end of town," or in the more newly fashionable sections of Washington—and rounding the great circle, flanked with beautiful houses, about the statue of the famous General from which it took its name. Dozens of children, watched by elderly "mammies" or, less frequently, by youthful French governesses, were playing around the marble base of the splendid, vital, bronze figure. More than once, the chauffeurs driving the limousines called out sharply to the old balloon man, whose bunch of many-colored balls shone like huge jewels in the afternoon sun, as he crossed and re-crossed the street, selling his wares first to the small persons who were spending the afternoon with the military celebrity, and then to those who were merely walking or motoring past to some less lovely spot. The organ grinder, too, jerking out "Dixie" and "Yankee Doodle" alternately, kept obstructing the traffic, kept playing, indeed, under the very windows of Mrs. Edward Appleton's house, as if he were trying to compete with the stringed orchestra inside it. The butler came out, and gave him two dimes, telling him to move on. As the organ grinder moved on, grinning cheerfully, he saw a little old woman whom he often encountered, a woman with a gray shawl over her head, and a small frayed basket full of dingy cake, which she tried to sell to passers-by. He gave one of the dimes to her, and turned across the bridge, starting "Dixie" again.

All afternoon, the great door of Mrs. Appleton's house, with its beautifully polished brass handle, its iron grill, and its crimson velvet curtain had been swinging open and shut. On the left, inside the basement entrance, was a small room where two maids took charge of wraps, and where a toilet table, with a great gilt-framed mirror over it, set with a gold service, and also supplied with hairpins, pink powder, fresh absorbent cotton and various other things, stood ready to serve Mrs. Appleton's callers quite as attractively and efficiently, and scarcely more silently, than the well-trained servants. The second man preceded the guests up the curving marble staircase, the carpet of which matched the curtains on the door, bent toward them as he neared the drawing room with a murmured, "What name, madam?" or "Whom shall I say, sir?" and then announced, importantly, "Mrs. Gregory, Miss West,

Madame de Solles, Major Wing," and walked slowly down again to repeat the process with the newcomers who had arrived during his brief absence.

Just inside the drawing room door stood Mrs. Edward Appleton, receiving alone. "Floaters" she always had in plenty, young, pretty women, dressed in dainty pale frocks, chatting lightly, preventing blockades and boredom, and luring guests who were inclined to chat too long with the hostess into the dining room, where at the lace-covered, flower-decked, candle-lighted table, slightly older and much more important women "poured." Mrs. Edward Appleton was famous, among other things, for the persons who were always glad to "assist" her. Today the Spanish Ambassadress was at one end of the table, and the wife of the Secretary of State at the other. But no one was ever asked to stand with her as she received her guests, though the most jealous of women—and many women in Washington were jealous of her—could hardly have said it was because she was afraid of having her own radiance dimmed. She did not belong to the type apparently most popular at the present time—at least with novelists! She was not "dark and small, with a pale though warm complexion, her only ornament a string of pearls, and dressed entirely in black." Not in the least. She was as tall and as beautifully made as Juno must have been, with deep blue eyes, and color in cheeks and lips as vivid as a sunset. Her turquoise-colored dress was shot with silver, her slippers were silver, and there was a silver fillet in her coppery hair. And, for the rest, there were diamonds—long, pendant earrings hanging from the small white ears partially covered by the low coiffure, diamonds around the white throat and on the folds of tulle against the white breast, below the extreme décolletage, diamonds, quantities of them, on the welcoming white hands.

"Sally, I haven't seen you in the longest time! Yes, I know, Florida is wonderful, but to stay there until April! Oh, Mrs. Letheridge, I think the ball for the Balkan Relief was the greatest success, how do you accomplish so much? Captain Hatley, I've just been telling someone what a capital dinner partner you are, someone who I'm sure you'll be glad to hear drank in every word I had to say with evident pleasure. I think you'll find her in the dining room. Ah, Monsieur, *quel plaisir—il y a longtemps que je n'ai pas—vous connaissez bien* Madame la Marquise, *n'est-ce pas?*"

"People used to say," a woman standing by the white marble mantel remarked to another, "people who envied her, I mean, that Gloria Appleton owed her popularity to her husband's position. I wonder what they say now."

"Well, he *was* a power."

"You mean *she* was—and still is! And a wonder! Think of her when Edward Appleton picked her up in the course of a summer vacation and brought her here —a little mute, red-headed thing, eighteen years old, who had never been out of the Middle West in her life! It took a good deal of solid gray matter underneath that great mop to learn the ropes of Washington in one year, and handle them herself in three. I wonder how many men owe their positions—or loss of them —to her! I wouldn't dare guess. It makes me tired when I hear that Edward Appleton was the most brilliant cabinet member of his time. He had the most brilliant wife, that was the whole story!"

"I sometimes wonder why she doesn't marry again."

"My dear, why should she? She has everything already that the most wonderful marriage could give her, and her freedom besides. I think she likes being able to have all the masculine attention she wants, too, without the disagreeable comments that would arise if she weren't a widow."

"There never was a breath against Gloria," said the first speaker sharply.

"Oh, my dear, *of course not!* But still—mightn't there have been, if she hadn't, as you say, been so powerful? She always shines out like a great light wherever she goes, and you know that moths are forever getting singed at that sort of an illumination."

"I never noticed that the singeing hurt the light any," said Mrs. Letheridge dryly.

"No, but for instance, look at the flowers here today! Dozens and dozens of them, all the most costly kinds—American Beauties, orchids, Easter lilies! There isn't a debutante of the winter who had at her coming-out party as many as Gloria has every time she has an 'at home.' One can't help wondering where they all come from."

"Perhaps she buys them herself," suggested Mrs. Letheridge, still more dryly, "she buys the silver vases that hold them, I presume? Suppose we go into the dining room and get some punch."

As they passed through the brocaded portieres, a large woman in mauve broadcloth and a picture hat, top-heavy with plumes, rushed up to them and addressed them gushingly.

"Oh, my *dear* Mrs. Letheridge! My *dear* Mrs. Pallison! Such ages since I've seen you! I do hope you're both quite well! I've worried, *not* seeing you, for fear something might be the matter! There *isn't!* I'm *so* glad! You *will* come in to my next day at home, won't you? The twenty-sixth. Perhaps you'd *pour* for me! Oh, of course I know you couldn't tell me now, without consulting your calendars, such *popular* ladies! But *if* you could! I've got to run along now, I owe about a *thousand* calls! I mustn't allow myself to linger, even in this *charming* spot. One's social obligations are *such* a burden, aren't they? But then I feel they're a *duty* as well!"

"There ought to be some law," said Mrs. Pallison savagely as the effulgent lady lumbered off, "to protect Washington hostesses from having 'climbing' females like that coming and spending the afternoon with them! And there's that awful Mrs. Kipp, with her woolen scarf and her scarecrow hat, over there in the corner eating everything she can lay her hands on! If it weren't for what she gets at teas, she'd starve to death."

"I'm sorry for poor old Mrs. Kipp," said Mrs. Letheridge kindly, "I'm afraid she *is* dreadfully hard up. But of course the mauve lady is awful. And it does seem too bad that when we open our doors to our

friends, we have to open them also to so many who are
not our friends."

Her companion glanced at her a trifle suspiciously,
but the placid face of Mrs. Letheridge was noncommit-
tal. Mrs. Pallison turned her attention to the really excellent punch.

Gradually the crowd began to grow smaller, the second man's trips up and down the red carpeted stairs
grew farther and farther apart, the waiters in the demolished dining room began to clear away the remains
of the feast. The "pourers" and "floaters" assuring
their hostess what a wonderful success her "day" had
been, suggested that they might safely leave; no one
else would be coming in so late. Gloria Appleton, who
had been standing on her feet for more than three
hours, walked over to one of the long windows, flung it
open, and sat down beside it, her hands relaxed in her
lap, fine lines of fatigue showing under her eyes and
around her lips. No, there would be no one else in
now; she could sit quietly for a few minutes before she
went to dress for her late dinner, looking out over the
Circle, at the shadows gathering about the bronze
statue, deserted now by the playing children, at the
stream of lighted cars passing up and down the broad
streets, at the bronze buffalo and shining lamps on the
bridge, at the tiny moon glowing in the soft sky.

"General Sheridan."

Gloria rose quickly, conventionally cordial.

"General Sheridan, I'm so glad—" she began, but
the man interrupted her quickly.

"Why, Gloria, don't you know me? Have I changed
as much as that? It—it's Roger," and, without further
preamble, he walked swiftly over to her, flung a pair of
vigorous arms about her, and kissed her heartily on
both cheeks.

For a moment she stood quite rigidly, shocked and
startled by the sudden surprise and by the slower recognition that followed it. Then, before she freed her-

self, she relaxed, laughed softly and, raising her face, gave him back his kiss.

"Why, my dear boy! I thought you were three thousand miles away at least."

"You mean you didn't think about me at all."

"And I didn't know you were a General."

"I wasn't. I used to be a Lieutenant."

"Oh, you know what I mean! I didn't know you were a *soldier!* Tell me all about it."

"I'd rather not, if you don't mind. It's all such ancient history. I left America when the war broke out. And I stayed in Europe until now."

"Is that all?"

"Yes, practically."

They both laughed, and Gloria motioned towards the sofa.

"Suppose we sit down for a few minutes," she said. "There must be something you could add to that. You arrive here with as much suddenness as your great namesake, whose statue is out there on the Circle."

"Yes," interrupted her caller, "I stopped to look at that. Isn't it a wonder? He was the chap who came 'up from the South at the break of day,' wasn't he?"

"No—that was 'the terrible grumble and rumble and roar,' " she corrected, "Sheridan came 'from Winchester, twenty miles away.' "

"So he did. Say, do you remember when we spoke that piece together in high school?"

"You still begin your sentences with 'Say,' don't you, Roger? Even becoming a General hasn't cured you of that!"

"Nothing will ever cure me of that. But do you remember?"

"Yes," she said slowly, "I remember."

"And in the end he 'saved the day.' "

"No," she corrected again, "it was the *steed* that saved the day—'by bringing Sheridan into the fight, from Winchester, twenty miles away.' "

"I guess you remember the poetry best, and I remember some of the things about our saying it together best," the man said dryly. "But after all, the main thing was that he got there."

"In other words you mean to say 'I too have arrived.' "

Sheridan nodded.

"Is there any special reason why you wanted to 'enter the fight'?"

"I wanted to see you," he said bluntly. "And I guess it amounts to about the same thing, doesn't it? To get near you at all?"

The clock on the mantel chimed the half hour. Gloria rose.

"I'm so sorry," she said, "but I've got a dinner engagement."

"*Dinner* at this hour?"

"Yes, some of the dinners are at half-past eight now, but most of them are still at eight o'clock."

"Gosh! Why, I had my supper at six, on the train, before we got in from New York. I thought you'd be all through, and that. . . ."

"I'd love to have the evening with you," she said swiftly, "that's what you started to say, isn't it? But I can't. This is an official dinner. I mustn't even risk being late to it, and I've very little time to dress."

"Can I come tomorrow then?"

"My dear boy, I haven't a free evening in six weeks."

A brick red color rose slowly under the tan in the man's cheeks.

"Is that just a way of saying you don't want to see me at all?" he asked after a minute. "Because if it is, I'd rather you said so right out."

"Indeed, it isn't! But life here is so awfully full, so involved. I have all these engagements, and I must keep them. But of course I can have you included in some of them, if you're to be here some time."

"I didn't come here to be 'included in engagements.' I came here to see you. I was a little afraid it was still too soon, you know, I thought you'd be—"

"Of course, you've been picturing me all in crepe, with a long veil," answered Gloria. "Oh, I *did* wear all that! I was absolutely conscientious and conventional about it. And I'm told that the costume was very becoming."

"Gloria!" exclaimed Sheridan, with genuine horror in his voice.

"I'm sorry to shock you. I really did play the game awfully well, before he died as well as afterwards. He never was sorry, I'm sure, that he married me. But I'm through with it all now, and there is no reason why I should sit by the fireside grieving. You're not 'too soon,' as you delicately put it."

"Am I too late?"

"Mercy, no! You're simply too funny!"

"I see," he said. "I guess I do seem sort of funny to you. Do you have engagements in the morning, too?"

"No, I stay in bed, so that I'll be rested enough to keep the ones I have for luncheon, tea and dinner. And no matter how much I stay in bed—"

"Yes?"

"I'm tired."

The clock chimed again.

"Look here, Roger," said Gloria abruptly, "you've simply *got* to go. But come again. Let me see, this is Wednesday—Sunday, if you feel like it. To lunch. There'll only be a dozen or so here, very small and informal."

"I've got to get back to California as soon as I can. Couldn't you make it tomorrow?"

"All right," she said, almost desperately, "tomorrow then. At twelve. I'll get up early for once. You may stay until half-past one; I'm going out then. But that ought to give you time to say a good deal."

"To make a good beginning," said Sheridan lightly. "Good night then," and taking her swiftly in his arms again, he kissed her a second time—less heartily and much more slowly than upon his arrival, and upon the lips instead of the cheeks, and swung himself out of the room.

He was still peacefully sleeping the next morning,

when the telephone bell jangled in his ear, and he turned over with a muttered "damn" to answer it.

"Is this General Sheridan?" asked a formal voice with an English accent.

"Yes—what in hell do you want at this hour?"

"This is Mrs. Appleton's butler, sir. Mrs. Appleton wishes to speak to you. One moment, sir."

"The deuce she does," muttered Sheridan, sitting up in bed, and scenting trouble. But the voice that floated to him over the telephone was honeyed in its sweetness.

"Is that you, Roger?"

"Yes. I thought you never woke up early."

"I never *get* up early. Often I don't sleep at all."

"I'm sorry. Did you call me up to discuss insomnia? I'm not troubled with it."

"No."

"How did you find out where I was, anyway?"

"That wasn't hard. I simply had the butler call up various hotels until he located you. You ought to be at the Shoreham or the Willard."

"Why ought I?"

"Oh, that's where everybody goes."

"This humble inn seems to be pretty well filled."

"Of course, but—"

"Well, did you call me up to talk about hotels?"

"No. Just to say that if you're thinking of coming to see me—"

"*If* I'm thinking of it!"

"You must behave better than you did yesterday."

"Didn't I behave all right?" asked Sheridan innocently.

"You know you didn't."

"Well, then, you didn't either."

"What do you mean?"

"You kissed back," he said bluntly. Then, as there was no reply to this, he asked after a moment, "Didn't you?—Gloria—Are you there—Oh, damn!"

She was quite capable, he knew, of refusing absolutely to see him. But he was admitted, when he reached Sheridan Circle for the second time, without question. The man at the door was expecting him, and had quite evidently had his instructions.

"Mrs. Appleton will see you in her own sitting room, sir," he said, "this way, if you please, sir. It's two flights up."

He found her stretched out on a chaise longue before a sunny window, dressed in a sea-green negligee, with a vase of flowers, a cup of black coffee, and a new novel beside her, and a cigarette between her lips. She held out her hand without rising.

"Can I kiss this?"

"I suppose you can, but you may not."

He grinned, dropped her hand, and drew up a big chair. "It's no use, Gloria," he said. "I shall always keep on talking like that. And eating supper at six o'clock. And going to the wrong hotel. And so on. Breaking all your ten commandments."

"Have you kept Moses'?"

"Most of them. I've never slipped up on the popular seventh, even though I did on the tenth."

"I've forgotten which is which."

"Thou shalt not covet," he began; then, as she still looked a little vague, "thy neighbor's house, thou shalt not covet thy neighbor's wi—"

"Oh, yes, I remember now. And I remembered 'Sheridan's Ride' better than you did anyway."

"We had good fun, the night we said that together."

"Yes."

"And at the Senior Prom, and the School Picnic, and going home after the baccalaureate sermon."

"Yes."

"And then I went off to college. And you got married."

"You're terribly fond of ancient history. Tell me about California for a change, if you won't talk about the war."

"At first I didn't do very well there. You know, when I came here, eight years ago—"

"Yes, I remember that perfectly, too. But I want to hear about *California*."

"Well, I was getting to it. I went to California, of course, in the first place, to get as far from—from where you were as possible. There wasn't any other special reason. And nothing went right. I didn't get to love it right away, as most people do, and—and everything. And at last I thought, 'What's the use anyway?' and came East again, eight years ago, as you remember perfectly, and then went back after a while, as you remember perfectly too, of course. Then, the second time, I put my back right to it, and worked like the devil. To keep myself from *going* to the devil mostly, I guess. But anyway, I began to prosper. I was out of debt before I went to war, and had a nice little place of my own, and some money in the bank. I—I began to love it out there, too. I grew oranges and lemons and olives, you know—my, but it smelt good all around every time I stepped out on the piazza. That had roses crawling all over it. It was just a bungalow of course—six rooms and a bath. But it was mighty pretty. I had a good Jap, too, to work for me. I suppose it'll be hard to get another like him. And a Dodge car—'Dodgey,' I always called it. I paid five hundred dollars for it, got it second hand. I didn't sell it when I left. I'd got to feeling it was sort of—like a person. It'll be worthless now of course—I'll have a new one. 'Dodgey Second.' My business'll need building up some, too; perhaps it's all gone to pieces. But I don't care much. It seems as if I couldn't wait to get there. Home! After four years! Say, Gloria!" he broke off, almost shamefacedly. "You must think I'm an awful fool, talking like this."

"Indeed, I don't. I like it."

"Do you honestly? Well, I've figured out that, after the first I ought to get back on my feet pretty quickly. That money in the bank's been drawing interest, of course, and I've saved some out of my pay, too—didn't have anyone to spend it on. So I've got capital now, which I hadn't before, and then my war record is going to count for me—not that I want to trade on it,

but such things do help. And just now, in the spring
—gosh, it's going to be paradise!"

He got up quickly and came and put his arm over
the back of the chaise longue. "I'm not going to kiss
you again," he said, "don't worry. I wouldn't have
done it the second time yesterday if I hadn't thought
you were willing, and the first time was just because I
was glad to see you—like I would have kissed a kid,
you know. But I've been thinking things over since. I
knew you were rich, of course, but I didn't realize how
rich until I actually saw all this—Sheridan Circle—and
I'd pictured you as kind of lonely and quiet, and I
thought—but I see it isn't like that at all. So, if you're
not ashamed of me—"

"Ashamed of you?"

"Sure. You were a little bit, yesterday, weren't you?
I don't blame you. You're 'adaptable'—you got used
to this sort of thing—took to it like a duck to water,
from the very start. You've got an awfully long way
from my kind."

She turned her head away a little. "Yes," she said
slowly, "I have—got an awfully long way from your
kind."

"That's what I said," he went on cheerfully. "But if
you don't mind, I'll stay and play around here for a
week or so, and be with you when I can, and then I'll
go along."

"I see," said Gloria, more slowly still.

"That'll be all right, won't it?"

"I think it will be very nice. What shall we do first?"

"Well there are those damned engagements of
yours—"

Gloria laughed. "I think we'll have to juggle with
those engagements a little," she said, "if you're only
going to stay a week. I've already wriggled out of the
one for luncheon today. If you'll go down to the drawing room and wait while I dress, I'd like very much to
have you stay here and lunch with me, while we discuss our plans for the future."

"Our plans for the future!"

"For the rest of the week, I meant, of course!"

"Oh," said Sheridan briefly.

Washington in springtime is a miracle of loveliness
—not only the Washington of sunny Sheridan Circle,
but the Washington of shady avenues with trees interlacing overhead, of white marble buildings seen
through feathery boughs, of pink cherry blossoms
blooming along the Potomac River beside the Speedway, of fragrant gardens behind stately old houses, of
overflowing brooks and masses of white dogwood in
Rock Creek Park. And for a week, together, and for
the most part alone, Roger Sheridan and Gloria Appleton watched this miracle unfold. They went, to be sure,
to a few dinners and dances, and Gloria's "set" if inwardly no more than amusedly tolerant of her "new
beau" were outwardly at least cordial and even effu-
sive. Sheridan met diplomats and congressmen and justices; he left the "wrong hotel" and was "put up" at
the Metropolitan Club; he was offered a seat in the
Senators' Gallery, and given freely to drink of everyone's private stock. But much of the time he and Gloria wandered about like tourists "doing" the capital for
the first time, though in a more leisurely fashion, and
perhaps with more sympathy and understanding. They
went to the top of the monument, and took the boat
down to Mt. Vernon, returning by road; they explored
every corner of the Congressional Library, and ate their
lunch in the restaurant on the top floor; they walked
through Rock Creek cemetery and stood silently before
St. Gaudens' statue of "The Peace of God." Only once
did a troublous ripple mar the calm of their contentment. They had been playing golf and had had tea,
and were sitting on the paved loggia at the back of the
Chevy Chase Club watching the sun, a magnificent red
ball of fire go down beyond the soft green fields, when
Roger spoke suddenly and rather awkwardly.

"Gloria—there's no danger, is there—that people
will talk about you running around alone with me all
the time when we're not engaged or anything?"

She thrust her feet out a little further in front of her, dug her hands further into the deep pockets of her sport suit, and stretched herself, lazily comfortable.

"No, there's no danger."

"I'm glad. I had a sort of feeling——"

"There's no danger of it, because there's an absolute certainty."

He jumped up, turning the dark brick-color that was so strangely becoming.

"Then I must stop," he said hotly, "I can't have you——"

"My dear boy—people have been talking about me for years."

"Then I'd like to cut their damned dirty tongues out of them and see them all in hell!" he cried vehemently.

"Thank you, Roger," said Gloria slowly.

"Thank me! What for?"

"It doesn't seem to have even entered your head that, that there might be any good reason why they should talk."

There was a hint of tears in her voice, but there was more than a hint of them in her eyes. Sheridan found himself gulping.

"Say, darling—I mean, look here, Gloria. You know you've been the one woman for me always, and that you always will be. But that doesn't mean that I'm a fool or a baby. I can see, of course, that you move with a swift set here. Probably you've done some things that you wouldn't have if you'd kept right on living in Greenville, married to some ordinary man there. You wouldn't have worn your dresses so low or so short, or seen men callers in your robe——"

"Negligee," murmured Gloria, smiling a little again.

"I don't care what you call it. That kind of a garment—you know—upstairs or—or——"

"Let us leave something to the imagination," suggested Gloria helpfully.

"Yes. All that. But though I can see all that plain enough, do you think I'd ever doubt that you were good? Why, I'd stake my soul on it."

He was far the more upset of the two. She tucked

her hand into his, "I know you would, Roger," she said softly, "and I am—the way you mean. And you don't need to give up anything we've planned this week, either. It'll be all right. I was only teasing you a little. Before we start home, let's go for a little walk over there in the trees."

On the last night of the week, they dined together, alone, at Gloria's house. And, over the cigarettes and coffee, Roger leaned across the table, and took her hand again.

"You've given me a wonderful time, honey," he said, "I'll think of it all the way across the continent. I've got my ticket for the Sunset Limited tomorrow. Tickets, I should say. I took a stateroom, and found that I'd have to pay double fare for that. But I don't care. I figured out I wouldn't feel like talking to a carful of strangers. It'll be worth the extra price to be rid of them, instead of being in a section. And I've bought some books—Zane Grey's got a new story out. I like his things. I asked for a Rex Beach, too, but there was nothing doing. So I got one or two others and a whole raft of magazines. But I guess mostly I'll sit and look out of the window, and think about Sheridan Circle."

Gloria drew away her hand and pushed back her chair.

"You didn't tell me before that you were going tomorrow," she said.

"Why, you said a week. You've been awfully generous, but the week is up."

"I want to get outdoors," she said suddenly.

"Outdoors! Where?"

"Oh, anywhere! It's stifling in here. We can go and sit beside the statue."

"We'll be taken for a chauffeur and his best girl."

"I don't care."

"You must have something around you."

"I mustn't either. This scarf will be plenty. It isn't cold."

It was not, indeed. It might have been June instead

of April. The slender moon of the week before had grown to a substantial quarter. The magnolia bushes had burst into sudden fragrance. From one of the lighted houses came the sound of music, and the great globes on the bridge shone with a quiet radiance.

"Roger," said Gloria quietly, "are you going to let me go a third time?"

He stammered something, neither of them ever knew quite what. She went on without giving him time to recover himself.

"After we had been graduated from the high school in Greenville," she said rapidly, "and had done all those things together that you apparently take great pleasure in recalling to me, I supposed you were going to propose to me. Why didn't you? Didn't you care enough?"

"Didn't I care enough?" he burst out, still stammering, "I cared a darned sight too much to spoil your chances with Appleton! It isn't every day that an honest-to-goodness member of the President's Cabinet and a millionaire to boot stumbles into a little one-horse place like Greenville! And he was dippy over you from the first time he ever set eyes on you, we could all see that! So of course I cleared out. If I hadn't you might have been there yet. Instead, you're one of the great ladies of the country."

"Oh!" she said a little bitterly, "it didn't occur to you, did it, that I might care a little for you, too! And that when you went away without saying anything, and simply left me in Edward Appleton's hands, I supposed of course you didn't care—and so—"

"Wasn't he good to you?" asked Sheridan savagely.

She ignored the question. "And then," she went on, "after I'd been married a few years, and you had moved to California, as you say, to try and get me out of your mind, you suddenly stopped trying, and came on here to see me, and stayed several weeks. We saw a good deal of each other, first and last, but you went away again without saying anything."

"Good God! What could I say? You were a married woman, and I was breaking that tenth commandment just as hard as I could—coveting my neighbor's wife, and all that was his! I fairly ran away, when I saw that instead of making things any easier to see you, it made them worse."

"You certainly did run away. Everyone noticed it, including my husband. It didn't leave my pride much of a pedestal to stand on."

"But, Gloria, what could I—?"

"I don't know. I'm only trying to make you see that there are at least *two* sides to what's called the everlasting triangle! And then you wait eight years, until I've been a widow more than three, and am getting old as the hills—"

"You aren't quite thirty!"

"You are painfully exact. And come back expecting to find me sitting like patience on a monument smiling down on grief, and to wipe away my tears, apparently ready to do a little real love-making at last, and then because you find I'm able to totter about without weeping, and that I won't fall into your mouth like a ripe cherry, even if I did kiss you once, you—you— Oh, you make me so angry that I could break every bone in your body!"

She sat down suddenly on the marble seat, half laughing, half crying, her hands clenched. Roger strode over to her.

"Gloria," he said huskily, "I did mean this time to ask you to go back with me. I didn't ask you the first time because I thought it wasn't right. And I didn't ask you the second time because I *knew* it wasn't right. But I did hope that now . . . and then I saw how wonderful you were, and how commonplace I was, and I knew that nothing I had to offer could compete with Sheridan Circle."

"Men are unfair to women in lots of ways," said Gloria, even more bitterly than she had spoken before. "But I think they are most unfair of all when they don't give the women they love the *chance* to say—"

"No?"

"*Yes!* How can you tell whether what you have to offer is worth anything to us or not? You won't care if you ruin our lives as long as you save your own pride! It's more than unfair; it's wicked and cruel."

"But Gloria—"

"There are three things," she said distinctly, "that I have never had."

He put his arm around her shoulder. "What are they, my dear?" he said gently. "If I could give them to you—"

"The first is rest."

"*Rest!* Why, every breath you draw is made easy for you!"

"The mechanical part of living is smoothed out. Do you think that necessarily means inner peace?"

"What is the second thing?" asked Sheridan awkwardly.

"Love."

"Love! When every man that sees you falls at your feet—"

"I did not say I had not had admiration, even affection; neither did I say that I had not seen both desire and lust."

In the moonlight Gloria could see the brick red color flooding Sheridan's face.

"What is the third thing?" he asked, after a long silence.

"A child—"

He did not answer her. When she looked at him again, the flush had gone, and he was very white.

"I thought," she said, faltering a little, "that in that little house in California, I might find all three."

He leaned over her, his cheek touching her hair. Then suddenly he pulled her toward him, burying his face in her soft white breast.

"Do you know," she said, some minutes later, "that you haven't asked me, even now?"

He laughed, "I'm not going to. This time I'm not asking. I'm telling.

"That train," he went on, "leaves at ten o'clock tomorrow. Well, I'll be here with a license and a parson about eight-thirty. That will give you time to pack all you'll need beforehand, and we can make the Union Station in half an hour from here, can't we?"

"But my darling boy, I can't get ready to leave here overnight."

"You bet your life you can!" he cried. "Because you've got to! Say, Gloria—"

But whatever it was that she was to say, of course she never said it. And when he finally released her, she was trembling, but he was trembling too.

"I'll watch you across the street," he said unsteadily, "but I'm not coming any nearer your house than this. If I did, I shouldn't be able to let you go, even 'til to-morrow."

He folded his arms and watched her as she crossed the wide, smooth street, and let herself in through the heavy grilled door. When she had closed it behind her, without a backward glance, he looked up at the splendid bronze statue towering above him.

"Some day, General," he said aloud, "I'm coming back here to decorate you with the biggest laurel wreath you ever saw! But not for a long while. We're going fast away from Sheridan Circle, Gloria and I."

MERIDIAN HILL

ELSIE Noyes was pretty, she was intelligent; she was "nice"; and yet—

That was what everyone said about her; what is far worse, it was what, in moments of bitterness, she said about herself.

She had married Sam Noyes when she was twenty-two, and he was twenty-six; and even then, though Sam's family was "nothing much" in the eyes of West-field, the small city where he lived, it added that "and yet" about Elsie. She had come from a small suburb of Boston—not one of the "right" suburbs; and if there is anything more damning than to be called "poor white trash" in Virginia, it is to come from one of the "wrong suburbs" in Boston. She had been graduated from the small local high school, and then, having displayed some gift for reciting, she had gone to a College of Elocution and had been tremendously thrilled to obtain, almost immediately after her graduation, an engagement to "read" at some of the big summer hotels. She sat up most of the night for two weeks sewing on a wardrobe to take with her and, when it was done, she spread it all over her little bedroom, and gazed at it with tearful pride. But she had not been filling engagements for a week, before she realized that the new wardrobe, like everything else she had and did, was not quite right somehow. This would have been almost more than she could have borne, for she was sensitive, and high strung, and badly overtired, if Sam Noyes had not heard her read. He was staying at that particular hotel with a grouchy old uncle who had paid his way through college and law school, and was quite ready to continue his allowance so that he might indulge in his taste for politics before his budding law practice had produced even the greenest kind of fruit. She really "read" very well indeed; and Sam, though properly attentive and truly grateful to his useful relative, was now finding time hanging rather heavily on his hands. So he had leisure to observe how intelligent, and pretty and nice Elsie was, and promptly fell in love with her.

It took two years to reconcile the elderly uncle to the match, and during that time Elsie worked hard at the profession to which he objected (since it was her only means of sustenance) and improved steadily all the time in her work; but her heart was very heavy, for she realized that it was keeping her and Sam apart. Sam's father and mother "came around" before his uncle, but this did not really help matters much, because they were having hard work paying for their own rent and groceries, and could hardly be expected to help with Sam's. But the uncle "came around" too, in the end, and when Sam had brought this about—the reconciliation was actually accompanied by quite a substantial check on which to start housekeeping—he felt no further doubts of his fitness for a political career.

His self-confidence seemed to be justified; he served in the State Legislature, he became Mayor of Westfield; finally, with a comfortable majority, he was elected to Congress. Just then the elderly uncle died, leaving his modest fortune all to Sam. He would not be able to splurge in Washington, it was true, but he was not faced with the hideous necessity of trying to live on the salary which an otherwise extravagant government deems sufficiently large for its public servants. And all this time Elsie had remained exactly as pretty, and intelligent, and nice, as when Sam had fallen in love with her; and yet—

They settled themselves, temporarily, upon their arrival in Washington at one of the hotels near the Capitol. It was convenient for Sam, and Elsie, at first, was perfectly satisfied with it. But time hung rather heavily upon her hands. She wandered aimlessly through the parks, she went sightseeing alone, she sat in the gallery of the House of Representatives and tried to make herself understand that the turbulent body of men to whom she listened was making the laws of the nation. Sam, enthralled with his new position, poured out an enthusiastic account of his day's work, of the men he was meeting, of the committees upon which he had been placed, of the hearings he had attended, every evening over their dinner. She listened attentively, praised him, gloried in him. Still, though she did not admit it to him, hardly to herself, she had never been so wretchedly lonely in all her life. At last, one night when he was almost asleep, she rather timidly asked him a question.

"Sam, dear."

She had to repeat it. The second time, though drowsily, he answered her.

"What's the matter, old lady? Don't you feel well?"

"I—I wish you wouldn't call me 'old lady.' You know I'm not old at all."

"I know you're not, honey, and neither am I! That's the dandy part about all this—no telling where I'll end

up, with all the time I've got ahead of me! Well, what's
the trouble?"

"Hasn't it seemed to you—sort of queer—that neither of our senators' wives—or any of our delegation
have been to see me? I should think they'd—want to
welcome us in some way."

"Gosh! I've been too busy with *real work* to bother
about little things like that."

"Well, I haven't been awfully busy!"

Being a man, it was not until the next day that the
full import of what his wife was trying to say to him
dawned upon Sam. Conscience-stricken, he hastened
home earlier than usual intent on proposing a theatre party, *à deux*—and found her curled up in a little
crumpled ball on her bed, crying as if her heart would
break.

"My precious girl, what *is* the matter?"

"Oh, Sam! I ought to have gone first!"

"Gone first!" he echoed in bewilderment.

"Yes. To call. On our senators' wives—and *all* the
senators' wives. And all the representatives' wives who
have been here longer than we have. And the cabinet
officers' wives. And the justices' wives. And the ambassadors' wives. I've counted them all up, and there are
about a *thousand* of them. I shall simply die going
around to all those strange houses and explaining who
I am! Why, I never went to call on a stranger in my
life! And what is worse, while I've been wondering
why no one came to see me, those women have been
thinking I was terribly rude and—and ignorant because I haven't been to see them."

"Most of them haven't thought about you at all,"
said Sam sensibly but unflatteringly. "What women do
you mean?"

"Well, Mrs. Shaw for one. I met her in a shop this
morning, and from what she said *to* me, I can guess
what she's been saying *about* me."

"Well, yes, I know just how Mrs. Shaw would let
you—and other people—know about your shortcom-
ings."

"And she's our Senior Senator's wife! Oh, Sam, it's awful!"

"It does look like a rather stiff proposition, especially now you've queered yourself with Mrs. Shaw. I ought to have made inquiries, about what you were expected to do, and helped you out. But I didn't realize that the social game was so tied up with politics here. Of course it isn't at home."

"No."

They were both silent for a few minutes, thinking—though from a different angle—of the years that Sam had been forging ahead in politics, and that Elsie, giving up her "reading" entirely, had kept their little home so trim and neat and cozy with no help at all, and had taken care of the two babies, for whom she had paid so dearly physically, and who, in spite of her care and her paying had not lived very long. She had seldom gone with him anywhere, but that, though he would have been glad to have her, had not handicapped him in the least politically. Now it seemed things were different. Certain things were expected of Elsie on account of Sam's position, and she must do them, or he might suffer.

"It's all my fault," he said at last, "I'm sorry, honey. But I've had so darned much to do—"

"And besides, Mrs. Shaw intimated that we weren't living in a fashionable neighborhood at all. That we ought to have a house, or at least an apartment, in the northwest part of the city."

"Thoughtful of her!" said Sam dryly. Then, after a brief pause, "Would that suit you better than this? I thought we were pretty comfortable here, and that it might be a relief for you to get out of a kitchen for a while; but if you'd like to move, and keep house."

"Well, don't you think we *ought* to?"

Sam reflected for a minute. Then he put his arm around her and kissed her.

"Maybe," he said pleasantly. "Well, yes, I guess we better."

So Elsie went house hunting, or rather apartment hunting very happily, and at last secured an unfur-

nished housekeeping suite in one of the big, new fashionable apartment houses on Meridian Hill. Then, still
more happily, she bought furniture—a shining oak
dining room set, a brass bed and curly-birch dresser, a
three-piece parlor suite upholstered in emerald green,
and a brilliantly-hued collection of American rugs. She
sat up late at night hemming lace curtains and em-
broidering centerpieces with American Beauty roses;
she climbed stepladders, and hung "A Yard of Roses,"
and "Venice by Moonlight" and "St. Cecilia" on her
gaily papered walls. And when everything was in perfect order in the shining little new home, she took time
to buy herself a new wardrobe, having, during the process of settling, allowed herself to get frankly soiled and
shabby—and set out to pay her first official visits in her
new Ford sedan.

Sam had been interested and helpful all through the
transition period, cheerfully moving chairs about from
one position to another which might possibly be more
effective, pounding in nails, washing the new china as
it arrived dusty and gaudy from the shops, so that it
was often late at night before he could sit down to read
his Congressional Record and his home paper. He admired all the results of Elsie's efforts whole-heartedly,
and when she returned from her round of calls, day
after day, too exhausted to prepare supper, though it
did not occur to him to suggest that they should engage a maid, since they had never had one, he cooked
it himself, or insisted on taking her down to the café
which was in the building. But as time went on, he
began to worry over her constant fatigue and lack of
spirits.

"Look here, honey, you're not taking this calling
game too seriously, are you? It can't be worth getting
sick over."

"I've got to do it."

So Elsie went from Chevy Chase to Alexandria,
from Capitol Hill to Cleveland Park, grimly and con-
scientiously, starting out every day at half-past three
and returning at seven. At last she announced, in a
tone of triumph, that she was through and that now

she must have a "Tuesday" of her own, and a new dress to wear to it.

"Sure," said Sam with interest, "what kind of a dress?"

"I—I don't know. That's the trouble." Her lips, he saw, were quivering. Her moment of triumphant feeling had passed. She not only looked fagged—he was used to that—she looked unhappy.

"Isn't there someone who would tell you?"

"Oh, Sam, whom can I *ask?* That would be a confession that I didn't know what to do myself!"

"Well, anything you want," he said awkwardly, "We don't need to stint ourselves any more, you know." But Elsie interrupted him with a flood of tears.

"I don't know *what* I want!" she sobbed, "Everything I've bought so far has been wrong—I can tell that by looking at the other women—and still I can't seem to choose what's right. And—and this apartment, too. No one has rugs and furniture and pictures like these. I've spent a lot of money, and worn myself all out, and still—I'm—I'm not a credit to you. I can't help you with your career. Some people are even saying that I'm a stumbling block to you."

"Who has been saying that?" asked Sam, quietly enough, but with murder in his heart.

"I've—I've overheard it in several places."

"Was Mrs. Shaw one of the persons you overheard?"

"Yes. I keep forgetting to turn down our cards at the corner to show that I have called in person. And I went in a door once in front of an ambassador's wife. And another time I left a luncheon before the guest of honor. Oh, Sam, she talks about these things as if I might better have broken the Ten Commandments!"

Sam drew her into his arms, and sat down with her on one of the green brocade "parlor pieces."

"I want to talk with you," he said, "right from the shoulder. The way I'd talk to another man. Do you mind?"

"No. I guess not. As long as you keep on holding me as if I were a woman."

"Well, listen. All these customs and rules that bother you so have got some meaning—some meaning that's worth while. They haven't just happened. They've grown out of something that was important and necessary. So we ought to try to learn them and observe them. You can do that all right. You're smart. But you're scared. And you've lost your sand. You've cried more since we came to Washington than in all the years I've known you put together. And because you keep thinking about how scared you are instead of how smart you are, you're not doing as well as it's in you to do. I want you to buck up and do better."

Elsie stiffened a little and snuffed a little. Sam began to stroke her hair.

"But I've noticed," Sam went on, as if he had not noticed the stiffening and the snuffing, "that the people who really count don't agonize over all these customs or make newcomers miserable about them. It is the ones who've been pretty small potatoes themselves, or who think their own position is a little wobbly, that stir up all this fuss that makes you so unhappy. Ever hear the story about a guest of Queen Victoria who drank out of his finger bowl? The old lady didn't lay him out telling him in a murderous kind of voice that it was a sort of washbasin! She drank out of *hers!* She was a queen, you see, so she could afford to act like one. Do you want to know the real reason why Mrs. Shaw is mean to you?"

"Because I'm not her sort."

"Thank the Lord you're not! But that isn't the reason. It's because her husband got into the Senate by the skin of his teeth, and neither of them made good after they got here. And he'll never be re-elected. I'm going to run against him at the next primaries."

"You're—going to be senator!"

"It looks that way."

"Then I haven't handicapped you?"

"Gosh, no!"

"You're too generous to tell me," said Elsie in a low voice, "that it's because you're so strong yourself that I

—couldn't. That you don't need me to help you. That I
—just don't count at all."

"You count to me," said Sam huskily. "You always
have. I think the world of you."

"But no matter how much a man thinks of his wife,
he likes to have other people proud of her too—
doesn't he?"

"That doesn't matter much," answered Sam loyally.
But he turned away from her, and pushed back one of
the carefully hemmed lace curtains, and looked down
Meridian Hill. Elsie walked out of the room, and went
into the kitchen, and laid her head on the hard, spotless white enamelled table that stood by the gleaming
kitchen cabinet, and sat there for a long, long time.
Sam had been able to climb Meridian Hill—and to
climb it alone. He would climb more hills—always
alone. She would remain forever at the bottom. And
though he loved her, he would never be proud of her,
and by and by, he wouldn't miss her.

When she finally rose it was to go into her own
room and sink on her knees beside the brass bed.

Our prayers, if they are sincere, are usually
answered, though sometimes we do not recognize the
replies when they reach us because they do not take the
form we expect, or because we do not really expect
any kind of a reply at all. The telephone bell, jangling
unmusically across Elsie's petition, brought her to her
feet, but it was with no sense of thanksgiving that she
answered the disturbing summons.

"Is this Mrs. Samuel Noyes?"

"Yes," Elsie steadied herself.

"This is Mrs. Moore speaking—Mrs. Hillary Moore,
Senator Moore's wife. I'm the third Vice President of
the Congressional Club. Perhaps you remember me."

"Yes," said Elsie again.

"I wonder if you could possibly help us out of a
very awkward situation."

Elsie's heart missed a beat. She could not imagine
any situation in which she could help Mrs. Moore,

whom she had admired tremendously at a distance; neither could she imagine that poised and elegant individual in an awkward situation.

"Mrs. Shaw has told me that you once studied elocution. Is that so?"

"Yes." Elsie's voice hardened. She could imagine the reason for this information, the manner in which it had probably been given. "It was a long time ago. I've never kept it up at all since I was married."

"Oh, I'm so glad—I mean I'm so glad you've studied it, not glad you gave it up—no one ought to let marriage interfere with a real gift. We haven't known to whom we could turn until I remembered that you had this one. Mrs. Hastings, who had the principal part in the entertainment after the spring breakfast of the Congressional Club has fallen and broken her leg —and you know the breakfast is only two days off. No one without special training and talent could possibly fill in—and I've been in despair. Would you—could you—"

"I'm afraid—" began Elsie stiffly. Why should she "help out" these women who had snubbed her and sneered at her, with the very talent which they had made a laughing stock? But Sam was beside her, pressing her shoulder. "I heard," he whispered. "Say yes. Surprise them. It's your big chance. Every one gets their chance, only they don't have sense enough to see it. Say yes, I tell you."

Elsie hesitated and gritted her teeth. Then she went on in a very different voice. "I'm afraid I couldn't do it as well as Mrs. Hastings," she said, "but if you really need me and want me, I'll try, of course. Shall I drive over to her house and get the part right away?"

There were four hundred women—women from every state in the Union—at the annual spring breakfast given in honor of the President's wife at Rauschers' the day before Ash Wednesday by the Congressional Club, and more than half of them, when it was over, came to Elsie and told her that she was "the best thing they ever had." Most of them went home and told their husbands the same thing, for they really meant it; and the next day, in the cloakroom at the Capitol, many of these same husbands passed on the words of praise to Sam, who glowed with pleasure, and went home to tell Elsie all about it.

"Mr. Hastings says his daughter told him herself that her mother couldn't have begun to play the part as well as you did! Coming from that quarter, compliments mean something! Of course it was nothing short of a marvel to get the lines letter-perfect in the time you had, but in addition to that, I've heard that your voice was beautiful, and that you looked pretty as a picture, and that you not only *saved* the day, but *made* the day. It's fine!"

Elsie beamed over the tea tray that she was dismantling. "Mrs. Moore has been to call," she said happily, "and she didn't seem to mind a bit that I opened the door for her myself and hadn't changed my dress. When I asked her if she'd let me make her some tea, she said why yes, she felt just like having a cup, and then she told me how awfully capable she thought a woman was who could do her own housework and still cultivate a—a talent like mine. Wasn't that sweet of her?"

"It was true," said Sam, devouring the last remaining sandwich.

So things took on a more rosy hue, and Elsie, forgetting to be frightened and self-conscious began to fit into her niche, and to fill it capably and contentedly—not the niche that Mrs. Moore, with her white marble palace near the apartment house where the Noyes lived and her shining limousine, and her lovely French clothes filled, to be sure, but a suitable and useful one for all that. She was asked to "recite" again—that after her first success, was inevitable, and with Mrs. Moore's drawing room for her next background, she not only repeated, but eclipsed, her first triumph. She began to study again, to spend long morning hours in practice by herself, to go to a famous teacher in New York twice a month. Before long, she found herself, in a modest way, almost a local celebrity. Mrs. Shaw ceased to be a disturbing factor in her existence; and Mr. Shaw, as the months went on, grew less and less of a disturbing factor in Sam's. That the young representative would wrest the seat of the middle-aged senator away from him became more than ever a foregone conclusion. When Congress adjourned, and both families went home, it was generally conceded that a brief whirlwind campaign of brilliant speeches was all that was needed to clinch the matter.

Then, in the middle of this brief whirlwind campaign, when every hour counted, Sam was suddenly smitten with typhoid fever.

Elsie listened to the doctor's verdict of absolute quiet—no worry, no excitement—with a blanched face. Sam had climbed and climbed and climbed with never a setback, and now, for a mere physical disability—

"If he doesn't win that seat in the Senate," she said to the amazed physician, who was talking to her about ice bags and carefully shaded lights, "he'll—he'll—it will be an awful shock to him. He won't be able to bear it."

"He'll have to bear it," said the doctor shortly. "You don't expect a man with a temperature of one hundred and three to get up and talk about the tariff, do you? The drops, Mrs. Noyes, in water, every three hours, and the capsules the last thing at night."

"I'm going to finish the campaign for him," said Elsie suddenly.

"You're *what?*"

"Going to make his speeches—fill his engagements. I've had some training. I can tell the audiences." All that she could tell them seemed suddenly to shape itself before her like clay moulding under a sculptor's hands. Much, much more than Sam could say about himself, she would say about him—of his courage, his perseverance, his integrity, his ability. And now he was lying stricken, ill—her dramatic sense showed her that this, too, might be made to count for him, not against him, in the telling. And as for what needed to be said about his opponent—was there anyone on earth who could say that as well as she? "I've got a good voice," she went on aloud, "that'll help. It won't be hard for me to make myself heard, even in large halls." Then she remembered the doctor again. "I 'saved the day' once for a silly woman who fell down and broke her leg," she said scathingly, "a woman I didn't even like. I guess I can try to save it for Sam whom I—no woman in the world ever had such a husband as Sam," she ended abruptly. "Go and engage two nurses for him instead of one. I'm not going to have time to put ice bags on his head. It's more likely, before I finish the amount of studying I've got to do tonight, that I'll be putting one on myself!"

When Sam Noyes returned to Washington after a long, slow, convalescence, it was as Senator-elect. But when Elsie returned with him, it was as the most widely known and extravagantly praised woman in the United States with the possible exception of the President's wife. People had stopped saying that she was pretty and nice, and intelligent, and yet—They were saying instead that she had succeeded in doing something which had never, in the history of the country, been done before, and which might never be done again.

The door of the apartment on Meridian Hill was opened for them, on their arrival, by a sleek, white-coated servant; and the apartment was miraculously transformed with soft draperies and rugs, with dull mahogany furniture and slimly-framed etchings. And Elsie, standing on the threshold of the room from which the brass bed and curly-birch dresser had vanished, to be replaced by ivory-colored woods and old rose hangings, laughingly told Sam—who had his arm around her—that she had written to Mrs. Moore and said "straight out" that she knew everything was all wrong and asked for help.

"I don't seem to mind admitting my ignorance a bit any more," she finished happily. "Isn't it funny? Mrs. Moore telegraphed back that she 'would consider it a privilege' to be allowed to help me, and that she would engage a servant and send in an interior decorator. Apparently she has. Isn't it *lovely?* And she's sent me the name of a dressmaker she thinks I'll like, and a caterer—I'm sure you'll never need to feel that things aren't just right again, Sam."

"Good Lord," exclaimed her husband, "you turn a trick like what you've done this fall, and then you worry for fear of what I'll think of the *furniture!* I never saw anything equal to you in my life!"

"Well, anyway," said Elsie, "we're still on the top of the hill, and we're there togther—that's the main thing."

"You bet it is," said Sam.

COMPENSATION

MYRTLE EVANS "just missed being pretty." She "just missed" being popular and prominent and prosperous. It seemed to her as she approached thirty, that she had "just missed" almost everything that really counted, that a long, drab, empty existence was stretching out ahead of her; and it was partly to fill these vacant days, partly in memory of a boy whom she had cared about in high school (though that boy had never cared about her, had indeed married another girl three days before he left for France, never to return) that she began to interest herself in the cause of compensation for disabled soldiers.

She had grown up in a Midwestern state, in a town of some five thousand inhabitants, where her father's "residence" on Prospect Street, squarely and solidly built, with a cupola, hamburg-edging trimmings, and stone deer and urns filled with geraniums—in season —on the front lawn, was the show place of the community when, as a rising young lawyer, he had built it and brought his bride to it. Myrtle was their only child, the pride and delight of her parents' heart. It was in order that later on Myrtle might have everything that,

during her childhood, they did not quite live up to the
stone deer and cupola in point of lavishness, but pru-
dently saved for the future. They did not even send her
away to school, though they often talked of it—always
deciding, in the end, either that they couldn't spare her
when she was all they had, or that after all, a good
home was the best place for a girl, if she had one. So
she progressed through grammar school, conveniently
located only two blocks away, with hardly a glimpse
beyond Prospect Street, except when she turned the
corner into Elm Street, where the Baptist Church
which she attended every Sunday was located; into
high school, where her parents at first frowned upon
"frats" and "proms" because they thought she was too
young for them, and where later she had no spirit for
them anyway on account of her bruised heart; was
graduated late, owing to several interrupting illnesses,
slim, colorless, painfully shy; and suddenly, with a
feeling of panic rather than of pleasure faced the fact
that her father, who had become more and more of a
"leading citizen" with the passage of years, had been
elected to Congress from his district, and that they
were all going to Washington to live.

From the beginning, George Evans blossomed and
flourished in his new position, a little self-consciously,
and a little pompously, but genuinely happy and absorbed in his work. For the first time, he, and not Myrtle, became the center of interest in the family; and his
wife and daughter, proudly appalled at his prominence,
rejoiced in it without either seeking or desiring to share
in it. Mrs. Evans ordered her life in much the same
way on lower Massachusetts Avenue as she had on
Prospect Street; Myrtle helped her mother in the ordering of it. It took a good while to find a comfortable
house to live in—a house, that is, that resembled the
one on Prospect Street in its essentials; longer still to
find reliable shops to trade with, a general maid who
would "do." They missed the informal neighborliness
of home, but they made no effort to replace it by a
round of official calling—when their first winter in the
Capital melted into spring they had not even joined the

Congressional Club. There was a Baptist Church not
far away, and for this they were thankful; but it did
not seem, somehow, to take the place of the one at
home. During their second season, youth asserted itself
over shyness, and Myrtle—with her mother's help—
had bought some new clothes, of a cut and texture
very different from those to which she had been accustomed in her native town, and had begun to learn,
when, where and how to wear them; then her mother
died of pneumonia, and the dresses were laid away,
with tears and camphor balls, and replaced by garments of somber black, which reflected only meagerly
at best the gloom and depression and aching loneliness
in which the spirit of the girl was shrouded.

There was a second period of readjustment now, for
Mrs. Evans had, emphatically, possessed a much
stronger and more assertive character than her daughter; Myrtle missed not being told what to do at every
turn, not only because she had loved her mother, but
because she had leaned on her; initiative was abhorrent
to her. And yet, it was absolutely necessary that she
should develop initiative. She could no longer "ask
Mother." And Father—who had been re-elected—
must be kept comfortable, and not "pestered" when he
came home from the House Office Building, late and
tired and hungry, glad to talk about what he had
achieved during the day—the committees he had
served on, the speeches he had made, even the enormous and unreasonable amount of correspondence he
had received—but he did not wish to discuss missing
laundry and exorbitant prices of meat, and the short-
comings of Ella, the colored general maid. His tastes in
food, in service, in household appointments, were changing, too, as he mingled more and more with his colleagues. He no longer suffered the use of napkin
rings and bone dishes. He wanted iced orange juice before breakfast and black coffee after dinner; he stored
the pictures of "still life" which had hung in the dining
room, in the attic, and told Myrtle to get rid of the
chenille portières, and the Parian marble groups which
had ornamented the parlor mantel. These changing

tastes had to be interpreted, followed, filled. By the time the period of mourning was over, the Congressman was going out a good deal; he had become interested in golf, bridge, and moving pictures; he was in demand as an "extra man" to "fill in" at dinners and Sunday luncheons. His daughter was going out less and less.

She was not, after the first shock of loss, acutely unhappy; she did not suffer. She did not even resent her father's increasing neglect and criticism, or the indifference with which official Washington, crowded with women much more attractive than she, had passed her by. She did her appointed task uncomplainingly and well, and it filled her life. Then, suddenly, her father announced his engagement to a girl younger than she was, the daughter of another Congressman who had been in the Capital no longer than she had, but who had spent her time in a very different way—a brilliant, worldly, hard little creature, the embodiment of chic and sophisticated charm.

Myrtle did not need to be told that there would be no place for her in the new ménage. In fact, she became conscious of the inappropriateness of such an arrangement before her father did, and broached the subject herself. He was righteously indignant; but as the time for the wedding approached, she noticed that, though no less righteous, he was not so indignant. And when the parents of his prospective bride offered them a house on Sheridan Circle for a wedding present, he compromised with his conscience, thanking Heaven that so easy a way to do it had been opened before him. He came home one night, and handed Myrtle the deed to the little red brick house on lower Massachusetts Avenue, in the quarter which was already ceasing to be fashionable when they had bought it, a quarter which was now being frankly invaded by boarding houses and small shops.

"I'm going to give you a wedding present, Myrtle," he said and laughed at the idea of Myrtle's having a wedding present, it seemed so humorously impossible. "You've made it plain you didn't want to leave here,

or to live with Gwendolen and me. Of course we're
hurt that you should feel that way, but we've finally
decided not to keep pressing you against your will. So
I've decided to give *this* house to *you*. And the little
property your mother left will be yours, too. I feel it's
proper that you should have that now. You can't be
extravagant"—again he chuckled, it was so humorously impossible that Myrtle should be extravagant—"but
you can be comfortable, very comfortable. And if
you're not, of course, you can always come to me. I'm
not one to deny my own child, even if she won't stay
by me."

"I shall be comfortable," said Myrtle, "and I shan't
need to come to you."

Looking at her, standing before him in the inadequate gaslight—her skin and hair colorless, her colorless dress hanging limply about her flat figure—her
father became vaguely and abruptly aware of a hidden
and undeveloped strength and beauty in her. She had
been a pretty little girl, a bright little girl; but somehow
the prettiness and the brightness had all faded away.
Was it possible that they had not really gone, that they
were merely submerged, that something might yet
bring them to the surface again? The idea made him a
little uncomfortable.

"Well, if you should," he continued.

"I shan't," said Myrtle.

She looked very well at the wedding, really very well
indeed. She went to one of the specialty shops on Connecticut Avenue, and put herself, unreservedly, into
the hands of the proprietress. And this plump and capable person, besides doing an excellent piece of work
herself, recommended a hairdresser, a corsetière, and a
shoe shop, all excellent also. The knowledge that she is
well turned out will often give a woman a degree of
composure and self-confidence which no sense of stern
application to duty can impart. Thus armored, Myrtle
made a favorable impression during the marriage festivities upon persons whom, hitherto, she had not impressed at all; and after they were over, before her
youthful stepmother could suggest that it was rather

late in the day for her to begin to bloom out in this fashion, she began her compensation work.

During the war she had taken, with her mother, some of the Red Cross courses in home nursing and surgical dressings, and had knitted mufflers and wristlets according to the directions of that organization, because it seemed the thing to do. But her interest had never been very vital, and it had died entirely with her mother's death. Now, however, for lack of a better plan, she decided to go to the National Headquarters and offer her services. She stated her case falteringly, with the apologetic postscript that she didn't know how to do much, and that anyway, she supposed there wasn't much to be done any more. But before the business-like person, sitting trim and capable behind her office desk, to whom Myrtle had applied, could answer her, another woman who had come in almost at the same time and was standing near her, interrupted her with a vehemence that frightened her almost out of her senses.

"You're wondering whether there's anything to be *done,* any more," she snapped out. "Good heavens! where have you been living since the war?"

"On Massachusetts Avenue," said Myrtle, with painful literalness.

The stranger laughed. She had a rather pleasant laugh, for all her fierceness, hearty and wholesome and sincere.

"Where have you been living *mentally?*" she asked.

Myrtle flushed. "I've been shut in a good deal," she said. "My mother died, and—and—I'm afraid I didn't even read the papers very faithfully for a while. I didn't seem to be interested in anything except doing for Father as nearly like Mother did as I could. A Congressman seems to need to have a good deal done for him."

"Your father is a *congressman?*"

"Yes—Mr. Evans—and now he's married again, so I'm not so busy, and I thought—is there really something I can do to help?"

The stranger had, by this time, literally seized her.

"Help," she exclaimed. "You are an answer to prayer." Her tone was not particularly religious, but there was no doubt that she meant what she said, that she really wanted Myrtle, that she was glad to have met her. The girl's courage soared, "I've come over from New York on purpose to see if I could find someone —someone with official connections—who wasn't already so involved in reconstruction work that she would consent to serve as Washington representative on my Committee for Disabled Soldiers. I thought the Red Cross might help me out, but now—you come right over to the Shoreham for lunch with me, and we'll plan your special field of usefulness at once. Have you any idea how many men haven't got any compensation at all yet?"

"No," said Myrtle, "but I'd be happy to hear."

When she did hear, it made her anything but happy. But it shook her, once and for all, from her apathy, fired her with the zeal for service. Mrs. Thompson— this, she learned, was her kidnapper's name—leaning across the table over a chicken pâté and a romaine salad with Thousand Island dressing, spared her so few of the dreadful details that she grew faint and sick; but she did not waver from her new-made resolve. Before they had finished their baked Alaska pudding she had promised to serve on Mrs. Thompson's committee.

It was the beginning of a new life for her. Every morning the postman's cheery whistle, which hitherto had presaged the arrival of nothing more exciting than a few circulars and advertisements, brought her hastening to the front door before Ella could reach it, to seize the pile of mail which he stretched out to her. Once a month at least she went over to New York to take her appointed place at Mrs. Thompson's committee meetings, and because her work meant more to her than it did to any other member on the committee, she soon did it better than any of the others; much oftener still she went, as the need arose, to see the men in whose service she had enlisted, or their families, to the Capitol and Veterans' Bureau in their behalf; she entirely forgot that it was a torture to meet strangers.

She went back to the specialty shop on Connecticut Avenue, and invested in an outfit worthy of her new task; she bought herself a Ford sedan, and learned to run it, that she might get about more quickly, might accomplish more in a given time. The dusty pigeon-holes of her mind were brushed clear. She began to prove her intelligence, her worth, her importance even. Her father, amused and condescending at first, began to take a grudging pride not so much in what she was accomplishing, as in the manner in which she had developed. The nonentity who had been his daughter was, in her own way, becoming a power.

For a long time she was entirely satisfied; then, at first vaguely, and then more definitely she realized that her work did not, after all, fill her life as completely as she had expected. It was all so impersonal.

The poignancy of this feeling swept over her more strongly than ever before as one afternoon late in April she was walking home, loitering through sheer joy in the beauty of the Washington spring—feathery boughs of trees interlacing across broad avenues; magnolias blooming in dooryards, wisteria hanging heavy over porches; balloon-men releasing their grouped, multi-colored balls, floating at the top of a network of fine white strings, one at a time, to the crowding children who sought their wares; vendors of violets and daffodils blinking in the sunshine, their sweet-scented burdens outstretched. If only she could transfer some of this color and fragrance, some of this budding promise, into the dingy little house towards which she was walking, she would not feel that life had passed her by. Even the broken and mutilated men whom she sought to help had, most of them, known more of its bitter-sweet fullness than she had, she reflected; how happy she would be if even the least of these would share with her, in some intimately personal way, his experience!

Dreaming, wistfully rather than resentfully, she turned up the steps to her doorway, fumbling mechanically in her handbag for her latchkey. It was not until she was about to insert it in the lock that she saw that her progress was blocked.

At her feet sat a soldier, his khaki-clad figure huddled wearily against the lintel, his cap in his hand, a small and dilapidated handbag, stained and roughened with age, by his side. A pair of dark eyes, uncannily bright and searching in a narrow, white face, raised to hers from under a thatch of tumbled dark hair, widened with relief at her approach as if he recognized her mentally, to be the person for whom he had been waiting. Stiffly and clumsily he arose.

"Are you-all Miss Evans?" he asked in a soft southern drawl, from which suffering had not been able to banish the music.

"Yes, let me help you—you wanted to see me?"

"I sho'ly did want to see you, ma'am, and I reckon you sho'ly can help me. I didn't have any doubts of that, not for a minute."

"Will you come in and tell me how?"

"If I wouldn't be intruding on you' valu'ble time."

"My time isn't so very valuable," said Myrtle, realizing that he could not possibly know how true this was. "We'll sit down in the parlor and talk things over. Will you have a cup of tea with me—or"—after an instant's hesitation—"something a little heartier perhaps?"

The white face flushed. "You sho'ly are kind. But I didn't mean to make that much trouble."

"If you happened to lunch early"—the fiction that he had, of course, lunched must, she saw, be maintained—"perhaps you'd stay and have supper with me. I'm alone. It would be a kindness—to *me*. You're from the South, aren't you? I believe you'd enjoy my Ella's cooking—she's a Carolinian."

It was a long time since Myrtle had had a guest. She left this one in the most comfortable chair which her ugly little parlor afforded—she had restored the chenille hangings and the Parian marble groups after her father's marriage—a steaming cup of tea beside him, while she slipped from her street suit into a simple housedress, lighted candles for the table, gave Ella hurried instructions for augmenting her frugal supper, telephoned to the nearest drug store for cigarettes and candy. While they waited for these to arrive, she sat

down near him in front of the leaping blue flame of the
gas log, and gave him an opportunity to tell his story.

"It was Harrison told me about you. Do you-all remember Harrison, the drunk that was discharged from
that hospital in New York? He said he went to a lady
named Mrs. Thompson, who is at the head of some
committee who helps men even if they don't always
behave very well, and she told you about him, and you
believed in him, and got him transferred down to Aldeen."

"You were in the Aldeen Hospital?"

"Yes, ma'am. In the same ward with Harrison. I'd
been there eighteen months. And all that time I hadn't
been paid any compensation money. Harrison said he
was sure you'd help me get it. He gave me your address when he went away. He's doing right well again
now, had a good job and a sweetheart—did you know
that, ma'am? He writes once in a while. I kept your
address, but I thought likely it wouldn't be necessary
to bother you, just the same. I thought if I could just
get to Washington, and go to the Veterans' Bureau,
and explain how I'd been—overlooked—everything
would come right. The other fellows in the ward
thought so too. We used to talk it over, evenings. So,
when I got well enough to travel, they took up a collection to help me get here. I didn't have much of my
own, you see."

"I see."

"And then I came. I went right over from the Union
Station to the Veterans' Bureau. I tried to tell where
I'd served, and when I'd been wounded, and how long
I'd been sick. Nobody seemed to want to listen to me.
It seemed almost as if some of them didn't believe me.
Of co'se they have to be careful. Of co'se there were
crooks and bums in the service same as there are
everywhere. It wasn't that I minded—that they should
be thorough, looking me up. It was that they didn't
seem to care—didn't want to look things up."

"I know."

"I went to about fifteen different offices. I'm not
right smart yet, you see, and I got kind of tired. I

stayed there all that day, and all the next, and all the next. And then—well, you see we hadn't figured, the other fellows in the ward and I, that I'd have many expenses *after* I got here. We thought if I could just get here, like I told you—"

"I know," said Myrtle again.

"So then I came to you. Your maid didn't want to let me in either. She didn't seem to have any mo' friendly feelings towards me than the officers down at the Bureau. I wasn't sure whether she was telling the truth or not, when she said you were out, but I reckoned I'd sit down and wait. I reckoned, if I waited long enough, you'd either come in or come out. And anyways—"

Myrtle knew what the end of that sentence was going to be, even before he uttered it.

"I didn't have anywhere else to go."

After he had told her this, quietly, he fainted away.

"And, in view of the heart complications, I think it would be most inadvisable to have him moved at present."

"I hadn't thought of having him moved at all."

The soldier opened his eyes to pleasantly unfamiliar surroundings. He was lying between soft sheets in a huge black walnut bed, his head resting on a pillow so immense and puffy that it seemed to be bulging out of its case, his fingers touching the fuzzy nap of thick blankets. The sun, streaming in through the long, primly-curtained windows on either side of a black walnut bureau, slanted across the two figures standing beside the bed—his hostess of the evening before, and a man who was evidently a doctor. He closed his eyes again, not because of any deliberate desire for eavesdropping, but because he did not yet seem to possess sufficient energy to make his consciousness known.

"You mean to have him remain here indefinitely?"

"Why not?"

"No reason, I suppose, if you want to. But, from your own account you know almost nothing about him

—no details about his record, not even his name. You have—ah—literally picked him up off the streets."

"I know that he is ill—dangerously ill."

"Well, yes—of that there isn't of course the slightest doubt."

"That's all I need to know."

"Very well. You've consulted your father, of course. I'll be back later in the day. Meanwhile I'll send in a nurse, but I may not be able to get one right off. There's an unusual amount of sickness about just now. But you can't do this poor chap much harm if you practice some of that home nursing you learned during the war on him. Quiet's what he needs principally. No excitement or worry."

"I don't intend that he shall worry," said Myrtle.

There was the sound of a door opening and shutting gently, of someone coming towards the bed again. The soldier opened his eyes.

"I'm sorry," he said awkwardly, "I've been awake —sort of—for the last few minutes. My name's Joe Symmes, and I'll tell you all the rest—as soon as I feel a little more spry. There's nothing to hide or to be ashamed of, not in my war record, ma'am. Only I don't like you should be put to all the trouble. I never guessed—"

"It isn't any trouble," said Myrtle truthfully, "it's— it's wonderful to have someone to take care of." She sat down beside him. "You're not well enough to tell me about yourself yet," she went on, "but I'm going to tell you about myself, so that you won't fret, so that you'll understand how much it meant to me that you wanted to come to me." Her inarticulate shyness had dropped from her like a cloak. This man, a misfit, even as she was, would understand. She told him about the house on Prospect Street, about the cupola and the stone deer and the Baptist Church which she never saw any more. She told him about the boy she had loved in high school, who had not loved her, and who had died "over there." About her pride in her father's success, about her mother's death, and the silent years that had followed it. About her pretty stepmother.

When she had finished the tired man lying before her had forgotten his own burden, and was looking at her with his dark eyes soft with sympathy.

"You've had a hard time, ma'am, haven't you?" he said gently, "and not much to compensate for it, seems like." He gave a little laugh. "Compensation! That's what we both want, isn't it?"

"I'm going to try to see that you get yours," she said.

She was as good as her word. She went, first of all, to her father, as soon as the nurse arrived, and laid the meager facts of the case that she already knew before him. He was inclined to regard the matter in the light of a huge joke, an escapade.

"Why, Myrtle, who'd have believed it of you! It all goes to show that you can't tell by the looks of a frog how far it will jump! So you picked this man right off the doorstep, and put him in your bed." He had anticipated that she would cringe at the coarseness of his jest. But she did nothing of the sort. Instead, she corrected him calmly, as if he did not have the facts perfectly straight.

"Oh, no; it was not until after he got in the parlor that he fainted. And I couldn't pick him up myself—he's thin, very thin, but he has quite a big frame, much too heavy for me to lift. I had to wait for Dr. Lorimer to come, and then Ella helped him. And I put him in the room that used to be yours and Mother's. It's ever so much sunnier than mine."

"You seem cool as a cucumber about it."

"Why shouldn't I be cool? You will help, won't you, Father?"

"Good God, girl, how can I help till I know what needs to be done? You'll have to wait till he can tell you the whole story and then take that to the Bureau."

A few days later she accordingly told a more complete tale at the Information Desk on the first floor of the Bureau, and asked to which office she had better go about it.

She was given the name of a certain major, and informed that he was out just then.

"I can wait till he comes in."

The two stenographers in the Major's office did not give her a particularly cordial welcome. They were chewing gum and passing the time of day with each other and, for the moment at least, seemed to have no pressing professional duties. Myrtle reflected, as she waited, that their salaries would have gone quite a distance in paying Symmes what he needed. She had ample time for reflection before the Major came in. When he did come, he was pleasant to her, exceedingly pleasant. Myrtle was never aggressive in her work, and she did not antagonize him. But he gave her no definite encouragement, and finally dealt her hopes a blow, with the air of endeavoring to make it as light a one as possible.

"My dear lady, this case can't properly be dealt with here, now that decentralization has taken place. It must be handled from Atlanta."

"It could be brought here, couldn't it?"

The Major was doubtful about that, very doubtful. But her father helped her that much. The case was, after a time, brought to Washington. Then a fresh difficulty arose.

"The case isn't compensable," the Major told Myrtle, "it isn't 'incident to the service' as we say—that is, not acquired in line of duty."

"You mean that he was a sick man—that he had T. B. *before* he went into the service."

"Very possibly."

"Then why was he passed by the Medical Examination Board? As fit for active service overseas? He was well enough to fight in the Argonne for several months."

The Major became more stiff in his manner than he had hitherto shown himself. "I can't argue with you, Miss Evans, about Medical Boards."

"I'm not trying to argue. I'm trying to get information."

"Well, one piece of information that I can give you is that one doctor diagnosed his case as chronic bronchitis. If that diagnosis is correct, he wouldn't be compensable in any case."

"But he was put in a ward with tubercular men."

"As I said before, Miss Evans, I don't wish to argue with you."

"Let me see Mr. Symmes' papers myself—perhaps then I could understand a little more clearly."

"I'm sorry, we don't allow that."

It was hard to keep going home and telling Joe Symmes that she had not, as yet, succeeded. The fear that he might lose his faith in her caused her the only terror that she knew in those days. But his confidence was implicit.

"I think you're wonderful to have done as much as you have, Miss Myrtle," he insisted. He had stopped calling her "ma'am" at his own request, saying shyly that if she didn't mind, he would say "Miss Myrtle" instead of "Miss Evans"—"like we do in the South—and then Myrtle's such a pretty name." Pretty! She had been thinking it ridiculous these many years now, but she decided that she had been mistaken, that it was, after all, rather pretty, perhaps. "Funny that major should say I only had bronchitis. The first time I applied for permission to come no'th and present mah case, the doctor that looked me over said I sho'ly had T. B. bad —that permission couldn't possibly be granted for such a trip."

"Well, there must be a report of that examination, too, somewhere. I've got to see those papers myself. I don't think they really mean to be careless or unfair, but of course there are so many—"

"I know, Miss Myrtle, I know."

"You didn't go into service from the South, did you?"

"No, Miss Myrtle, I hadn't lived south for quite a while befo' the war. I'd gone west—" he stopped, and laughed mirthlessly. "I wished I'd gone west the way we meant it 'over there,'" he said with bitterness, "it would have been a heap sight better."

"You mustn't say such things," said Myrtle so sternly

that he looked at her in surprise, "I'm going to see your own congressman about you."

His own congressman proved to be one of the unattached guests upon whom she had made so pleasant an impression at the time of her father's wedding to Gwendolen. He welcomed her at his office with real cordiality, and listened to her story with genuine interest.

"And how did you think I could help?" he asked when she had finished it.

"I think you could arrange to have me see those papers."

"All right, I'll try. I'll go down to the Bureau some day next week."

"I thought perhaps you'd get in my Ford and let me drive you down there now."

He protested, but after a moment's hedging, laughingly acquiesced. Then he tied a string to his favor.

"If I succeed, will you take lunch with me afterwards?"

"Will I—" Myrtle could hardly believe her ears. She managed, however, to conceal her surprise, "if you're sure you're not too busy," she finished demurely.

"It's just as I thought," she said two hours later, as they were lingering over their coffee, "out of six examinations, the report is the same in every case but one —and if that one were correct, Mr. Symmes deserves compensation for being put in a ward where he'd *catch* T.B.! There isn't any doubt in *my* doctor's mind as to what that poor man has been through. He'd gladly testify." A new idea flashed into her mind, "Mr. Weld," she asked, "you could arrange, couldn't you, to have Dr. Lorimer and me appear before the Board and plead Mr. Symmes' case?"

"You want to *make a speech?*"

"If I could do any good."

"By Jove, I believe you could! You've dovetailed the thing together pretty neatly, and you've got some rather unanswerable arguments—and the faith which removes mountains. Besides, you're a congressman's daughter—not that that ought to matter, but it does.

And"—he hesitated, wondered if she would think him "fresh," decided to take a chance on it, and continued, "you're the kind of a woman those men would be likely to listen to. Not only sincere and intelligent, but awfully feminine and sweet and attractive."

"Mr. Weld!"

"Well, I'm game to do anything I can to help, anyway."

Harry Weld was not the only man who saw how sweet she was. She blossomed before Joe Symmes' eyes like one of those pale roses which does not reveal how much color there is on its petals until it begins to unfold. Her stepmother, meeting her on the street, could hardly conceal her surprise.

"When you get rid of your lame duck, my dear, I hope you'll let us see more of you," she said, taking in Myrtle's improved appearance with a practiced eye. "We're having a dinner for the Secretary of State on the sixteenth—will you come? Harry Weld will be there. You certainly have 'vamped' him, you sly little thing. He was talking to your father the other night about the speech you made before the Board, and he said it was perfectly wonderful—absolutely unanswerable, you were so convincing. He seems to think there's no doubt that Mr. Symmes will get his compensation now."

"Yes, so he says. He's been in to see Mr. Symmes several times lately, to talk to him about it himself. He's really been awfully helpful."

"You don't mean to say you think he's wholly disinterested?" Even Myrtle was not unsophisticated enough for that. But she evaded the issue.

"I'll come to the dinner gladly if my lame duck, as you call him, is gone by then. I don't want him to be lonely."

"What are the prospects that he *will* be gone?"

"Pretty good, I think. He's gaining every day, and I'm hopeful that within a week or so his check will come."

It was even less than that. But when the mailman, heralded by his cheery whistle, brought the slim, official envelope which contained, at last, as she knew, the precious money which should have reached Symmes months before, she stood holding it in her hand for a long time before, very slowly, she mounted the stairs and handed it to him as—promoted to an armchair at last—he sat by the sunny window looking down into the street.

The check was larger than he had expected. His slim fingers shook as he looked at it, and then he raised his dark eyes, and let it flutter to the ground.

"You've given me my compensation, Miss Myrtle," he whispered, "I never should have got it if it hadn't been fo' yo' efforts. I'd have been dead befo' it reached me. Now I can pay back the fellows in the ward, and go to some warm dry place fo' a while, like Dr. Lorimer says I must to get entirely well, and have something left over to begin life on again afterwards—thanks to you. But I can never pay you back."

"You have," said Myrtle softly, "you have already. Can't you see that you've given me my compensation, too?"

"You mean that if it hadn't been fo' me, maybe you and Mr. Weld wouldn't have come to see so much of each other?"

"No, I didn't mean that. I like Mr. Weld very much, but—"

"You ought to like him. He's a powerful fine man, Miss Myrtle. And he'd put you right where—if you'd give him the chance—all these folks who haven't appreciated you would see right soon they'd made a great mistake, and come crowding 'round—"

"I've thought of that," said Myrtle honestly, "any woman would, if she were human. It would be, of course, a kind of compensation. But I've decided it isn't the kind I care the most about. And it isn't the kind I meant when I said you'd brought mine to me."

The dark eyes travelled towards her, and rested there, testing her sincerity. At last the man spoke.

"You're a lady," he said, "pretty and sweet and good. A *real* lady, yes, ma'am. I've never seen one so real, not even in So'th Carolina. And I'm nothing but a common soldier—po' white trash they'd call me where I came from, if I went back there. They'd call me that even if I'd never done anything to be ashamed of—and I have—lots of things. I'm not saying I'll do them any mo'—"

"You won't," said Myrtle.

"But I've done them. Things I wouldn't soil yo' mind telling you about. I've had a good education. But I haven't used it to any account. And the war didn't make a hero of me. It just broke me."

"You're mended now."

The man struggled to his feet, and laid his hand on her shoulder.

"Would you give me a year," he asked, "a year to see what I can make of myself with the compensation you've given me? And write to me while I'm gone? And at the end of it let me come back and tell you what I've done? That I'm fitter to stay, maybe, than I am now? That I've earned—a little bit—what you've done for me?"

"Would you be happier," she asked faintly, "to go and come back than not to go at all?"

Symmes hesitated. Then he bent his head and laid it against hers.

"You're powerful sweet, honey," he whispered, "I'll miss you a lot. I love you a heap mo' than you guess, a heap mo' than I'm going to tell you—fo' the present. I want to stay—the way you're giving me a chance to stay—mo'n a woman like you can guess. But I've got to get well, so that I wouldn't harm you that way if— And I've got to prove to myself, even if you don't ask me to prove it to you, that I'm fit to be with you—other ways than on account of this old lung. It's right I should go for a while if after that we're going to be together for always. Some day you'll see it that way, too."

"I see it now," said Myrtle.

MOUNT VERNON—
THE STORY OF A HOME

"THIS IS a spacious mansion you have built for yourself, Colonel Blackburn. I wish I had for myself one half as seemly."

"You compliment me, Mr. Washington. When all is said and done, Rippon Lodge is but a simple abode—and yet, I hope, suitable as the country seat of a gentleman."

The two friends, who had changed from tight-fitting coats to loose, flowered banians, were taking their ease in the cool of the evening, under the pleasant shade of coffee trees. Before them, the Potomac curved to form a great crescent beyond the spreading lawns; behind them rose the portico of the sturdy, wide clapboarded house which Richard Blackburn, late of Yorkshire and now a Member of the Virginia House of Burgesses, had built for himself on a clearing in his twenty-thousand-acre land grant. Most of this land was still given over to virgin forest, through which wild animals roamed; but the clearing itself already had that cultivated look which comes with the advance of civilization. The paths were paved with homemade bricks, the flowerbeds were abloom with roses and bushes of box were clumped about the house.

"Perhaps you are giving thought not only to a country seat which would be suitable for a gentleman, but to one which would be suitable for a lady," Richard Blackburn went on, with a knowing smile. According to reliable rumor, Lawrence Washington was courting Anne Fairfax, the lovely daughter of Colonel William Fairfax of Belvoir. If she decided to accept him, then Lawrence would indeed soon have to put both his mind and his hand to building. For the Washingtons' house at Little Hunting Creek had recently burned down and Augustine Washington had not cared to rebuild. Instead, he had taken his second wife, Mary

Ball, and her young children, George and Betty, to Ferry Farm, turning over to his eldest son, Lawrence, the demolished Hunting Creek property. In its ravished condition, this certainly could not be used for the accommodation of a bride reared in the state to which Anne Fairfax was accustomed.

"Perhaps I am, Colonel Blackburn," Lawrence Washington answered noncommittally; but the suspicion of a smile flitted across his handsome face. He was certainly a fine figure of a man, Richard Blackburn reflected. Lawrence had been educated in England and had profited in every way by his advantages. It was no wonder that his young half-brother, George, so idolized him and that Anne was lending him a willing ear.

The visitor, undisturbed by his host's scrutiny, lifted the silver goblet which stood convenient to his hand and sipped its contents slowly. Then he took up the long pipe which he had temporarily laid aside, and filled it with his home-grown tobacco; when this was lighted, he began to puff with deep breaths of satisfaction.

"If I had a mansion comparable to yours, I should feel it fitting to name it, as you did, after our hereditary home in Yorkshire," he observed, reverting to the topic which still occupied his mind. "Except that my ancestors forestalled me in so doing—as you know, their homestead in the Northern Neck was called Wakefield. But I take it the name of a human being might properly be commemorated in the same fashion. I have long cherished a great admiration for Admiral Edward Vernon, under whom I served in the Royal Navy. Would Vernon do for the name of my mansion, think you, Colonel Blackburn?"

"Vernon—yes—I like your thought and its expression. But swell the sound a little! Vernon Park, perhaps? Or Vernon Manor?"

"These do not seem to be precisely what I am seeking. But wait—I believe I have it! *Mount Vernon* shall be its name and you shall help me to build it!" He sprang up, his face kindling. "I have evidence of my own eyes, here at Rippon Lodge, that you know how to build!" he exclaimed. "So I will have no other architect! And let us hope that, in the years to come, descendants of mine may wed descendants of yours and that the builder and the owner of Mount Vernon may thus ever be united. I give you a toast; to the Blackburn girls and the Washington lads and to the home which we will give over into their keeping—Mount Vernon on the Potomac!"

Such, in substance, was a conversation which took place around 1740 between a prosperous landowner and a naval officer who was weary of seafaring. Their conference proved even more portentous than either of them could have well foreseen. Mount Vernon was indeed built, as they hoped and planned; and the story of it, as a home, is the story of their two families and those allied to them through friendship, kinship and wedlock—a landed gentry which lived luxuriously, entertained lavishly—and all unconsciously made American History as it did so!

The Mount Vernon to which Lawrence Washington took his bride, and which they called Mount Vernon Villa, contained eight fair-sized rooms, comfortably furnished; but in spite of its agreeable attributes, it was not the grand mansion into which it was later converted, nor was it the center of fashion which it afterward became. This was located at Belvoir, the home of Anne's father. Like the Washingtons and the Blackburns, the Fairfaxes had originally come from Yorkshire; and like Lawrence Washington, Colonel William Fairfax had served in the British Navy. Belvoir was the favorite resort of his innumerable friends, who never failed to seek it out when they came to America. In addition to these visitors who came and went, there were others whose sojourn was permanent: Lord Fairfax had come over from England to escape the scene of an unhappy love affair and William Fairfax proffered hospitality to his stricken kinsman after the prodigal manner of his time; when the Colonel's eldest son, George William, married Sally Cary of Cellys, he brought this fascinating creature to Belvoir and she acted as hostess for both her husband and her widowed father-in-law. Moreover, the young Washingtons were constantly going back and forth to Belvoir; and with Lawrence and Anne, George, who was spending more and more time with his idolized brother, usually went also.

It was on the growing boy—gray-eyed, auburn-haired, straight-mouthed—that these visits made the most impression. Life at Ferry Farm had been simple and here it was sophisticated. He knew he lacked the grace to fit into the picture and strove to achieve this. He was self-conscious about his large hands and feet and ashamed of the awkwardness of his bearing, for he had not yet learned to carry off his immense height. He wondered whether he would be able to overcome the inadequacies of his education, which the straitened circumstances of the family, after his father's death, had greatly curtailed—why, he did not even know how to spell! But he was quick and active and eager and everyone liked him. Presently, Lord Fairfax, who had observed his natural aptitude for surveying, offered him a job.

"How would you like to go down to the Valley, George?" he asked. "I could use you there to fix the metes and bounds on my place."

So young George went off to the Shenandoah Valley and did very well there—so well that Lord Fairfax helped him to get other surveying commissions. He was gone a great deal from Mount Vernon and consequently from Belvoir also, and this was just as well—for he had fallen head-over-heels in love with his sister-in-law's sister-in-law, Sally Fairfax!

She was fond of her husband and conscious of her obligations to her father-in-law; but she was one of those irresistible women who, without effort, so radiate enchantment, that their magnetism draws every man who sees them into their charmed orbit. George Washington was a wholly normal youth, in spite of the fact that history has persistently misrepresented him as being inhumanly austere. But he was also what is still known as a man of honor. He strove sincerely to put Sally out of his mind; and because it was easier to do this when there was no ever present temptation to row down the inlet from Mount Vernon to Belvoir, he welcomed the work which took him into the wilderness. Moreover, he offered, with eagerness—which was more than Anne had done—to go with Lawrence into exile when the balmy climate of the West Indies was suggested as a possible cure for the ill health of this idolized brother. So they set sail together for Barbados, where they were effusively received; but Lawrence was not cured of consumption and George contracted smallpox. With a scarred face and an aching heart, he started back to Virginia, bent on persuading Anne to join Lawrence. But her life still revolved around Belvoir and she could not believe that her husband's life was actually jeopardized. In the end, it was he who returned to her. A few months later he died at Mount Vernon.

In making his will, Lawrence had bequeathed a life interest in the estate to his widow, but provided that if his only child, Sarah, did not live to marry, it should go to "his beloved brother, George." Sarah died a few weeks after her father; and in less than six months, Anne laid aside her weeds and bestowed her hand and what passed for her heart on Colonel George Lee. Her brother-in-law grimly came to terms with her: he agreed to pay her a suitable annual income if she, in turn, would agree to his immediate possession of the estate. At the age of twenty-one, George Washington became the undisputed proprietor of Mount Vernon.

He enlarged it by buying back the old "Spencer Tract," which had originally been part of the property, but aside from this, he did little to it during the next six years and he was absent from it much of the time, surveying on the Northern Neck and campaigning in the French and Indian War. He had not forgotten Sally Fairfax. Indeed, he kept up an intermittent correspondence with her and even after his troth was practically plighted to Martha Custis, the pretty little widow

whose manner was so demure and whose fortune was
so substantial, he wrote Sally several impassioned letters. Then he steadied himself and never again failed
his chosen bride. In writing to her, during their betrothal, he signed himself, "Your faithful and ever affectionate friend," and this he always was. He recognized
the supreme suitability of this alliance with a woman
slightly his senior, somewhat his social superior. He
brought to it fidelity as well as dignity and devotion.
And this was the kind of tribute which Martha wanted.
She too had had her moment of high rapture, culmi-
nating in a June wedding, held in a bower of roses,
when she had married Daniel Parke Custis ten years
earlier. Now he was dead, and so were two of the children she had borne him. Romance itself was dead for
her. But she was a sensible woman. She knew that
though this was so, she still had before her the most
lasting joys of conjugality—comfort, companionship,
confidence and all else that springs from these sources.
She was content.

She was married to George Washington in January,
1759, wearing a pearl headdress and "an imported
gown of yellow brocade, flamboyant in design." Her
coach was painted in the Washington colors—red and
white—drawn by six horses and directed by liveried
postillions. Her bridegroom, seated on a "richly capari-
soned charger" and accompanied by a "cortege of
mounted gentlemen" rode at her side, wearing a suit of
blue and silver. The days when he had reason to de-
plore his awkwardness were gone forever; he carried
himself superbly.

All the great and near-great of Virginia came to the
wedding and the festivities were prolonged. When these
were over, the bride and groom settled down at the
"White House," Martha's old home, for the rest of the
winter. Its location made it convenient to Williams-
burg, the colonial capital, where, as a member of the
Virginia Assembly, George had to be in constant attendance. But when the winter session was over,
Martha's household goods were loaded on a vessel to
be transported first down the York and then up the

Potomac, while she and George and her two children started overland by coach, sending advance riders before them with their baggage. They arrived at Mount Vernon in May, when the grounds are a miracle of bloom and the house is gilded with radiant sunshine.

George had been meticulous in his consideration for his bride's well-being. At his request, William Fairfax had come over from Belvoir to supervise reconditioning and George had also written minute instructions to his most dependable carpenter. No woman could possibly have been more gratified by the results than Martha. She was a born housekeeper. After an early breakfast, she began her day with prayer and meditation; then she set the domestic machinery in motion and made the rounds of her gardens. Though she was well acquainted with the arts of dress, she preferred homespun and there was plenty of it for her to wear; in one year alone, thirteen hundred yards of goods were woven on the place. The laundry, the kitchen, the dairy, the distillery were all kept humming with activity, for Martha, like her Biblical namesake, was "careful about many things." She did not waste a minute.

While she was variously occupied, her husband rode over the plantation. There was much for him to supervise and he was especially concerned with the rotation of crops, to which Lawrence had not given much attention. But at half-past two he came back to the house for dinner. This was followed by a brief social period; and though afterward he retired to his library, to do accounts and attend to correspondence, he could be induced to interrupt these occupations for a rubber of whist, which he enjoyed. He imported his cards from London, as he did other elegant accessories for his establishment and paid his losses with a good grace. He was rapidly becoming a very rich man and whist was a gentleman's pastime. So were fox hunting and horse racing and he enjoyed both.

For fourteen years the tenor of life at Mount Vernon was idyllic. Then the shadows began to fall over it. The first one came in the sudden death of Martha's little daughter, Patsy; the second in the precipitate mar-

riage of her son, Jack. The third sorrow, which was
probably harder for George to bear than for Martha,
came when William Fairfax left Belvoir. He had come
into the title when the love-stricken kinsman, who had
befriended George, finally died, without ever having
married. Now it behooved William to take up the re-
sponsibilities of a peer; and with him to England went
his son, George William, and his son's wife, the incom-
parable Sally. They never returned, and with their departure the disintegration of Belvoir began. Eventually,
the mansion's ruins were destroyed by fire and only a
small cleared area remained where Sally's "posy garden" had been. Here thousands of daffodils continued
to bloom perennially and a legend arose that in them
the sunshine of Sally's smile and the gold of her hair
were perpetually preserved. But in the year of grace
1774, George Washington had no leisure to concern
himself with legends. The first rumblings of the coming
national storm were already troubling the air; and within a twelvemonth, he had been chosen Commander-
in-Chief of the Continental Army. Martha, accompanied by her son and her daughter-in-law, set out to
join him in Cambridge; and over six years went by before General and Mrs. Washington were in residence
at Mount Vernon again.

They returned to it with heavy hearts, for Jack had
died of fever shortly after the surrender of Yorktown;
but he had left four children and, as their mother soon
remarried, two of these, Nellie Custis and George
Washington Parke Custis, were adopted "as the wards
of Mount Vernon." With them, it was possible to
recreate, in a measure, the glad atmosphere of earlier
days, but this joy was fleeting. George, who had determined to retire "not only from all public employment
but within himself," was swiftly dislodged again, this
time to assume the presidency and to be absent for another eight years. The pomp and circumstance of high
office was extremely irksome to both him and his wife,
but especially to her. More than once she gave vent to
her irritation; and finally, when she had returned to
Mount Vernon for good and all, she wrote to a friend:

"I cannot tell you how much I enjoy home, after having been deprived of one so long. . . . I am fairly settled down to the pleasant duties of an old-fashioned Virginia housekeeper, steady as a clock, busy as a bee, cheerful as a cricket."

The later years which George and Martha spent at Mount Vernon brought about their own productiveness. It was immediately after the Revolution that George set out the lovely trees, over half a hundred of which are still standing. The enlargement of the mansion had already been completed. Celebrities from all over the world came flocking to the door, and also near-celebrities, less well accredited. With slight acrimony, George compared Mount Vernon to "a well resorted tavern." He still rode over his estates, still on occasion took an active part in the labors which he never ceased to supervise. His correspondence was vast and it required several secretaries to help him keep up with it. When Nellie Custis, his beautiful and beloved godchild, was married to his nephew, Lawrence Lewis, he gave her in marriage, touched and pleased that she had chosen to celebrate his birthday in such a manner. But ten months later, his bier stood where her bridal altar had been.

Perhaps he had a premonition of this. I do not know. But I do know that one day he rode along to Belvoir to look at the daffodils blooming amidst the ruins. And there was one letter which he did not dictate to any of his secretaries, but which he wrote himself to Sally Fairfax, who was living in widowed seclusion at Bath.

"Mt. Vernon,
16 May, 1798.

"My dear Madam:
"Five and twenty years have nearly passed away since I have considered myself as the permanent resident at this place, or have been in a situation to indulge myself in a familiar intercourse

with my friends by letter or otherwise. During this period so many important events have occurred and such changes in men and things have taken place as the compass of a letter would give but an inadequate idea of. *None of which events, however, nor all of them together, have been able to eradicate from my mind the recollection of those happy moments, the happiest in my life, which I have enjoyed in your company."*

Did Martha ever know of this letter? I doubt it, but I also doubt whether, had she known, the knowledge would have greatly disturbed her. She had not had the romance, as far as George Washington was concerned; but she had had the man. She stood steadily by his bedside, on the December night when the house was steeped in stillness, except for the sound of sobbing from others who kept watch. The night before he had come very late to bed, in spite of the fact that he was suffering from a severe chill, and she had chided him gently. "I came as soon as my business was accomplished," he had replied briefly, and she had known in her heart that before he lay down, all that he had to do must be done.

Life ended for her with his death. Her mind reverted with scorn to the thought of Lawrence's widow, remarried almost before he was cold in his grave. It was not thus that she, who had been wedded to greatness, would conduct herself! She shut the door of the death chamber after her, and ordered that it should stand empty, according to custom, for three years. Then she betook herself to a small attic room, where, from a dormer window, she could look out on her husband's tomb. Before the three years of mourning were past, she herself had been laid to rest beside the object of her veneration.

It was the end of an era at Mount Vernon. George Washington had died in the last month of a dying century; only Martha had been left as a link with a new one. Now this link had been severed. Bushrod Washington, the nephew of George and the heir to the estate, belonged to the new order. So did his wife, Anne Blackburn Washington. The cycle of Mount Vernon and Belvoir was finished. The cycle of Mount Vernon and Rippon Lodge had begun again.

The two "wards of Mount Vernon" were well provided for; there was no reason why they should cast covetous eyes upon Mount Vernon. However, they went out of their way to make Bushrod feel uncomfortable. When he came to his aunt's funeral, he was not even asked to partake of the baked meats set out in the state dining room; a slave prepared a simple meal which he ate alone in a cabin. Such a breach of hospitality had never occurred at Mount Vernon before.

Bushrod, however, took the slight calmly. It was against his principles to harbor resentment or to make disagreeable remarks. And, after all, he could afford to be generous. The estate, which by this time consisted of five farms, was indisputably his and, though he did not dine there that day, he soon took possession of it and held it for twenty-six years.

He was not an impressive looking man. He had a slight figure, a sallow complexion, straight hair and peculiar eyes—one apparently sightless, the other "having more than the fire of an ordinary pair." But his career was notable and he achieved it himself, for his famous uncle was not given to nepotism. He was educated at William and Mary College, served as a private soldier during the Revolution, studied law in the office of James Wilson of Philadelphia, and practiced it successively in Alexandria and Richmond. When he was only thirty-six, he was appointed to the Supreme Court by President Adams.

From then on, Bushrod's occupancy of Mount Vernon was interrupted by his attendance at Court sessions, which were still held in Philadelphia; and his plan of entertaining, when he was at home, was patterned with a view of making his associates on the bench especially welcome there. Long legal discussions took the place of those which centered on the arts of war, on statecraft, on scientific farming and on sports. If Anne Blackburn Washington had been of a sprightlier nature, she might have rescued Mount Vernon from the slight stodginess which permeated it at this period. But she was one of those "delicate females," typical of her time, who "enjoyed poor health. . . ." "This was never robust," a kinsman of her husband tells us, "and was greatly impaired, shortly after her marriage, by a shock occasioned by the sudden death of her sister under peculiarly trying circumstances." A modern husband would probably feel that however great a shock his wife had sustained, she should eventually pull herself together. But most of the fair victims of invalidism, at this period, contrived to imbue it with elegance and fascination. There is no doubt that Anne Blackburn did this, and that Bushrod was as much in love with her, after forty years of marriage, as when he first walked with her among the teaberry trees at Rippon Lodge, which had furnished the Blackburns with their favorite brew throughout the Revolution.

In spite of her fragility, Anne always accompanied Bushrod to Philadelphia and he saw to it that she made the trying trip in a luxurious private carriage. But during the autumn of 1829, he was thankful to take the journey as easily as possible himself; for he was seriously ailing, though he said little of this—not for worlds would he have given Anne cause for alarm about *his* health. But for all his solicitude, he could not save her from another shock; he died, suddenly, uncomplainingly, and far from home. He had been her bulwark against an unfeeling world. When she looked down at his face and saw it unlighted by its bright glance and its whimsical smile, she collapsed completely. She did not live long enough herself to take his body home. She died on the rough road, no longer tenderly smoothed for her, that led back to Mount Vernon.

Anne Blackburn Washington had not fulfilled herself through maternity; but her niece, Jane Charlotte Blackburn—more fruitful than her aunt, more hardy than her husband—had married Bushrod's nephew, John Augustine Washington, the heir to the estate. He died when he had been in possession of it only three years. His widow, a woman with a serene brow and untroubled eyes, continued to live there quietly with her children. She had hardly ever left it when her eldest son came to tell her that he was going to be married to Eleanor Love Seldon of Exeter.

He was his father's namesake and the idol of his mother's life. He had recently been graduated from the University of Virginia where he was a tremendous favorite; he had a brilliant mind, pleasant ways and laughing brown eyes. Life seemed to stretch out before him, full of beauty and promise. He asked nothing of his mother, and yet, looking at him, she felt she could not give him enough. Her husband had left Mount Vernon to her unentailed. She could do with it what she chose. And suddenly, she knew what she wished to do.

"It is just one hundred years," she said softly, "since Mount Vernon was built for a bride. You would like to bring your bride here, too, wouldn't you, John? Well, it shall be my wedding gift to you. And since I believe that young couples are happier alone, I shall go to your father's old home at Blakely, for the rest of my life. But I want your promise that at the last, I shall lie in the vault here, beside your father."

He promised readily, his heart full of gratitude; and, in the next few years, it was the angel of birth, not the angel of death, which hovered over Mount Vernon. Jane Charlotte's namesake was soon toddling about there and, after her, came six other children. But before the last two were born, the vault had been opened —and shut—for the last time.

When Jane Charlotte Blackburn Washington had been brought home, to rest beside her husband, her son saw that the vault contained room for only one more coffin. For whom should this be reserved? Surely not for him, since when he died, he would lie beside Eleanor, his wife. For one of his sons? They, too, would wish to be buried with their wives and, in any case, how could he choose among them? It was better that there should be no occasion for a choice. He closed the vault and locked it. Then he walked slowly down to the river with the key in his hand. An instant later, the waters of the Potomac rippled over it.

As a family center, Mount Vernon survived the death of Jane Charlotte Blackburn Washington only three years. John Augustine, the younger, and Eleanor his wife were happy in each other and in their children; but they were eaten nearly out of house and home by importunate strangers, and with their shrunken fortunes *they* could not support a "well resorted tavern" as the free-handed George had done. Both the Federal Government and the State of Virginia were given the opportunity to acquire the property, but neither took advantage of it; the mansion seemed destined for the same fate as Belvoir.

But as this had perished with the passing of a woman, Mount Vernon was saved by the coming of one. A young invalid, Ann Pamela Cunningham, was coming up the river from South Carolina in search of health, when the sound of tolling bells arrested her attention. The ship had stopped to pay the customary tribute to Mount Vernon, and she beheld it, not rising in grandeur, but battered and weatherbeaten and worn, surrounded by encroaching underbrush. Then and there, she determined that Mount Vernon should be restored and preserved.

Even those who have found similar undertakings almost overwhelming in the present day and age can hardly visualize the magnitude of her task. In the fifties, "delicate females" were still supposed to recline perpetually upon sofas, as Mrs. Bushrod Washington had done; and the name of a true gentlewoman appeared only three times in print: when she was born, when she was married and when she died. But Ann Pamela Cunningham was undeterred by such obstacles and such traditions. She sent out an appeal which she signed "A Southern Matron." She organized a society, called the Mount Vernon Ladies Association. Mr.

Washington himself at first declined to consider a proposal for purchase by such an organization; he could not bring himself to believe in its reliability. But eventually he agreed to sell the mansion and the two hundred acres surrounding it for $200,000, giving the ladies four years in which to pay for the property. The final payment, like all preceding payments, was made on time. In 1860, the Mount Vernon Ladies Association took over the property; and in 1874, Miss Cunningham, in resigning from its regency, imposed a sacred charge upon it:

"Ladies, the home of Washington is in your hands; see to it that you keep it the home of Washington."

The regents of Mount Vernon have been faithful to their trust; Mount Vernon is still a home—a home to which all the world may turn with admiration and affection. Like a benign presence, the spirit of the men and women who loved and lived there rests over it. Their human failings bring them closer to us. Their qualities of grandeur make us strive to come closer to them. Mount Vernon is still theirs. But they share it with us. It is ours, also.

THE DIXIE DOLL

"HOUSE CLEANING time—why do we always think of it as that instead of appleblossom time?"

"We don't—except in New England. If you were a Virginian instead of a Vermonter—"

The man laughed and, pausing in the act of pushing a heavy, battered old secretary further under the eaves of the attic, tipped up his mother's chin with one dusty hand, and kissed her on both cheeks, in the fashion which he had learned in France.

"Is that where you want that thing? Sure you got every speck of dust out of that corner before I moved it in?"

"Yes—what do you know about Virginians? You seem to refer to them so often since you came home."

"There were—some in my regiment. I learned enough to know that instead of doing all this scrubbing and scouring—you'd be a game little rebel and fare forth and pick appleblossoms instead!"

"House cleaning seems to me a strange subject for soldiers to discuss."

"Mummm—where do you want this trunk? I take it for granted it's got to be moved—moved somewhere, anywhere, rather than allowed to stay quietly where it is."

"John, you—"

"Whose trunk is it, anyway? It looks as if it dated back to the Civil War."

"It does."

"Honestly? Was it Grandfather's?"

"Yes. His uniform is in it. A few old papers, too, I believe. He left the entire contents to your father in his will—mentioned it particularly. 'To my eldest son, John, I bequeath my army trunk, and all that it contains, including the gift made to me during the campaign in Virginia.' "

"Gift?"

"I daresay that was his manner of referring to his medal. I know that one at least—I really thought there were several—was awarded him. He was decorated for conspicuous gallantry."

"Have you ever been through the trunk?"

"Yes, once, with your father—but that was very long ago."

The woman turned toward the tiny window from which every trace of dust and cobweb had been scrupulously removed, and looked out again at the boughs of appleblossoms swaying against it, fluffy pink and white against a hard, clean, blue sky.

"It was soon after we were married. My first spring house cleaning in my own house. Your father helped me with it, just as you're doing now. We talked about you a good deal, that day. I think we did more talking than cleaning. You see, we were expecting you, and I grew rather tired, so he said, 'Let's stop pulling furniture around and look at Father's things for a while.' "

"Couldn't *we*, Mother?"

"I thought you didn't like to see anything that reminded you—of war."

The man winced, ever so lightly, then colored.

"I'm getting over that. I think it would be rather jolly to see all the old boy's trophies. Gosh, he must have been even younger than I am now, when the whole thing was settled. What kids they sent off, in those days."

He was lifting the leather cover as he spoke, folding back the yellowing towel laid neatly over the tray, sniffing the faint mustiness of old linen mingled with camphor and lavender. The blue uniform lay neatly folded, the gold braid and buttons shining still in spite of a dimmed and tarnished glory, the sword in its sheath placed slanting across the cuff of one sleeve and the shoulder of the other, medals pinned firmly in a straight row across the breast. The man's lips twisted a little as he lifted the coat and heard the crackle of papers underneath it.

"His commissions!" Lieutenant—Captain—Lieutenant-Colonel—Colonel—say, he was in through it all, wasn't he? Four years of it."

"My dear, if looking at these things brings back your own memories so vividly—"

"Was he ever wounded?"

"Oh, yes. Don't you know that part of the story? I supposed your father had told it to you."

"Was it very bad?"

"Very. He wasn't expected to live for months. But I didn't mean that. I meant about the girl who nursed him."

"The *what?*"

"He fell in love with her."

"Grandmother was a nurse?"

"Oh, no! Your grandmother never left Hamstead at all, as far as I know. She was just a little girl when the war began. He didn't marry her until several years after it ended. And she made him a splendid wife. But the girl—the other girl—the Real Girl, I suppose you'd call her—was a Virginian, a Rebel. She wouldn't have him."

The man moistened his lips. He was, his mother saw, very white, but, like most mothers, she had learned to pretend to see less than she really did. He was not very strong, even yet, she knew—he was emotional, easily upset, merry, then sad—but still, it had amused him, taken him out of himself, to come with her to the attic, to open this old trunk, and anything that amused him and took him out of himself must ultimately be good for him.

"Her name was Sally—Sally Blair." The man grew whiter still, the mother went steadily on. "I think there wasn't much doubt that she loved him, too. It was in a skirmish near her father's plantation that he was so badly wounded, and in her father's house that he was taken care of, by her and her mother—not in a hospital. He had to stay a long time before he was well enough to leave, and the Blairs were very good to him, there's no doubt of that, even though Mr. Blair and both the sons had been killed, fighting on the other side. The southern women didn't think much about what color uniform a man had worn, when they were trying to keep him from wearing a shroud, any more than the northern women did. And it was a lovely old place, lovelier than anything he'd ever seen in Hamstead, though it was stripped and poverty-stricken—those Virginia estates must have been very beautiful, before the war."

"Yes, I guess they must have been," muttered the man, "and—and so Grandfather fell in love with a girl named—Sally Blair. And she wouldn't marry him."

"No, she wouldn't marry him, but, as I said, I think she loved him. She pleaded for his release once when he was a prisoner. She went to the general in command and told him she wanted him to give her a present. She coaxed him into promising to give her anything she asked for, if it was in his power, before she told him what she wanted. And when he had promised, she said, 'I want a Yankee soldier.' He roared with laughter, and said they weren't giving away any

Yankee soldiers in Virginia those days, not if they *knew* it. But at last she wheedled him into saying he'd give the man a chance to escape. He'd let John Gray go out to meet her with a guard who wouldn't be especially watchful, and if she happened to meet him with a horse, why, there was no way of stopping that—though of course, as an escaped prisoner—if he *did* escape—he'd be pursued. She met him with the horse all right—and they never caught him after he'd said good-bye to her on the top of a hill looking down over the valley. Sometimes I think those valleys in Virginia must be nearly as pretty as the one here, John."

"I shouldn't wonder."

"And peaceful looking. It must have been terrible, having them ravaged that way."

The man winced again, at the word, "ravaged." His mother went on, quickly.

"But he went back to see her once after that. I don't know how he got through the lines. Of course he was taking his life in his hands to attempt it. He must have wanted her pretty badly. She let him stay a day or two. Then she sent him away, forever. And when he left, she gave him—"

Suddenly, Harriet Gray sprang up from the dilapidated stool upon which she had been sitting, and bent over the little army trunk, lifting out the tray with its folded uniform and its clean, yellowing linen.

"The gift," she said, her voice thrilling. "The gift he received in Virginia—of course! I was so tired that day your father and I opened the trunk together, and it was so important that I shouldn't get *over*tired that we never lifted the tray. But it must be here—oh, John, that white satin box in the corner!"

They took it out together. It was wrapped in a napkin, an old, soft napkin, as heavily monogrammed as it was finely darned. The box itself, as the napkin fell away, was covered with satin, ivory white with age, splitting under their touch. The rusty clasp stuck. As she wrestled with it, Harriet Gray finished her sentence.

"She gave him a doll. A doll dressed like a bride.

And, instead of a bouquet, it carried a Confederate flag with a little scroll wrapped around the handle. Sally Blair had written on the scroll."

The clasp gave suddenly, the tiny nails which held it crumbling in dust—a powder the color of an old blood stain. The cover sprang back. Inside lay the doll —the yellow-haired, blue-eyed, waxen doll of the sixties, which only rich little girls were fortunate enough to possess, her hooped skirts of ribbed white silk extending over frilly petticoats, her satin slippers laced with straps across her ankles, her bodice cut low over the breast, finished with a tiny bertha of lace and caught with orange blossoms, her full lace veil crowned with them. The Stars and Bars lay across her heart, firmly clasped; but the tiny paper with which they had been wrapped fluttered loose, and John Gray caught it in his hand.

They took it over to the window and read it together. The appleblossoms kept beating against the window, beating as if they were trying to force an entrance through the glass. But neither Harriet Gray nor her son noticed them.

"You say you want a Southern bride. I am giving you the only bride from Dixie that you will ever get." How finely cut the clear, small letters were, sharp as daggers!—"To take back north with you. And I hope the bones of every Yankee soldier will whiten between here and Richmond. Except yours."

"She couldn't help adding that—she simply couldn't." Harriet Gray turned to the man beside her with brimming eyes. "And your grandfather kept it all his life— and willed it to his eldest son. It has never been talked about—he didn't want your grandmother or any of her family to be hurt because—but of course he kept it. And your father was the only one of the children who knew the story. It wasn't until long after the day when we cleaned the attic together that he told me. And then he didn't say that the doll was still in existence, that he knew where it was. Perhaps he didn't. Perhaps he never looked, either, to see what the 'gift' was. Aren't you glad, now, that you came to help me?"

She stopped abruptly. The man had taken the doll in his arms and, closing the lid over his grandfather's blue uniform, had sat down upon the little army trunk, holding it. He did not seem to be listening to her. And, suddenly, he bowed his head over the tiny flag, and burst into tears.

Appleblossom time in Vermont is rose time in Virginia, a time unrelated to house cleaning. The dust lies undisturbed in the attic; but the roses—thorny and yellow, top-heavy and red, pink and freighted with fragrance—clamber and tangle in sweet neglected gardens, beside moss-grown brick walks shaded with weeping willows, around tall stately columns from which the paint is peeling. And roses and columns screen together sometimes the ladies who, unmindful of mops and brooms, rest quietly on their verandahs through the hot haze of early afternoon.

A lady resting so—an old lady, fragile and fair, her full, silk dress falling softly about her—stirred slightly at a faint sound, opened her drooping eyes, looked through the tangle of flowers and shield of columns down the brick walk. Someone was coming towards her, someone whose step was vaguely familiar, whose face and figure, she saw, with clearing vision, were vaguely familiar too. He was advancing without hesitancy, as if he knew the walk well—a slim tall man, rather fair, rather finely-drawn as to face—a man, she decided quickly, who was not sickly by constitution, but rather, recovering slowly from some long dreadful illness or shock. Where had she seen that face —when had she listened to just that step—before? Was this some friend of Sally's whom she had temporarily forgotten, with that failing memory which annoyed her so? She must give him no hint that she did not recognize him, since he seemed to have no doubt of his welcome—had even, perhaps, come to visit. He had a bag in his hand.

"This is Miss Sally Blair, isn't it?"

So he didn't know her, or wasn't sure he did, after

all! He seemed to recognize her, through a glass, darkly, just as she recognized him. And that voice—surely she had heard that before, too! She gave back a welcoming smile to the one with which he had greeted her.

"There are two Miss Sally Blairs. I am one of them."

"Yes—I know the other one—I thought I might find her with you."

"My great-niece does live with me. But she is not at leisure at this time of day."

"Then perhaps I'd better come back in the evening."

"I'm very sorry—but she isn't at leisure in the evening, either."

The man shook his head, smiling again.

"I know that's your way of saying that a stranger shouldn't intrude upon you like this. But I've brought a—a kind of a letter of introduction with me."

Miss Sally was opening her lips to reply, to tell him —for he seemed so friendly that she could not help but wish to be friendly too—that what she had said was not an evasion, but the literal truth, even though it hurt to let him know that Sally Blair—whose mother had been a Page and whose grandmother had been a Randolph—worked for her living in a department store where she sold ribbons during the daytime, and at a moving picture theater where she sold tickets at night. But glancing at him, her speech was checked as he leaned over his bag. He was opening it, and taking out a box. He was handing the box to her—a box wrapped in a linen napkin, daintily darned, magnificently monogrammed—a napkin yellow and fragile with age, folded over splitting satin and a drooping, rusty hinge the color of old blood....

"Won't you take it, Miss Sally, and open it?"

She tried to put out her hands and found she could not. The man laid it in her lap and dropped down beside her.

" 'I'm giving you,' " he whispered, " 'the only bride from Dixie that you will ever get. And I hope the bones of every Yankee soldier—' "

"You're—you must be John Gray's grandson."

He slid his firm hand between her trembling ones.

"Don't tell me you're sorry I came."

"No, my dear boy, no. Somehow, as you came up the walk—"

"I looked familiar, didn't I? And still you couldn't quite place me? I realized that, as soon as I saw you looking at me. That wasn't so strange, perhaps. But what *is* strange—you're not going to think I'm crazy, are you, telling you this?"

"I—no, surely not."

"It was familiar to *me!* It seemed natural to me to come. No one even told me the way out from the town."

"You found Golden Springs yourself?"

"Yes. It's meant, you see, that I—that this—" he touched the box gently—"shouldn't happen twice."

He lifted out the doll, straightening the fabric of her veil, uncurling the folds of the Stars and Bars.

"Let's put her beside us where we both can look at her, if you don't mind, while I talk to you. There are quite a number of things to say. But they'll all boil down in the end, to one. You made Sally promise when she was a little girl, that she'd never marry a Yankee. You've kept it before her all her life; you've talked to her about the Civil War as if it happened yesterday; if you haven't actually poisoned her mind, you've misdirected it. I'm a Yankee—and I've come for Sally."

The old lady looked from John Gray to the doll, and back again without speaking.

"She's never told you about me?"

"No."

"We met during the war. At a hospital—a base hospital in France. She was my nurse."

"You still look very young—to have gone to war in 1916."

"I was older when I went across than the other John Gray was when he came home."

"It's taken you a long time to get over your—the war."

"Not so long as it's taken you to get over the Civil War!"

"The War between the States."

"All right," he amended, cheerfully, "the War between the States. The very fact that you pick me up on a phrase like that shows that you haven't got over it yet—after sixty years! And I've spent only a fifth of that time trying to recover from shell-shock and being gassed, and having a big hole in my side—and a few other things. Among them being turned down by a wonderful girl I was in love with—for no better reason than that her great-aunt turned down my grandfather! I didn't know that was the reason, of course, and neither did she, but it was. You've kept on trying to hate us all because you wouldn't let yourself love one of us! I haven't done a very good job, I know. But I've done a better one than you have, in spite of ten years in a hospital. I don't mean to be rude, honestly, Miss Sally, but—"

"You're not rude," she said a little faintly. "I think perhaps it's a family failing to speak rather abruptly."

"And truthfully—"

She hesitated, then smiled at him. What glory that smile must have held, he realized, in those years so long ago!

"Yes," she admitted, "—and truthfully. I have never recovered from the War between the States. Many of us never have. We never shall."

"Do you try to?"

"Why, of course—"

"Honest?"

"Mr. Gray—you—"

"It'll be John from the start," he said quietly, "because that it is going to be in the end. Well, I've had to face the fact, lately, that I might have got well sooner if I'd tried to—consciously—hard—instead of letting myself think all the time of all that horror—" The sweat suddenly broke out on his face. "That's held me back. I've lived it, not the once I had to, but over and over again when I didn't have to. My mother's tried to keep me from it—she's been a wonder. She's helped me all she could. But I couldn't seem to help myself. Until —until I found your doll.

"And I can't help feeling, sort of," he went on, after a minute, "that some of you have been like that, down here. I don't mean to say that you've consciously liked to think of all you went through—but you consciously *disliked* to! It seemed to me, as I came down your walk, that you were enfolded with memories. Not unwrapping them and clothing yourself with hope."

He took a tiny frill of the doll's dress between his fingers, pleating it and unpleating it. "Perhaps I'm wrong. But Sally used to talk to me about the South —about Virginia—a lot. And I got to love it."

"It?"

"Yes—and her. While I was pretty flat, you know. And I got to know it—and her—to sort of feel it—and her. I'd never been here, never been told about you and Grandfather, but I was pulled towards it—her. She was very kind to me, as long as she was sorry for me. What makes women like that?"

"God, I suppose."

"And does He make them unkind, too, when they are not sorry any longer?"

"He makes them loyal."

"Loyal to what?"

"Ideals."

"Ideals—or merely memories?"

"You are not fair. What you are pleased to call 'merely memories' were bleeding realities when—when your grandfather and I were young."

"Yes, but they aren't now. And you've bound Sally, my Sally, with your memories. You may have been right to send my grandfather away. I don't know. I can't judge, of course. I'm sure you thought you were doing right, that you suffered in doing it. But that Sally should shut me out of her heart because of something that happened more than sixty years ago, is wrong, dead wrong. I hadn't realized that you still thought so much about the Civ—the War between the States here until I talked with her. We don't, any more—"

"My dear, it is easy for victors to forget and forgive. You won."

"And do you mean to say that Southerners aren't good losers? Why, that's being awfully poor sports!"

"Have you been a good loser?"

The man laughed. "You've got me there. But all the rest of what I said was true. No, I haven't been a good loser. I was a poor loser first, to let it take hold of me the way it did—the fact that Sally wouldn't have me. I proved unworthy of her all right, being so weak. And now I'm a poor loser in another sense—in a sense that I utterly refuse to be a loser at all! There was an old South that was wonderful—your South. It suffered. It died. I can understand that you feel it was murdered. But not before it had given birth to the new South—different, but very wonderful too—full of a new promise, a new patriotism. Sally's South!"

"Is there a new North, too?"

"There will be, when you let the new South come to it. It needs your glory to add to its own."

"Our glory—?"

"The glory of the conquered—is there any so great? Have you forgotten the story of the Resurrection? Should anyone think of Calvary on Easter Morning?"

He was kneeling beside her now, pressing his face against the soft silk of her dress, against her delicate hands.

"At home," he said, "everyone is in the cemeteries today, decorating them with appleblossoms and flags. Stars and Stripes. It's Memorial Day—a month later than your Memorial Day, you know—our flowers come so much later. It's the first Memorial Day that I've missed, since I was a little boy—except those years in France and in the hospital—going to my grandfather's grave and putting the flag and the appleblossoms on it myself, thinking I'd try, when I grew up, to be like him, to be worthy of him—"

"My dear boy, you are."

"Praying a little, I guess, though I never told anyone that before—I've always thought of it as *his* day—"

"That's why, this year, instead of going to the cemetery, you came to me—"

"Yes—to ask you to help to make it, more than ever, his day—"

Across the tangled garden came the sound of a singing voice, a woman's voice, fresh and clear, drawing closer.

" 'Away down South in the fields of cotton—' " the girl was singing, " 'Cinnamon seed and sandy bottom—away, away!' "

The man sprang up to his feet. His hand went up in quick and formal salute. Then, picking up the refrain, he walked out between the pillars to meet Sally Blair.

" 'In Dixie Land I'll take my stand,
And live and die for Dixie Land—' "

The two young voices rose together, merged, fell with one long, choking intake of breath, to sudden and profound silence.

An hour later, the two came up the moss grown walk together in the warm dusk, and pushed back the yellow roses screening the verandah. Miss Sally had gone into the house. But in her chair, proudly erect, the Dixie Doll was standing, with the Stars and Bars still in her hand. But over her head was floating the Stars and Stripes.

THE CARDINAL'S NEST

MARSHALL SINCLAIR, a Virginian and an aristocrat—which is enough by way of description—married, directly after his graduation from the University, Isabel Atwood, who was neither, and who therefore requires more explanation. She came from New York, without even an invitation as far as anyone knew, to visit her uncle, recently installed as a professor, during Easter Week, bringing with her three trunkfuls of beautiful clothes, a great deal of spending money, and unlimited assurance. She was nineteen years old, and her striking, if rather too obvious beauty, made an immediate impression in a place which is so used to pretty girls that it requires something very extraordinary indeed to score in that line. Before her bewildered relative had succeeded in accounting for her presence, she was partaking in all the festivities of a very festive ten days; and before his colleagues—and more especially their wives and daughters—had finished commenting on the fact that she was not at all their kind, and could, therefore, have no lasting attraction for any of their young men, she had announced her engagement to the very flower of them all and gone back to New York to buy her trousseau for a June wedding.

If Marshall Sinclair even guessed, in the first flush of a feeling that was very powerful and very beautiful, the criticisms which his choice aroused—or, to put it more exactly, Isabel's choice, though they certainly did not guess that—he disregarded them with an indifference that was almost insolent. Every week-end he rode back over the Blue Ridge hills to Mock Meadow, the beautiful old place which had belonged to the Sinclairs for seven generations, and which his dead parents had left him as their final trust to their only child; and worked all day to put it in fitting order for his bride, and then sat up most of the night writing—at an inlaid desk which Thomas Jefferson had given his great-grandmother—long, dreamy, ardent letters to the vivid young creature who had startled him into such a tumult of rapture. They were charged with all the eloquence and all the sentiment which had stamped him as the poet as well as the orator of his class, and Isabel enjoyed them and was flattered by them; but she did not entirely understand their delicate sensitiveness, and smiled over parts which were not meant to be funny. But, when they returned from their wedding trip—an extravagant, hasty tour through Europe, conducted entirely in accordance with her wishes—and arrived, late in the afternoon of a bronze and golden October day, at Mock Meadow, she did not even smile. She found the preparation which had been so proudly made for her wholly inadequate, and said so, in tones of curt dissatisfaction which cut her husband as if the lash of a whip had suddenly been snapped across his finely-molded face when he had expected a caress.

"I did the best I could for you, honey, but the old place *is* run down, and there wasn't much time or"— "or money to do with" were the words he left unsaid, cursing himself because the truth of them was still there in spite of his silence, and the offering that he had to make to his goddess so inadequate.

"I should think it *was* run down! Why didn't you give me more idea? We can't possibly live here!"

"Not live here?"

"Of course not! Doesn't it ever occur to a Virginian to go and live somewhere else? Well, anyhow," she ended, a slight feeling of compunction pricking her at the sight of the stunned grief in his face, "we can't live here until it's been made habitable—decent plumbing and heating and paint and paper and new furniture and new—servants."

"New furniture! New servants!"

"Oh, Marshall, you are positively archaic! There isn't a single comfortable sofa in the house, or a servant under sixty about the place! I can stand it for a few days, I suppose—we'll wire for an architect and a landscape gardener to come straight down from New York and make plans for remodelling—I assume that we can send wires, or is that too much to hope for in this medieval place?—and we'll go back to Washington and stay while the work's being done." Then, noticing that her husband still looked hurt and hesitant, "You're not going to refuse—when you know how bad it is for me to be uncomfortable or unhappy just now?"

Of course he yielded. And instead of the autumn and winter of idyllic solitude which he had planned for them—long rides over the tranquil hills, long evenings with old books before a glowing hearth, the weight of old silver and the fragility of old china on their candle-lighted dinner table, the fragrance of old linen on their great four-poster bed, sunrise and starlight reflected in each other's eyes—there were a few unsettled, hectic days with the sense of strain between them, and then a silent trip back to Washington, Isabel's hatboxes and dressing bags and huge jewel case piled up at their feet.

"What is the matter with you?" she asked at length, as they drew near Alexandria, and still Marshall had said only "yes" and "no" when she spoke to him through the three-hour trip.

"I reckon I feel the way I would if I had a young one who was sick—and went off and left it for a strange doctor to operate on."

"Oh, Marshall, you're too silly—and anyway, you wouldn't want the child to die for lack of an operation, no matter how much you love it, would you?"

"No, honey; but I'd hate to have it hurt. I reckon I'd stay right there and see that the strange doctors did right by it."

"Well, if you love Mock Meadow better than you do me, you can go down there any time, you know, and see what the 'strange doctors' are doing. I'd rather wait until everything is over—neatly cleaned up—and the smell of ether all gone!"

To do them justice, the 'strange doctors' were remarkably wise and kind in their treatment of Mock Meadow; and Isabel, when it became impossible for her to go out in Washington any longer, yielded to her husband's wish that she should return there before her child was born. But she tied a string, neatly and firmly, to her concession.

"I'm crazy about Washington—it's a wonderful place. I never had any idea I could have such a good time anywhere. If I go back to Mock Meadow now to please you, will you promise to come back here in the fall to please me?"

"By next fall—do you mean—every fall? Are we to start in with that—for a definite arrangement?"

"Ye-es. I'd like to buy a house here, entertain a lot myself. It's been a nuisance living in a hotel, and having to be careful about getting overtired, and all that! I want to make up for it. Surely you can't object to my spending something here, after all I've spent on Mock Meadow."

Marshall winced. Then he brought out a question, which had been puzzling him for some time.

"If you didn't like Virginia—and all that it means to me—why didn't you tell me so before we were married?"

Isabel hesitated. She could hardly tell him the truth —that she had been shrewd enough to see that his birth and breeding would be an open sesame to doors locked before her wealth; that she had also practically taken a dare flung her by those "old snobs"—as she mentally designated them—at the University that she could not make him love her, and had "shown them"; finally, that his charm had really lifted her off her feet for a time, but that now those small feet were firmly fixed on earth again. Then she had a sudden and happy inspiration. "I do like Virginia—and what it means to you. That's one reason why I want to come to Washington—it's more for your sake than for mine. I want you to run for Congress." And, as he colored quickly, she went on swiftly and tactfully, "It's perfectly simple. There's going to be a vacancy in your district—our district, I mean. Old Mr. Fairfax doesn't want to run again. He isn't well enough—I've been told on very good authority. You wouldn't hurt his feelings by taking his seat away from him—in fact, he'd help you get it—he'd feel you'd carry on his policies worthily. And I'll help too—I can do a lot for you —after a few terms in the House, you could try for the Senate—and make it, I'm sure. And after that—why, there's no telling—the Cabinet, an ambassadorship. I know how you can write—I'm sure you can speak the same way. Haven't you ever thought that you'd like to enter public life?"

"Yes," said Marshall slowly, "I have, of course. It was clever of you to guess. But I'm too young—and too poor—"

Isabel laughed. There was no doubt of it, she had touched the one vulnerable spot on the heel of her Achilles. "You're growing older every day," she said, flinging her arm around him, "and I'm growing richer —it's perfectly scandalous how much money there is in those patent snap-fasteners that Father put on the market. It's settled then, isn't it? Kiss me."

Isabel's first son, vigorous and beautiful, was born early in May, when the white dogwood blossoms in the woods at Mock Meadow were beginning to fall lightly to the ground, and the pink and yellow roses, thick and thorny, which grew in great clusters of bushes about the tall pillars of the manor house, were opening in scented profusion. There had been little discomfort during the period of her pregnancy, and there was no horror in her confinement; her convalescence was a period of lazy and luxurious contentment. Dressed in a lacy negligee, she lay on the deep, pillowy couch in the new sun parlor, which she had built the winter before, facing the mountains, and made love, alternately, to her husband and her son. By the time she was on her feet again both had expanded, the former mentally, the latter physically, to such a degree under this agreeable treatment that they were entirely ready for what she had decided was best for them to do next. Neither one caused a hitch in her plans; and the following winter Marshall Junior was installed in his new and palatial nursery in a corner house on Massachusetts Avenue only a few months before his father, who had been duly elected to Congress the autumn before, took his seat in the House of Representatives. And when the summer adjournment came, and Isabel decided that she wished to take another trip to Europe, she was ready for Marshall's objection that they could not leave the baby.

"I thought of asking Ruth to spend the summer at Mock Meadow," she said, "you remember my cousin Ruth, don't you, at our wedding? She's terribly poor —much poorer than you ever thought of being—and has done some sort of stupid clerical work in New York for years. Now she's had the flu, with a horrid aftermath of physical ailments, and has lost her job, and really isn't well enough to try for another, even if she were trained, which she isn't. She's so proud that she shies at anything that looks like charity. But if I could tell her that her coming to stay with Junior would release us to go to Europe—why, she'd come like a flash! And the restful, pleasant summer would —why, there's nothing it *wouldn't* do for her! She's run down, and tired out, and discouraged—she was so pale and thin the last time I ran over to do a little shopping and caught a glimpse of her that honestly, I wondered if she weren't going under altogether."

Marshall remembered Ruth—so curiously unlike Isabel, in spite of the nearness of their relationship— with her soft, smoothly banded hair, her pale heart-shaped face that flushed so easily, her wide gray eyes. He remembered, too, the shabby little dress she had worn in the midst of all the wedding finery, the deep, violet circles of fatigue on her cheeks—it seemed to him very hard that a girl like Ruth—Isabel's cousin— should be so tired and so poor.

"Would she accept a salary, do you think?" he asked tentatively.

"Well—I could make her see that she'd need pretty frocks, and all that, and give them to her—and when we came back, I'm sure I could make her a present, just to show our appreciation of her helpfulness and splendid care of the baby."

"She wouldn't come and stay with us if we didn't go away?"

"No, no! She'd think she was imposing—and intruding. And she would be. I like to have you all to myself." Isabel's hand stole softly around his neck. "It'll be like a second honeymoon," she whispered, "you and I in Venice, all alone."

So Ruth came to stay with the baby, and Marshall and Isabel started for Europe, and again everything went as Isabel had planned it, and went well. It went so very well that Isabel, who was by this time expecting to present Marshall Junior with a little sister, made another plan which seemed to follow in natural sequence.

"What would you think," she asked her husband one evening, "of suggesting to Ruth that she should stay at Mock Meadow altogether? It isn't as if she were a young girl—she's older than I am, you know —and I don't believe she'd mind the winters there a bit. In fact, I honestly think she'd like them. Then we could keep the house open, and a couple of servants there all the time, and run down weekends whenever we felt like it."

"Do you think you'd feel like it very often?" interrupted Marshall whimsically.

"Well, you could go whenever *you* felt like it! I know you'd love it, and I think of what pleases you more often than you give me credit for. You need more relaxation, as you work harder and harder at your career—I'm so proud of the name you're making for yourself! I always knew you could do it! And the children could be there a good deal."

Marshall flushed; there was something about the word "children" that seemed to him full of a rosy glory, and yet Isabel used it quite casually, and he knew that it was in thinking of them, and in the desire that they should not be "under her feet all the time," that the real reason for her scheme lay.

"Do you like my idea?" she asked impatiently.

"I think it's a wonderfully clever idea," he said a little dryly.

But Ruth *really* thought so, without any reservation at all. After her first shock of grateful surprise was over, she settled down contentedly and unquestioningly, to the life which Isabel mapped out for her. With extraordinary ability she ran the house and supervised the grounds; neither solitude nor storms, the sudden departure of servants nor unexpected houseparties seemed to disturb her; and, in the sun parlor which Isabel had built she showed an initiative for improvement which delighted her employer-hosts; it became, under her skillfully loving hands, an increasingly charming spot, where all sorts of plants and flowers grew and blossomed. Isabel had fitted it with wicker furniture upholstered in bright chintz, had caused an effective system of shaded lighting to be installed and a small fountain built in the centre; but it was her cousin who put tiny boxes of seedlings everywhere, who trained vines along the walls, and coaxed pansies and hyacinths and daffodils into bloom long before they pushed up through the damp red earth outside. When Marshall motored down there on Sunday, alone, to make sure that everything was in readiness for Isabel's homecoming, and the reception of the heiress to the throne, Ruth led him out there, after their quiet lunch, to show him a new treasure.

"A cardinal bird's nest? In the sun parlor—or perhaps you'll insist on my calling it the conservatory, now that you've developed it so! You're joking, Ruth!"

"No, really. I was sitting here alone one evening not long ago, with all the windows all open; when the gorgeous red creature flew in, I closed the windows, I wanted so much to keep him. He stayed several days, and grew very tame. He seemed happy, too."

"Yes? And then?"

"Then one of the servants forgot and left a window open, and he flew away. I missed him terribly—one does, you know, a beautiful, brilliant presence like that. It was silly of me, but for the first time here, I felt lonely. And then I had a wonderful surprise. He came back—and brought his mate with him! I don't shut the windows any more, the birds fly in and out as they like, but they've built a nest. There are little eggs in it," she finished softly.

They went to look at it together, and Marshall reached into the nest, and, ever so gently, stroked the eggs with the tip of his finger.

"I like to think of them here at Mock Meadow under your care, Ruth," he said, "the cardinal's nest —and the eggs. They seem so safe."

"I'll try and keep them safe," she answered quietly, so quietly indeed that Marshall, noticing that her little heart-shaped face had flushed suddenly, wondered if he could in any way have hurt or offended her.

"What's the matter?" he asked, "aren't you happy?"

"Oh, very happy! I've grown to love it here—last night I stood between the while pillars on the porch, and watched the moon come up over the mountains, beyond the weeping willow and horse-chestnut trees—then I walked down across the lawn, so still and sloping and silvery in that lovely light, to the swimming pool—the bridal wreath and purple iris are in bloom around it now—the snow-balls are just beginning to scatter—I wondered if anyone had ever had such a beautiful home—anyone except your ancestors, who lived here before we came."

"I don't think anyone ever did—I watched those same things nights myself, Ruth, and had those same thoughts—but you *must* be lonely sometimes—"

"No—everyone at the University—and all through the county—has been so kind. I don't see what Isabel meant when she said—"

"When she said what?"

"That people weren't especially cordial. Oh, she must have misunderstood—and of course she hasn't been here much. But they've been so good to me that I don't even mind the roads I have to travel over to go to see them."

Marshall laughed. "That is a triumph. If our Virginia mud looks good to you—"

"It's so rich and red and fertile. It—it brings forth such wonderful things. The last time I went to see old Mrs. Fairfax she told me with pride that the road from the station to her house had been built by George Washington when he was a young engineer working for one of her ancestors—and I feel perfectly sure that nothing has been done to it since!"

Marshall laughed again, but he was not to be sidetracked. "Tell me what you were thinking about," he said, "when you told me that you would try to keep the cardinal bird's nest safe."

"It's only a fancy."

"I like your fancies."

"Just that you seem to me—like the cardinal bird."

The words once out, she did not seem to regret them. In fact, in the face of his grave silence, she poured out the full explanation of her thought.

"You're very brilliant and—and beautiful. I don't think any one has recognized it fully yet, anyone except

—that is, I don't believe all your talents are realized. But they will be. You're so young yet, and have been so —so hurried—in different ways this year or two that you haven't had time to prove how worthy you are of recognition. But you will."

"It's Isabel who is brilliant and beautiful."

"Of course. A fitting mate for the cardinal. And, after the first captivity, and then the flying back and forth—this is the place where the nest is built."

"With you to watch over it."

"It just happened that way," said Ruth.

This time Marshall did not answer her. He stood, silently, beside her for a few minutes, looking out towards the mountains, and then he said, a little satirically, that no matter how much she liked the roads, they *did* take a long while to travel over, and that it was time he started back to Washington.

The following spring, the cardinal bird and his mate came back to the little conservatory, and Ruth, with Marshall Junior at her side and little Bella in her arms, showed the new nestful of eggs to the children, who had been sent down to Mock Meadow as soon as the weather grew warm. The winter had been an unusually gay one, even for Washington, and there seemed to be no diminution of festivities during the "little season." So Isabel, whose picture was beginning to appear more and more frequently in the Sunday supplements featured as "one of the most beautiful young matrons of the Capital's smart official set" showed no inclination to leave the handsome house on Massachusetts Avenue; and Marshall, who was beginning, as Ruth had predicted, to make himself felt in Congress, stuck closely to his all-day and sometimes all-night-sessions, and his important committee meetings on Capitol Hill. Almost too closely, people began to say; for though he went less and less into the kaleidoscopic society which his wife loved, she went more and more, and she never went alone. The vivid beauty of her girlhood had grown even more striking, and she had learned to conceal the slight hardness and aggressiveness which had marred it somewhat, her scheming was less obviously done. She attracted as inevitably as a sweet-scented, scarlet flower. Ambassadors and Justices, Senators and Cabinet officers, hovered around her, eager to pluck and wear the tropical bloom. Her husband, though he could scarcely be unaware of this, apparently did not regard it seriously. When Isabel herself called it to his attention, he received the information in a manner that was less flattering to her than it was surprising. They were dining out, and he had returned so late from the House that she finished her toilet before he was ready and, drifting into his dressing room, her chinchilla wrap slipping from her shoulders, she sat down by the window and lighted a cigarette as he busied himself with studs and brushes.

"Can't you stop long enough to kiss me?" she asked lazily, "I haven't seen you all day."

He laughed pleasantly, as if she were jesting with him, and went on with his tie.

"I meant that, you know," she said at length, a trifle less casually.

He turned from the mirror, brushed her forehead lightly with his lips, and turned back again.

"And I didn't mean that kind of a kiss, either."

Marshall was slipping on his coat. "We'll be late," he admonished. "All ready? Let's go then."

Isabel moved across to the door and stood in front of it.

"Do you dare to tell me," she asked, "that you're tired of me—after all I've done for you?"

"I've done something for you, too, Isabel." The words were true enough, and she had been aware of the truth all along. But she never dreamed that he had become so. "Do you insist on discussing it?"

"Yes," she said angrily.

"You know I'm not tired of you. I wouldn't be human if I didn't find you—utterly desirable. But when I married you, I thought you something more than that—I thought you something to worship. I don't any longer. I know that you're not. And since you're my wife, I refuse to degrade you by giving you—passion without reverence."

"Reverence is rather out of fashion. Has it occurred to you that other men might not feel the same way?"

"Of course. I'm not a child—or an idiot."

"Then you had better exert yourself a little to hold me."

"Against your will? No, my dear, not that. You have reminded me how much I owe you. I have not forgotten it. And if you want it, it seems to me that I owe you your freedom."

"In your house?"

"This house is yours. Mock Meadow is mine. If you had been willing to stay with me there, if it had become ours, I should have felt differently."

"Also you would not have been in Congress."

"Not yet, certainly. If I really have the talent for statesmanship, it would have made itself felt, sooner or later. But meanwhile I would have had more chance to mature, and we would have had some quiet years together with the children first. As it is, the children are with Ruth, and you and I are—apart."

"Do you realize how far apart?"

"I think I do," he said steadily, "come, Isabel—it is not fair to keep our hostess waiting."

Perhaps as all Washington said, what happened next only "served Marshall Sinclair right." No husband of a beautiful wife, it declared, should be a visionary; no man engaged in practical politics should be an idealist. He declared himself, openly and unreservedly, for a policy as unpopular with his party as a whole as it was with his constituents; a policy which Isabel did not hesitate to brand as "absolutely crazy" and, refusing to assist at all in a campaign which "no sane man would have undertaken on such a platform," departed to spend some months traveling in California while he fought it out for himself. The wrath of those in high places, and the wrath of those in small country seats met together, crashing over his head and he was defeated in his race for reelection by an overwhelming majority. The returns were scarcely in, before he received a letter from Isabel, written from Del Monte, but saying that she was on her way to Reno; and, on the neatly folded and clearly written sheets she told him without circumlocution the reason for her journey.

"I've kept hoping that you'd come through a success," she wrote. "I think you've got it in you, but you haven't made good anywhere. I've tried to give you every chance, politically and with me personally, and you failed all along the line.

"If you want them, you may have the children. I should have to admit, if you contested the case, that I'd forfeited the right to them, and I'd rather not have a scandal about it, which I'm sure would be your feeling, too. Of course, you know who the other man is. He and I will be riding on the top of the wave, when you're stagnating at your old manor."

Marshall put the letter in his pocket, and rode back over the hills to Mock Meadow. He had avoided it during the campaign, and had made his headquarters in town. Now he knew that there was nothing else which would rest his tired spirit and heal his bruised soul. Ruth was standing at the door almost as if she had been waiting for him; but she met him with so blanched a face that he wondered whether, in some inexplicable way, his bad news had preceded him. It was, however, a grief of her own that she had to lay before him.

"The children's Persian kitten—oh, Marshall—"

"Steady, Ruth. That beautiful, sharp-clawed treacherous little devil that—that—" he hesitated over his wife's name, and then brought it out firmly—"that Isabel sent down to them? What's he done?"

"He's killed the cardinal's mate. I went into the conservatory and found it, dying, on the ground, and the kitten—just ready to devour it. And Marshall—the nest is full of baby birds. They haven't any mother. And the cardinal—"

"Suppose," he said gently, "that we watch the cardi-

nal, you and I, and see what he does next. The baby
birds won't suffer—he'll find some way to manage. I'm
going to have plenty of time now to sit and watch
birds. I've been defeated."

"I know. I've seen the papers. I'm so glad."

"You're so *glad*—"

"Yes, because you were defeated fighting for something you thought was right. That's what we mean
when we talk about the glory of the conquered."

"Ruth," said Marshall Sinclair solemnly, "you ought
to have been a Virginian. But if you don't tell, people
may take you for one."

Ruth laughed. "Thanks," she said, "that's a real
compliment. When I lived in New York, I used to be
told that no one would ever take me for a New
Yorker. I'm beginning to think maybe that was a compliment, too. I'll make a prophecy; you'll go back to
Washington two years from now stronger than ever.
The very men who are opposing you now will be glad
and thankful to help you then. Meanwhile, come and
see the children. You'll have time for that, too. It'll be
a good thing all around."

It was then that Marshall remembered again that he
had something dreadful to tell her, something that her
trouble and then her comfort had made him forget for
a minute. And Ruth, her gray eyes fixed steadily on
his, listened until he had finished without a word.

"It would be easier for you if she were dead," she
said at last, "if she had died when you could still have
had a beautiful memory of that first, wonderful love of
yours."

"Yes."

"Or even if she had died—like the cardinal's mate."

"I think it is something like that. Something cruel
was too strong for her and overpowered her. Perhaps
—the cardinal should have been more watchful."

"Perhaps. But I don't think so. I think it would only
have meant that the cruel thing would have killed him,
too—and then there would have been no one left to
watch over the little birds. Wouldn't you like to stay in

the nursery tonight with Junior and Bella? There's something very comforting about a sleeping child."

"I know," said Marshall.

He wondered as he drifted, very late indeed, into unconsciousness, whether he had done right to stay. Strangely enough, it never occurred to either of them, that Ruth should go. He and she were not children, of course, he argued to himself, there was no reason why they should be unduly influenced or troubled by *les convenances* and yet, one must remember *les convenances,* even if one did not worry about them. And he *was* worrying, worrying lest anything should happen to hurt Ruth, who asked so little, and gave so much. He must get hold of Miss Fairfax—dear old soul—the first thing. He could not seem to rest, though he clasped Junior's moist, limp little hand in his through the bars of the crib, and tried to derive comfort from the nearness of the sleeping child. Perhaps it was worry that made his head ache so abominably.

By morning he knew that it was something more than worry, that it was something very serious indeed, when he tried to get up and found that he could not. He sent Junior to call Ruth.

"I'm afraid I'm ill," he said, when she came very quickly, and stood, with the morning freshness all about her, by his bed, "very ill. Something seems to have happened to my head."

"Yes," said Ruth in her quiet way, "I know. I thought it might. I knew last night how tired you were, how everything had crumbled away around you. But everything's going to be all right. Miss Fairfax and the doctor are coming—and I'm *here.*"

It was weeks later before, very white and shaky still, he was able to leave the nursery and walk, leaning heavily on Ruth, to the deep couch in the sun parlor; and when she had settled him comfortably he looked about with a question.

"We didn't watch the cardinal bird together after all, did we?" he said, "What happened? I hope the little birds didn't starve!"

The deep flush which he had learned to watch for swept swiftly across Ruth's white, heart-shaped face.

"Oh, no," she said, "they kept quite strong and well, and at the right time, they flew away. And the cardinal has gone, too. But he'll come back."

"How did he manage to look after them alone?"

"He didn't. I suppose ornithologists would tell us that what happened couldn't, but it *did*, because I saw it. He—he found a stepmother for them. She came—right away when he needed her—and stayed and took good care of the little birds until they flew away—and then, when he went, she went too. I suppose next year she'll come back with him—and that maybe there'll be another family in the cardinal's nest."

It was very still in the long Virginia twilight. Over the Blue Ridge mountains the sun had gone down, and a crescent moon was shining; the valley beneath them lay bathed in peace. From the weeping willow trees that Ruth loved came the sounds that little outdoor creatures make as they are preparing for rest. The leaves of the privet hedge stirred, quivering in the breeze. Marshall reached over and took Ruth's hand and found that the soft slim fingers curled up contentedly inside his own as if they had been waiting to welcome his touch.

"My dear," he said, and found his voice was breaking. But Ruth answered him steadily.

"I know. And it doesn't frighten me."

"I'm ruined. I don't mean penniless, I'm that, too, of course, but disgraced and shattered and sick and disillusioned."

"I know," said Ruth again.

"I gave the best that was in me to Isabel, and she found it worthless. Now I've only the husks left to offer any other woman. What can those be?"

"Priceless, to her."

"I can't even offer anything yet. I'm not free."

"You're going to be."

"And you don't believe—neither of us believes—in divorce—"

"I believe in love," said Ruth, "and in God and his goodness. And in you. I can wait. But by and by I want to help the cardinal build his nest. Because—"

She hesitated, her flush spreading. Then she went sturdily on again.

"Because I know I *can* help. I used to think it was a girl—a wife—like Isabel who could help a man the most—a girl who is rich and strong and brilliant and beautiful—a girl who had everything! I used to think —because I had nothing at all—not only that no man would ever want me, but that even if he did, I wouldn't have any right to marry him, because I'd have to go to him so empty-handed. I've grown wiser, in these years among your mountains. I've got a better sense of values. I see more clearly what really helps a man, what a woman needs to do for him. I see—what *I* can do for *you*. What I can give you—besides my love!"

"As if that weren't enough!"

"I believe it is, there's so much of it," said Ruth huskily, "but I've got more than that. I'm not even humble about it. I'm proud. So proud that I can forget the chain of grief that first linked us together, and only remember that it joined us, inseparably, in the end, so proud that I can stand the waiting, and the criticism and misunderstanding that are likely to come from almost everyone while we wait, and even after the waiting is over. So proud that when you go back to Washington I'll probably stand on the Capitol steps and shout for joy because I helped you to fly after Isabel made you fall to the ground with broken wings and a bruised breast. For, in spite of her, that nest is going to be built in a very lofty place!"

"My dear," said Marshall softly, "I believe you've built it there already. It only remains for you to share it."

THE SPIRIT AND THE VISION

> "Where there is no vision the people perish."
> —Proverbs 29:18

THE BATTERED Ford runabout, three years old and never repainted, its shabby top thrown back, its hinges creaking, looked strangely out of place as it drew up at the brilliantly lighted entrance of Mr. Thomas Hamlin's town house, and came to a noisy and abrupt stop. Mr. Thomas Hamlin was a dignified and imposing personage, and his residence certainly reflected its owner's characteristics; only the most expensive, silent, and shining limousines stopped there as a rule, and impassive chauffeurs sat staring stolidly in front of them, while the owners of the marvelous machines walked with quiet assurance up the broad, low, gray marble steps. The young man who had been driving the Ford, however, jumped out, shut the door of his car with a bang, and pushed the house-bell with considerable determination. He was tall, lean, and frankly shabby, from the crown of his rough, weather-beaten gray cap to the soles of his heavy leather boots. Nevertheless, the face of the very correct manservant who opened the door changed its expression to something not unlike a smile, and he spoke with real cordiality, mixed with surprise, before the visitor had so much as stated his errand.

"Mr. Garland! I'm that glad to see you, sir! It's a long time—begging your pardon, sir—since you've been here."

"Rather!" The visitor smiled, showing some very white teeth. "I'm glad to see you, too, Thompson—convinces me *somebody's* been taking good care of the family, anyway."

"Oh, as to that, sir—"

"I know. Is Miss Gloria in?"

Thompson coughed, and his expression became

doubtful. "Yes, sir, she's in; but very much engaged, I'm afraid, sir."

"Very much engaged!" thundered the caller, his bright smile quite gone.

"Oh no, *not*—that way—*not as* I know of, sir. But there's been a dinner, and there's quite a crowd in for dancing afterwards, besides, sir—you'll hear the music beginning again just now. But if you'll step into the reception room, sir, I'll see what I can do—I'll tell Miss Gloria, anyway, that you're here."

The boy pulled off his shabby cap, and followed the servant into the white-panelled room with its gilt furniture and its glare of light; then, as if attempting to escape as far as possible from it all, he crossed to the window, threw up the shade, and stood staring angrily out into the street. What an atmosphere! It wasn't sour grapes—he was honestly glad that he had never lived in it. Did anyone really *live* in it?—Did Mr. Thomas Hamlin, with his heavy correctness, and his manner of uttering bromidic nothings as if they were the brilliant and original inspirations of his own dignified brain? Did Mrs. Thomas Hamlin, with her lorgnon that shut with a click, and her carefully regulated smile, and equally carefully regulated figure? Did Thomas Hamlin, Jr.—and all the friends that he brought home with him—with their silk socks, and their imported cigarettes, and their taste for musical comedy? Yes, and their ability to buy long-stemmed roses and big boxes of chocolates for Gloria! Did Gloria herself really live? —Gloria, who at sixteen, her years divided between a country boarding school in the winter, and a very quiet seaside resort in the summer (that was before Mr. Thomas Hamlin had pulled off that last enormous deal in copper) had been so wholesome and sunshiny and generally delicious? Not that he meant to be unjust to Gloria, in her later development, or bitter about her— not in the least—only—

"*Steven!* Where on earth did you drop from? And —and—*why* if you don't mind my asking?"

The boy turned abruptly. Gloria Hamlin had come into the room quietly and quickly, pulling the pink brocade portieres together behind her as she did so. Her golden hair was piled up high, soft and fine and shining, on her erect little head; her sleeveless dress, with its mere apology for a bodice, was of gold-spangled tulle; there were gilt slippers on her feet, and a small gilt fan in her hand; and out of all this dazzling glitter, her face and neck and arms shone all the whiter and lovelier than he had ever seen them.

"Good heavens, Gloria, you startled me; I didn't hear you come in—must have been thinking about something pretty hard, and you're—sort of dazzling—"

"Sorry to have interrupted a valuable train of thought—I suppose I'm quite the most expensive looking creature you've seen lately and that it was too much for you!"

"Exactly. Thank you for supplying me with just the right phrase," the boy retorted in a voice as hard as hers, the honest admiration entirely faded from it. She stamped her foot.

"There you begin, quarrelling with me again, and you haven't been inside the door five minutes! Do tell me what you want quickly! Didn't Thompson tell you —I'm having a party?"

"He said you were very much—engaged—are you?"

"Is that what you came to find out?"

"Partly."

"What else?"

"Is it really necessary to treat me quite so much like a tramp asking for a job? Well, mostly to ask you if you wouldn't go out for a ride with me—just once more?"

The girl burst out laughing. "Just once more!" she mocked. "I wonder how many times I've heard you say that, as the ending to all kinds of sentences! Gloria, do dance with me—just once more! Gloria, do let me come and see you again before I go back to college —just once more! Gloria, forgive me for losing my temper—and being cross and jealous—and disagreeable—just once more! Gloria, let me kiss you—just once more! All that went on for two years, and you know how it ended—two silly children, wrangling and making love in one breath, and then getting found out, and very properly separated by their parents! I think your mother was as angry as mine, and your father has a truly Biblical hatred of the idle rich! And now that it's all been *over* two years, you suddenly turn up, without any warning whatever, when the house is crammed with people, and calmly ask me to go out to ride with you—as if you expected me to accept!"

"Aren't you going to?" asked Steven quietly.

"No—no—*no*—of course I'm not! It wouldn't be just once more at all—even if there were nothing else to be said against it! . . . It would mean starting the whole thing all over again!"

"So you're afraid of that?"

The girl stamped her foot again. "Of course I'm not —what makes you twist my words so? But I know perfectly well what 'just once more' means with you."

"This time it happens to mean exactly that. I've ridden all day—over all kinds of roads—to get here tonight, hoping you'd say yes. I've got to get back home tomorrow to stay with my mother till Saturday."

"If it's the same old Flivver"—the boy nodded— "you must have put in an awfully uncomfortable, jiggly, jolty, wild-goose chase—for nothing!" said Gloria flippantly. "May I inquire where you're going on Saturday—just to assure myself that I shan't have to turn down another preposterous invitation from you?"

"I'm going to France," said Steven Garland.

Afterwards—it was not until he was on shipboard —Steven realized how suddenly the lovely mocking face grew pale and quiet, and that Gloria, catching hold of the portiere, dropped the little glittering fan, and that it lay for a full minute on the floor between them as neither stooped to pick it up. At the time he was only conscious of how rapidly she spoke and acted, after that one silent moment.

"Don't bother; let it stay there—I shan't need it." Her fingers were on the electric bell. "Why are you going?"

"I can't help it."

"Father says the United States may not get into the war at all."

"I hope that isn't so; but that wouldn't make any difference."

"Are you going into the Ambulance Corps?"

"No—Aviation."

Gloria stooped over, and picked up the fan herself; her hands were trembling—Steven remembered that afterwards too; then she flung open the portiere; Thompson was standing outside.

"You rang, Miss?"

"Yes. Ask Marie to give you a heavy coat and scarf for me and bring them to me in the vestibule—you'll hurry, please. Come, Steven."

She put her hand on his arm, drawing him after her, switched off the entrance lights, and closed the front door after them. Before Steven found his voice, the servant had reappeared, holding her wraps. Breathlessly, she slipped into the coat, and wound the scarf about her head.

"I'm going out with Mr. Garland, Thompson. I may be late getting back."

"Yes, Miss."

"You'll please tell my mother."

"Er—just that, begging your pardon, Miss?"

"Yes, it isn't to be a secret this time—*after I get away*. But thank you, Thompson, just the same."

And then she was climbing into the car, and asking, "Will you drive, or shall I?" and he was answering "I will," and watching her, stupidly, without offering to help her, while she tucked herself in beside him. They were in the suburbs before he was able to realize fully that it had really happened—that they were together —and alone—again and that the chance he had hoped and waited for so long had come. He turned to her.

"Warm enough, Gloria?"

"Yes."

"Rather have the top up?"

"No."

"Care particularly what time we get back?"

"Not in the least."

"You're a good sport, same as always, aren't you? Because if you don't, I thought we'd get straight out into the country, to that little lake we found once—remember?—and climb out, and sit beside it for a while —there's an awfully jolly moon, and it isn't cold—and —and—I think it would be rather fun, don't you?"

"Anywhere you say."

"Look here, Gloria, you're awfully quiet! Is anything the matter?"

They were already past the lighted streets, and her face, shadowed by the scarf, was turned away from him. Steven gave a little laugh.

"There were advantages to that little old brown horse I used to have, after all," he said. "I could drive him with one hand, and he didn't need much driving, at that! On a pinch I could drop the reins entirely, he went along about the same. But I've got to hang on to this blamed wheel, or we'll go into the ditch. So please be a good girl, and look round at me just this once!"

The words were out before he could stop them, and he tried to catch them back, fearing another bitter answer. But Gloria surprised him—she turned around, to be sure, but quite silently, and in the dim light he saw that she was crying, as if her heart would break.

His own suddenly stood still; less than an hour before she had been standing before him so hard and glittering and erect, making him hot and cold with bashfulness, and resentment, and shame—and now she was out alone with him, this glorious spring night, her shimmering dress covered with a rough serge coat, her hands bare and cold because in her haste she had not stopped for gloves, her wilfulness and self-assurance all gone—crying! Was it possible that this was the same girl? Or was it the old Gloria, miraculously come back? He steered the car to the side of the road and stopped it.

"Gloria," he began, his voice trembling a little, "you mustn't. I shall be most awfully cut up, if you do. I had no idea you'd take it like this. I didn't think you'd care a bit. I didn't feel I could go off without seeing you just—without saying good-bye, that's all," and timidly, almost awkwardly, he put his arm around her. He was rewarded with a flash of the old spirit.

"You do that very badly."

"I'm out of practice."

"Too bad," flashed back Gloria. "Let me help you" —and she threw both her arms around his neck; he drew her towards him, and without speaking, looked straight into her eyes.

"Yes," she said. "If you don't hate me too much—I should think you would," and began to cry again. Then Steven surprised *her;* he let her go, and started the car again.

"I'm not going to," he said stubbornly, "not until we get to the lake, and sit down, and thrash things out. Then maybe you'll say no."

"Aren't you taking rather a long chance?" asked Gloria.

"Yes, I am; but I've got to take it. I can't get near you when you're making fun of me, because you hurt me too darned much—nor when you're crying, because that also hurts too much—I don't see things straight. This may be the last chance I'll ever get to talk to you, and I've just got to get them straight— see?"

"I see," said Gloria, and sat staring ahead of her for a long time; then at last, "but I think you might have kissed me—just once more!"

"That tiresome old phrase," mocked Steven; but Steven's mocking was very different from Gloria's. He managed to get one arm around her again, for a minute, in spite of the wheel and then he laughed very happily, showing all his white teeth. "There's not going to be any just once more about that, darling, if I get started at all, but I'm not certain that I'm going to get started."

"Aren't you?" asked Gloria lightly, "why not?"

"Because, as I've kept trying to tell you, I asked you to come out here with me tonight so that I could have a chance to talk to you—alone and—away from—all that stuff you live cluttered up with. I haven't the least

idea of trying to get you to change your mind about—
well, about marrying me. Of course it was a mistake
that we ever thought of that—I know that now just as
well as you do. But I did care an awful lot for you,
and so—"

"You *'did'*?"

"Oh, I *do*, then! you know I do! But that's beyond
the mark. The real point is, that because I did—and
do—I can't bear to go off to France and perhaps—get
—hurt—and have to lie still for a long time thinking
of you doing the sort of thing you've been doing the
last year or two, without even attempting to make you
see that you're built for something much better than
that. It won't amount to much—my going over, I
mean—except to me personally. It'll be a tremendous
satisfaction to me to go, but there are hundreds of
other fellows who can accomplish five times as much
as I can, and who are doing it, right along. Whereas
you"—he broke off, and brought the Ford to a stop—
"well, that's what I came to talk to you about. Here we
are—climb out."

Steven made her very comfortable first. There were
pillows tucked away in the back of the car ("He must
have been pretty certain I was coming!" said Gloria to
herself, as she watched him taking them out) and he
spread the rug that had been around them on the
ground, and piled the pillows up in one corner of it,
and then he unearthed a blanket to put over her; and
when she was all settled, he took out a battered old
pipe, filled and lighted it, and sat looking down on the
quiet lake shining in the moonlight for a long time
without speaking or moving. At last he reached for her
hand, which was very smooth and small and cold, and
trembling a little, and taking it in both his big rough
warm ones, held it fast.

"Isn't this wonderful, Gloria?" he asked softly. "All
this silence and space and water and light, the open
bits of pasture and little pointed fir trees, and—you
and I alone? I'll never forget it, or get over being

grateful to you for coming with me. I know it was a lot to ask of you; but while I'm flying around up in the clouds 'over there,' I'll live it over and over again in my mind, just as long as I live myself.

"If that shouldn't happen to be very long," he went on after a short pause, during which Gloria did not stir, "I think we'll both be glad that we parted differently from—from the way we did the last time—that we did go out together 'just once more!' "

"Steven—won't you believe me when I tell you that I'm sorry—oh, *desperately* sorry—for everything I said and did that day. I've been paying for it ever since, if that's any satisfaction to you. I *did* care!"

"You—'*did*'—"

"I—*do!* Oh, I can't let you go to France! There are lots of other men to go, just as you said. What difference will it make in the winning of the war if you stay home? And aviation, of all things! Why, I never heard of an aviator except to read that he's been *killed* and that's the way you feel about it yourself—don't you suppose I can tell? You know you'll never come back, if you go—but I won't let you go; I'll do anything— *anything*—you ask me to now, if you'll only stay with me!"

"I'm going on Saturday," he said quietly, "and I'd rather you talked to me the way you did the last time than like that. It doesn't mean much to me after all, to have you care for me, if that's the way you feel."

He dropped her hand, and turned a face towards her from which all the youth and gentleness seemed to have gone, leaving it stern and white and cold.

"Listen to me," he said, "if this war hasn't done anything else good, it has at least brought back to most of us the capacity, which we seemed to have lost, of being able to distinguish between what really matters, and what only seems to matter. I understand now— which I didn't before—why everything went dead wrong with us from the beginning—we kept letting non-essentials get in our way; and the non-essentials, in our case, were that you were beautiful and rich and clever and worthwhile, and that I was just an ignorant no-account, stupid boy from a little one-horse country town, where my father is a teacher in a two-by-four college, and supports his entire family on less than your father pays his butler! I'd never even *seen* a girl like you until that day I found you changing a tire—quite capably and all by yourself—on the road between Meriden and Boston, and stopped to see if I couldn't help you. I couldn't, of course—you were perfectly able to do it yourself, and I saw that, after the first minute; but I couldn't help hanging around—just for the pleasure of watching someone so lovely—and so efficient—and when you asked me perfectly casually, after everything was in order again whether you mightn't give me a lift—well, I nearly jumped out of my skin with joy. I was crazy about you from that minute.

"We'd saved for years to take that trip to the seashore; none of us had ever seen the ocean before—and of course we all expected wonderful things of that vacation, but nothing half so wonderful as what *did* happen. When I wandered into that dance at the Casino, the Saturday night after I met you, I felt just like what I was—a great big country boob, and then some—I was dressed all wrong, and I didn't know any of the new dances, and I was sure not a girl there would look at me. Then suddenly, as I was leaning against the veranda rail, wondering whether I'd better go home, or drown myself right then and there, and rid the earth of such a cumbersome object, you came along, with half-a-dozen fellows at your heels, and stopped and shook hands, and said you were glad to see me again, and hoped I was having a good time; and while I was wondering how on earth you *did* it—spoke so easily and pleasantly, and as if nothing could possibly embarrass or disturb you—the music began again, and I blurted out 'May I have this dance?' and then went hot and cold all over because I'd said it. And—the next minute you were in my arms—do you remember, Gloria?"

"I remember how angry the boy was to whom the dance really belonged," she said with a little laugh, "and that you danced very well indeed—so well, that I was glad to have another with you. Go on."

"Well, I'm not going to bore you reviewing the whole thing. You were kind to me at first because I was such an absolute outsider that you could afford to be; and by the next summer—you'll never know how I worked to scrape together the money to go to Meriden a second time—you were kind because—someway—in spite of yourself—you cared. Didn't you?"

"Yes," said Gloria, very low, "I cared—quite a lot."

For an instant it looked very much as if Steven were about to forget his strong-minded resolutions; but he pulled himself together and went on. "Now, if we'd only had sense enough to face the non-essentials right then and there, and thrash them out and stick them behind us once and for all, we'd have been mar—we wouldn't have come to grief the way we did. But although we both knew they were there, we tried to ignore them and shirk them. So, as a result of our cowardice, we quarrelled about them. And since you were my superior in every way—and I knew it—and you knew it—and we each knew that the other knew it—I was constantly in the position of a starving dog who's grateful for any meager bone that the little girl who lives in the big house he's always hanging around will throw him—and that's not a suitable attitude for any man to have towards the girl that's promised to marry him."

"Steven!"

"Well, that's the way things really were, if you'll only be sincere enough to admit it. You said this evening that you thought my mother was just as angry as yours when we were found out. She wasn't angry, but she was pretty nearly heartbroken. She thinks a lot of me, just because I'm *hers,* you know, and she said she'd never get over the disgrace of having her only son making love to a girl secretly—with the help of a friendly butler—when he didn't think he was good enough—and the girl didn't think he was good enough —to go and ask her father for her, like a decent man, and then, if he were refused, put up a good fight for her! In the open! She said she didn't wonder that I turned tail and ran, instead of *making* you stick by me, for my whole behavior had been just as dishonorable and cowardly, as if I'd—"

"As if you'd—what?" asked Gloria, for he stopped and turned his head away.

The boy swallowed hard, and flung back his head. "As if I'd ruined some poor little creature in the streets," he muttered, "she said the only difference was that a girl like you was safe, and the other kind— wouldn't be—that didn't make *my* share any better."

"And didn't your mother ever say that *I* had behaved disgracefully?—led you on, and played with you, and then thrown you over after I'd got over the fun and excitement of a new plaything—the prerogative that any idle, rich girl has over the man she considers beneath her?"

"No, she never said that—I don't believe she ever thought it. You see, I'd told her about you."

"Told her what?"

"Why, how wonderful you were—how capable and self-confident and fearless—and how sweet and noble and lovely, too."

"Did you feel that way about me—*afterwards?*"

"Of course—why not? We had let the non-essentials spoil things for us, but the essentials were there just the same, weren't they? Those qualities in you I've just described—and the fact that we loved one another."

He took her hand again, and this time kissed it gently and laid it against his cheek and held it there for a minute.

"Listen, darling," he said, "men—like me—can go out and fight, and die if we have to, but women—like you—have got to win the war—same as they always have. Aren't you ready to begin to do your share?"

"But I don't know *how* to do anything! What *can* I do? What *is* my share?"

"You ought to be able to decide that better than I can; but I'll tell you what I think, if I may."

"Please; only Steven—"

"Yes, dear?"

"Don't—hurt any more than you can help. Whatever you tell me, don't say it in that voice you used when you said it didn't mean much to you, after all, to have me care if I was such a coward."

"I don't want to hurt you; but I do want to bring you to your senses—if I can." He stopped, as if seeking for just the words he wished to use. "I'm not a clever talker, and I *feel* an awful lot, and between the two it's hard for me to express myself."

"Do you mean you think I ought to stop dancing, and playing cards and all that, and go in for Red Cross work and food conservation, and Civic Reform?"

"Partly that, but not entirely. It isn't all in what you *do*. Red Cross work and Civic Reform are mighty good things; but there's nothing wrong—per se—in playing cards and dancing, if you've got the time and strength for them, after you've done more important things—the way I look at it anyway. It's the spirit—and the vision—back of it all that really counts."

"The spirit—and the vision?"

"Yes—the vision to discover not only the right and the wrong, but the essential and the non-essential; and having been granted the vision, the spirit to follow it faithfully—at all costs."

"How?"

"I can't tell you that. Every woman must decide that for herself. I suppose sometimes it's making bandages, and sometimes it's taking some fellow's job outright, and keeping it for him while he goes to the front, and sometimes it's giving up dinner parties so that you can send food to France. Women can't all work the same way, any more than men can. Now you know that I can tinker with any kind of machine, and I'm light and quick and strong; I know a good deal about higher mathematics and astronomy, which I've been considering rather useless for a long time, when suddenly I discover that I've all the qualifications for an embryonic aviator! Whereas Bill Smith, who weighs two hundred, and doesn't know a triangle from the Dipper, or a lawn mower from a locomotive, may in some other mighty efficient way of his own be exactly what General Blank is looking for to serve as a non-com. in the heavy artillery."

Steven laughed a little, and then sat quietly for a few minutes looking off into space, as if dreaming that the new work had already begun for himself—and Bill Smith of the heavy artillery. Gloria waited. At last he turned, his face shining with a radiance which did not seem to come wholly from the moonlight, but from the clarity of such a vision as he had tried to express to her.

"Excuse me, darling," he said, "I was Somewhere in France for a minute, I guess. I hadn't finished what I was trying to say, though—there's something else. Whatever women do—and whatever they do without —I think they ought someway to make the men who've gone to fight *feel* that they're trying to do their share—taking their part of the work and the pain and the sacrifice—and not entirely for the sake of one man whom they love, but for *all* of them—every single man that's gone. Have you read anything about the women in France who are still safe—the work *they're* doing? Why, there's nothing—*nothing*—that seems too much, or too hard! Don't you suppose that our soldiers will do more, when they know that their women are helping like that? Have you read anything about the women in *Belgium*—I don't mean wild-cat reports, but perfectly authentic accounts? Well, our men are trying to save you—yes, women just as rich and lovely and safe as you, Gloria—from horrors like that.

"When you came into the room tonight," he went on in a low voice, "of course the only thing I could think of at first was how beautiful you were, and how glad I was to see you, and how I hoped to get you—in my arms—and—kiss you, all I wanted to, just once more before I went away. And then—a new feeling seemed to sweep over me like a flame and drive out everything else. I saw that your dress wasn't useful, or warm, or—or even modest, but just a glittering, alluring wisp of gauze; and that you were coming to me, straight from some man with whom you'd been dancing—who'd had you in his arms—some man who's probably just as young and strong and able to fight as those fellows over there in the trenches; and when you spoke to me, it was to jeer at me, and mock the way I used to plead with you, and tell me to go away and leave you to go back and dance some more, dressed like that, when I'd ridden a hundred and fifty miles on the chance of seeing you, and in the hope of asking you to think—more gently of me before I went away for good." His voice sank almost to a whisper, "Oh, Gloria, darling, please don't think I'm venturing to preach, or even criticize, I never did amount to much, and for a little while—when you first threw me over —I did things that were so weak—and mean—and bad that I couldn't tell you about them. I'd been pretty straight, as men go, until then; but with the memory of that time in my mind, still pretty fresh and bitter, I know I'm not fit to consider myself even half as worthy of you as I used to be. But I couldn't help thinking —if hundreds of others, already over there had seen you, just as I did, wouldn't they have felt—just as I did—that it wasn't worthwhile to go out and fight for women, if all they were going to do in return was to stay at home, and make themselves lovely for the slackers!"

Steven sprang to his feet and, walking away, stood for a full minute with his back towards Gloria, his shoulders shaking. The radiance of the night had dimmed a little; the moon had gone under a cloud, and a slight chill wind, foreboding rain, had sprung up. The boy shivered. Then he set his teeth, and turned again. Gloria was standing beside him.

"Steven," she began, but he interrupted her.

"That's why I wouldn't kiss you, even when you gave me the chance much sooner than I expected," he said gently, "even when I found you still cared, and had been suffering too; I had to tell you all this first— and ask you if you wouldn't give your own self—the girl I told my mother about, you know—a fair chance to do her share. I'm sorry if I've hurt you—I haven't meant to—have I?"

She hesitated, but only for a moment. Then, unasked, she slid her hand into his.

"You've hurt me dreadfully," she said, "but that doesn't matter—what matters is that you've brought me out here, and talked to me, and shown me your whole soul—and my own. I've been yearning for you —all these two long years—but I've been too proud to send for you and tell you so, and say that I was ashamed from the bottom of my heart at the way I had treated you and ask you to take me back—and give me another chance to show you how much I loved you. When you came, I tried not to let you see how glad I was—I didn't want to throw myself into your arms before you'd even asked me to—and then—when I found you were going to France—that I'd got to lose you right straight off again—I felt, just for a minute, as if I couldn't bear it. But of course, now, I know I can. I want you to go. Only before you do—I must tell you—though I don't know whether it means much to you now—I've been silly and idle and proud, but I've —never for one instant forgotten—how much you meant to me. *Engaged!* Oh, Steven, you ought to have known better than that without asking! I never cared for anyone else, and I never shall—no other man has ever touched me—my darling, won't you kiss me now?"

How long they stood there, his arms around her, her wet cheek against his, they never knew; and when at last Steven raised his head again, he found himself looking into such a new strange beauty in the pale and tear-stained face still raised to his, that he was frightened.

"Gloria—dearest—I didn't mean to let myself go," he said, "but—you never kissed me—we never kissed *each oth*er I mean—like that before, I don't see now— how I can give you up. You belong to me now, whatever happens. I've got to have you for my very own."

"Will you—take me?" she whispered, "will you marry me—and take me home with you? I know it's an awful lot to ask of your mother to share you with me, but somehow I think she'll understand—and forgive me. I don't think my father will mind as much as you imagine—now—but if he does—well, I was twenty-one last week, and I've got a little money of my own —enough to keep me from being a burden to your family if you shouldn't—I mean, until you come back. I won't keep you from going on Saturday—I *want* you to go—but before you do—"

"Gloria," began Steven huskily, and stopped. "Gloria," he said again, and again found that he could not go on. "I—I—mustn't," he breathed at last, "I haven't any right to. Aviation isn't as dangerous as you imagine, and much less—less dreadful than the trenches, but still I'm—sure I'm never coming back—"

"I know. I—feel that way, too. And so—if I could be yours—your very own before you go—

"All the rest of my life," she went on, when he would let her speak again, "I can remember that. I'll feel so rich—and safe—and proud—compared to all the other women whose husbands are with them at home. We may be mistaken—you may come back safe and sound—or perhaps I might—perhaps I wouldn't be alone all the rest of my life after all. But even if I am—I'll *exult,* every time I think of you because I've had so much more than—those others. And after you've gone—after Saturday—I can find my work— whatever it is—and do it well, because you've given me the spirit—and the vision—for ever and ever."

THE SECOND BEST

STRETCHED at full length on the sand, the sun of a mid-September afternoon shining upon him, but tempered by the brisk breeze blowing up the Sound, Edward Middleham lay with his hands behind his head, his eyes half closed, a blessed feeling of contentment permeating his whole being. There were several substantial reasons for his state of mind—aside from the fact that being very full of good food and fresh air—a combination hard to beat in the mind of the average male—he was inclined to view his condition in life from a favorable angle; but at this particular moment he was not thinking of any of these substantial reasons; but principally of the seemingly unimportant and carelessly spoken statement, made by Mrs. Carruthers some hours earlier, that, provided nothing more pleasurable or important presented itself to her, she might join him on the beach between four and five.

It was twelve years—or was it even more than that? —since he had first seen her. Then, as now, they had been fellow guests at the house of their common friends, the Percy Drakes, meeting for the first time, in that incubator of modern flirtations, a week-end house party. She was a country cousin of Mrs. Percy's, on her first long visit away from home, younger than any of the others, miserably shy at the mere prospect of meeting so many strangers, ill at ease in the unaccustomed atmosphere of luxury, painfully conscious that she did not "fit in"—even a little shocked at the women's cigarettes and low-cut dresses and the men's frequent cocktails, and the easy camaraderie which existed among all the other guests. Middleham was at that time, an unimportant young man, just out of college, with no record of athletic glory behind him, and no large fortune ahead of him. He was, moreover, quite unencumbered, not even nominally attached to Nancy Hutchinson, the reigning belle of the occasion. Mrs. Percy found him an easy prey.

"Do be nice to that poor child, if you don't mind too much! She's so frightened, it's positively painful, and I can't do anything with her; she has no idea how to dress or dance, or talk, or—anything! Not a man will look at her except out of charity."

"And I struck you as being the most charitable of the bunch!"

"Well, I thought you wouldn't mind as much as some of the others, and besides it would be a personal favor to me."

"Oh, well, of course, Hester, if you put it that way—" He laughed good-naturedly, and rolled off to be victimized.

The first attempts were certainly discouraging. Mrs. Drake had hardly overstated her cousin's lack of attractions, and Lucy Miller was only seventeen, and had scarcely been outside of Millertown, New Hampshire, in her life. But she was neither diffident nor stupid, and once having gained a little self-confidence, she made rapid strides in the right direction. Middleham was staying over till Tuesday, longer than most of the others, and when he left she displayed a frank regret which was very flattering.

"I hate to have you go. I suppose you won't be down again."

"On the contrary, Hester has asked me to spend my vacation here, a week, and that's only ten days off— shall you still be here then?"

"I think so."

"I'm very glad." There was no question about it, he really meant it. It was interesting to watch such rapid development. He sent her a five-pound box of candy and a frivolous note as soon as he reached town. Having done this, he instantly regretted it. It would never do to trifle with the poor little thing's young affections; and not being very old himself, he gave way to some complacent reflections about his charitable, and scrupulously platonic conduct, and resolved to adhere closely to it during the approaching vacation. He was therefore somewhat piqued—such is the inconsistency of man—when Lucy neglected to write to thank him for the candy for several days, and completely ignored the tone of his letter, both in her own reply and upon his arrival at Meriden.

She seemed to have spent the interval very profitably; even the critical Hester confided to him that she was encouraged.

"The Haven boys came in to call Tuesday, and she really did very well. Will you actually believe it, they came again last night, and George—the younger one you know—asked her to go to the dance at the Casino with him this evening. She's been to Boston and bought some new clothes—quite pretty—and if she can only get the hang of how to wear them, she'd look very well. I suppose you haven't noticed what wonderful color she has, and what lovely hair—if she could only do it properly."

"Well, I have," said Middleham.

So Lucy went off to her party with George Haven, looking not quite like the other girls, to be sure, but very fresh and blooming for all that; and Edward, who came in late with Hester and Percy, found her enjoying herself very much, with only one dance left for him, and the next day he did not see much of her, either, because she went on a long sail with the Havens and some friends of theirs whom he did not know. Monday morning he cornered her, and complained.

"I came down here on purpose to spend my vacation with you," he said in a grieved tone that was not half so platonic as it might have been.

Lucy opened her eyes very wide. They were gray eyes, and they were fairly large anyway, with long, soft brown lashes that curled most engagingly over her rosy cheeks.

"Why, no, you didn't," she stated quite frankly, "you had planned to come anyway."

Edward decided that it would be wiser to waive this question.

"I hope you'll go sailing with me today," he remarked, still very cordially for a careful young man.

"Just us two?"

"Why, yes."

"I think it's more fun with a crowd, don't you?"

"No."

The monosyllable was intended to carry a good deal of weight. Lucy stood twisting her handkerchief around her hands, looking down at the piazza floor with evident interest. Then she smiled and turned away.

"Aren't you coming?" asked Edward.

"No," said Lucy in her turn.

"Why not?"

"I have some sewing I want to do, and some letters to write and—"

"Oh, well, of course, if you don't want to—"

"I don't," said Lucy quite calmly.

"If that's the way you feel about it I won't bother you any more."

Even this dark threat proved ineffectual; and Monday, like Sunday before it, was wasted; on Tuesday Edward attached himself to Nancy Hutchinson, who had returned, with her usual suite. Lucy apparently did not notice; and this, though it appeared strange to Edward at first, seemed naturally less strange in the light of the fact that Nancy's suite was noticing Lucy more than at the previous party.

Edward was piqued nay, more, he was grieved; here was a raw little country girl, whose hair was untidy and whose belt sagged and whose petticoat showed; who had been educated at the high school at Millertown, and gone to the Congregational Church there every Sunday, and whose idea of a ball was a "hop" at the Town Hall in her native village, and she had been just as shy and inexperienced and uncultivated as such an upbringing would lead anyone to expect, and he had gone out of his way to be nice to her—and now —almost directly—she was acting as if she were not under any obligation to him at all—to Edward Middleham, who was born on Beacon Street and reared in the atmosphere of culture and refinement!

It is probably not fair to blame either Millertown, or Beacon Street, for what happened next. Accidents have been known to occur in every locality. Lucy and Edward went out in the garden after supper and sat down on a stone bench. There was a moon, and stars, and nobody else around—in fact, all the accessories for a successful accident. So it happened, and Edward discovered that Lucy's fresh cheek was even softer than it looked, and experienced sensations that filled him with great satisfaction, for a minute. Then he found that it would require considerable ingenuity to restore peace, not to say amicable relations.

"You nasty, fresh, hateful thing! Go back to the house this minute—"

"But Lucy—"

"I don't care! Keep your hands off me! No. I won't

forgive you! I think you are horrid—no, no, no! I said no!"

"I'm no end sorry—"

"You are not! You'd do it again if you had the chance! Oh, I wish I'd never come here at all!"

"Please don't say that. I think the world of you—"

"You do not. You are only teasing me. And you imagine that because I come from the country you can do any sort of an inexcusable thing, and I won't mind. First you make fun of me behind my back, and then you look after me just to oblige Hester, and then you expect me to be *grateful* to you—I *hated* that letter you wrote me! I *hate, loathe* to have you touch me— Oh, I just *despise* you anyway!" Lucy stamped her foot and wept big, wrathful tears of injury and rage; then she fled to the house leaving a very astonished young man behind her.

It would take too long to follow in Edward's footsteps as he walked—figuratively speaking—from the Drakes' garden that July night—to the Millers' parlor some six months later. Millertown, on a cold, sleety December day, the bare trees swaying in the bitter wind, the streets almost impassable with icy puddles, the gray, angry sky threatening snow at any moment, was not a particularly cheerful and inviting spot; and the room into which the stout "hired girl" ushered him revealed nothing to raise his spirits. There was a blocked up fireplace, with an air-tight stove in front and a mantel adorned with wax flowers above it, there was horsehair furniture, and pillows of patchwork plush. There were large crayon portraits—presumably meant to resemble Mr. and Mrs. Miller; there was a carpet, and over it some bright rugs with startling designs—wreaths of roses, and barking dogs, and sacred mottoes, not of course all on the same rug, but still all in the same room, and it was frightfully chilly, and smelled as if it had not been opened in months. He sat on the shiny sofa, and waited and waited. Then he waited a while longer; the "hired girl" came back with an armful of wood and said she would light a fire; and finally Mrs. Miller came and greeted him very doubtfully, and he felt that the artist who "did" the crayon portrait had been lenient with her. She was just on her way to a meeting of the Ladies Aid, she said, and Mr. Miller was off in the back part of the town seeing a man about a horse he was thinking of buying, but still he wasn't sure—and—

"Isn't Lucy here?" asked Edward Middleham at last, almost desperately, considering his upbringing.

"Yes, she'll be down in a minute."

A minute! There was no doubt about it, that girl kept him waiting at least an hour. . . . Now, twelve years later, a little smile began to play around Middleham's handsome mouth as he thought of it; but then, it seemed very far from funny, and when she finally appeared, she looked very much more tidy and stylish than the summer before, to be sure, but very grave, too.

"Why haven't you answered any of my letters?" said Edward, bursting into the middle of things without a word of preamble.

"I didn't know just what to say."

He softened at once—poor little Lucy! Poor little bewildered untaught child.

"Then you do believe that I'm sorry I hurt your feelings, and that I never meant to?"

"Yes, I believe that now."

"And you know that I like you a lot?"

"Yes, I know that, too."

Lucy no longer twisted handkerchiefs. Her hands were folded quite calmly in her lap.

"And don't you like me?"

"Yes, I like you—pretty well," she said.

"Is there anyone else you like any better?"

"My, yes—several people—Mother and Father and—"

Edward almost gave up in despair. This girl needed everything spelled right out to her, like a child in kindergarten.

"I didn't mean that way. I meant any man—"

"Oh, I knew what you meant, but you interrupted me. I was going to say, and Henry Carruthers. I am going to marry him next fall. I am at boarding school in New York this winter, but I'm home just now for the Christmas vacation."

It was impossible. He, Edward Middleham, had come all the way up from Boston in the dead of winter to see this girl, and she informed him that she was already engaged. He could scarcely believe his ears. There was a long silence, which embarrassed him very much, and which did not seem to trouble Lucy at all.

"Who," he asked at last, "is Harry Carruthers?"

"Well," replied Lucy, "he's the boy that lives next door. He's a nice boy—that is, I think he is. If you want to stay to supper, I'll ask him over, too, and you can see for yourself. His mother died this spring, so he's awfully lonesome—that's one reason why we're going to be married instead of waiting until we're a little older—he's only twenty himself. His father's been dead a long time. He's got plenty of money, so we haven't got to think of that—and he seems to be—sort of in a hurry." The rosy cheeks grew suddenly pinker. She paused a moment and then went on, in a slightly different voice. "If I'd known just how to say it, I would have written to you—but maybe, now you're here, I can tell it to you. I did like you a whole lot—at first. And you helped me, ever and ever so much. I'm awfully anxious to learn—all those things you and Hester tried to teach me. I'm going to, some day, too. I've learned quite a good deal more this winter already, I think. I'm going to be—just like Hester, only more so—do you know what I mean? If you'd only kept on the way you began I—" She came to a full stop.

"You mean you might have cared the way I want you to?" he asked, very gently, considering how strangely raw he felt inside.

"Yes; but you were making fun of me, and you thought I was cheap—oh, yes, you did—and I'm not, I'm not! I'm all the other things you thought, but not that—and Harry was right here, and he—"

Edward rose, holding out his hand. "It's all right,"

he said, "I understand. I've been a horrid ass. I'm sorry."

"Are you going away?"

"Why, yes," he said, smiling a little, "there really isn't very much for me to stay for, considering—er—Harry and everything, is there?"

Then Lucy, with the fickleness of woman, softened; she could not, it appeared, let him depart in this fashion. She sought for words of comfort.

"I'm sorry, too," she said, and it was evident that she meant it—"I do like you—after all—a whole lot —I think—honestly—I like you second best."

Edward smiled again. "Thank you," he said, "but after all, second best doesn't amount to much, does it? I'm afraid that wouldn't ever satisfy me. I wanted more than that, you know."

And so he left her.

It would be overstating the case to say that Middleham was still a bachelor at thirty-five because a little country girl threw him over for the "boy who lived next door." But the incident, slight as it was, at least taught him two valuable lessons. Successful as he became in many directions as the years went on, he never again overestimated his own importance, and he never again made the mistake of taking for granted that an untrained mind was necessarily a stupid or silly one; and so it chanced that he saw or heard of Lucy Miller—or Lucy Carruthers, as she had now become —just frequently enough to keep him in touch with her development, and just infrequently enough to make him wish that their paths might cross more often.

Meantime, he had become a very fair specimen of the type of American man who succeeds in business, who uses his muscles enough to keep physically fit and his brains enough to make him an interesting dinner companion; doing nothing very great and good, but nothing very small and bad either—well-bred, well-educated, well-nourished, and pleasant to look upon, more with the good looks that result from these advantages than from any physical beauty. Essentially normal, too, with an even and sunny temper, and no signs of "nerves"—the stumbling block over which many of his associates ingloriously tumbled. In short, he was a good sort to have around.

Hester Drake was among the many who always found him so; and having urged him to come in early one evening so that she might have "some chance to talk to him," before her other dinner guests arrived, she entered her drawing room to find him standing with a large framed photograph in his hand, looking at it very intently.

"Have you had this long?" he asked with his old abruptness.

"It just came. Lovely, isn't it?"

He nodded, without taking his eyes off it—"How old's the kid?" he asked at last.

"Six months—a beautiful boy. You know Lucy persuaded Harry to take her to Europe on their wedding trip—and then to remain a year. This little chap was born in New York soon after they got back, and they've stayed on there since; but they're going back to Millertown in the spring. Harry's pining for his native heath. Lucy's planning quite extensive improvements on the house, which she writes ought to keep her busy and interested there for the present."

"You haven't seen her?"

"No, but I've persuaded them all to make me a visit before they go to the country."

"I'll be in to dine," said Middleham briefly; then as an afterthought—"What's the matter with Harry that he can go wandering around the earth like this—hasn't he any business, and isn't he enough—with her—with the kid—to keep her 'busy and interested anywhere?"

"Oh, I don't know," Hester gave a little laugh, and taking the photograph from him set it back on the table. "I only saw him, very casually of course, at the wedding. He seemed a good enough sort—nothing extraordinary. He was very young, you know, just out of some small college. I believe he expects to farm—that's what his father did. But he's fairly well-to-do, for a country boy, and the result is that he probably won't work very hard at anything. He'll have lost the habit, anyway, after all this idleness."

"Trips of the sort you describe, and winters in New York are fairly expensive, even for a 'well-to-do' country boy."

"Well, they may have used capital. Lucy was bound to have her 'chance' as she called it; and he was perfectly crazy over her—that's one sure thing. What is there about her that—?"

"Purpose and sincerity and—purity," said Edward Middleham quietly, and he took up the picture again, but even the photograph and the information that he was able to gather from Hester did not prepare him for all that he saw when he met Lucy face to face again.

Yes, the husband was commonplace—there could be no doubt of that; and, even allowing for the passion that he must have felt, and the admiration that he must still feel for his wife, there was bound to be so little congeniality between them, soon, if not already, as to be a serious drawback to their happiness together. Lucy had always possessed the sterling qualities in which he was totally lacking, and it was not strange that, at seventeen, she had failed to realize that he would inevitably disappoint her in his mere standards of actual right and wrong, still less strange that she could not have known that she would so rapidly outstrip him in all the more superficial requirements and social graces. Still her behavior as an affectionate wife, no less than as a delightful individual, left nothing to be desired, and her devotion to her baby was so wholeheartedly joyous, that it was a revelation to see them together. While the Carruthers made their visit at the Percy Drakes, Middleham not only dined there. The hours that he spent in sleeping, at business and occupied by other social engagements were mere steppingstones to the time when he should be free to sit quietly beside this starry-eyed, rosy-cheeked, grave young mother, who seemed so simple, lovely, successful and serene. He had not the lack of taste to attempt to make love to her; in fact, it may be quite truthfully said that he had not the slightest desire to do so. With all her loveliness she possessed none of the natural coquetry necessary for the equipment of a married belle.

Then, suddenly, the visit was over and the Carruthers were gone. Two summers later, motoring through the White Mountains with George Haven, Edward suggested that they should call in at Millertown. George made no objections, rather the contrary. He, too, had seen Lucy on that memorable visit.

"Do you remember what a queer little kid she was?" he asked, as they were speeding along over the hilly but excellent roads of the Granite State. "Scared to death, and always with the look of being half put together. . . . Gosh! I nearly fell on my face when she sailed into Hester's drawing room in white satin and tulle only three years later, looking as if she'd never been dressed by anyone less than Worth from her cradle up. I liked best seeing her with the youngster though—he was a bully kid. That must be the house —great, isn't it? Look at those piazzas—and the view you get from 'em—she must have done wonders. I wonder if she'll have changed a lot again—and what way, this time?"

They were destined to find out very soon—and to leave Millertown more silently, and with soberer faces than they had approached. The little boy had died only a month before, so Lucy—dressed all in deep black —told them herself, quite calmly, and the six weeks old baby girl was sleeping, and was so fragile that she did not dare run the risk of taking them to see her in her cradle, for fear of waking her; and there was something in her voice when she told them, in response to their civil inquiry, that her husband was not at home, that caused them to feel no astonishment when they overheard two strangers talking about him at the little inn where they stopped to eat their dinner.

"Harry Carruthers? a good farmer? Lord, he hasn't been sober enough to walk straight, let alone farm straight, for the last six months. He had always had it in him to go that way—but he hasn't been downright bad at it till just this last year. Trouble with him is, he hasn't any pride—never did have—or he'd have hung on to decency like grim death for the sake of that wife of his. Darned hard on her, I call it. He had a good property, too; but between her ambition, and his lack of it, they must have made ducks and drakes of it by now—she'll blame herself for that too, more than she ought to—she just naturally couldn't seem to help wanting the best of everything, and that don't mean just money's best, either."

Middleham avoided George Haven's eyes all that day; and suddenly, in the dead of night, the fierce desire to go to Lucy and crush her in his arms, and kiss the color back into her white cheeks, and the dark circles from under her eyes, to take her away from the sickly baby and the drunken husband, and the dreary guest of poverty, already knocking at her door, swept over him like a surging fire, and made him hot with shame that he should have such thoughts, and still the thoughts persisted, and gave him no peace. All the old evil arguments that made black look white—or at least a delicate pearl gray—swept through his mind, almost convincing him as it has convinced many—and possibly better—men before that the thing he wanted to do was the thing that was right to do. Lucy would resist, of course. But still, she was surely too weak, too broken, too disillusioned and embittered, to resist long. That he would ruin the very qualities which had made her so dear to him if he succeeded did not of course occur to him then; he thought only of her deliverance and his possession.

But when morning came, it found him with his mind master of itself once more, and his face turned sternly towards the city.

That night was now mercifully far behind him. In the years that lay between he saw her from time to time, when she went to visit Hester in Boston, or school friends in New York; but she did this very seldom, and even then the meetings were only accidental and casual. For by this time he realized that the only

safe and decent thing for him to do was to avoid her.
Each time their paths crossed, his heart was wrung
afresh by the black clothes that she never laid aside
after the little boy's death; by her increasing thinness
and pallor; and by the silence and reserve that had supplanted her radiant poise, just as that, in its turn, had
supplanted her awkwardness and shyness. She never,
in any way, referred to her situation; but Hester did
not fail to comment on it.

"If it weren't for the baby I think she'd lose her reason—and of course she just *mustn't* with that delicate
child to consider—so she doesn't; and leaving Harry
doesn't even seem to occur to her—though he's given
her causes enough, Heaven knows!—more than one—
she'll stick it out if it kills her—and some times I think
it will kill her—if it lasts long enough."

And so matters stood for a long time, changing only
to grow gradually worse. Then, suddenly, came the
news that Harry had died, under circumstances too
disgraceful to dwell upon; that Lucy had paid all her
debts, sold the farm, and with little Angela abruptly
left for Europe. The first distant rumbling, threatening
a great war, brought her back again, after she had
been there over a year; and, apparently with great contentment, she fell in with Hester's suggestion that she
and Angela should spend the summer in Meriden,
while she considered what she should do next.

So there, in time, Middleham came, too; and having
come once, and been made welcome, he came often;
and now the summer was almost gone, and he lay on
the sand waiting for her to join him for one of those
long, quiet talks, sometimes alone, sometimes with little Angela between them, that had become almost a
daily custom with them.

"Hello! I'm a little late, I'm afraid! But George delayed me. Now he's taken Angela off for a ride in his
car, and I'm quite at your service for the next two
hours."

Middleham sprang to his feet. She had come up so

softly that he had not heard her, and now stood quite close beside him, all in crisp white, her soft hair blowing in the wind, her cheeks tanned and rosy. How well she looked again, how wholesome and content; how alive in every fibre of her being, how lovely and desirable.

"George never did have any idea of the value of punctuality," he remarked duly, "but after all, I don't blame him much. You look good enough to eat—you remind me of all kinds of pleasant, fragrant things, someway—fields of clover, and orchards with the apples all ripe, and blue salt water in the sunshine."

"How nice of you!" she returned gaily, sitting down on the sand and tucking her feet underneath her, "I never should have thought of comparing a woman to any of those things—and they're all delicious."

"So," he said, sitting down beside her, "are you—I don't know any word that describes you so well."

"I'm nearly thirty," she remarked irrelevantly.

"Balzac's *Femme de Trente Ans?*"

"That wasn't half as nice as your other compliment. Balzac's Julie *was* a—well, she *was* attractive, but some way—."

"Oh, she didn't come up to you, I know," retorted Middleham, laughing, "few do—."

"Did you want me to come out here just to talk to me in this silly way?"

Her tone was light enough, but for some reason he grew instantly grave.

"No, my dear," he said soberly, "I wanted to speak to you of grave things—things that I think matter to us both—I've waited a good while to do it." He paused, and as she made no reply, "Twelve years," he added slowly. "Lucy, you know how much I care for you. Don't you care for me—at least a little—too?" And as he still received no answer, "Surely it can't be hard for you to answer—you must have been expecting this to happen for a long time."

"Oh, yes," she said. "I have, but still it's hard to answer just the same." The weariness in her voice, in striking contrast to her happy manner a quarter of an hour earlier filled him with quick alam.

"What is the trouble? Why, my darling, I wouldn't have hurt you for the world. Is it too soon—I thought—"

"Oh, no," she said, "it isn't too soon—it's too late. I care for you—not a little but a great, great deal—in a way more than for anyone in the world except Angela —but it's no use."

"There's someone else—again—whom you're planning to marry?"

"No, it isn't that—I'd be glad—this time to say yes —but I *can't*."

"My dear," he said, still more gently, "you've never told me—but I know you've suffered—that you've undergone great grief and shame. Don't make the mistake of letting that cause you to be afraid of marriage —to think unfairly of it."

"It isn't that, either," she replied, so low that he could hardly hear the words, "it's because it wouldn't be fair to you. It's a case of—second best—for you again this time. You told me before you wouldn't be satisfied with that—and I won't give it to you."

"I shall be thankful for whatever you will give me now. But I don't understand—."

"I will tell you," she said.

For some minutes, she sat very still, looking out at the water, her lips trembling in spite of the great self control which he knew she possessed. Then she faced him squarely.

"When I had been married about four years," she said, "I fell in love, deeply, violently, passionately in love—and the man—loved me."

Middleham felt his throat grow dry.

"I was wretchedly unhappy at home—you say I've never spoken of it—well, I will today! I married a weak, ignorant, vicious boy. He was attractive and he was rich, and he was eager to marry me when I felt that the people whose opinion I valued looked down on me. I was ambitious to attain all those little, little things—all that veneer, which looked like solid mahogany to me then, and he could give it to me and longed to. So I let him. He broke my heart, if you like to put it that way—he certainly degraded my body and smirched my soul; and it was when things were at their very worst—when the money was nearly gone, and my little boy had died, and I had come to the realization that my own false ideas had brought me to this pass, that I had no one but myself to blame, it was then that I met the other man.

"I met him in New York—I had scraped together the money, in the face of violent opposition from my husband to take Angela to see a doctor there, a great specialist. I went to stay with an old school friend. It happened at her house.

"I loved him from the first moment I ever saw him; I never shall get over loving him as long as I live—and he loved me, too, as I said before—but—he didn't love me enough."

"Enough for what?" asked Middleham, stupidly, speaking with difficulty through that dry throat of his.

"Oh," she said bitterly, "he loved me enough for what you are imagining. He loved me enough to want to buy me from my husband—and he was rich enough to do that, for he had a great deal of money. He urged me to—to divorce Harry and leave him to drink himself to death alone—and I could have kept Angela. There wouldn't have been any trouble about that, for Harry had been unfaithful and—and cruel, too. Those things usually come, with the other. That's why it's worse than anything else, because it drags so many other horrors in its train. But I wouldn't go. You see, I had made my own bed, and I had to lie in it. I *had* to. I couldn't leave him, no matter how bad he was. I *couldn't*. Do you understand?"

"Yes," said Middleham hoarsely. "I understand—most women could, but *you* couldn't. So this man wanted to have you marry him after a divorce, but when you wouldn't—what then?"

"He suggested that I should stay with my husband and—" The bright head sank, and then came bravely up again—"And oh, I *wanted* to! You shan't think me one bit better than I really was—Just seeing him, and looking into his eyes was heaven, and when he touched my hand! But I *couldn't*. I couldn't do that either. Of course, you know that."

"Of course, I know that."

"So then, he thought I didn't love him. He didn't believe me. He was angry and harsh, and he went away. He didn't love me enough to trust me, and wait for me, even to the end of his life, if it had been necessary. That's the way I loved him. He didn't even love me enough to keep decent for me, and now that I'm free I can't marry him—he isn't fit for me to marry. I'd have to go through all that—that mire of hell a second time. I've just got back to—to feeling like a human being again after all these frightful years, and Angela would see the very things that her father's death saved her from. He says now it was my fault that he went down hill. I don't know, perhaps it was, but I don't believe so—and even if I knew it were, I'd have to do the same thing right over again. Of course I realize that he's made of very different clay from Harry, and that I understand so much and—and want him so that it wouldn't be quite the same. It would be *worse* because I love him so much. I'd let myself be cut into little pieces for him gladly. I often lie awake all night thinking what bliss it would be to belong to him, but I won't marry him."

"Lucy," Middleham found that his own voice was breaking. "Don't you know how safe Angela would be with me? Don't you know that I love you so that in time I can make you even forget that this ever happened? Don't you know that you've come through sorrow and suffering and sacrifice to be one of the noblest women that ever lived? My dear, I don't deserve you —but won't you come to me just the same? Don't let this spectre of the second best come between us again. It was a mistake that we allowed it before. We mustn't repeat that mistake—Dear Lucy, can't you see?"

"I've thought of all you've said," she answered dully, "hundreds of times. And it's partly true, largely true perhaps. But it doesn't matter. I can't marry you.

I can't go to him; but I'm his, all that part of me—in my mind—just the same. It would be a—a sacrilege to forget that for one single moment."

"By-and-by, my dear, I hope you may feel differently."

"I never shall," she said. "Dear friend, don't pain me by speaking of all this again; and now, let me go back to the house."

Twice, looking fully at her, realizing as never before how vitally precious she was to him, Middleham opened his lips to speak, and each time something in the steady eyes looking into his checked him.

For a full moment they faced each other, both white with determination; then silently he bowed his head, and raising it an instant later, still silently, he stood and watched her out of sight as she walked slowly away across the sand.

WORTH WHILE

PETER BRUCE was the Hamstead correspondent for the *Wallacetown Bugle*. The *Bugle* was issued only once a week, and the demands which it made upon its rural reporters were not heavy (Wallacetown, having two thousand inhabitants was not rural, but Hamstead, five miles away, with only seven hundred, was, of course in a different class). Yet Peter chewed the end of the stubby pencil with which he invariably wrote his first copy, before, carefully revised, it was typed on the ancient machine—a Smith Premier with a double keyboard which Prue Fielding had once told him was undoubtedly manufactured before the Civil War—which stood on the kitchen table beside the breadboard and the alarm clock, and allowed long pauses to elapse between the items of interest which he laboriously jotted down after careful thought.

"Joe Elliott is having his barn shingled and building a new henhouse. Good for Joe.

"Sol Daniels has had a bay window with colored

glass panes added to his dining room, which is a great improvement to his residence."

This seemed to cover the improvements in real estate. It was necessary to turn to other topics.

"Thomas Gray has resumed his studies at the Agricultural College in Burlington. We shall miss Tom around here.

"Mrs. Watson entertained the Village Improvement Society in the vestry of the Congregational Church last Wednesday evening. A pleasant time was had by all.

"Sawyer has a new line of cotton dress goods and bungalow aprons in his store, received from Boston last week.

"A pretty home wedding took place at the Hunt Farm on Friday when John Merrill and Sally Hunt were united in marriage by the Reverend Mr. Jessup. Miss Prudence Fielding of Washington, D. C. acted as bridesmaid. The bride was attired in—"

The stubby pencil stopped moving. Peter was a bachelor, and a sisterless orphan to boot. He was not versed in the lore of the materials from which wedding garments are usually made. After some pondering, he decided to evade the issue.

"—becomingly attired in white, and carried a bouquet of sweet peas. The wedding presents were handsome and numerous. Supper was served, consisting of ice cream, cake, coffee, doughnuts and pie. The happy pair left to pass their honeymoon at Niagara Falls followed by the good wishes of their many friends. They will reside in Washington, where Miss Hunt has been employed in one of the government offices for the past two years, and where John has a fine position as secretary to a senator."

Again the stubby pencil ceased moving. Peter's thoughts wandered to Washington, to fine positions there with senators, to the weddings that such fine positions made possible for Hamstead boys, to John Merrill, who had been in his class both at the high school in Hamstead and at Middlebury College, and who had made no more brilliant progress there than he had; to Prue Fielding, who was Sally's best friend, who came often to visit her, and who had come now to help with the wedding festivities. And when his thoughts reached Prue, they stopped there abruptly.

Prue Fielding was an assistant to the Society Editor on one of the big Washington papers; and when Sally Hunt, lonely and bewildered, had first gone to take up her work in the War Risk Insurance, she had stayed for a few days—until she found she could no longer afford it, to be exact—at the small and comfortable hotel where Prue lived. Two or three chance meetings in elevator and lobby had been followed by solitary dinners at adjoining tables; and before they were half way through, the girls had joined forces. The casual acquaintance developed before long into a very real friendship; the sophisticated little reporter and the farmer's daughter from the Connecticut Valley found themselves strangely drawn to each other. And when Sally went home on her first vacation, Prue went with her. Hamstead remembered—still with something of a gasp—her first appearance at the railroad station— crinkly black hair bobbed about a rosy face, under a perky little hat; a black frock that was simple enough, but somehow wickedly "different" from anything ever worn in Hamstead, and all of twenty inches off the ground; transparent stockings; slim black patent leather slippers; a slim black patent leather bag in one hand. Peter Bruce, who, finding nothing more pressing to do at the moment, was sitting on the "depot" steps watching the train come in, stared at this apparition in reluctant fascination. Sally, an old and privileged friend, intruded on his contemplation.

"Oh, hello, Peter! How are you? If you're just sitting around—"

"The same as usual," interpolated a voice beside her, a voice as smooth as the patent leather with which its owner was shod.

Sally laughed. "How did you know it was 'as usual,' Prue?" she asked.

"Haven't you heard that reporters have to learn to

be quick observers?" the patent leather voice continued. "Were you going to suggest that your friend—"

"Peter Bruce."

"Peter Bruce should help the station agent with my trunk?"

"Prue, you're a regular mind reader. Would you, Peter?"

Without betraying undue energy, Peter acquiesced. The trunk was a "wardrobe," the largest trunk, the heaviest trunk, that he had ever seen. With its contents, as the days passed, Peter Bruce and the rest of Hamstead made astonished acquaintance. Miss Fielding entered, apparently wholeheartedly, into the social life of the village, thereby causing a slight pang of disappointment to those who had been awaiting the opportunity of saying that she was "stuck-up." She went to Thursday evening prayer meeting and *walked* home afterwards. She went to the movies in Wallacetown, to the card parties of the Village Improvement Society, to the dances in the Town Hall; and at each of these functions she appeared in a different costume. She wore dainty and demure white to church; fragile and fluttering scarlet to the ball; jade green embroidered in gold to the movies; turquoise blue trimmed with tiny pink rosebuds to the card party; and there were slippers and scarfs and sweaters, hats and capes and even earrings and necklaces to match the dresses. Peter, who almost from the first, seemed frequently to be her escort, pondered deeply on the economic side of this finery, and finally hazarded an indirect question about it as they were "sitting out a number" on the Town Hall steps.

"Rich? Me?" Prue laughed outright at the humor of it. "What makes you think so?"

"Why, pretty things like yours cost a lot—that is, I suppose they do."

"You think they're pretty?" The patent leather voice was velvet now.

"Yes, lovely."

"I'm glad. But they're not so awfully expensive, really. I see the new fashions, as soon as they're out, doing the kind of work I do, and I learn to copy, and to shop at the right places. And I have to be well-dressed, or I'd lose my job—it's nothing to my boss whether I eat or not, but if I go to the British Embassy to report a party, looking shabby, well, that would be another story. However, I earn enough to have what I need. I do quite a little writing, special features, and interviews, and things like that, besides my society reporting. It means long hours, of course, but—"

"You earn all the money you spend on your clothes *yourself?*"

"Naturally. And all that I spend on food; and for a 'room and bath' at a decent hotel; and for movies and taxis and French scent and other necessities of life."

Peter had not hitherto considered the exotic and exquisite apparition which had so startled Hamstead in the light of an industrious and successful wage earner.

"I shouldn't think, to look at you, that you could earn a dollar to save your life," he said in some bewilderment.

"That's meant as a compliment, isn't it? Thanks—a lot. But I can. In fact"—the velvety voice grew, if possible, even more velvety—"what would you like to bet that I don't earn more in a month than you do in a year?"

"Nothing," said Peter, gulping a little, "you probably do."

"I hope," said Prue without apparent connection, "that Sally isn't going to be such an awful fool as to marry John Merrill."

John Merrill was considered the greatest "catch" in Hamstead. Peter was honestly surprised.

"Why, she'd be an awful fool if she didn't," he exclaimed, "what do you mean?"

"She'd have to give up her freedom—going out when she pleased and coming in when she pleased, and all that. Perhaps she hasn't got as used to being her own mistress as I have, but anything that tied me up, kept me from running around and meeting clever, stimulating people—would drive me stark, raving crazy. I don't see how the girls around here live. They don't live—they just exist. And she'd stop earning money of her own if she got married, wouldn't she? She's just beginning to make good at her job and she'd lose it. Then, she couldn't have pretty dresses and French scent."

One of Peter's hands slid silently out, and touched a frill of the pretty dress beside him. How sheer it was, how soft and fragile! He drew a deep breath, and his nostrils seemed full of French scent—or something sweeter still. He was not sure which. Yes, Prue was right—no Hamstead man could give a girl things like these. No Hamstead man had brains enough to earn them. Prue's hand, in the dark, suddenly touched his. He drew his own away.

She left for Washington soon afterwards; but in midwinter she returned for a few days, because she had been ill, and had been ordered to the country to recuperate. Strangely enough, she selected Hamstead for the scene of her convalescence, and stranger still—since it had never occurred to him to venture to write to her—she sent Peter a little note, telling him of her impending arrival. Sally was not at home, so Prue went to the village inn, which was not a very sheltered spot in which to foster a friendship. However, Peter took her sleighing two or three times, and in the course of these rides learned that the job which meant fortune and freedom was not a bed of roses after all.

"I'm up until three in the morning most of the time," she admitted, "going to parties, and then rushing back to the office and hammering out a description on the typewriter of what everybody wore and how 'beautifully appointed' everything was. 'Among those present were Senator and Mrs. Brown. Mrs. Brown looking unusually charming in a beautiful Paris creation of red *pailletted* in green; the Minister from Dulmania and Madame Spavoski, the latter very *recherchée* in orange and pink. A fountain which unfortunately was out of order was the *pièce de resistance* of the table decorations and the refreshments consisted of *bombe glacée* into which a little salt had leaked and—"

"You're making fun of something," said Peter patiently, "I'm not sure whether it's me or your job."

"Of myself, stupid. Well, that goes on night after night. And while Mrs. Brown and the Minister from Dulmania and the florist and the caterer are all peacefully sleeping, I sit up and write about them. Then I have to be back at the office by nine the next morning gleaning wheat in a reaped field in the way of who is going to be at home that day."

"At home?"

"Receiving—serving tea, chocolate, coffee, sherbet, sandwiches, cakes, candy and salted nuts for anyone who wants to come and eat it. The offici_l women do that once a week, from four to six or four to seven, you know."

"I didn't."

"Well, you ought to. But all this isn't so bad. I don't mind doing it for the ones who 'belong,' though some of them are pretty nasty to us—they seem to forget that a society reporter is a human being, that her bread and butter depends upon finding out what they're doing, that as soon as their husbands take official positions, the public feels that it has a right to read about them. They seem to forget too that in order to *be* a society reporter, a girl has got to have some social background herself, or she wouldn't know how to go about it. I had a grandfather who was one of the Justices of the Supreme Court, and my father was an assistant Secretary of State—but now that they're dead, and didn't leave any money, people have forgotten that! But some of the official women are so nice it makes up for the others—and you better believe that we're ready to do all we can for *them*. It's the 'climbers' I mind most of all—the ones who want to 'belong' and don't, who offer us all kind of inducements, if we'll mention them in the social column."

"What do you mean, 'inducements'?"

"Oh, pretty trifles—vanity cases and flowers and candy and seats to the theatre; invitations to parties to which we wouldn't naturally go as reporters—even money sometimes."

"Are you cold, Prue?"

"No—what makes you think so?"

"I thought you were sort of shivering a little. I guess I was mistaken."

"I guess so. And, well, I don't have time for many special articles in the season, so I don't make much money, and I need more. Besides I want to begin to do something else gradually."

"I thought you loved to write."

"I do. That's just it. I want to write something worth while. We mostly all do, we society reporters. We get to know human nature pretty well, you see, and we're not free to write about it the way we'd like to. 'The School for Scandal' couldn't teach me anything, but I mustn't ever say a word that hints at criticism of anyone prominent—freedom of the press stops short of the social column! And when I've got that 'copy' ready, I'm too dog-tired to do anything else. Now magazine work—"

"Yes?" encouraged Peter.

"It pays much better, but it has to be much more finished. Not slapped out in a hurry, with one ear at the telephone, and one eye on the clock. And novels —those take years, sometimes—"

"You'd like to write a novel?"

"There was a woman novelist came to one of our Press Club luncheons once," said Prue abruptly, "who made a little speech afterwards, talked darn well, too, about her work; how she'd made a solemn pledge with herself never to let anything leave her hands unless it was just as good as she could make it—not as good as she'd like to make it, not as good as she hoped to make it sometime, but the very best she could do then. She 'got' me, that woman did. She loved her work, same as I do—and the work she turns out is worth while. But she doesn't have to do hers in a dirty clattering office whether she's sick or well or alive or dead. She had a nice husband and a lovely baby, and she writes when she feels like it, in a lovely quiet house on top of a hill. A fat chance I have of ever writing a novel."

"But you said when you were here last summer—"

"I do hate people with memories. If I could have a newspaper of my own, I'd like that best of all—but I'd write the novel, too. Sally has gone and got engaged to John after all, hasn't she? I knew she would. He kept after her until she couldn't help herself."

There seemed, Peter reflected after he had left her at the inn and was putting up his horse, very little connection to a good many of the things Prue said.

And now Sally, radiantly happy for a girl who was making a fool of herself, had been getting married, and Prue was in Hamstead again, staying on at the Hunt Farm, looking after old Ephraim as capably—Hamstead admitted it grudgingly—as his niece had ever done, and paying her board besides. She was going to stay indefinitely. Her paper considered her so 'invaluable' that as she had never really pulled up after that winter illness they were giving her a vacation with pay until she could. There was nothing unhealthy, or even "pindling," about her appearance, to be sure, though she was very slight, almost elfin; and there was something elusive, something incomprehensible, which made Peter uneasy, which tantalized him.

His reflections were interrupted by the sudden and unexpected appearance of the young lady upon whom they were centered. She banged on the kitchen door, opened it without waiting for an answer to her knock, and confronted her startled host before he had fairly risen from his chair.

"Hello," she said cordially, swinging herself up on the table beside the typewriter, "It's such a lovely afternoon, I thought I'd go for a tramp. I've been almost to Wallacetown and back. And then it occurred to me to come in here and ask for a cup of tea on the way home."

Peter could never quite decide whether Prue tortured him intentionally, or whether she really took certain things so much as a matter of course that it did not occur to her that anyone could be tortured by them. The pang of delight which her presence in his house had given him was succeeded, almost immediately, by a pang of wretchedness.

"I'm afraid my fire is out."

"Well, we could light a new one, couldn't we?"

"Ye-es. But you see I'm all alone here."

"What's that got to do with the fire?"

"Why nothing, exactly. Nothing at all. But you see—"

Light suddenly dawned upon Prue. Or else—horrible thought—the light had been there all the time, and the dawn was an imitation one.

"You mean you think it isn't proper for me to have tea with you?"

"Of course I don't think that. But you see—"

"Do stop saying 'but you see.' I suppose you mean that Mrs. Elliott, or Mrs. Weston, or one of your other neighbors might see, and—"

"Yes," replied Peter almost eagerly, "I wouldn't want you to get talked about. Folks do talk, you know."

"Yes, I know," she said casually, "that's what I've come here for—to talk to you." She had lifted the stove cover, and was poking at the coals that glowed beneath it. "There's quite a little fire there, after all," she went on, pushing in a fresh stick, and pulling the kettle forward. "There—that'll boil in a minute. Get some cups, and sugar and lemon—"

"Lemon?" queried Peter blankly.

"To put in the tea. I forgot; you'd have cream in yours, of course. Exactly as you'd say 'pleased to meet you' when you were introduced to anyone, and refer to your wife—if you had one—as 'my little girl' even if she weighed three hundred pounds."

"I don't see—" began Peter.

"Of course you don't. It's all true to type, that's all—are there any cookies in the house?"

"No."

"Any crackers?"

"No."

"Goodness, Peter, how lavishly you keep house! Have you any bread?"

"I guess there's half a loaf. Being Sunday, I'm kind of short."

"I'll make it into sandwiches. We're going to be ever so cozy, aren't we?"

The coziness of the situation did not seem to loom as large in Peter's eyes as it did in Prue's. With visible reluctance, but with no further protest, he set out some nicked and battered china, silver spoons from which the plate had partly gone, tea in a broken paper package, granulated sugar, a single shriveled lemon, bread that was dry and hard, highly colored butter oozing over a cracked plate. Then he drew back with a slight start, as Prue took a cigarette out of a slim silver case, put it in her mouth and extended the case towards him.

"I don't smoke much—a pipe, once in a while, after supper. That's all."

"Well, light mine for me, will you?"

He struck a match and bent over her. Her rosy face, still cool from her walk in the wind, with the dark, crinkly hair about it, was as freshly fragrant as a flower. His hand shook a little, and the tiny flame scorched it. He dropped the match suddenly, and straightened up.

"So you didn't dare do that either?" Peter had not known that so sweet a voice could be so taunting.

"Do what?"

"Kiss me."

"You don't mean to say that you asked me to light your cigarette for you *on purpose* so that—"

The taunting voice broke with exasperation. "Honestly, Peter, I don't know why I bother with you at all!"

"I don't either," said Peter simply, "It's terribly good of you. You were sweet to me the day of the wedding. I've been thinking about it ever since. Say—" he interrupted himself suddenly, "you don't happen to know what Sally's dress was made out of, do you?"

"Of course, crepe meteor. Why?"

Peter produced his copy. Prue took it, read it

through almost at a glance, and dropped it to the floor, shaking with laughter.

"Peter—why don't you do something worth while?

"What do you mean, 'worth while'?"

"Are you planning to spend all the rest of your life in Hamstead? Living all alone on this fourth-rate farm? Writing items—" she choked a little—"for the *Wallacetown Bugle*?"

"What else can I do?"

"Why don't you come to Washington? John Merrill did."

"I know. I was thinking about that when you came in. But John's smarter than I am, I guess. He passed a Civil Service Examination. I don't know what I could do there."

"You might enter the field of journalism." Prue's glance strayed towards the sheet of pencilled paper on the floor. "I'm sure after what I've seen of your—ah —work—that you'd make an awfully snappy reporter; I'll say a good word to my boss about you, if you like."

"Are you just making fun of me, or do you mean that?"

Prue hesitated. And, in that moment of hesitation, Peter plunged headlong, with a discernment and a courage which neither of them had known that he possessed, into topics which he had not meant to touch.

"Because," he said, "if you mean it, I'm coming. I'll sell the farm—there isn't a person or a thing to tie me to it—and if you think I don't know it's a fourth-rate one, or that I want to live here alone all my life, like you said a few minutes ago, you're mistaken a lot. It wasn't so bad when Mother was alive. Since she died it's been pretty dreary. I could leave it tomorrow. And I'd have enough money to keep me going for awhile. I'm not poor. I guess you thought I was, because I told you once I knew I couldn't earn as much money as you could. But Father and Mother were both well to do for the country, and of course they left me all they had. I'd just as lieve go to Washington as anywhere else, if that's what you'd like to have me do. The thing that really matters is you. You know how I've felt about you ever since I first set eyes on you. I'd never seen a girl like you before. I never expect to again. You think it's silly and countrified because I don't want you talked about. I don't want you talked about because I love you. If I didn't, it wouldn't matter to me whether you were or not. I guess customs are different in big cities and little villages. I've heard that country folks who go to the city try awfully hard to act like the people who've always lived there so they won't get laughed at. But I notice that when city folks come to the country they seem to think it's kind of smart *not* to do like country people. It's a poor rule that doesn't work two ways. The country people don't always think they're so smart. Mrs. Elliott can be real mean. If you *needed* to come here, if it was part of your job to get news out of me, of course you ought to do it, and not care a hang what she said. But you know perfectly well that wasn't the reason you came. You thought I was stupid not to kiss you. Don't you suppose I thought of it? Don't you suppose I wanted to? But I think a fellow who kisses a girl when she isn't willing is a pretty poor kind of a skunk. And I didn't know you were willing. I didn't suppose a girl was ever willing—a nice girl—unless she cared for a fellow. And I didn't think you cared about me. I didn't see how you could. *Do you?*"

Prue, for the first time since he had known her, had no answer for him. Instead, the panic which he had felt in his heart earlier in the afternoon seemed now to be all transferred to her face.

"If you don't," he said sternly, "it's—it's cheap for you to be here at all, for you to try to tempt me into kissing you—"

"Well, it isn't cheap for that reason, anyway," flamed Prue suddenly. "I've cared about you, from the first, too!"

Something inside of Peter flamed also. But he went steadily on. "Well, if you do," he said, "I shouldn't think you'd mock me by telling me you'd get me a job on your newspaper. You know that I can't write. That

I couldn't if I lived to be a thousand years. I could sell the farm, and go to Washington, same as you say, but that doesn't mean for a minute that it would be worth while for me to do. It would be damned no-count, and you know it. The thing that *would* be worth while would be for me to stick right here, and make this fourth-rate farm into a first-class one. I could do that if I weren't shiftless and lazy. I know *how* to do it. And I wouldn't be shiftless and lazy, if I didn't have to live all alone, and feel that it didn't matter a hang to anyone whether I was or not. I wasn't when Mother was alive. Maybe you don't believe me, but—"

"I do believe you," said Prue quietly.

"I'd work hard—if *that* were worth while. But I haven't felt that it was. I haven't had anyone to work *for*. But if I have, if you do care for me, the thing for you to do," he went on, gulping a little, "that would be worth while for you would be to stay here with me. There are dozens of other girls who could do what you're doing in Washington exactly as well as you can. It's all very well for your paper to call you 'indispensable' but you know very well that you're not, that they could find someone else to take your place. And you know you haven't been happy, that you don't think what you're doing is worth while. You as good as told me so yourself last winter. And yet you have the face to pretend to me now—"

"I haven't meant to pretend anything."

"All right. Then stay here. I don't mean that I think you ought to settle back and vegetate like some of the women in Hamstead do. But you talked to me once about that woman writer who first made you feel that what you were doing wasn't worth while—or who made you *admit* it. If you stayed here you could write your novel."

"And have it refused by every publisher in the country!"

"It wouldn't be—it couldn't be. If you put yourself into it the way you talked that day, it would be *good*. But even if it wasn't—"

"I'd have my happy home, I suppose you were going to say!"

"I wasn't. I wasn't going to say anything of the sort."

Prue slid off the table upon which, for a long time, she had sat motionless, and put her hands on his shoulders.

"Peter," she said softly, "I am a perfect beast. What were you going to say?"

She half expected him to raise his own hands, and take hers down. Instead, he put them over hers, and held them there.

"You ought not to be sarcastic about a 'happy home,'" he said, "even though I wasn't going to say that. I might have, perfectly well. A 'happy home' is a pretty good thing to have. There'd be plenty to eat in this one, whether there were any pretty dresses and French scent or not; there'd be no slights and no insults, even if there wasn't much excitement; there might not be many prominent people—who didn't care a rap about you—coming here, but there'd be one person, not at all prominent, to whom you meant the world and all. And all that being so, I might perfectly well have asked you if it wouldn't be worth while to write your novel, whether anyone else in the world believed in it except you and me, if that's what you really want to write. But what I meant to tell you was that I heard today that the *Wallacetown Bugle* was for sale, and I was sort of wondering when you came in—remembering that you'd said you'd rather have a newspaper of your own than anything else in the world—whether you'd let me buy it and give it to you for a present?"

Prue would have dropped her hands herself, in her amazement, if Peter had not, by this time, been clutching them much too tightly for her to do anything of the sort.

"You meant to buy a newspaper and give it to me for my own?" she gasped. "A whole newspaper to do just what I wanted with—for a wedding present?"

"No, I didn't. I didn't mean to tie any strings to it at

all. I thought you never wanted—any wedding presents. But I thought it would be good for you to stay in the country for a while, anyway, till you got strong and well again. I thought you could go on living at Ephraim's and go back and forth in the Ford. Of course you could go back and forth from here just as well. And it seems to me it would be just as worth while for you to take a little no-count country weekly and make it over into a real newspaper—to handle the tools you know how to use, and be your own boss while you're at it—as it would be for me to take a little no-count farm and pull it up to scratch—"

Suddenly Peter knew that Prue had wrenched herself free, that she had laid her head down on the battered bread board beside the ancient monumental typewriter, and was crying as if her heart would break, but crying, as he knew very well, with joy, with that starved and lonely and valiant little heart full of gratitude towards him and love for him. He picked up the alarm clock, and set it down upon the cooling stove, where it would not tick in her ear, and swept the soiled tea dishes into the sink with one reckless movement; then he picked up the sheet of paper with the Hamstead "items" scribbled on it, and tore it into pieces.

"This doesn't seem to suit the new editor," he said whimsically, "I guess I'll have to try again." And, as no answering laugh came back to him, he knelt beside the girl and put both his arms around her.

"Prue," he asked, "Prue, darling, do you think it worth while to cry like that—when everything's going to be so wonderful for both of us?"

BAYOU D'AMOUR

FOR over an hour, Rose Celeste had been glancing desperately toward the little baroque clock which stood on the mantelpiece between the French flower prints, almost as if she thought the appeal in her look would make the dragging hands move more rapidly. The day had been tedious and trying, too, and she felt as if she simply could not wait any longer to switch out the lights in the plate glass bay window and turn the big key in the old-fashioned lock and close the perfume shop for the night. She could stand up bravely under a day that was trying or a day that was tedious, but when it was both, she found that was very hard to bear. Especially when they needed money so much, now that her mother was sick. If there were no more sales than there had been that day, Rose Celeste really did not see. . . .

The weather had been beautiful, too. She had kept the door of the former carriage entrance, through which customers entered the shop, wide open, so that the sun could pour in, and in the morning she had felt sure that, since the weather was so propitious, and since there were so many tourists in New Orleans now, she would make a great many sales. But though numerous tourists did go by, most of them were hurrying, as if they were trying to see the French Quarter between trains.

About the middle of the afternoon, two lovely young girls came into the shop, and Rose Celeste's drooping spirits revived. Those girls were not tourists. She knew them both by sight, for she had seen their pictures repeatedly in the society columns of the *Item* and the *Times-Picayune*. Their arms were linked together and their heads were tilted back as they laughed. They were obviously in the sort of spirits conducive to the lavish spending of money and they were both dressed exactly right, one in a beautiful red sweater and a tan tweed skirt, and the other in a perfectly tailored blue suit. These were the kind of clothes that Rose Celeste would have liked to wear herself, and could not, because they were so much more expensive than sleazy serges and silly silks. Girls who wore clothes like that could afford to buy any amount of perfume. Rose Celeste laid down the little gilt bottle tops she had been arranging and went forward, smiling herself, to greet them. But before she could ask what she could show them, they began to chatter.

"We've heard there's a fortuneteller somewhere around here. But we can't seem to find her. You don't happen to know where she lives, do you?"

Rose Celeste, still smiling bravely, told them the fortuneteller was just across the street, that there was no sign because there had been trouble with the police, or something, but that they would be able to find her in a little room back of the bar. They went out again, still laughing, their arms still linked together. They did not stop to look at perfume at all. They did not even thank Rose Celeste for directing them to the fortuneteller.

The sunlight streaming in through the big doorway was obscured again, and again Rose Celeste looked up hopefully. But the obscurity was caused by a shambling unshaven mechanic, who said in a surly voice that he had been sent to fix the linoleum. His manner was so truculent as to imply that no one should have linoleum in the first place, much less permit it to get out of order. Rose Celeste felt acutely miserable as she led the way through the former carriage entrance to the patio, flanked by the little apartment made out of the old quarters, which was rented to a young couple who had come to New Orleans to work at the Delta Shipyards. She was terribly sorry, she said, to bother the store which had sold her mother the linoleum. But apparently it had been laid too tight, or something. It kept curling up. They were afraid it might crack, if it went on doing that—Rose Celeste knew that the linoleum was not paid for yet, which made her feel all the more apologetic, but the young couple had not paid their rent, either, and she and her mother had depended on that.

When she went back to the shop, she found two tourists who were just going out of the door. They were both very belligerent-looking women, and one of them spoke to her harshly.

"We came in here intending to place a large order with you," she said. "Of course, we expected a reduction if we bought in quantities. But we can't fritter away the afternoon waiting to be served. We've been

nvited to hear a very instructive lecture at the Orleans
Club and we've got to get there."

"Oh, please!" Rose Celeste said pleadingly. "I'm
very eager to serve you. I'd be glad to make a reduc-
ion. But I haven't anyone to help me in the shop, and
I had to leave it, just for a minute, because the man
came to fix the linoleum and . . ."

"You Southerners have no sense of system," the bel-
igerent woman said scornfully. "Now in Peoria you
would have someone to help you. You'd realize that
lecture. . . . I hope I taught that girl a good lesson,"
she added to her companion as she went out. "She's
pretty, if you care for the small dark type they have
down here. But she doesn't look to me as if she had a
particle of will power."

Resolutely, Rose Celeste began moving bottles
about and restacking them neatly in the big white cup-
boards under the encircling mirrors. The work steadied
her hands, and she steadied her lips too, when she
answered Susie, the country girl who did a little housework and casual nursing.

"Miss Rose, all de 'lectric lights upstairs done gone
off. De light by Miss Lily's bed and de light in de parlor and de light in mah kitchen. De Refrigidaire's getting right wahm too and all dat food in dere boun' to
spoil lessen you get someone in to fix de lights. Effen
we only had a real icebox lak we used to do, de food
wouldn't spoil when de lights went off, but now you
done buy dis Refrigidaire. . . ."

"Is there a fuse burnt out, Susie?"

"Lan's sake's, Miss Rose, I don't understan' nothin'
'bout fuses. All I know is, dere ain't no light by Miss
Lily's bed, and all dat food in de Refrigidaire is gettin'
mighty wahm."

"Call up Public Service for me, Susie, and ask them
to send someone. I simply can't leave the shop again."

"Miss Rose, you knows I don' understan' dat new
foam you done had put in. All dem little letters and
figures on de dial, dey strains mah eyes. I never did see
letters and figures so good. Besides, I ain't got time to

foam dis ebenin'. It'll be five o'clock now afore I get mah uniform changed."

The telephone was in the covered passageway between the patio and the old dining room which had been transformed into a laboratory. The laboratory in turn led into the perfume shop. Rose Celeste managed to keep watch while she called Public Service.

"It's an emergency," she said earnestly. "My mother's ill, and when our maid goes home, Mother's all alone. If she has to lie in the dark alone, she'll be frightened. And all the food in the electric refrigerator will spoil."

Rose Celeste finished telephoning and went back into the shop, feeling relieved that no one had come in while she was out of it, and at the same time feeling rather guilty. It was true that her mother would be frightened if there were no light by her bed. But Rose Celeste was not really worried about food spoiling in the refrigerator. It was a very good refrigerator, which, like the linoleum, had been bought in anticipation of the rent money overdue from the young couple in the patio apartment. Food kept in it, well, for a long time. That is, if there were food to keep. But this evening, three eggs and a pint of milk and the shrimp gumbo left over from Friday's supper made up the total of its contents. Not enough to worry about, from the viewpoint of spoiling. That was why Rose Celeste felt so guilty as she sat in the empty shop, from which the sunshine had faded away, waiting for the Public Service man and watching the lagging hands of the clock.

"I beg your pardon, ma'am. I wonder, could you advise me about a present for my mother?"

Rose Celeste jumped. She had been so busy watching the hands of the clock that she had neglected to watch the doorway. Now, at the eleventh hour, someone was standing there: a tall, rather gangling young man, whose clothes were shabby and who spoke hesitantly; nevertheless, unmistakably a customer. She slid from the gilt chair behind her inadequate little desk and went forward briskly.

"I'd be very glad to. What sort of present did you want for your mother?"

"Well, she said not to bother. But you see, ma'am, the only time I was ever in N'Orleans before, I wasn't but ten years old, and I was fetched along to a missionary convention because there wasn't anyone to leave me home with. This time I aim to do a little stepping out myself and I made up my mind I was going to send my mother something too. I told her so, and not to forget it. An apron or a handkerchief or the like of that. Then I was walking past and I saw that bay window with all those bottles on the glass shelves and the mirrors back of them. They looked so pretty I thought perhaps—"

"I'm sure your mother would like some perfume. You know women buy aprons and handkerchiefs for themselves, as a matter of course. But sometimes they think of perfume as a luxury. Though ours are very reasonable, really."

The gangling young man smiled. Although he carried his height so awkwardly, there was something very pleasant about his face. It was fresh colored and frank; his brown eyes were bright and his teeth were white and even.

"I guess you're not acquainted much among Baptist missionaries," he said. "If you were, you'd know their wives don't have so much money to buy things for themselves, as a matter of course, not even handkerchiefs or aprons. My mother makes hers last a long while. Probably she'd think I was plumb crazy, buying perfume. But somehow—"

"These containers with three small bottles in them are only a dollar," Rose Celeste said practically. She held up one of the crested boxes as she spoke, lifting the three bottles, one after the other, from the white velvet in which they were imbedded. "You can have a different perfume in each bottle too, if you like—Tea Olive and Magnolia and Vetiver, for instance. All our perfumes have the real scents of Louisiana. My mother and I prepare them ourselves, in our own laboratory. No one else touches them."

Rose Celeste extended the small container and the gangling young man took it from her, lifting out the bottles in his turn. But he did this silently, and Rose Celeste began to be afraid he was not vitally interested in them after all. She turned to the shelf which formed the top of the white cabinet, where strips of absorbent paper were laid out on a flat rectangular mirror.

"If you don't care for those, there are plenty of other scents to choose from," she said. "For instance, there are Vervaine and Grandee and Belle Chasse and Bayou d'Amour—if you'll tell me which you think you'd like, I'll dip one of these strips of paper into a big bottle and you can smell the perfume that way."

"Say, lady, did you send for Public Service or didn't you? I'm kind of a busy man these days."

Rose Celeste jumped again. In her absorption with her strange customer, she had forgotten all about the fuses, and her discomfiture increased when she saw that this mechanic was grinning broadly. Apparently he had misconstrued her eagerness to serve her client.

"I'm afraid you'll have to excuse me for a moment," she said to her customer. "There's something wrong with our lights, and I'll have to show this gentleman where to go. I'll be back as quickly as I can. You won't leave while I'm upstairs, will you?"

"No," her customer said slowly. "But if you don't mind, I sure would like to smell some of that perfume, the way you said, while you're gone. The Bayou d'Amour."

Hastily, she saturated a strip of absorbent paper and handed it to him. When she came back to the shop, he was still thoughtfully sniffing in its scent. He did not speak to her immediately, and she did not like to be the first to break a silence which somehow was strangely companionable. She was rewarded for her patience when he finally looked up with his pleasant smile.

"I guess that's the one I want," he said. "Bayou d'Amour. I guess she'd like that. I do. But if it would be all right, I won't buy but one bottle. That would be thirty-five cents, wouldn't it? If I did that, I could play safe and buy her a handkerchief and an apron too.

Just in case she didn't like the perfume after all. And if she did, then she could put it on the handkerchief, see? That's what women do when they have it to put it on, isn't it?"

"Sometimes. Or sometimes they put little dabs of it behind their ears. Of course it's quite all right to buy one bottle. I'll wrap it up for you."

While she was doing so, her customer extracted an old-fashioned purse from his pocket and began to count out coins—first two nickels, then two dimes, finally a third nickel. Meanwhile he went on talking.

"When I told you I wanted a present for my mother," he said, "that wasn't quite true. It isn't for my own mother. My own mother's dead. I'm—well, I'm sort of adopted. The Baptist missionary and his wife who brought me up are the very best people in the world, and it's a funny thing—their name, Martin, is the same as ours, except that they don't pronounce it like we do. They say *Mar*tin and of course we say Mar*tanne*. That is, the rest of my family does. But everyone calls me Chris *Mar*tin, and I've fallen into the habit myself, because the Reverend Caleb and his wife like me too, and I like to do most anything that suits them, I think so much of them. But they're not my kin."

He paused, and Rose Celeste, gazing at him with veiled intentness under her long lashes, waited eagerly for him to go on. She did not know why what he said should sound so thrilling to her, or why it should seem so natural for a complete stranger to talk to her in this intimate way. But she *was* thrilled and during that companionable silence which had preceded his soliloquy, her customer had somehow ceased to be a stranger. His next words indicated he felt the same about this that she did.

"I don't know why on earth I should be telling you all this," he said. "But you're so nice and everything, it's easy to talk to you. And this shop kind of fits you, it's so pretty and pleasant. I never was in a shop anything like it before. And I never met a girl anything like you before, either."

Rose Celeste wanted to tell him how happy it made her to have him say this, but she did not quite dare. She flushed and remarked that she would be very pleased to have him tell her about his own mother, if he felt like it, hoping that her voice did not sound too eager.

Chris Martin closed his purse and picked up the neatly wrapped bottle.

"My own mother lived in the cypress swamps," he said. "I don't suppose you ever got to go to them. But of course you've heard about them. You know there aren't any roads running through them. Just bayous. And you know the lumber is taken down the bayous in boats. The fish and the game and the skins and the moss, too. But perhaps you've only thought of the bayous as trade routes. They're more than that. They're life lines."

"I never did think of them that way before," Rose Celeste said slowly. "But I see what you mean. That is, I believe I will, if you go on explaining."

"I don't know that I can explain exactly. But when you told me the name of this perfume was Bayou d'Amour, I began to think about the way my father had courted my mother. He went through the forest in his pirogue, up the bayou, from the houseboat where he lived with his family to the one where she lived with her family. I don't know as they ever put it into words. Left to themselves, swamp people aren't apt to be as talkative as missionaries. I got my gift of gab from being with the Reverend Caleb. But whether they ever said it or not, I guess my father and mother thought that route was a bayou *d'amour*—a sort of love channel. Don't you believe they did?"

"I'm sure they did."

"Well, yes. And they were right happy together, for a little while. A year or so. Then my mother was going to have a baby, see? And she was sick. No one had thought she'd be that sick. Most of the women they knew got on all right with a neighbor taking care of them. So my father put her in his pirogue, and started down towards Plaquemine with her. The missionaries didn't have a regular hospital there then, like they've got now. But he knew they'd take care of her as well as they could. Better than anyone in the swamps. He did the best he could for her too. He made a good bed of moss for her to lie on and lifted her into the pirogue as carefully as he could. He never heard her groan or scream or anything, while they were on their way. But when he lifted her out again, she was dead. Her baby had been born already."

"But the baby was alive?"

"Why, yes, sure. I thought you understood. The baby was me."

"Listen, lady, I can't do a thing with them lights. You've got to have more than Public Service to get them fixed. You oughta had called a regular electrician in the first place. It's too late to get one now, tonight."

The mechanic was back again, grinning more broadly than ever, but with a certain gruffness now behind the grin. Rose Celeste could not blame him for being gruff. This was the second time within half an hour that she had completely forgotten about him. She apologized, swiftly and sincerely.

"I'm terribly sorry," she said. "I'll manage some way. I wouldn't have bothered you in the first place except that I couldn't leave the shop then and my mother's sick, as you know. But I can go to her now. And—" She looked from the grinning mechanic to her strange customer, and as she did so, in one mysterious moment, she stopped feeling baffled and frightened and helpless. "*You* don't know anything about fixing fuses, by any chance, do you?" she inquired boldly.

"Why, sure," he said. He said it so casually that she wondered why she had not asked him such a natural question long before. Apparently he wondered, too, for he nodded towards the mechanic, as if to tell him to go ahead and keep his union hours, if he wanted to; in the swamp country and up Plaquemine way, no one bothered with anything like that. "Is this how you get upstairs?" he inquired, turning towards the laboratory. "It's lucky your lights didn't go out here, too, isn't it?

That would've left you in the lurch, with all these jars and tubes and bottles around! My, but it smells good here! You show me how you make that perfume I'm sending to my mother, won't you, by-and-by? But we'll get your mother fixed up first. If you just happen to have some wire, left over from trimming a Christmas tree, or anything like that, I can get along fine."

As simply as that, Chris Martin penetrated for the first time to the quarters above the perfume shop where Rose Celeste lived with her mother. He remedied the trouble, as he had thought he could, with the wire left over from last year's Christmas tree; and after he had done that, he went from room to room, testing all the lights to make sure they were in good order. When he reached the room where Lily Landry was, wide-eyed and pale and fragile in a huge carved bed, he drew up a chair and sat down beside her. He asked her if there were anything else he could do for her, telling her he was right handy in a sickroom because his own mother—that was to say, his foster mother—was ailing pretty often now that she wasn't so young any more, and he did for her himself, all he could. When his father—that is, the Baptist missionary—wasn't home. The Reverend Caleb was away a good deal, because he held services in so many isolated houseboat communities in the swamps. He had made himself a little floating chapel out of an abandoned barge, and he towed it with a launch through the waterways of the marshes. There had been no schools or churches anywhere thereabouts, Chris told Lily, when his foster father started this work; lots of the children had never seen an automobile or a telephone or an American flag, and most of their parents couldn't read or write.

"My own parents couldn't," Chris said. "Lots of couples live together, too, and raise families, without being married. There wasn't anyone to marry them. My own parents—well, anyway, everyone gets married now, or most everyone. There are seven mission stations in the Atchafalaya Swamp, and there's a big

crowd of trappers and fishermen and moss gatherers
with their kids and womenfolk watching for Father's
floating chapel whenever it comes swinging into sight
down the bayou. They can hear it coming before they
can see it, because Father has a loudspeaker on it too
and he always starts a good rousing hymn when he's
getting near a landing place. The swamp people just
dote on those hymns. They sing right well themselves.
And you couldn't keep the young ones away from
school with a club. When it gets real cold, winters, the
big boys and girls, who paddle pirogues, put their little
brothers and sisters down in the bottom, wrapped up
in quilts, to keep them warm, while they're going to
the schoolhouse; but you better believe they get them
there. It's something like the way my father took my
mother into Plaquemine. Well, I told your daughter
about that already, ma'am. I won't tell you all over
again."

"I'm sure I would like to hear it," Lily said earnestly.

"Some other time then, maybe. But anyway, the
kids all go to school now, and last year, when the
school teacher at Hog Island Pass got married in the
schoolhouse, you just ought to have seen the presents
those kids and their families brought her. She married
one of the missionaries who's working with Father.
The Reverend's got three men helping him now, and of
course their wives help, too. They do right well,
preaching and teaching down there in the swamps, and
they feel for it. One of them said to me last year, 'We
get to feeling awfully close to God, out here in the
marshes.' Well, I could see what he meant. I sort of
felt that way myself, while he was talking to me. But I
wanted to get away, just the same. I always wanted to
get away. I don't belong to the missionaries, or the
swamp people, either, any more. I guess I'm kind of a
maverick."

Lily Landry kept very still, watching Chris Martin
intently while he told her all this, her eyes big and
black in her white face and her hair soft and black
against her white pillow. She was wearing an old fash-

ioned nightgown, made of white lawn, which covered her completely, as Chris Martin was accustomed to see his foster mother covered when she was abed; but its tiny tucks and little scalloped frills gave an effect of daintiness and delicacy as alien to everything in his customary environment as were Mallard furniture and Aubusson rugs and family portraits. His eyes strayed, every now and then, from the fragile figure in the bed to the carved crucifix above it, the first one he had ever seen in a private room, and to the turquoise tinted ornaments on the mantelpiece which were the first he had ever seen anywhere. But he kept on talking to Mrs. Landry while he looked at her surroundings, and by the time Rose Celeste, who had gone into the kitchen to make coffee, came back to her mother's bedroom, he and Lily were already friends. She had been born near Plaquemine herself; the fact that her birthplace was a stately chamber in a famous plantation house instead of a blood-soaked pirogue had not deterred her from feeling that she and Chris were essentially neighbors. She knew any number of Martins—they and the Landrys, not to mention the Fortiers, her own family, were always intermarrying. Didn't he know her Uncle Dieudonné, whose first wife Eloise—there, she had been certain of it!

Rose Celeste saw that Chris Martin had made her mother feel better, just by coming into the sickroom, exactly as he had made her feel better, just by coming into the perfume shop, and she wished she could think of some way to prolong his visit. She would have liked to ask him to stay for supper. But she knew that the leftover gumbo could not be stretched for three persons, and she had taken in no money all day, except the thirty-five cents which Chris had paid her for the bottle of Bayou d'Amour. That would not go very far for three persons, either; and though she had a little cash hidden away in a china bonbonnière underneath the handkerchiefs in her top bureau drawer, she could not very well burrow for it and bring it out without attracting attention, any more than she could slip forth to shop, without some explanation. But just as she was beginning to wonder what to do, Chris Martin solved the problem for her also.

"When I came in this evening," he said, "I was just loitering along, waiting for it to get to be supper time. I'd made up my mind I was going to eat my supper at Antoine's. I've been hearing about Antoine's ever since I can remember. I suppose I may as well tell you the truth again: One of the reasons I figured I couldn't buy more than one bottle of perfume was because I didn't want to cut too far into what I'd saved up, to have a good time with, these next few days. Well, and I was hoping I could find someone who would go with me to Antoine's. There isn't any dinner, I don't care how good it is, that tastes the same if you eat it all alone. I thought maybe I'd meet a girl, see? Now I have met one, a sight nicer than I figured on. But I know this one wouldn't go out with me, right off like that, even if she didn't have a sick mother." He stopped, looking first at Lily and then at Rose Celeste with his disarming smile. "But I don't see why we couldn't have a party right here. I'm good at marketing. I've done a lot of it for my own mother. That is, I mean . . . Well, what I'd like to do, if you'd let me, would be to take part of what I've set aside to eat at Antoine's and buy things for supper here. I could help cook it. I'm handy in a kitchen, too. And it would show you how much I appreciate. . . "

It was amazing how much better Lily felt the next day—so much better that she insisted on having Rose Celeste telephone their *Cousine* Elodie, asking her to come and sit with the invalid—who had moved, for the first time in weeks, from her big bed to her chaise longue—while Rose Celeste herself went out with Chris Martin. It seemed as if the little supper party, instead of tiring Lily, had done her no end of good. She had talked freely to Chris, telling him how she happened to make over part of her home into a shop, when she was left a young widow, and how the perfumes of which she had once made a hobby for her own pleasure had been developed to furnish a livelihood for herself and her daughter. In turn, Chris had told her how his own father had been killed in a logging accident, not long after his mother had died in childbirth, and how the missionaries, who had kept him with them, had wanted him to be a preacher, because he had "the gift of gab," and how they had scrimped and saved to send him to Centenary College in Shreveport with that end in view. But he hadn't taken to book learning, or religion, either; he had left school and got a job in a sugar mill, not a bad one at that, though deadly dull. That was why he had given it up. Now he had come to New Orleans to enlist. He didn't have to because he had been deferred on account of working in an essential industry. But he wanted to join the Marines and see some excitement. He didn't think they'd turn him down. After all, he had grown up with a gun in his hand, he could shoot anything, any time, so why not Japs in the Solomons? But just in case a Jap had the same idea about him, he was going to have a helluva good time before he went around to the recruiting office. He hoped Mrs. Landry and Rose Celeste didn't mind having him refer to it that way. The Reverend Caleb and Mother Martin did mind; they minded having him say it and they minded a lot more having him do it. That was one reason why he'd been so set on buying a present for his foster mother, to make her feel a little better, if he could. He didn't like making her unhappy, not one little bit. But he was going to have his helluva good time just the same, for once in his life. It was right pretty country, around Plaquemine, but things were sort of slow up there. After all, there was a limit to the number of times you could get a kick out of weighing yourself on a penny machine in an ice cream parlor.

He said this in such a droll way that Lily laughed and laughed, and when she stopped laughing, she told him that since apparently he had no other friends in New Orleans, she and Rose Celeste must help him have his—well, his good time, before he went to the recruiting office. She really did not see, she said, speaking thoughtfully and looking at Chris thoughtfully too, why Rose Celeste should not go to supper with him at Antoine's, the next evening, and the movies afterwards, if *Cousine* Elodie would come in and stay with her meanwhile. *Cousine* Elodie was not willing to help in the shop, but she loved to gossip; Rose Celeste would telephone her the first thing in the morning.

So now Rose Celeste and Chris Martin were sitting opposite each other at a table with an old-fashioned carafe in the center and well-worn plated silver scattered on either side of their white plates. They were both smiling and both feeling very happy, though their little feast had begun with a slight contretemps: when a jovial garçon first submitted an enormous menu for their inspection, Chris said with satisfaction that they would leave the selection of their dinner with him; it could cost a dollar apiece. A shadow came over the garçon's beaming countenance and he shook his head sadly.

"I'm sorry, *monsieur*. There are many restaurants in New Orleans where you can get a good dinner for a dollar, but Antoine's is not among these."

"Let's go to another, Chris. I won't be disappointed, really I won't."

Chris did not stir. "Girls don't notice what they're eating, half the time, just so long as they get something sweet and sticky," he said. "Maybe you wouldn't be disappointed. But I would. I've been counting on this dinner for weeks. I'm going to have it—could you give us a good dinner for a dollar and a half apiece?" he inquired doggedly, turning from Rose Celeste to the garçon. "Well then, two dollars—two and a quarter?"

"If *monsieur* and *ma'mselle* would take it without wine—"

"Sure we'll take it without wine. I never had wine with dinner in my life—I'm going on a real binge, sometime before I leave here," he added. "But it doesn't have to be now."

Rose Celeste had never had a dinner without wine, except the one Chris had provided the night before. She had been brought up to believe that food and wine made a civilized combination, just as she had also been brought up to believe that drunkenness was barbaric as well as disgusting. But it was only after the garçon had gone that she leaned forward and made a hesitant suggestion, blushing deeply as she did so.

"Chris, couldn't I—couldn't we—I mean, if we are going to do things together these next few days, I think it would be fair,' and fun too, if part of it were—what do you call it?—Dutch treat. I've had lots of customers today. I believe you've brought me good luck. I've sold two big bottles of Imperatrice and three of Pirate's Gold, and those are both expensive perfumes. I'd feel a lot better about coming out with you if—"

"And how do you think I'd feel?"

"I hope you'd feel better too. I hope you'd think it was a good idea."

"Well, I wouldn't. I'd think it was a rotten idea. I'd feel like a *macque* man."

"Please, Chris, don't be cross. I didn't mean to make you angry."

"I can't help what you meant. I don't take money from girls. Not for anything. Not ever."

"Chris, I—"

"Look, I didn't mean to hurt your feelings, either. There—"

It was only because he had seen the sudden tears in her soft eyes that he leaned forward and took her hand. But when he had taken it, he did not want to let go, and she did not want to have him. He forgot that he was trying to make amends because he had spoken sharply, and she forgot that there was any need of atonement. They were only aware that in each other's touch, as preciously as in each other's words and looks, they had found something new and wonderful. They did not notice the amused but tolerant glances from the people who were dining at the adjacent tables. It was not until a little busboy came up and offered them a long loaf of hot bread, wrapped in a folded napkin, that they drew their hands slowly away from each other. And while they were eating the bread, rather thoughtfully, Chris leaned forward again and whispered to Rose Celeste.

"Listen, when we get to the movies, we can hold hands all the way through. That'll beat any show there is in town. And it won't take us so long to eat dinner."

It was the realization of this, rather than the dinner itself, that made them feel increasingly happy, though the rubicund garçon had outdone himself to produce a feast worthy of Antoine's which still fitted within the limits Chris had set. And when they had finished, they walked through St. Louis Street and up Royal, entering the first moving picture theater to which they came on Canal. They were thinking only of reaching a dark and quiet place where they could again hold each other's hands, this time for a long, long while; and very soon they discovered, simultaneously, that the hand holding, which only a little while before had seemed so wholly satisfying, was inadequate after all. Chris had never been so glad that he had two arms, for without releasing his hold on her fingers, he could still encircle Rose Celeste's shoulder; and then he let his free hand slide down gradually until it pressed against her waist. For a moment she seemed to shrink and stiffen a little, but this did not trouble him. It rather pleased him, because it indicated that she had never received a caress like this before. So he did not take away his arm, and presently the involuntary resistance was over; he felt her lean back compliantly and contentedly. He knew then that if they had been alone he could have kissed her, and he wanted desperately to feel the softness and warmth of her lips under his. He tried to think of a place where they could be alone, and where they could stay until this strange new hunger had been appeased.

The final feature had already begun when they reached the moving picture theater, so they could not sit through a second show. They were startled to see that the audience was streaming out and the ushers were beginning to snap back the seats and extinguish the lights. Chris and Rose Celeste trailed out after the last stragglers. For a moment they loitered on the sidewalk, while Rose Celeste looked trustfully at Chris and he looked vaguely off in the opposite direction. He almost wished, for a moment, that he had not wandered into the perfume shop, which was just as proper, in its own way, as the parsonage where he had been raised. If he had kept out of it, he would not have met this gentle girl who had become an integral part of his life before he could stop her and who was so innocent and at the same time so desirable. He had not wanted to share his life with anyone, he had not wanted these last days to be complicated. He had only wanted them to be full and free and lusty and joyous. Now, instead of being well on his way to raising hell, he had gone to work and fallen in love. Finally, he cleared his throat, and after the immemorial manner of man, caught in such a predicament, tried to shift the burden of responsibility to his companion.

"Would you like me to take you home now?"

"Why, no. Not unless you want to. *Cousine* Elodie is going to stay all night. *Maman* will be all right. And she won't worry about me. She knows *I'll* be all right, with you."

Chris made an inarticulate sound, waited a minute and tried again.

"Well, is there any special place you'd like to go, that wouldn't cost too much?"

"I'd like to go anywhere you would."

"But I don't know what places to go to. I've told you that already."

There was a note close to irritation in his voice. He knew that this would hurt Rose Celeste, as she had been hurt when he rebuked her for offering to pay for their dinner, but he was not feeling happy himself, only thwarted and confused and resentful.

"We could go to La Lune and see the Mexican dancers. It's not as expensive as most of the places in the French Quarter," she answered, without showing that she was hurt. "We could order just beer and still have a nice little table. Or we could go and sit on a bench in Jackson Square. It isn't cold. We could sit there as long as we liked, and not buy anything at all."

"Would you mind just sitting on a park bench?"

"No. It's what I'd rather do."

"Right. It's what I'd rather do, too."

Rose Celeste could not leave the shop in the daytime. She explained this to Chris, very earnestly, when he finally took her home, hours later. But she did not seem to doubt, for a moment, that he would come to see her there the next morning, and run up to see her mother, too, or that at closing time, he would come back to take her out again. She thought it might be a good plan, she said soberly, for him to tell her exactly how much money he had to spend, altogether. They could make up a budget. He had not told her yet where he was staying, but she felt sure she could find him a cheaper room. And she thought they had better go to Tujaque's, where the table d'hote was very filling and very reasonable.

He had not expected her to show such a practical strain, and he was not sure that he admired it; romance was one thing, budgeting quite another. He was also faintly resentful of Rose Celeste's assumption that she was to monopolize his time. It savored of possesiveness, and that was one of the complications with which he had not reckoned, and against which he rebelled. So he told her, as they stood in the covered passageway, saying good night to each other, that he did not know if he could get around in the morning. After all, he ought to do a little sightseeing. He would make it in the afternoon if he could, though she had better not count on it.

She accepted his verdict unprotestingly, and then she raised her face to his for a good night kiss. It was while he was kissing her, this last time, that he knew if he did stay away, it would be out of sheer obstinacy, and not because he did not want to be with her more than he wanted anything else in the world. But he also knew that they could not continue sitting on a park bench under the stars, kissing each other ecstatically, but stopping there. Not for two more nights. Not for even one more night. So he decided definitely that he would not go to see her next morning. And then perhaps, when he went to the perfume shop in the afternoon—for he did decide to do that—she would receive him coolly, and say she could not go out with him after all. That would give him a chance to be cool, too, and after sitting around for a few minutes, just to prove he could take it or leave it as well as anybody, he would go out by himself and proceed to raise hell —as he had meant to do in the first place—at least as much hell as he still could, considering all the money he had spent on that dinner at Antoine's. He kept remembering that some Jap might be a better shot than he was and he was determined to get everything he could out of life before he joined the Marines.

So if Rose Celeste had only reproached him, when he reached the perfume shop, his course of action would have been very much simplified. But instead, she came forward to greet him with a shining face. She did not refer to the fact that he had not come in the morning. She told him that the young couple in the patio apartment had paid their rent at last, so that she herself had been able to pay for the linoleum and the refrigerator, and that her mother had sat up nearly all day, and that a dozen bottles of Radiance, the most expensive of all their perfumes, had been sold to a lovely lady from New York. She said all this as if she expected him to feel it concerned him personally, and the worst of it was that it did. Then she asked him to go upstairs and see her mother while she closed the shop and cleared the table in the laboratory so that they could make up the budget.

She was already seated at the table when he came downstairs again after another friendly visit with Lily. The laboratory was dim and rather dusty and cluttered, but it was permeated with fragrance, and the glass jars and bottles and measures on its encircling shelves caught the gleam from the one overhead light. This also shone on Rose Celeste's dark hair and on the sheets of paper which she had spread out. Chris could not refrain from putting his hand on her hair and stroking it for a minute and it felt even softer than it had the night before. Then he smoothed it back from her forehead and tilted up her face, so that she would have to look at him.

"Do we really need to make up a budget?" he

asked, voicing his aversion. "I meant to go on spending money as long as it lasted. I don't see why we can't still do that."

"We can, if you'd rather. But we could make it last longer if we budgeted it. How much are you paying for your room?"

"A dollar," he said, and at that he was sharing it with a shipyard worker. It was a dingy room facing St. Charles Street, in a house that did not look so bad from the outside; the prettiest iron grille work on the block was all over the front of it. But inside it was scabby. Rose Celeste shuddered a little when he said this, and she was forced to confess that she could not think of any way for him to economize further on his lodging. She wrote down, "Room, one dollar," on her list and looked up again with persistent hopefulness, as she asked him about his meals. But the next information Chris imparted was not encouraging: he was getting coffee for five cents at the nearest drugstore when he went out in the morning, and lunching on a "poor boy sandwich." He had heard a great deal about poor boy sandwiches before coming to New Orleans, and he had thought that these long loaves of bread, slit lengthwise and stuffed with meat and relishes, would solve a major problem for him, especially as he had been told that these also cost only five cents. But they had gone up in price; they were fifteen now, sixteen counting the tax. Well then, there was a dollar twenty-one every day already, and though he walked all he could, he averaged about twenty-one cents more for carfares. Then the apron and the handkerchief together had come to eighty-nine cents. Rose Celeste knew all about the perfume and the movies and the dinner at Antoine's. There was no use in talking any more about those.

"No, but you can tell me how much you've got left."

"Just under six dollars. I told you there wasn't any use in bothering with a budget."

She rose resolutely, pushing the sheets of paper, still so woefully blank, away from her.

"All right. We won't any more. And we won't go to dinner at Tujaque's either. We'll just walk over to the

French Market for coffee and doughnuts. It's a beautiful evening. We'll enjoy the walk. And we can sit outdoors when we get there."

There was something almost stubborn about her cheerfulness. She chattered gaily all the way across Jackson Square, calling his attention to the Cabildo and the Pontalba buildings along the way. He was not interested in these points of historic importance, but after they reached the French Market, she made a suggestion that was a distinct improvement on the one about the park bench, as she sprinkled sugar liberally over her doughnuts.

"I don't see why I didn't think of it before. *Cousine* Elodie has divided her house into three apartments, and she's moved into the top one herself, because she could get better prices for the other two. It's a studio apartment with a little terrace back of it. She has potted plants growing there, and small tiled tables and a swing seat that an artistic tenant left behind him. It's pretty and it's comfortable. And the view is lovely. You can see the spires of the Cathedral and tiers and tiers of roof tops. We could go and sit on *Cousine* Elodie's terrace after dinner. No one would bother us because she would be staying with *Maman*."

"But how would we get into the house?"

"I have a key. When one of our customers asks general questions about a place to live, I'm supposed to intrigue them with the studio. Because if *Cousine* Elodie could rent it, as well as the other apartments, she could live with us, and it would be more economical all around."

"I see. Well, I really think you have got a swell idea at last. I like the sound of that terrace."

He liked the actuality even better. He sat on the swing seat, with his arm around Rose Celeste's yielding waist, and talked to her while he looked out over the city. The scene was so tranquil and so beautiful that he found he could talk fairly quietly as well as very earnestly, despite the feeling of chaos with which he was still beset. He told her that he loved her, but that he did not think it was fair even to say so, because there was nothing he could do about it. He was going to enlist the next day and he felt sure he would be accepted, because there was nothing on earth the matter with him, and he could shoot like anything. He would be sent straight off to camp, and then pretty soon over to the other side of the world, and when he got there, probably a Jap bullet would get him. In the meantime, he thought he ought to send most of his pay to his foster parents. That was what he had done while he was working in the sugar mill, because he was bound to make up what they had wasted, sending him to Centenary College, and he wasn't half through doing it yet. This was why he was hard up. So he could not ask her to marry him, because that would be still more unfair than telling her he loved her, and of course he could not ask her to—it was different in the swamps, when there wasn't any chance for people who were in love to get married. There was some excuse for them if—but there wouldn't be when—well, anyway, that was the way things were. It was tough luck, but he hoped she would understand. He thought perhaps she would, because she had seemed to understand everything, right from the beginning.

Rose Celeste answered him just as quietly and earnestly as he had spoken himself, and very reasonably too, which was more than he had dared to hope for. She said she was glad he had told her that he loved her. Of course she knew it anyway, but she wanted to hear him say it, and she had been terribly afraid he would go away without doing so. That was the way with girls. They were not like men. They always wanted to be told, and they were always terribly afraid they would not be, until they actually were. They thought it was unfair only when they were given no chance to answer. There was only one thing that troubled her: she wished he would let her decide, or at least help in making a decision, instead of doing this all by himself.

"Decide what?"

"Why—about getting married."

"I'm sorry, but I've told you that I can't."

"Well then—"

"Well then what?"

"Well then, you might let me help decide about the other, that you said you wouldn't ask."

He released her, abruptly, and getting up, walked over to the terrace railing. The stillness of the night had deepened. Its radiance was intensified. But its tranquility and its beauty ceased to quiet him; all his tenderness was engulfed in tumult. Rose Celeste went up to him and put her hand on his arm.

"We could stay here," she said in a low voice. "I think there'd be some excuse for us, just as there was for your father and mother."

"I never told you that my father and mother—"

"Yes, you did, almost. Anyway, I guessed it, when you talked about the swamp people in the old times, before the missionaries went to them. We could come back tomorrow night, too, if you should happen to decide not to enlist until the day after. Since you're sure we can't get married, it would be better than nothing. I know how you feel. I know you think that if—if a Jap bullet should get you, and you hadn't . . . just because I'm not the sort of girl you planned to meet in New Orleans, I don't think that should spoil everything for you."

"*Spoil* everything for me!"

"Well, everything hasn't been spoiled, of course. Because we have been very happy. But we could be a lot happier. Not just you. Both of us."

"You don't know what you're talking about. You'd be a lot happier, wouldn't you, if you disgraced your mother? She's trusted you. She's trusted both of us. And she's been very ill. If anything happened to you, it might kill her."

"My mother wants me to be happy. If she didn't, she wouldn't have let me go out with you. And she won't die. Don't you worry about her. You might think about your mother instead."

"God, I don't need to think about her! She'd never know."

"I meant your own mother, Chris."

"My own mother!"

"Yes. Don't you remember what you told me about her, the first day you came into the shop? She couldn't have been so brave, Chris, if she hadn't had lots of happiness to look back on, if it hadn't meant everything to her that your father loved her and that she was going to have his child. She didn't mind dying, because they'd been together on the bayou *d'amour*, because they'd been part of a love channel, of a life line. You explained about that too, don't you remember? Well, I wouldn't mind living, no matter how, if you and I had been part of one, too, even for a little while. But if we're not—"

She stopped suddenly. Chris heard her sob once. Then she was very still. There was something about the sob which was like the momentary shrinking that had come before her gentle yielding. It was over just as quickly, and it was primitive and inevitable, like the other. Now she would not sob any more, she would not protest even if he told her he was going to take her home and that they would never see each other again. She had not asked for homage or security or loving kindness or any of the other prerogatives precious to women; she had asked only for a share in his decision. She had been groping toward her destiny, just as he had been groping toward his, though their understanding of what destiny meant was different. Now he had denied her fulfillment and she had accepted the fact that she could not have even that. It was all over.

He put his arm around her once more. She was still unresisting, still quiet and controlled. But she did not respond to his embrace. Her joyous spontaneity was all gone.

"Listen," he said. "I'm sorry. I've made a mess of everything. I didn't mean to. I wouldn't have hurt you like this, not for the world. I didn't know you cared so much. I still don't see how you can. But I know you do. And that makes me feel different, too. I couldn't go off, leaving you like this. Unhappy. Thinking I didn't care as much as you did. That all this hadn't meant a lot to me too."

He waited, hoping that now she would answer him.

But she was deeply silent. She had said everything there was to say, already.

"I think we ought to get married after all. I mean, I want to. Couldn't we get married right away?"

"No. Of course not."

"Are you sure?"

"Of course I'm sure. People don't get married in the middle of the night, right on the spur of the moment."

"Seems to me I've heard that some of them do."

Again she failed to answer him. But this time he felt there was not the same hopelessness and finality to her stillness that there had been before. He waited, and then he repeated his statement in the form of a question.

"Are you sure you haven't ever heard that, honey?"

"I've never heard of people doing it in New Orleans. I've heard of people going to Gretna sometimes."

"Well, couldn't we go to Gretna?"

"No."

"Why not? Don't you know how to get there?"

"Of course I know how to get there. You get there on the ferry."

"Couldn't we take the ferry?"

"No. Nice people don't go to Gretna to get married, Chris. Only drunks and people like that."

"Well, we could be the nice people who started the custom. We could prove that it was possible to do it. If we go right away, there ought to be quite a lot of the night left when we get back. I think it's a grand idea to spend it here. But I think it would be grand to go to Gretna first, too."

"You don't really. You're only saying that because you think you've hurt my feelings, or because you think I couldn't manage if I had a hard time. I'm used to having my feelings hurt. They get hurt every day. I'm used to having a hard time, too. I can't remember when I've had anything else. But if you don't mind very much, I wish you'd go away now."

"I am going away. But you're coming with me. We can argue about what I think afterwards. That is, if you still believe we need to. I should think you'd guess how I feel by what I'm doing. Will you tell me how to get to the ferry from here, or are you going to make me ask someone on the corner?"

The ferry, it appeared, was at the end of Jackson Avenue. They could get to it on the street car, if they changed twice. Then they would have to go across the railroad tracks on the levee, and up the steep ramp, and through a turnstile to the float. Chris did not learn all this easily or quickly.

It was a long time before he could persuade Rose Celeste to leave the terrace and go down into the street and, after that, information came out little by little, in reply to persistent questioning. Even when they reached the upper deck of the ferry, and Chris commented, admiringly, on the cotton warehouses and the big steamers loading at the grain elevators, and the way the lights along the waterfront brought out the crescent shape of the river, she did not respond. She had come with him because she could not prevail against him, but nothing that he had said or had done so far had made her happy, in the way she had been happy when he first talked to her about the bayou *d'amour* or when they sat together on the bench in Jackson Square.

There was another steep ramp on the further side of the river. It was not really hard to climb, but Chris realized, as they went up it, that Rose Celeste was very tired, and he said he supposed they did not have much further to go. No, she told him, there was a little park with a victoria in it, just beyond the ramp; the courthouse was at the other end of that. But of course the courthouse was closed up now; this time they would have to speak to someone on the corner, and ask where Judge Armance lived.

The park was deserted, the courthouse a looming bulk of darkness beyond it, but a bar was still open, so Chris went into it, telling Rose Celeste he would only be a second. He knew she did not want to be left alone on the street, and yet he did not want to take her into the bar, for he could see through the open doorway that some of the men in there were very drunk. Afterwards he thought it would have been better if he had taken her in anyhow, for while he was gone, two loiterers appeared from nowhere and spoke to her. She was trembling all over when he pushed them out of the way and urged her along.

"It's no distance at all," he said. "We turn left and go two blocks, and turn right, and we'll see a coffee-colored house with a bay window and oleanders in the front yard, just beside a fire plug. The Judge lives with his married daughter. She can be one of the witnesses. And the Clerk of Court can be the other. The barman said the Judge would ring him up, that this was an old story to him. I guess it's an old story to the barman, too. He was so glib about it, and grinned so, I knew he'd heard it pretty often—look, honey, those bums didn't really frighten you, did they? I don't see how they had time to. I wasn't gone but a second, just like I said I'd be."

"No, they didn't really frighten me. I guess it's just that I'm sort of generally frightened."

It was the first remark she had made on her own initiative since they left the terrace. She followed it up with one that was even less encouraging.

"Would you mind very much, Chris, if we didn't go to the Judge's, after all? I'd like to go back to my own house. I want to see my mother."

"Of course I'd mind. You can see your mother by-and-by. We're almost to the Judge's anyway. You haven't got anything to be afraid of. We'll talk about that by-and-by, too."

The Judge's coffee-colored cottage was as dark as the courthouse. Chris and Rose Celeste groped their way up the steps leading to the gallery, and Chris felt around for the doorbell. It was some time before he found it. Then a still longer time elapsed before it was answered. Finally a light was snapped on somewhere in the distance, dimly illuminating the hallway. They heard footsteps coming down the stairs. A key turned creakingly in the lock and the door was opened by a big bearded man wearing a dingy dressing gown over his rumpled pajamas.

"This is a great hour to be getting a hard-working man out of bed," he said gruffly. He looked from Chris to Rose Celeste and back to Chris again. "No need to ask what you're after. Come in."

He led the way into a stiff ugly parlor, with enlarged family photographs in heavy frames on the brown walls and a tasseled plush cover on the center table.

"I'll telephone the Clerk of Court," he said. "He won't be any more pleased to see you than I am. But then it's all in the day's work if you do the *kind* of work we do. Or perhaps I should say the night's work —have you got a ring?"

"No," Chris answered in a rather startled way. He had not thought of a ring before and the realization of this omission embarrassed him. But the Judge's next comment embarrassed him far more.

"Well, you can just hold hands then. I take it you do have the eighteen," Judge Armance said, speaking less sleepily and more sharply. "That's what you need. Three for the license and fifteen for the wedding fee. That's only a little more than the day fee—I'm letting you off easy. Unless you've got the eighteen, you can't be married tonight. You'll have just wasted your ferry fare."

There was a moment of dreadful silence. Once more the Judge looked from Chris to Rose Celeste and from Rose Celeste back to Chris again. Then he gave a short bark.

"Well, you are a couple of young fools," he said. "You didn't expect you could do this sort of thing for nothing, did you? You better get back wherever you came from and let me get back to bed. There isn't anything more to talk about."

"I've got enough to pay for the license," Chris said earnestly. "And two dollars for your fee. I'll send you the rest as soon as I can. I'm going to enlist in the Marines tomorrow. I'll get paid regularly every month. I won't need to spend much of anything on myself. I can send you thirteen dollars the first of December."

The Judge shook his head. "I've heard a lot of that kind of talk before," he said. "I fell for it, too, when I was younger. But not any more. I got stung. Weddings in Gretna come C.O.D. now."

There was another dreadful silence. While the Judge had been looking from Chris to Rose Celeste and back to Chris again, they had not once looked at each other. But now that he was turning away, they did. They looked each other full in the face and Chris drew a deep breath. Rose Celeste saw that whatever he was trying to say represented a hard struggle. But he got the words out at last.

"Honey," he asked, very slowly, "have you any money on you?"

"Why, yes," she said. She said it brightly, smiling again as she spoke, for the first time since they had left the French Market. And as she smiled, her whole face began to glow, not because she was blushing, but because it was illumined with recaptured joy. If Chris were willing to take money from her, after all, feeling about that as he did, he was not marrying her because he was sorry for her, but because he loved her and wanted her, as much as she loved and wanted him. "I have the twenty dollars that lovely lady from New York spent on Radiance. I didn't take time to put it in the safe before we went out—I'm Rose Celeste Landry and my mother and I own a perfume shop that's named for me," she went on, turning to the Judge. "Perhaps you've heard of it. Lots of people think it's the best one in the French Quarter. My fiancé's a little short of money because he's been under such heavy expenses while—during our engagement. We hadn't expected to be married quite so soon, and I guess I've let him splurge a little too much. Here's your money. He'll pay it back to me later on. I know I'm not going to get stung. I know I can trust him."

It was astonishing how different the river looked from the ferry on the way back. Rose Celeste called attention to it this time, to the loveliness of its lights and to its great curving sweep. She nestled close to Chris and held his hand hard, the way she had at the movies, while she talked about it.

"It doesn't look anything like the swamp rivers, does it, Chris?"

"No. Not a bit."

"You'll take me to see those when you come back from the war, won't you?"

"Sure. I'll take you wherever you want to go. Of course, I must take you to see the Reverend Caleb and Mother Martin first of all. They'll like you a lot. I think you'll like them, too."

"I know I shall. But most of all, I want you to take me on the bayou *d'amour*."

"I sort of thought we'd found our own bayou *d'amour* already, honey."

"Well, I guess we have. I guess different people find them in different ways. But just so long as they find them—"

"That's the idea."

He kissed her. They did not mind the other passengers on the deck at all. Then he laughed. Afterwards Rose Celeste knew that nothing he ever did would hurt her again.

"We found our Dutch treat, too. I'll say you're a great one for having your own way. But I'll tell the world it's a good one. I don't see why I ever thought I wanted to raise hell. I guess I haven't got much sense. If I had, I'd have known from the beginning that what I really wanted was to marry a girl just like you."

". . . AND SHE WORE DIAMOND EARRINGS"

PRUE Morton picked up the evening paper and shook it open, even before letting herself into the house with her latchkey. Then, without stopping to remove her wraps, she went into the living room and, slumping down in a big shabby chair, spread the paper out on her lap. When she found the society column, she read, with avidity, the description of what had been worn at the Carnival ball the night before.

She knew about the tableau already; there had been an account of that in the morning paper. And she knew about the favors. Marianne Newton had come in the office of the Great Blue Fleet, where Prue was employed, to get literature on the spring cruises, and had stopped long enough to talk to Prue about the favors. The Newton family fortunes had been rising steadily during the last few years and Marianne had been the queen of one of the first balls that season and a maid in the court of several others. The Morton family fortunes, on the other hand, had fallen quite as steadily; there had not been money enough, after Mr. Morton's death, for Prue to make a formal debut, and she had not been invited to the Pacifici Ball—the one which had taken place the night before—though she had been to a few less important ones. The worst of it was, a word from Marianne, in the right quarter, would have meant an invitation. That was what really hurt. Because once Marianne and Prue had been such good friends.

Oh, well, Prue thought. She would read about what had been worn by those whose families had not lost their money and their social standing. Then she would talk about it, with authority, to her fellow clerk, Julio Fernandez, who, as far as she knew, had not been invited anywhere in New Orleans. At least she had never met him at any of the few houses where she was still asked to cocktail parties and *brûlots* and very large buffet suppers. Once she had hinted to her mother that they might invite Julio to their house, and her mother had recoiled as if Prue had made a highly improper suggestion.

"You mean that strange looking boy from somewhere in Central America, who's been sent to the New Orleans' office of the Great Blue Fleet so that he could pick up a little English?"

"I don't think he's so strange looking. I think he's quite nice looking. He wasn't just sent up from 'somewhere,' either. He'd been in the Blue Fleet office at Puerto de Oro and he'd done very well there. When he came to New Orleans, it was a promotion and Mr.

Foxworth, the president of the company, gave him a personal letter of recommendation. And Julio speaks beautiful English. He didn't have to come to New Orleans to 'pick it up.' He'd been to school in the United States already."

"Well, I'm not going to have a strange man from some mongrel Central American port coming to this house, no matter where he's been to school or how many languages he speaks. As for Orson Foxworth, he hasn't any background himself, he doesn't even recognize the lack of it in anyone else. I'm certainly not going to help some protégé of his to worm his way into good society. I have some pride left."

Prue had never again suggested bringing Julio home to dinner. As a matter of fact, she realized that it *would* have hurt her pride to do so—not because Julio was a social inferior, but because she had gathered he enjoyed good food, and dinner at the Morton mansion was no longer a gourmet's delight, to say the least. Several times he had suggested that, perhaps, Prue would dine with him, at Antoine's or Brennan's, or some other good restaurant; but at her mother's insistence, she had declined—regretfully, because she had a feeling Julio might be quite good company at dinner, and besides, she herself could have done with one that was a gourmet's delight. This was one of the evenings when she had declined a dinner invitation from Julio, not merely because her acceptance would have displeased her mother; but because he expected her to tell him about the Pacifici Ball, and she had not gathered enough, from the morning paper and from Marianne's tittle-tattle, to describe it convincingly. So she devoured the social column instead.

"Among the stunning gowns seen at the Pacifici Ball last night was the one worn by Mrs. Alexandre Brugiere, the mother of the queen," Prue read, holding the limp page close to the inadequate light. "'Mrs. Brugiere chose metallic brocade, made in surplice style, and she wore diamond earrings. Her cousin, Mrs. Richard Eppes, of Richmond, Virginia, was in lavender satin, the full skirt caught up with bunches of violets. Miss Natica Livingstone, a former Queen of the Pacifici, was in white tulle with pearl trimmings. Mrs. Shirley Townsend was in bouffant changeable taffeta and she wore diamond earrings. Miss Mary Bruse, a maid in last year's court, was in coral-colored crepe and wore an antique necklace of carved coral which blended beautifully with her dress. Mrs. Malcolm Towne was regal in black velvet and she wore long diamond earrings."

Prue thrust the paper away from her and then snatched it up again. No two of the gorgeously gowned women who had arrested the society editor's coveted attention had been dressed alike; every style, every fabric, every color had been different. But three of them had worn diamond earrings—three whom she had read about already, and she had nowhere nearly finished the column. She began it again, and this time she read it through to the end. Apparently, there had been only one gown conspicuous for its "plunging neckline," only one with a "tiered skirt," only one with a "wide crushed band of material across the hips." What was more, only one girl had worn pearls worthy of attention, only one, carved coral. But there had been three fortunate possessors of diamond earrings, the ornament of all others which Prue had longed to own, ever since she could remember . . .

Belatedly, she took off her weather-beaten hat and tossed it onto a nearby sofa. She knew she should have taken off her jacket, too; it was bad for tailored clothes to lounge around in them, and this was the only well-cut outfit she had left. At that, it wasn't smart enough, any longer, to wear to a good restaurant. So, on account of it, she was glad she had declined Julio's invitation. She didn't want to tell him about the ball, either. She was tired of pretending—that it didn't matter she and Marianne weren't great friends any more; that it didn't matter whether she was invited to balls or not; that pretty clothes and lovely jewels didn't matter. Such things were important in every girl's life and all the other girls she knew had them. . . .

Her mother came into the room and realized, after

one swift glance, how Prue had been occupied since returning from the office. "You've been reading about last night's ball!" she said accusingly.

"Yes, Mother."

"I shouldn't think you'd want to, when you weren't invited. I didn't."

"I know. I found the paper, all wet, on the front gallery."

"I think I'll stop taking the paper. It's a needless expense. The less I learn about all the dreadful things going on in the world, the better it is for my peace of mind. And I certainly don't want to read about the good times my former friends—my *false* friends—are having without me. I've too much pride."

"I know," Prue said again. "Mother . . . didn't anyone in our family ever have any diamond earrings?"

"Why, yes, of course. In my mother's day, every lady used to have diamond earrings."

"Well, what happened to them all?"

Mrs. Morton began to look rather vague. "I'm not sure. I think some of them were made over into engagement rings—one pair of earrings made two very nice solitaires. And, of course, in my day, every young lady expected to have a solitaire engagement ring."

"There weren't any *long* diamond earrings?"

"No, there weren't any long diamond earrings, as far as I know. Why should there have been?"

"No reason why there *should* have been. I just thought there *might* have been. And in that case, they couldn't have been used up very fast to make solitaire engagement rings. As a matter of fact, I don't see how they all could have been used up anyway. You just said every lady had a pair, and every pair made two engagement rings, and in Grandmother's family alone, there were seven sisters. Were there fourteen engaged girls in yours that had no other way of getting rings?"

"No-o. I think, perhaps—well, I think, perhaps, some of the earrings were disposed of."

"What do you mean, disposed of?"

"Prue, don't snap at me like that! And don't ask such embarrassing questions! As if it were necessary.

As if you didn't know we had to sell them, as we did lots of other things. But if you had any regard for my pride. . . ."

Now she was crying. There was a time when Mrs. Morton's tears had been very moving to Prue. But that was long, long ago. She picked up her hat and turned to leave the room.

"Where are you going?" her mother asked suddenly.

"Just to put my things away. And then to get some cookies, unless you meant to have supper right off. Why?"

"There aren't any cookies in the house. And I didn't mean to have supper right off. I came to tell you something and then you distracted me, talking about diamond earrings."

"I'm sorry, Mother. What was it you came to tell me?"

"Rodney Tucker telephoned me late this morning. He wants to come and see you tomorrow evening."

"Was he sober when he said so?"

"Prue, what makes you ask such a question? Of course, he was sober! He sounded very much in earnest."

"Well, he isn't always—sober, I mean. Or very much in earnest, either, for that matter. Did he tell you what he wanted to see me about?"

"Yes, he did . . . I wish you wouldn't stand there, by the door, Prue, as if you were trying to run away from me."

Prue sat down silently. Her mother drew a deep breath and went on.

"He said he realized you weren't making an official debut, that you were so serious minded you didn't care much for frivolous society. Of course, that was just his nice way of putting it. He knows you couldn't afford to make a debut. But he said a lovely girl like you ought to be in at least one court. He—he said it could be arranged."

"This late in the season! Now I know he wasn't sober!"

"Prue, you're the most uncharitable creature I ever

knew! The girl who was to be Queen of the Helvetians is down with scarlet fever. So one of the girls, who was to be a maid, could be queen, instead, and that would leave room for one more girl in the court. Or else, the Helvetians might leave the court as it is and select another queen."

Prue looked at her mother without answering. Again Mrs. Morton drew a deep breath.

"He said you could choose, Prue. If you didn't care to be queen, you could be in the court. He said of course he realized there was less expense connected with being a maid than with being a queen. But he said, since you're earning a good salary, it would be easy for you to get a loan—he could arrange that, too. Oh, Prue, if you only knew what a disappointment it's been to me that you never . . . I told Mr. Tucker that you'd expect him at six tomorrow. I've been out and bought some Bourbon, so I didn't have any money left for other things. But you won't mind, just for tonight, will you, when tomorrow. . . ."

Probably it was because she was hungry that she couldn't sleep. She lay very still, thinking things over. She had never been especially popular with boys, as a teen-ager. Her gray eyes did not have much snap to them and her soft straight hair did not have much sheen. To be sure, she did have nice skin, but her pleasant smile and manner, which were considered a great asset in the office, went unnoticed in a group where loud laughter and much shouting prevailed. Besides, even in her school days, she had cared more about getting good marks than about having dates. If she had known a boy like Julio, that would have been different. But she never had, until she met Julio himself.

Still, Rodney Tucker, who was a good deal older, had gone out of his way to show her that he liked her. Prue had met him the first time at Marianne's house and he had invited her to a Sugar Bowl Game. All the other girls envied her. But they needn't have. She didn't realize, at first, what the matter was with Rodney Tucker, because, after all, she was just a kid, and this was her first date. But pretty soon she knew he acted the way he did because he had had too much to drink, even before they started for the game. And, on the way home, he not only drove very strangely, he took a very roundabout route; and when Prue called his attention to this, thinking he had made a mistake about the best way to get to her house, he laughed and stopped the car.

She had never told her mother about this, she had never told anyone; but she had never forgotten it, either. Nothing terrible happened. Rodney was not so drunk he did not realize, when she fought him off, that she was really frightened, really revolted. Suddenly sobered, suddenly sorry, he took her home. The next day, he sent her two dozen long-stemmed red roses. After that, he quite frequently sent her roses and, quite frequently, invited her to go out with him. She could not send back the flowers, because they always came anonymously; but she steadfastly refused to go out with him again. And, after she stopped visiting Marianne, because she was working and Marianne was making her debut, she had hardly seen him at all. And now, he had offered to make her queen of a Carnival ball!

Prue knew what this meant. She was sure he knew just how modest her "good salary" was, how impossible it would be for her to pay off a large loan with any degree of promptness. Although it would all be done tactfully and indirectly, Rodney would be underwriting her financially. She would be under obligations to him; and when he asked her to marry him, he would expect her to accept him, because that was what he wanted and he had given her what she wanted, or at any rate, what he had every reason to suppose she wanted. Prue did not believe there was a girl in New Orleans who would not have given her eyeteeth to be Queen of the Helvetians.

If she married Rodney Tucker she could go to all the balls after this. She could stop working in the office of the Great Blue Fleet and take one of those famous spring cruises herself, for a honeymoon. She could have a house on St. Charles Avenue and belong to the Orléans Club. She would have all the beautiful clothes she wanted. She could have diamond earrings.

Mrs. Morton was still asleep when Prue got up the next morning and, as she did not want to run any risk of waking her mother by moving about in the kitchen, she decided that she would go down to the French Market and have a cup of coffee and some doughnuts before she went to the office. It was a lovely mild morning and, as she sat on the open terrace of the Café du Monde, looking out on Jackson Square, where the azaleas were already in bloom, she began to feel better. She was just rising to leave when she heard someone calling out her name, in a very welcoming way, and saw that Julio Fernandez was hurrying in her direction.

"Prue! Please stay and have coffee with me."

"Thanks, but I've just had some. And I'm afraid I ought to be getting to the office."

"There's no law against having two cups, is there? And it's early yet."

He beckoned to a waiter and sat down at the table she had been about to leave, as if the matter were settled. "I wish I'd asked you to take breakfast with me, here, long before this," he said. "I come here almost every morning. It's very convenient, because I live at the Pontalba."

He lighted a cigarette and leaned back in his chair. "You promised to tell me about the Pacifici Ball," he said. "Why wouldn't this be a good time?"

"It was simply superb," Prue answered, trying to speak glibly. "The official favors were bracelets, copied from one a member of the Krewe brought home from Ceylon, when he took a trip around the world."

"I'm sorry you didn't wear yours this morning, so I could see it."

"It isn't the sort of thing you'd wear to work. But, Julio, I've got something to tell you. I think—I'm almost sure—I can get you an invitation to one of the later balls—one of the best."

"You mean that I'd take you?"

He sounded so happy at the prospect that Prue regretted her impulse to confide in him. She had found it an effort to speak about the Pacifici Ball and the change of subject had seemed like an inspiration. Now she realized it had been a mistake. But there was no help for it, she would have to go on.

"No, I don't mean that. I mean something a lot more wonderful. You mustn't breathe a word, it's a deadly secret. But I'm going to be Queen of the Helvetians. I'll have a limousine with a special police escort. There'll be an awning and a carpet at a private entrance of the Auditorium, on purpose for me and my court. I'll lead the Grand March. I'll sit on a throne with the masked king and everyone will come and bow to us—I mean all the members of the Krewe and all the girls in the call-out section. The other guests—the girls who aren't in the call-out section and all the male guests, except the committeemen—will be in the balcony looking on."

"That's where I'd be—in the balcony looking on?"

"Yes. I'm sorry, but that would be the best I could do for you. It's hard to get any kind of an invitation to the Helvetian Ball."

Julio rose, crushing the stub of his cigarette. "I do not think I would care much about just looking on from a balcony," he said thoughtfully. "Thank you for thinking of me, Prue. Truly my feelings have not been hurt by the lack of invitations to Carnival balls. It would have been wonderful if I could have taken you to one, that's all. . . . And now, I am afraid it is time for us to get to the office."

He was silent as they walked up Chartres Street and across Canal, and there was a strain to the silence. Moreover, the strain seemed to persist all through the day. Julio did not come over to Prue's desk, every now and then; it almost seemed as if he were avoiding her, and this troubled her. Presently, it would be time for her to go home, and Rodney Tucker would be there, drinking Bourbon and waiting to tell her that she was going to be Queen of the Helvetians and that she was not to worry about money or anything else. But she was worrying already. When Rodney Tucker had told her what he had come to say and she had thanked him, he would be on a different footing in the house. He could come there whenever he chose. And pretty soon she would be there all the time. She would not see Julio any more.

At four o'clock, she heard Mr. Forrestal, the manager, tell Julio that he was leaving for the day, but that there were still some memoranda on his desk that he would like Julio to look after. Julio went into the private office and closed the door. At first, Prue could hear him talking on the telephone and moving about; but after a while, there were no sounds. For some reason, this silence proved unendurable. At last, she could stand it no longer. She knocked on the door and then, without waiting for an answer, she went in.

Julio was sitting at Mr. Forrestal's beautiful big desk, but he did not appear to be doing anything about the memoranda. He appeared to be thinking about something which made him very unhappy. When Prue walked in, he looked up and rose. "What can I do for you?" he asked, rather formally.

"You can listen to what I'm going to say."

"All right, Prue," he said easily. "Shoot!"

"I didn't go to the Pacifici Ball," she said. "I didn't go to any of those other balls I told you about, either. I wasn't invited to them, any more than you were. I was just pretending. Somehow, I couldn't leave without telling you so."

Julio appeared to consider all this, carefully but not critically. Then he remarked, "Well, I'm sure there must have been some good reason for pretending. Were you just pretending about being queen, too?"

"No, that part was true. A man is coming to see me this evening who can make me queen—who wants to make me queen."

"I see. And then you wouldn't pretend any more?"

"No. Because I wouldn't need to."

"I see," Julio said again. "Well, I suppose this man you mention is very much in love with you—of course, that is easy to understand. But I don't understand whether you are very much in love with him."

"No, I'm not. I'm not in love with him at all."

Suddenly, she felt as if she were back in that parked car, suddenly she seemed to hear Rodney Tucker laughing at her and trying to take her in his arms. She had escaped that time, but the next time—the time that was so near now—she would be trapped. And nothing in the world would be worth that—not the fulfillment of her mother's ambition, nor the power of retaliation which would henceforth be hers, nor the preeminence of her future position. She felt humiliated because she had ever thought it would, so humiliated that she was afraid she was going to disgrace herself by crying. She might even fall, her knees were shaking so; in fact she was trembling, uncontrollably, all over. But she didn't fall, because Julio reached forward and put his arms around her; when this happened, she did not try to fight him off, she did not want to. She wanted him to hold her closer and closer and keep on kissing her and repeating what he was saying. She could not understand any of the words, because they were all Spanish words, but their meaning was very clear and it was music to her ears.

At quarter past six, Mrs. Morton, who was very angry, began telephoning the office of the Great Blue Fleet. She kept on doing so, at intervals, after Rodney Tucker, who was very angry, too, left the house. She did not get any answer, because the office had closed, as usual, promptly at five, and Prue had gone with Julio to his apartment at the Pontalba Building.

It was she who had suggested it. And then he said, well, perhaps he might be forgiven for following her suggestion, though he knew that, even in the United States, a gentleman did not—or at any rate should not—take his *novia* to his apartment, unless another lady were there to receive her. But they would stay only long enough, before they went out to dinner, for him to tell her again how much he loved her and to give her some kind of keepsake, as a souvenir of the day.

Prue was vaguely surprised by the appearance of Julio's apartment. Some of the old paintings on the walls were rather beautiful, and so were various carved chests and silver ornaments. Julio settled her on a big sofa and then excused himself, saying he would be back in a minute. As Prue waited for his return, she realized that everything she had coveted before seemed to have lost its glamour, and mingled with her newfound joy, there was suddenly a sense of thanksgiving.

Julio came back into the drawing room, carrying a small blue velvet box. "I must measure your finger for a ring before we go on to Brennan's," he said. "Unless you prefer something else, I should like to give you an emerald. But meanwhile, as I said, I want you to have a souvenir of today—my great-grandfather's first present to *his novia.*"

"As if I needed a souvenir to help me remember today!"

"But you will accept a gift, won't you, since it is our family custom to make one on such an occasion?"

He put his arms around her again and then handed her the box, still unopened. She turned it over, two or three times, with fingers that trembled slightly. Then she pressed the golden spring and the lid flew open.

Inside, on a bed of white satin that had yellowed with age, lay a pair of long diamond earrings.

IN NEED OF CONFESSION

I DO not think I realized, until I reached my brother's place in Kent, after an absence of several years from England, how thoroughly exhausted I was, how near a nervous breakdown which would have shattered my usefulness for years. Since I first came to the States, twenty years ago, I have allowed myself very few vacations, and my work, always hard, has been sometimes relentlessly so. The rector of a large church, situated on a city hill, just where the line between the very rich joins that of the uncomfortably straitened known as "persons in moderate circumstances," which, in turn, meets the line of those who stare poverty in the face daily, and drawing its congregation from all three; the representative of a Church Brotherhood of the greatest purpose and ideals, whose high name is entrusted to me to be carried like a standard in a land where it is less familiar and also less reverenced than in the mother country—the problems which I have had to meet and the tasks which I have had to accomplish have weighed me down, and at times threatened to crush me altogether. As far as I am able to tell, my own parish, the city of my adoption, and my brother-hood, have all judged my efforts leniently, not to say kindly. But I have never satisfied my own ideals of the highest service; in that, perhaps, is the explanation of the utter weariness and mental depression which men-aced not only my constitution, but my peace of mind.

England in springtime, however, revisited after years of exile by an Englishman to whom she is at all time and seasons the most beautiful and hallowed of coun-tries, holds peace and healing in her every hedge and lane, her sudden showers and soft sunshine, her blos-soming orchards and wide, serene fields. For several weeks after reaching the old manor, which I had never seen before, since my brother had only recently inherit-ed it from a distant cousin, my chief desire was to lie under a tree in a meadow, watching the buds coming out and the clouds floating by. I carried a book—sometimes several of them—about with me, but I sel-dom read them. I slept a great deal, and I dreamed even more than I slept. In time I was sufficiently rested to realize how intense was my fatigue; and when I reached this point I also saw that unless I were to prove myself the most unaffectionate of relatives, as well as the most boorish of guests, I must respond more gratefully to the anxious hospitality which my brother and his wife, the village rector, and the many kindly neighbors in the vicinity were so eager to lavish upon me. I had resolved to shake off my selfish inertia and show my deep appreciation of their interest, when something happened which I have never been able to explain, and the shock of which threw me for a time into sadness greater even than I had known before its occurrence. I am not yet able to account for the incident. But the time has come when I wish to tell it, in the hope that some other man or woman—blessed, perhaps, with deeper vision or more subtle understanding than I possess—may be able to help me unravel the mystery.

I had missed services the previous two Sundays of my visit for the first time since I can remember. I saw that my family was more troubled by this than by any other sign of lassitude which I had displayed. And I was conscious of the relief—I might almost say the joy —in their faces when I joined my brother and sister-in-law as they were leaving the house for early celebration on the following Sunday, and said I would go to church with them.

It was a rainy morning, not gray mist and pelting showers and sunshine, then showers and mist again, but a hard, steady, driving downpour, reminding one of the storms of late fall rather than those of early spring. There was something bitter and menacing about it. The little chapel, so imperfectly illuminated that the Eucharistic lights seemed to give the only glow in its darkness, was almost empty. There were three young girls, the fervor of their first Communion still high in their memories, coming almost shyly to the altar; an old couple, gray-haired and feeble, dressed in shabby black—it was easy to guess that some fresh sorrow, shared, as many others must have been shared, through the long years during which they had lived together, was bringing them to seek consolation; a few stolid villagers, their damp woolen clothing smelling musty and old; and ourselves.

After the service was over I knelt for a few moments, praying, the load of depression suddenly rolling from me. A clergyman taking communion as one of the congregation, instead of as the ministrant, is often

conscious of this sense of rest—at least so more than
one has told me. The other worshipers left one by one.
Even my brother and his wife, with the intuition of
affection, passed by me silently and went out of the
church. I could hear their footsteps slapping on the
stone walk leading through the courtyard to the high-
way, for, like most English country churches, this one
is set in the midst of its burying-ground. The rain beat
against the stained-glass windows, dimming their
brightness. I was quite alone. At last I rose and walked
down the aisle, happier than I had been in months;
and, as I pulled open one of the swinging doors to step
out, I felt a light touch on my shoulder and turned,
somewhat startled, to see what it could be.

A lady stood beside me in the vestibule—a lady so
tall that the gray eyes which were looking into mine
were almost level with them, though I am a tall man.
She was dressed in white, soft, costly garments—a delicate dress, a graceful, flowing cloak, a veil thrown
back from her face, floating from a small hat. Her
hands were bare and very beautiful. She had on a wedding ring, but no jewels. Her face, grave, finely chis-
eled, was beautiful, too; quite the most beautiful that I
have ever seen. She spoke immediately.

"Did I frighten you? I am sorry—but I did not like
to disturb your devotions, so I waited here until you
should come out."

"Were you at the service? I did not see you." The
words sounded stupid, almost discourteous, but I could
not restrain them. Surely I should have seen this lovely
creature if she had been there—she would have stood
out like a white lily among dull weeds.

"I came in late and knelt in the back of the church,
behind all the rest of you. I did not go to the altar, and
you seemed very much absorbed in your own reflections as you came down the aisle."

I hesitated. I could not conceive why she had
stopped me, a total stranger. It must be that she desired or needed something.

"Can I serve you in any way?" I asked.

She threw back her head slightly as if to make the

veil, which had fallen forward, clear her face. "Yes," she said quickly, "yes. I waited to ask you if you would go with me to receive the confession of one who needs you very much."

I looked at her in astonishment, almost in displeasure. Then I answered her rather coldly. "I am not the rector here, as you must know," I said briefly. "I am simply a guest, staying with my brother at the old manor for a much needed rest. It is neither my duty nor my wish to act here in my official capacity."

She touched me again, taking hold of my arm, almost eagerly. "You don't understand," she said. "I can't apply to the rector. He's a good man, but there are reasons. One of them is that he doesn't believe in confession at all—he's a Low Churchman. And the Judge is in such desperate need—ah, if you knew, you wouldn't refuse! You wouldn't even force me to waste time explaining to you—you'd come with me."

"Come with you?"

"Yes—I have my car here." She threw open the church door, and there, indeed, stood a handsome gray limousine at the entrance, its door held open by a slim man in livery which matched the color of the car to perfection. "Oh, *please*," she urged, fairly pulling me with her, "you won't be sorry—I promise you that."

"Madam," I said, "I must at least let my relatives know that I have been called away. I haven't, of course, breakfasted, and they'll be waiting for me—anxiously, for I haven't been well."

"The Judge doesn't live far away and you can telephone them from his house after you reach it."

Still reluctantly, but uncertain how it was possible to refuse her, I followed her and took my place beside her in the car. She was visibly relieved when we were actually on our way. I hoped for explanations, for more explicit directions, but none were forthcoming. We went very rapidly, and she leaned back in the corner of the car, her veil shadowing her lovely face again. She seemed, now that she had accomplished her purpose, momentarily exhausted. It was not until we turned through great carved posts into a wide, shaded driveway that she spoke again.

"Ask for Judge Gore. He'll receive you—I know he will, if you are very firm with Hastings—that's the butler. Simply say that you're the priest whom the Judge wanted to see. And when you've been taken into the library, say the same thing to the Judge—that you have come to give him the consolation he needs and to receive the confession which he desires to make."

"You're not coming with me?"

"I can't, just now. But you must trust me—it's right that you should come." The car stopped, and the gray eyes looked fixedly into mine for an instant, while, for the third time, she touched me lightly with one of her beautiful hands. "I haven't thanked you—aloud. But I'm doing it—in my soul."

Although my ring at the bell was answered promptly, the gray limousine had vanished before the door was opened. The manservant made no objection to admitting me. He took me into a stately, though rather bare—I might almost say empty—drawing room, and said he would tell his master that I was there. And in a moment after he had gone he returned again with the announcement that Judge Gore would see me if I would come into the library.

The library was a great raftered room, walled with books to the ceiling. I think I have never seen so many books in one room or in any private house. There were velvet hangings at the windows and doors, a fire on the hearth, immense leather chairs drawn up in front of it. Wealth, culture, learning, luxury—all these were manifest here, and yet, though it was full—almost crowded —it seemed curiously empty, just as the drawing room had looked. I had expected, vaguely, to see a man who was old, and probably ill as well, but the one who rose from one of the great leather chairs to receive me, throwing down a morning newspaper as he did, could hardly have been forty years of age, and his face, though there was a sort of tragic bitterness about it, was unmarred by any ravages of disease. I felt more and more bewildered, and utterly at loss to explain my presence satisfactorily.

"Good morning, sir," he said courteously, "you wished to see me?"

It was a question, not a statement. I tried hard to control my inclination to answer it in the same way.

"I was given to understand that you wished to see me."

He looked his amazement.

"I was told," I said, gaining courage, "that you had sent for me; that you had reasons for not wishing to apply to your own rector, but that you were in need of both consolation and confession."

His face hardened still more. "Who told you this?" he asked coldly.

"A lady," I returned, "a lady who attended early service at the village church," and I told him, as well as I could, what had happened. Then as he stared at me almost defiantly, I ended, "But if it's all a mistake, pray forgive me for intruding. I don't attempt to explain, but I do ask you to believe—"

Suddenly he sank down in the great chair again, burying his face in his hands. I saw, as he did so, that his hair was golden and wavy, like the hair of a young boy—a child. He must have been made a judge very early in life—must have great talents as well as great worldly possessions. When he looked up, the bitterness had left his face, but in fading it had left fear in its place, and the grief which I had seen vaguely before was so vivid that it seemed to have color and shape.

"Please," he said simply. My heart went out to him. "I do need you," he went on, "I do need consolation —and I must confess."

"If we are alone," I said quietly, "I am quite ready to receive your confession, my son."

"Oh, not now! I can't—so suddenly—I must have time to think—to prepare—to decide. But I'll tell the whole truth—everything—" He pulled himself together, realizing that his emotion was getting the better of him. "Will you come again tomorrow morning?" he asked more calmly. "I'll be ready for you then—I'm not, now. And meanwhile, may I rely on you to say nothing about this visit—or the one which you are to make? If you'll allow me, I'll ring for my car to take you back to the village—and I'll send for you, if I may, at nine tomorrow."

Although I accepted his offer of the car for that morning, I declined it for the next. During the intervening twenty-four hours I lived through a turmoil of indecision. Half a dozen times I nearly yielded to the temptation of going back to the Judge's house. The man's face, as he had raised it from his hands, haunted me. In remembering his I almost forgot that of the lady. He did not look as if he had ever committed a sin, except in as far as we all sin, trivially, from day to day. And yet the burden of one was there—a burden which had become intolerably heavy. The lady had been right—he was in need—great need—of confession. And yet the fear of losing his confidence altogether if I tried to force it—if I went to him a second time before he was "prepared," as he termed it—held me back. I passed a sleepless night.

The clock in the hall of the Judge's house was striking nine as Hastings opened the door to admit me.

"Judge Gore?" I said. This time it was merely the form of the announcement one makes in keeping an appointment.

"Judge Gore," said the man distinctly, "died during the night." He spoke with the expressionless tone of the well-trained English servant, but his face was stricken. "Heart failure, the doctor says. The valet found him when he went to call him, as usual, sir, at eight. Would you—come up and see him, sir? The doctor's just left, and he's alone now."

I followed the man up the thickly carpeted stairs. There was not a sound of any kind—none of the bustle and confusion that generally follows sudden disaster. The hall had the same emptiness which I had noticed in the drawing room and library the day before. I entered the chamber with bowed head and a contracting heart.

On a great canopied bed lay Judge Gore, the golden, wavy hair about the still, white, curiously youthful face. But on that face was an expression at which I could not bear to look, for the mask of death is usually a mask of peace as well, and there was no peace here. I glanced away quickly, horror-stricken. And as I did so my eyes fell on a portrait which hung over the marble mantel—the portrait of a beautiful woman, tall, with gray eyes, dressed all in white—the woman who had stopped me at the church door. Something made it difficult for me to form the question that rose in my throat, choking me.

"Who is that lady?" I managed to ask at length.

Hastings looked from me to the dead judge, lying on his white bed.

"Why that, sir," he said, as if surprised that I needed to ask, "is my late mistress, the Judge's wife—she died a year ago."

Sensational SIGNET Bestsellers

- [ ] **BRAIN by Robin Cook.** (#AE1260—$3.95)
- [ ] **THE DELTA DECISION by Wibur Smith.** (#AE1335—$3.50)
- [ ] **CENTURY by Fred Mustard Stewart.** (#AE1407—$3.95)
- [ ] **ORIGINAL SINS by Lisa Alther.** (#AE1448—$3.95)
- [ ] **MAURA'S DREAM by Joel Gross.** (#AE1262—$3.50)
- [ ] **THE DONORS by Leslie Alan Horvitz and H. Harris Gerhard, M.D.** (#AE1338—$2.95)
- [ ] **SMALL WORLD by Tabitha King.** (#AE1408—$3.50)
- [ ] **THE KISSING GATE by Pamela Haines.** (#AE1449—$3.50)
- [ ] **THE CROOKED CROSS by Barth Jules Sussman.** (#AE1203—$2.95)
- [ ] **CITY KID by Mary MacCracken.** (#AE1336—$2.95)
- [ ] **CHARLIES DAUGHTER by Susan Child.** (#AE1409—$2.50)
- [ ] **JUDGMENT DAY by Nick Sharman.** (#AE1450—$2.95)
- [ ] **THE DISTANT SHORE by Susannah James.** (#AE1264—$2.95)
- [ ] **FORGED IN BLOOD (Americans at War #2) by Robert Leckie.** (#AE1337—$2.95)
- [ ] **TECUMSEH by Paul Lederer.** (#AE1410—$2.95)
- [ ] **THE JASMINE VEIL by Gimone Hall.** (#AE1451—$2.95)*

*Prices Slightly Higher in Canada

Buy them at your local bookstore or use this convenient coupon for ordering.
THE NEW AMERICAN LIBRARY, INC.,
P.O. Box 999, Bergenfield, New Jersey 07621
Please send me the books I have checked above. I am enclosing $_____
(please add $1.00 to this order to cover postage and handling). Send check
or money order—no cash or C.O.D.'s. Prices and numbers are subject to change
without notice.
Name_____
Address_____
City _____ State _____ Zip Code _____
Allow 4-6 weeks for delivery.
This offer is subject to withdrawal without notice.

𝒮

More SIGNET Bestsellers

Buy them at your local

bookstore or use coupon

on next page for ordering.

Great Reading from SIGNET